I0594722

THESE DARK WATERS

KELSEY TREMAINE

Cover by Andy Payne (andypaynedesign.com)

Illustrations by FS Autumn (IG: @feelinstabbybyfaith)

Map by Cartographybird Maps

Proofreading by Melissa Stone

ISBN: 979-8-9997643-0-0 (paperback), 979-8-9997643-1-7 (ebook)

Library of Congress Control Number: 2025919279

1st edition 2025

To all the girls whose love wasn't enough.

PRONUNCIATION GUIDE

Characters

Aedi: Ay-dee
Aris: Air-iss
Anrena: Ahn-rey-nuh
Dínn: Deen
Ekris: Eh-kriss
Eli Crowley: Ee-lye Crow-lee
Etris: Eh-triss
Kiara: Key-are-uh

Places

Altean: Al-tee-unn
Breton: Breh-tun
Erama: Err-ahm-uh
Kornas: Core-nuss
Maia: My-uh
Nestad: Ness-tad
Reidde: Ride
Sudal: Sue-dahl
Sulesia: Sue-less-ee-uh

KYLESIA MOUNTAINS
ISLES OF THE DAMNED
ALDER
ALI
KURU
THE REIDDE SEA
PASSAGE OF D
JARVA
NESTAD
KOSNAS
MAIAN EMPIRE
KAKOS
BALMOEN
HURAN
LOKSA
ANTSA
MAJOR SETTLEMENTS
NOTABLE SETTLEMENTS
MINOR TOWNS & VILLAGE
THE KNOWN WORLD

MYTHSHADE
BRETON
NALI
KAMBA
SIMBIA
DFORD
MERDEN
A
EKAMA
BODENCETON
STANES
THE STANNING SEA
THROMIS
TAPTONBURY
THERMA
AKROS
PITRAT
DESSE
DUCHY OF
ULESIA
KORNESIAN
KINGDOM
RAINEN
SUDAL
ADREUS'S
SACRED
FOREST
BAY OF KORNAS

PROLOGUE

ARIS STANDS AT THE bow of *The Basilisk*, his chin high against the breeze off the water. The sea is calm, but Aris knows the calmest surfaces can hide turmoil. He feels like the sea today, calm and smooth from the outside, but his ever-present anger bubbles in his stomach. He grits his teeth against the thoughts of his mother and father, his sister.

Longing washes over him, pulling at his chest, and he takes in a sharp breath through his nose. He turns his head to the left and closes his eyes.

"Ramsey!" he calls.

Ramsey, a tall man with a scar through one eye, steps up beside Aris. "Captain?"

"Has *The Altean* been seen recently?"

Ramsey grunts. "They pulled out of Sudal this morning."

Aris nods and turns his face back toward the water. "Let's go find them."

PART I

ONE

WREN RUNS, HUGGING HER cloak tighter around her. Ducking her head and praying no one recognizes her, she stops at the end of the dock. The boats moored there rock lazily in the waves. They all look the same, masts towering high, furled sales rippling in the breeze. Wren doesn't wait, she chooses a boat at random, glancing over her shoulder to ensure no one has followed her from the church. When no one yells after her, she takes a deep breath and runs up the gangplank.

A black and white cat roots her in place at the top of the incline. The cat's green eyes follow her, but then they slide away and back down toward the dock. Wren turns and continues on, taking short, quick steps so her bare feet make little noise on the wood. She's never been on a boat like this and has no idea where to go, but she doesn't hesitate in doorways or at stairs. She just goes down, as far as she can until the steps run out and she's left in darkness.

It takes a few agonizing minutes for her eyes to adjust and her breathing to even, but once they do, she finds her way through the path of barrels and crates to a corner where she slides down the wall and tucks her cloak under her toes. She takes a few steadying breaths and closes her eyes, choking back a sob. She presses her palm to her mouth and then the heels of her hands into her eyes, shaking her head.

What am I doing? she thinks.

The barrels at her side press against her, squishing her body into the side of the ship. Her breathing quickens, and she has to fight against the blackness clouding her vision.

Just as she's ready to stand and leave the ship to make her way back to the church, a voice above her calls out, "Shove off!" and the ship below her shifts. She can feel the rush of the waves on the hull, can hear the creak of the masts on deck, can barely see her hand in front of her face.

Her chest heaves, and she presses her palms against the boards by her feet. The ship below her seems to hum, and she's calmed, like when her papa would make time to put her to sleep. The barrel pressing into her arm suddenly doesn't feel suffocating but like a warm embrace, and she leans her head against the wood, taking deep breaths in through her nose.

She wakes a few hours later, her neck stiff and her tailbone on fire. She peeks over the barrel to make sure no one sneaked down during her nap, but it's just as dark as before. Aside from the ship creaking above her, there are no other noises. No conversations, no footsteps, no gulls.

Her back protests when she stands, and she grimaces when she stretches. A soft glow of light forms in her palm, and she uses it to look around. The barrels and crates are unmarked. A few of them are bolted shut, but a few lids open freely. She lets out a breathy "Oh!" when one of the barrels is full of clear water. Wren claps her hand over her mouth, extinguishing the light, and crouches, holding her knees to her chest. She waits a few moments, expecting a pounding of feet to come down the steps. When no one appears, she cautiously stands again and dips her fingertips into the water. It's cool against her skin, and she cups her palm and drinks greedily.

She washes her face and takes another drink before returning the lid to the barrel and moving on. One of the crates contains leather books, and she pauses, running her fingers along their spines, the soft leather reminding her of the rows and rows of books in the estate's library. During rainy or lazy spring days, she'd curl up with one on the window seat in her room and page through, drawing her finger over the illustrations. She pushes her fingers between two of them to pull one free, but footsteps on the boards above her make her pull the lid over the crate again and dive into the space between the barrels and the wall.

Her heart jackrabbits against her ribs as the footsteps descend the stairs.

Lantern light illuminates the hold, and she wills herself smaller, pressing her hand against her mouth to quiet her breathing.

"Ezra, what are you doing?" a voice singsongs down the stairs.

A laugh reverberates off the walls. "I'm looking for the apples!"

Wren's foot slips and thunks against a crate. The light swings around, and she ducks her head, begging her heart to slow.

"Arden put them in the galley. All the food is there."

The light steadies, and Wren can see the shadows of the barrels next to her on the wall. "Okay," Ezra calls, seemingly uninterested in the apples.

"Ezra, I'm going to find the best ones and give them to Grace!" the voice taunts.

The light swings around again, and Ezra bounds back up the steps. Wren hears the woman ask him, "Everything okay?" but she doesn't hear his response.

She stays in her corner for the rest of the day, jumping at every sound above her. She cries, too, muffling her sobs into her cloak. Eventually, she falls asleep to the sound of the waves against the hull.

When Wren wakes, there's a moment before she remembers where she is, but her stomach sinks when her eyes adjust. She listens for a moment before slowly venturing out and finding the barrel of water. She drinks and washes her face of her dried tears and then settles back into the corner.

She rests her head against the wall and hugs her knees to her chest. Closing her eyes, she can almost imagine someone stroking her hair and humming.

No one comes down the rest of the day. Wren stays in her corner until her stomach rumbles loud enough to drown out the creaking around her. She crawls out and continues searching the barrels and crates. Despite the woman saying all the food is in the galley, Wren prays she can find something. One of the gods must be looking out for her because, in the smallest crate tucked in a corner and covered in a thin layer of dust, is a container of hardtack.

"Thank you," Wren breathes as she takes a few bars off the top. She takes another drink before settling in for the night in her corner.

The hardtack is stale, and it crumbles when she bites into it, but she forces herself to swallow and take another bite. Once she's finished one bar, she eats another. Her tongue is dry, but she doesn't risk crawling out for water.

Before falling asleep, Wren runs her hands along her arms and warms herself with her magics.

When she wakes again, there's a chill in the hold. Goose pimples raise on her arms and legs, and she shivers, tucking her bare toes into the cocoon she makes with her cloak. She warms herself a little, but her energy wanes as the day goes on. Not for the first time, she reminisces on the thick comforter of her bed. And also not for the first time, she wishes she were there.

Footfalls on the stairs make Wren shrink further into the corner. Light bathes the hold, casts shadows on the walls and floor. The footsteps and light come closer, casting the light closer to her. She prays to Emelia for protection as she wills her body smaller.

But, as Wren expected of the hard-to-convince goddess of protection, Emelia doesn't answer her prayer. Soon, the lantern casts its light over her, bathing her in a warm yellow glow. Wren blinks against it.

Someone kneels down, their dark arms covered in darker swirls of ink. Their hair and eyes are the same dark as their tattoos, and silver and gold rings crowd their fingers.

"And who are you?" This is someone different than before. Their voice is calm, curious. A smile pulls at the corners of their mouth.

Wren's heart races in her chest. She feels six years old again, sure the person in front of her can hear it hitting her ribs. "Wren," she croaks out. It's the first thing she's said in days.

Her finder lets out an amused hum. "A stowaway." They stand and hold out a hand. The lantern light glints off the metal on their fingers. "Let's go see the captain."

The captain's quarters are well-lit and warm. The person who had found her—Lex, they had called themselves—had gotten Wren a blanket and left her to find the captain. She sits in a chair in front of a large wooden desk, the heavy wool wrapped around her legs.

The room is large, with shelves along one wall. They're heavily laden with books and stuffed with jars of dried flowers and herbs, marble statuettes, and bronze figurines.

Wren's eyes are drawn to the door that leads back to deck. She's not sure how far from shore they are, and she has the sudden and fleeting thought of jumping overboard. But she decides she'd rather go back to Sudal and deal with the duke's anger than drown in the middle of the ocean, far from any place she'd ever called home.

Her eyes drift to the wall next to the door. It's crowded with miniature paintings of all different faces. Some have faded with age, but all of them were obviously painted with care and bright colors. Wren recognizes Lex, smiling widely, nestled in with other paintings that look recent.

Behind the desk in front of her are two tables. Light blue silk drapes the larger of the two. In a dried clay bowl is coarse salt and a dried stem of an herb with green-yellow flowers. Scattered on the silk are shells and pieces of coral, a black and white bird's feather. Half-burned candles sit at each of the four corners, their wicks trimmed and ready to be lit. An altar for Anrena, the goddess of the sea, and Iros, the god of travel.

Next to it, on top of the smaller table, sits another altar. Half the table is draped in black silk and the other half in white, with a piece of what looks like driftwood in the middle. White and black candles sitting on each corner look freshly burned. This could only be for Adreus, the god of life and death. Altars to Anrena and Iros are common on ships, but an altar to Adreus is unusual. Wren's eyes linger on it for a moment, and she wonders why the captain has set up an altar for the god.

Across the room, a makeshift curtain of deep green velvet has been draped from the ceiling. Through a small gap, Wren can see a bed piled high with blankets and pillows.

The door opens, and the room is bathed in bright light. Through it strides a tall woman with skin like midnight. The sides of her head are shaved, and the rest of her dark hair is in long locs, threaded with silver and gold. A piece of leather ties them together at the base of her skull. Wren sucks in a breath when the woman looks at her. Her eyes are bright green. Against her dark skin, her eyes remind Wren of the portraits of ancient Kornesian hierarchy hung in the king's halls. Wren knows this is the captain;

who else would enter the captain's quarters with such elegance and confidence?

Following her is another woman, this one shorter and thick-waisted, her light brown hair tied into a low bun. Her tanned skin is full of freckles, like constellations across her nose and cheeks, down her neck and arms.

Lex follows them, and the black and white cat that had greeted her at the top of the gangplank canters in after Lex.

Wren had stood when the captain entered, the blanket falling to the floor in a heap at her feet.

"Please, sit," the captain says, nodding at the chair Wren had been sitting in. The cat trots to Wren and sniffs her legs before continuing its way across the thick rug and jumping onto the bed behind the curtain. Wren watches as it turns a few times and then settles. It watches her with shining eyes.

Wren sits again, pulling the blanket back over her legs. She tucks it under her thighs and places her hands on her lap, linking her fingers together.

The captain introduces herself as Eleanor, and the other woman as Kiara. She flicks her green eyes at Lex, and they leave, winking at Wren before pulling the door closed behind them.

"Wren," Eleanor starts. "I assume we picked you up in Sudal." Her accent is vaguely Kornesian, but it's faded, as if she's spent a long time away from there. "Is that where you're from?"

Wren nods, hesitant. "Yes," she says, her voice shaky. She licks moisture back into her lips. "I was…" She trails off, pulling her cloak tighter around her shoulders, hoping to hide the dress underneath.

To no avail. "Getting married," Eleanor says.

Wren nods again, her chest sinking, her eyes on her hands. "Yes. I didn't want it. My papa"—she clears her throat—"the duke arranged it."

"And you ran. Aboard my ship." Eleanor doesn't indicate if she's noticed Wren's correction. She leans against the desk, mere feet from Wren. Wren can feel the captain's eyes on her as she talks.

Wren bites the inside of her cheek. "I'm sorry," she manages. She lifts her eyes and meets the captain's. "I didn't know what else to do. I didn't have anywhere else I could go."

Eleanor takes her eyes from Wren and locks them with Kiara, who stands behind Wren, leaning against the wall. Then Kiara nods and moves to the desk, pouring tea from a floral painted kettle into matching teacups. "Here," she says, holding the cup out to Wren. Her voice is warm, her smile soft and kind.

"Tell me the rest," Eleanor says, shrugging out of her green coat and draping it over the back of the chair behind the desk. When Wren doesn't, the captain sits and leans forward, her elbows on the desk.

Wren hesitates, holding the steaming cup in her hand. She breathes in deeply and takes a careful sip. "What do you want to know?" she asks when she sets the teacup back on its saucer.

Eleanor smiles. "Everything."

TWO

When Wren is finished and her mouth has gone dry, Kiara asks, "Why didn't you tell the duke you didn't want to be married?" She had set out a plate of cheese and bread. Eleanor holds out a small plate to Wren.

She gratefully takes it; her stomach has been grumbling loud enough that she's sure they've both heard. After days in the ship's belly with no food, the mere smell of the hard cheese in front of her was enough to make her salivate. She places a piece of it onto a slice of bread and stuffs it into her mouth. "I tried. He said I had no choice," she says around the food, too hungry and tired to bother with politeness. She shakes her head and takes a drink of her cold tea to wash down the bread. Softly, she adds, "I'm not sure why. He never forced me into anything before."

Eleanor and Kiara give Wren a few minutes of quiet to finish the food on her plate and refill her cup with hot tea before Eleanor says, "Do you know what happens to stowaways, Wren?"

Wren almost drops the plate. "Please don't send me back," she begs. "I'll do anything."

It's as if Eleanor hasn't heard her. "Stowaways become prisoners. On many ships, they're thrown into the sea."

The bread turns to stone in Wren's stomach. Her heart thumps against her ribcage. She thinks of the door leading to deck again, of jumping on her own before she can be thrown into the depths.

"But," the captain takes a drink of tea, "this isn't most ships. On *The Altean*, stowaways are not treated any differently than the rest of us. We can take you wherever you want to go. Maia, Jinsimbia, Kornas, Breton." She pauses, takes another drink of tea, and sets the cup on its saucer. "Or you can stay with us as part of our crew."

Wren forces herself to swallow the piece of cheese in her mouth. "Stay with you?"

Eleanor nods. "Are you a magics user?"

Wren pauses but then lifts her chin and straightens her spine. "Yes. I'm a healer."

"We could use a healer on our crew."

Wren sets the plate on the desk in front of her. "Why would you let me stay?"

Eleanor's bright green eyes flash as she smiles. "I've spent my life helping people, Wren. You will be no different."

If she stays, Wren won't be able to go back home. She thinks of the duke—her papa—alone in the estate. Had he been surprised when they found her gone? What had he told the guests? What had he told her betrothed?

The tea in Wren's cup has gone cold again, but she tips the rest into her mouth and swallows the way she would a shot of whiskey. She takes a deep breath, closing her eyes and letting it out slowly. "I'll stay," she says. She doesn't want to go back to Sudal, not yet. Maybe not ever. She hadn't wanted her life to change, but now, sitting in Eleanor's cabin aboard this ship, she thinks she might like a change of pace. A change of scenery. She nods. "I'll stay," she says again.

"Fantastic." The captain stands and holds out her hand. "Welcome aboard."

THREE

Eleanor takes Wren down to the crew's quarters, where she's given a change of clothes.

"You'll have privacy down here. Everyone's above," Eleanor says as she walks back up the steps to the deck. "Come on up when you're done." She smiles at Wren and disappears into the sunlight.

Wren is used to having no privacy. At the estate, she had a revolving door of maids and handmaidens to help her get ready for the day. They helped tie or zip her into dresses, helped pile her hair on her head, helped her strap shoes on her feet. Still, she's glad for the quiet.

And it is quiet, mostly. The waves scrape against the hull, there are shouts from people and cries of gulls overhead, a bell somewhere in the ship's belly. But her mind is quiet, and she's glad for that.

The clothes she'd picked out—dark linen trousers, a white shirt—are nowhere near new, their hems stitched closed, or holes patched with scraps of fabric or embroidered over with colored thread, but they fit her and she's glad to be out of the wedding dress. She doesn't know what to do with it, so she leaves it in a pile next to the trunk she dug through to find the clothes she wears now.

She steps into a pair of leather boots that are a nearly perfect fit and tucks the hems of her trousers into them. When she straightens, she pulls her cloak from the top of the trunk and swings it around her shoulders. There's a mirror hung on the wall, and she looks at her reflection as she clasps her cloak at her throat.

She combs her fingers through her hair and tries to untangle the knots as best she can until it hangs limply down her back. She runs her tongue over her chapped lips before gently pressing the pad of her thumb to them, healing the cracks before heading up the steps to the deck.

"All set?" Eleanor asks her as she steps into the sun.

"Yeah," Wren says. "Thank you, Eleanor."

The captain smiles and dips her chin to her chest. "Eli, please."

Wren smiles. "Thank you, Eli." Then, "Where did you find these boots? They're almost a perfect fit."

Eli laughs. "Kiara and I have been on this ship a long time. We've got clothes and shoes to fit almost anyone."

A long time? Wren thinks. Neither of them looks much older than she is. Before she can ask, Eli turns and starts walking across the deck.

Wren follows, shielding her eyes from the sun. Eli had put her green coat back on when they left her quarters and Wren's eyes stay focused on the starburst pattern embroidered over the back, centered over the captain's heart.

Lex walks past them, carrying a coil of rope in their arms, and Wren has to tear her eyes from Eli's coat to avoid tripping over the end of it. "Heard you're joining the crew. Welcome aboard." They give Wren a bright smile.

Eli laughs and tosses the end of the rope over Lex's shoulder. "Things travel fast on *The Altean*," she says. "I'm surprised it took us so long to find you in the hold."

She drags her fingers along the wood railing, then pats it lovingly. "She must have wanted to wait until we were further out to sea."

"You talk about her like she's alive." Wren pulls her hair out of her face and off her neck, twisting it so it hangs down her spine. There were no leather strips in the trunk below deck.

"She is," Eli says, digging into her pocket and handing a leather tie to Wren. "I won her in a bet fifty years ago. She's made of wood from Adreus's sacred forest."

Wren's steps falter as she secures the tie at the back of her skull. "Fifty years ago?"

Eli smiles at her. "Yep. C'mon, let's introduce you to the others."

Wren wants to ask about the bet, wants to ask how old Eli is. But she keeps her questions to herself, having been chastised as a child by her nannies that it was rude to ask too many questions, especially when the question was, "Why?" or "How?"

Though she had walked past the other crew members on her way to the captain's quarters with Lex, and again when she followed Eli down to the crew's quarters to get changed, she kept her eyes on her bare feet and not paid any attention to them. Now, she forces herself to meet their eyes, repeats their names in her head until she's sure she'll remember them.

Eli introduces her first to Arden, a big-chested man with ruddy hair and beard and moss-green eyes. Freckles dot the reddened skin over his nose. When he talks, his voice is gruff and weathered and he stutters a few times, drawing out the w and t in "We're glad to have you." Wren thanks him, tells him she's happy to be here, and smiles at him as she and Eli leave him to his work.

"Arden is our cook," Eli says. "But he's *very good* at setting things in pots to simmer all day, so he helps us on deck, too."

Though Wren has already met Kiara, she and Eli stop by the bench where she's sitting. She has a basket of sewing things next to her and a pair of green trousers on her lap. The cat from earlier sits on the bench next to Kiara, on what looks like a pile of folded clothing. It blinks at Wren before going back to cleaning its ears.

"You're wearing some of my best work." Kiara pulls the needle from the trousers and points to the shirt Wren is wearing. Holding up the trousers, she says, "If you need anything mended, just let me know." She winks and goes back to her work as Wren and Eli continue on. Eli scratches the cat between its ears before they walk away.

A few members gather by the mast. Jez, a skinny man with hooded eyes, dark hair, and a gap-toothed smile, throws dice with a girl that can be no older than twelve named Grace. Grace's curly hair bobs as she laughs and grabs a handful of colored candy discs from a pile. Watching their game is a woman named Clare, her long blonde hair blowing slightly in the breeze off the water. She has a bubbled scar that runs from her hairline and down her neck and shoulder before it disappears under her shirt. They're all friendly and smile at Wren. Grace offers her a green candy disc and Wren takes it, tucking it into the pocket of her trousers.

Then there are Ophelia and Ezra. Wren knows Ezra's name from his brief voyage to the hold where she hid, but she's glad for a face to go with the name. They sit by the bow, Ophelia cleaning under her fingernails with a silver-bladed knife and Ezra chewing on a piece of dried meat.

"Good to meet you, Wren," Ezra says, looking sidelong at her as if he remembers the noise he'd heard and can now attribute that to her. He holds out his hand to her, his honey eyes bright, a headband pushing stray hair from his angular face.

"Good to meet you, too." Wren takes his hand and shakes. His skin is rough and calloused. The olive skin over his forehead and nose is sunburned pink. His long curly dark hair is tied out of his face in a knot at the back of his scalp.

Eli leaves Wren with Ezra and Ophelia before joining Kiara on the bench.

"So," Ophelia says, her singsong voice high and light. She slides her knife into a holster strapped across her chest and sits forward. "What brings you aboard *The Altean*?" Her red-blonde hair is cropped short, showing off her pointed ears. They remind Wren of a creature out of a fairy tale.

Wren settles on the deck in front of Ophelia and shrugs. "It was time for a change of scenery.". She tells them she was adopted by the Duke of Sulesia at six and offers a few minor details of her life since. She doesn't go into details of the arranged marriage, and while they had to have seen her ratty dress on either of her trips across the deck, they don't ask about it. They only talk when Wren mentions she's a healer.

Ophelia holds out her hand, showing a small infection on her palm. "Got a splinter a few weeks ago," she explains. "I thought I got the whole thing, but it's festered, so I must've missed a bit."

Wren takes Ophelia's hand in hers and inspects the wound. She traces around it with her finger, feeling for the pocket of infection under the skin. She can't manipulate the wood, but she can pull the whole sac out if she's careful. Wren looks up at Ophelia through her light eyelashes. "This might hurt a little."

Ophelia waves her hand through the air. "Nothing I can't handle."

Wren goes back to the wound. She has to open the skin a little more to extract the infection, but once she pulls it free, she looks around for something to wipe her fingers on.

Ezra is there, waiting with a worn handkerchief. She rinses her fingers in a small stream of water Ophelia pours from a flask, then traces the hole in Ophelia's palm with her finger, feeling the skin knit together.

"I've never been healed by magics before," Ophelia says, admiring the thin pink line on her palm. "I wasn't gifted with healing."

"Can you use magics?" Wren asks. She had discovered her magics when she was young, and her healing just before her birth parents died. She tried healing her mother's lungs, but she didn't know how, and all she'd done was heat her hands as they pressed into her mother's chest.

Ophelia twirls a knife in her fingers. "Yeah, but my gift is a little...unusual." The corner of her mouth tugs up.

Ezra barks out a laugh from where he lies on the deck. "*Unusual* is right. Scared the shit out of me the first time she did it."

Ophelia shrugs and then turns back to Wren. "You wanna see?"

"There isn't much to *see*, honestly," Ezra says. Ophelia throws a dried piece of meat at him. He laughs, a deep sound that comes from his chest. "It's really cool," he amends. "But not much to see." He pops the meat Ophelia had thrown at him into his mouth and laces his fingers behind his head.

Ophelia huffs, but she's smiling. She stuffs the bag of dried meat into her pocket and sheathes the knife and stands, her arms hanging at her sides loosely.

Then she disappears.

Ezra shrugs a shoulder and closes his eyes, wiggling his shoulders to get more comfortable. "Like I said. Not much to see."

A loud pop behind Wren makes her swivel around. Ophelia squats there, a big smile on her face. "Hi," she says. She puts her lips together and makes another popping sound.

Eyes wide, Wren gawks. "How did you do that?"

Ophelia moves back to her spot near Ezra and sits down on the deck, leaning against the railing. "I can manipulate the light to bend away from me, so it doesn't reflect. I can do it to objects and other people, too." She laughs, bubbly and bright. "For the first few months after I joined, Lex thought they were being haunted by a ghost."

"It was not funny, by the way." Lex joins them at the bow and sits next to Ophelia, their legs stretched out in front of them.

"On the contrary, Alexandre. It was hilarious," Ezra says, his eyes still closed. "Even the Star Child laughed."

Lex playfully kicks Ezra's leg. "Shut up. No, they didn't."

"There's a Star Child on board?" Wren asks.

Wren had only heard stories of Star Children. Those with the ability to see perfectly in the dark are rare. It's rumored their vision is so clear, they can see into the future. There was never a need for them at the estate, so Wren has never seen one in person, just illustrations of them in her books.

Ophelia smirks. "Yep," she says. "They sleep during the day and keep watch at night. I'm sure you'll get to meet them soon."

They talk for a few more minutes until the sound of laughter floats to them from where Eli and Kiara sit. Wren is struck again at how young they are. It's not unusual for ships to be captained by young people, but the way Eli was talking, Wren thought she would be older.

I won her in a bet fifty years ago.

"So, what's Eli's story?" she asks.

Lex's voice is light when they answer, but Wren notices their shoulders square a bit when they say, "What do you mean?"

Eli and Kiara sit close together on the bench, their thighs touching. When Kiara looks at Eli, her eyes shine and she smiles the way Wren's mother used to smile when she looked at her father.

"She said that she and Kiara have been on the ship a long time. And when we came up on deck, she said she'd won *The Altean* in a bet fifty years ago." Wren turns to the others. "There's no way she's that old."

Lex laughs, their shoulders relaxing again. "You'd be surprised." Then they yell, "Hey, Captain!"

Eli stands and makes her way over to them, looking back at Kiara, who's smiling after her. Turning back to the crew at the bow, she says, "What's up?"

"Wren wants to know how old you are."

"No, that's not what I said!" Wren says, stumbling through the words.

Eli laughs. "It's okay," she says, holding up her hands. "It's a question I get from every new crew member. Lex still holds the record for the shortest amount of time passing before asking, though."

Lex hunches their shoulders, and Wren can't be sure the red over their cheeks is entirely the fault of the sun.

Eli tells Wren about where she grew up. A port town in the Kornesian Empire, more than three hundred years ago.

"Three hundred years ago?" Wren parrots, dumbfounded.

"Shh!" Ophelia says.

"Sorry." Wren mimes locking her lips with a turning key and then tosses the key over Ophelia's head and the railing.

Eli laughs and then continues.

She's the daughter of a judge and grew up near the sea. Her life was spent in classrooms, but her heart beat like the waves on sand. She begged her parents for sailing lessons since she was small, and they finally relented when she turned fifteen.

Then, she was given a boat for her eighteenth birthday, and she set sail. She met Kiara at a port town a year later and invited her along. They spent the next few years sailing the world, exploring cities, and hiking along coastlines.

Six years after Kiara joined her, they were caught in a bad storm, one that pushed their boat against the rocks and sent waves over the rails.

"We thought we were going to die. I'd never seen water that dark before," Eli remembers. "We prayed to Adreus, asking for his mercy."

Before they finished their prayer, the storm calmed. When they looked around, there was a tall man on the deck of their boat. His robes were half black, half white, split down the center. He introduced himself as Adreus, the god of life and death, and said he'd come to offer a bargain.

"I will give you your life, Eleanor Crowley. In return, you will give life to all that ask," he said.

"I didn't know what he meant. I asked him, 'How can I give life? I'm not a goddess. I wasn't born with magics.'"

"'I will save you and your ship,'" Eli recounts, her voice growing deeper to emulate Adreus's. "'You will treat it as a sanctuary and will give mercy and shelter to all who ask. You will have your life and, as long as you are on board, death will not find you, and you cannot be harmed.'"

The gift of immortality. From a god. Eli accepted. How could she not? To reject his offer would be an offense to not only him, but to all the gods.

Before Adreus left, Eli asked for one more favor.

"What right do you have to ask a favor after what I've already given you?"

Eli stood in front of the god, her legs wobbly and her voice shaking. "I'm not worth what you have given me, and I'm not worthy of what I ask for now. But I would give up any part of your gift for this."

Adreus softened. "Tell me your wish, Eleanor."

Eli held out her hand to Kiara and pulled her to her feet so they were standing together on their buffeted ship. "Let her come with me," she said to Adreus. "Let her stay with me, please. I'll give up anything you ask." Eli's voice would have shaken then, just as it does now.

Adreus smiled. He is the god of death, yes. But he is also the god of life. He could easily give Kiara the same thing he'd given Eli. After all, what is life without love?

"I will give her immortality, but she will not be invulnerable. Unless she is hurt beyond help, death will not find her. Will you still have her?"

Eli looked at Kiara. They had grown so much together over the last six years. They had seen so much of the world, had eaten food that made them feel alive and food that made them wish for death. They had saved each other's lives more times than either of them cared to admit. They'd become inseparable.

"Yes," Eli said. "I would have her forever."

Adreus nodded. "Then it is so." And he vanished.

Since then, Eli and Kiara have sailed the world hundreds of times over. They'd repaired and replaced their ship a few times, but each time, it was together. They had become soulbound, Eli says.

The Altean, though not the ship they'd had the longest, was the one they were most fond of. It had brought them the crew they had now. *The Altean* had been a rescue ship on more than one occasion and saved more lives than grains of rice in their bowls. It had served as a homecoming vessel, been a makeshift nursery when one of their guests had given birth, been a place for celebration and mourning.

Wren thinks back to the altar in Eli's cabin. Adreus doesn't have any specific symbols like Anrena and Iros do, but she can guess that the piece of wood on the altar to Adreus would have belonged to that original ship. The one Adreus had stood on and saved their lives. They had saved a piece, either as sentiment or to be reminded of the task that had been set upon them.

"We may appear to only be twenty-five, but we'll be celebrating our three hundred and fiftieth birthdays this summer," Eli finishes.

"That's incredible," Wren says. "I've heard stories—rumors—of you and your ship, but I never would have thought they were true."

"It's true," Eli says, lifting a shoulder. "It's hard sometimes. Watching friends leave is especially hard. But," she turns toward Kiara, "having someone to share it with is nice. It makes the hard times easier."

"Papa always told me there could be no good times without hard times," Wren says. He'd said that while rubbing her back when she was nineteen, lying in bed for the third week in a row, fighting her own storm and praying for reprieve.

"Your papa is very wise," Eli says. Then she nods at them and turns to rejoin Kiara.

Wren stays at the bow with the others, listening to stories and jokes that Lex and Ezra tell. Arden and Clare join them. Arden sits next to Lex, resting his arm on their knee. He'd brought a bottle of cheap whiskey with him and they all pass it around, taking swigs of it until their thoughts are fuzzy, their tongues thick.

A few hours later, when the sun sinks closer to the horizon, Eli, Kiara, and Grace bring around beat-up metal bowls of stew and pass them out. The cat—Penelope, Ophelia said when Wren asked—follows them, her tail straight up but for the very tip that's stuck at an angle.

Wren feels the thick stew clearing her mind as she eats. The carrots and potatoes are fresh from Sudal. Wren finds herself suddenly homesick, and she has to bite the inside of her cheek and look out over the water to keep herself from crying.

The duke had always treated her well. After she moved into his home, she never wanted for anything. If there had been even an utterance of anything she wanted, it would arrive within a few days, a bow of purple ribbon tied around it.

He made sure she grew up with a good education. She was enrolled in private tutoring sessions and had a pianoforte teacher. He never forced her to learn anything she didn't want to. When she was eight, she wanted to learn to ride. At ten, she tired of horses and a sword-fighting instructor replaced her riding instructor. During her training, she started an apprenticeship with the estate's healer and herbalist. After she thought her training in sword and herbology was done, she filled her time instead with reading and painting.

The only time he'd forced her into anything was when he told her she would be getting married. She wasn't interested in marriage. At twenty, when it was first brought up, she felt like she was too young. Her life without tutors and instructors and lessons had barely begun, and she was just starting to get out of bed without wanting to crawl right back in. Why should her newly won free time be taken by someone else? Especially after what had happened the summer before.

The duke relented, until her twenty-first birthday, then until her twenty-second, then her twenty-third. But by her twenty-fourth birthday, he had had enough of her avoidance. He told her he'd arranged a marriage between her and a Nestadian judge's son. He was making arrangements for his travel to Sudal, and the wedding would be in two months.

She misses her home. Her room at the estate. The gardens and marble hallways. Despite her anger and the sense of betrayal, she misses her papa, too.

Ophelia nudges Wren's foot with her own, pulling Wren from her thoughts, and raises her strawberry-blonde eyebrows slightly in question. Wren gives her a smile and a small nod. Ophelia smiles back and returns to her stew and the story Ezra is telling. She doesn't move her foot from where it rests against Wren's.

That night, after Wren helps clean up from dinner, Ezra and Ophelia show her down to the crew bunks. She'd been down here with Eli earlier, but she'd only seen the trunk of shared clothes and the mirror hanging next to it on the wall. The pile that was her wedding dress has disappeared.

There are hammocks hung in rows down the center of the room. Cots line the walls. Each cot is piled with blankets and pillows, some of them folded and others bundled or bunched. Grace kneels next to one that is so crowded with stuffed animals, it's a wonder a person would fit there at all. She rearranges the stuffies, stacking a few of them against the wall next to the cot.

Ezra and Ophelia's bed is at the end of the room. There's an unclaimed hammock near them, and Wren gratefully takes it when Ophelia offers it to her. She lies down and, though it's nothing like her bed at the estate, it's not uncomfortable, and it's infinitely better than the hold where she'd been hiding. The fabric is thick and will help keep her warm during the cool nights. Hanging from a nail in one of the posts the hammock is strung from is a leather satchel.

"You can have that, too," Ophelia says, sitting down on the mattress she and Ezra share.

Wren lifts the flap and looks inside. Apart from some lint in the corners, it's empty. It's large enough to carry her cloak when it's folded and a few other things. Maybe she'll find some crystal bottles at a market or a book she'd like to keep. "Thanks," she says and hangs her cloak from the same nail the bag is hanging from. Then she sits in the hammock and swings her legs in.

Ezra, leaning against the other pole Wren's hammock is tied to, points to a chest near the one with the shared clothing Wren had dug through earlier. "That one has blankets and a few pillows in it if you need some."

"Thanks," Wren says again. She unties her boots, leans over the side of the hammock, and sets them under her cloak and new bag.

"Sure," Ezra says. He bounces from where he leans and unbuttons his shirt, letting it fall from his shoulders. Across his chest is a bandage, layered a few times from his armpits to his waist.

"What happened?" Wren asks, pushing herself up. She's never healed wounds deeper than a shallow cut from sword sparing, and nothing so big it required bandages like this one, but if Ezra is up for it, she's willing to try.

He only laughs. "Nothing, which is the problem." Wren cocks her head to the side, knitting her eyebrows together. Ezra laughs again. "I'm saving up coin to get them removed." He motions to his chest.

"I offered to cut them off myself, but he hasn't taken me up on the offer," Ophelia says, twirling a knife in her hand.

"I've seen what you cut with those knives. They're not touching me."

"That's not what you said last night." She looks up at him from under her eyelashes.

Wren snorts, and Ezra puts his hands over her ears. Muffled, she hears him say, "O, we are in the presence of *royalty*. We mustn't be scandalized so soon after we've become part of her good graces."

Wren pushes him away. "Please, if you think *that*"—she nods to the knife in Ophelia's hand—"is enough for me to consider you *scandalized*, you've never spent any time in a duke's house."

"Well, no shit, Wren. I've spent my life in alleyways and the last three on a ship captained by someone gifted with eternal life trying to save enough coin to get my tits removed."

Wren isn't sure if Ezra is joking or not, so she just looks at him, but then he laughs and she lets out a breath and smiles.

They talk for a few more minutes while Ezra fluffs the pillows and rearranges the blankets on the mattress. Then Ophelia complains about how tired she is and leaves to dig through the shared clothing trunk. Ezra shrugs into an oversized shirt and removes the binding around his chest.

"Does it hurt?" Wren asks when he lies back.

"Binding?" His eyes are closed, his hands clasped behind his head. He'd pulled the headband and tie from his hair and his dark curls fan out on the pillow. "Sometimes, if I rush it. Ophelia helps. She makes sure it's not too thick or too tight. When I first started, it would cut into my sides." He opens one dark eye and looks up at Wren. "It's still not easy to fight in, but thankfully, we don't have to fight too often." He closes his eye again and settles further into the blankets and pillows.

Ophelia returns a few minutes later, carrying a flask. She sits down next to Ezra, who has started snoring, and takes a swig. She offers it to Wren.

"No, thanks. The whiskey earlier was enough." Wren's head had been fuzzy for hours after they'd finished the bottle on the deck, even after eating the stew Arden made for dinner.

Ophelia shakes her head, smiling. "It's only water."

Wren gratefully takes it. It's cool on her tongue. When she's finished, she hands the flask back to Ophelia.

They lay back, Ophelia next to Ezra, Wren in her hammock. Just before Wren falls asleep, Ophelia says, "Oh. Here." She tosses Wren a dense ball.

"Wax?" Wren asks.

"Yeah," Ophelia says. "Snores from the others can be pretty loud. Especially this guy's." She nudges Ezra's shoulder, and he grunts in his sleep.

"Thanks," Wren says for what feels like the hundredth time that day. She divides the wax and puts it into her ears. She'd used it occasionally at the estate, when the duke had parties or hosted royalty from the Kingdom of Kornas. Immediately, the noise from the other crew members quiets. She lies awake for a little while, tracing the whorl of the wood above her, until someone turns out the lantern and the room is left in darkness.

The waves against the hull of *The Altean* lull her to sleep.

FOUR

OVER THE NEXT FEW weeks, Wren helps out on deck and learns what she can about life on board. Every night, she has to heal the ripped blisters on her fingers, the sunburn over her nose. She heals the crew's pinked skin, a few splinters in thumbs, and a burn on Grace's hand from a hot kettle. They thank her in sweets, in spiced tea, by letting her have the sweetest strawberries at dinner. Two weeks after she joins the crew, Lex and Arden gift her a swath of purple fabric so she can tie back the short hair over her forehead that won't fit in the leather tie.

Her favorite days are the days they're docked. She walks the market square with Ophelia and Ezra, sings shanties with Lex sitting on the dock, their bare feet dangled over the water, takes laundry into town with Kiara and helps hang it to dry on the deck of the ship.

In Locksa, she gets a bout of sickness after eating food from a street cart, and Ophelia holds back her hair, and Lex brings her clean water to wash her mouth out. After sleeping the rest of the day and through to the next morning, she wakes feeling better but is wary about what food she orders from then on.

On days at sea, Wren and Grace sneak tastes of Arden's food. She pulls a piece of ribbon just out of Penelope's reach to watch her jump. Sometimes, she helps Kiara with the mending.

She sleeps in the hammock near Ezra and Ophelia every night. They'd hung a piece of old sail between them so the two could still have privacy when they wanted, but it was kept open most nights. When they can't sleep, Wren and Ophelia lounge together in the hammock, Penelope sleeping spread out on their laps.

One night, Ophelia tells Wren about her family.

"I grew up in a village in Breton called Nali with my parents and little sister. Our father died of sun sickness and our mother left for the market one day and never returned." Ophelia speaks in hushed tones to not disturb the others. "I was only eleven. Evey was six. We went to a children's home, but the winters were hard. A sickness went around the home once and Evey caught it. I thought she was going to die. She recovered but lost most of her hearing because of an ear infection." They had left a lantern burning low near them and it casts deep shadows over the angular planes of Ophelia's face. Her eyes shine in the glow.

"I worked jobs no one else wanted to do. I mended clothes from sunup to sundown, scrubbed floors after bar fights, shoveled shit. We couldn't stay in the home, so we slept in alleyways and abandoned apartments for a few years. It was cold, but it was better than passing sickness from kid to kid."

Her voice grows quieter when she says, "When I was fifteen, a man cornered us in a dark alley. I thought it was going to try to take her. We were careful to avoid the docks, where we were told pirates stole girls. But I guess pirates need to eat too and he came into town. I shoved her behind me and the man pulled a knife on us.

He ordered us to give him what we had—money, jewels, whatever. But I don't believe that's all he wanted. I pulled my own knife and stabbed him." She chuckles but there's no warmth behind it. "He must've been pretty drunk to let me get one over on him." Her long fingers move through Penelope's black and white fur absentmindedly. Her voice has hushed to a whisper, and Wren has to strain to hear her over the creaks and moans of the ship.

"The next morning, when he was discovered, I was so afraid they'd tie it back to us that we ran as far as we could. We braved the docks, where I paid our way onto a fishing boat going to Jinsimbia. It cost us all the money we had. When we got there, Evey found a job doing laundry, but she had to sign an indenture for food and housing." Ophelia has stopped petting Penelope and her fingers twist around themselves. "I worked still, doing whatever I could. Cleaning pots and dying fabric for dress shops, shearing sheep, trimming trees." She lets out a huffy laugh and wipes her eyes. "I ran into Ezra while on a delivery in the market. He took me for drinks at a cheap pub and I joined *The Altean* the next day.

"I told Evey I'd buy out her indenture." She shakes her head. "It's been seven years. I send her all my extra coin, but we're not even halfway to paying it off."

Wren can't imagine the heartache Ophelia must feel for her sister. She slips her hand into Ophelia's and lays her head on her shoulder. They stay that way until morning, falling asleep against the other, Penelope purring in their laps.

FIVE

THEY DOCK A FEW days later at a Kornesian town. Wren is worried about someone recognizing her, as it was the King of Kornas that appointed the duke to rule in Sudal in his stead generations ago, but after a quick trip through the market and surrounding areas, Kiara tells her there are no posters or conversations about the duke's missing daughter. Wren is relieved, but there's a pang in her chest. Had the duke not sent out search parties? Had he not wondered what happened to her?

She leaves the ship arm in arm with Ophelia, Ezra running ahead of them. They stop at a booth near the docks to exchange their money for Kornas crowns while Wren looks at the message board nearby. She had half expected a letter from the duke to be pinned there, or a letter that had his seal on it begging for any information on her. But there's only the standard work ads and notices pinned up.

When Ezra and Ophelia are finished exchanging their money, they meet her and they join the crowd of people walking into town.

Wren's mood had fallen when there was nothing for her from the duke, but looping her arms together with Ophelia and Ezra brings her spirits back up.

The market is dusty and people stand shoulder to shoulder between the stalls, ducking to keep their faces and heads in the shade.

Wren and Ophelia walk from stall to stall as Ezra runs ahead and then runs back, showing them something he bought, or calling from ahead and holding things up, asking Ophelia how she likes them.

"He's like a child," Wren says, laughing.

Ophelia nods and examines the hilt on a black-bladed knife. "Yeah," she says affectionately. "He gets excited about the little things."

"That's why he likes you." Wren bumps into Ophelia's shoulder.

Ophelia laughs and hands over a few crown bills to the vendor. She adds her new knife to the leather strap across her chest. "I can neither confirm nor deny if that's the reason he's kept me around."

Just then, Ezra runs up to them, a pink sphere clutched in his hands. "Ophelia, Wren, look!" He holds up the stone. He reminds Wren of the crows out her window at the estate when they'd found something shiny. "Isn't it pretty?"

Ophelia and Wren look at it. It is pretty, Wren thinks. The stone is varying shades of pink, from the pink of a baby's cheeks, to the smoky grey-pink of a sunset, to the lilies growing under her window at the estate.

Wren glances the way Ezra has just come and sees an angry woman with a red birthmark on her cheek shoving the crowd aside and coming their way. "You should take that back, Ez," she says, nodding toward the woman.

Ezra turns, sees the woman, looks back at the girls and salutes, tossing the pink sphere into the air and grabbing it back before he lets the crowd swallow him up.

The next few stalls are things Eli asked Ophelia to pick up—gauze and rope and wax. One at the far end, away from the crowds and tucked under a tree with twisted roots at its base, is a stall with a woman behind it. She's got a crown of yellow flowers on her head and a permanent twist to her lips. She reminds Wren of the healer and herbalist at the estate, an old woman named Mim.

When Wren had asked to train in swords when she was ten, the duke was hesitant at first, but his best friend and head counselor had said his son was learning as well, and the duke agreed. He gifted Wren a steel dagger with purple jewels encrusted in the hilt. It was perfectly balanced and just the right length. She impressed her sword teacher with parries and jabs. The first time she'd disarmed and knocked down the counselor's son, she beamed. At least until he swiped her feet out from under her. She was surprised but then they laughed together as the dust settled around them.

When they started sword-sparring with the trainees for the navy, Wren would go to bed covered in bruises and cuts, her knuckles bloodied, her knees scraped. She learned on her own to heal her bruises until they were faded yellow instead of dark purple. One day, after a session that left her arms covered in shallow cuts, the healer who lived at the estate invited Wren into her cottage.

Wren had seen the woman work around the grounds. She was an older woman with a wrinkled round face and middle. She was in the navy when she was younger and had been in an accident that left her chest mangled. The combat healers said they could save her breasts, but she'd opted to have them removed. She left the navy and gone back to Sudal, where she'd grown up. She started apprenticing under the then-current healer at the estate and, when they died, took over. She made salves and poultices, loose-leaf teas, and dried herb bundles. There were always sachets of lavender in Wren's closet made by her, and the fresh flower bouquets in her papa's study were made by Mim, too.

Mim asked Wren what healing she could do once they were sat in the cottage at a small hand-carved table. It wasn't much, but Wren had learned how to heal papercuts and pinpricks, along with more superficial wounds, like bruises and spots on her face.

Mim smiled. "That's very good, Wren. Have you ever had any training in your magics?" She was grinding up a few stalks of lavender in a marble mortar.

Wren was surprised at the woman's lack of formality. Everyone around the estate called her Lady Wren, even her sword instructor, her tutors, and her nannies. But she liked the informality; she didn't feel very ladylike sitting in the cottage, her hands and arms bleeding on the woman's table. She shook her head. "No. I just tried once and found I could. I've tried bigger things," she ran her fingers over a scabbed cut on her arm from the day before, "but I can't get it to work."

Mim set her mortar and pestle on the wooden counter that ran along one wall of the cottage and turned to lean against it. "Let's get started then."

Mim had no magics, but was gifted in herbology. She could make tinctures and salves, lotions and ointments. She knew just the right mix of herbs for a headache, for vomiting, for labor pains. She left the large wounds to the healers employed by the military, the ones that were magics users, but she had watched them working, watched as a new wave of healers was trained by the previous, and had picked up a few tricks.

She taught Wren what she learned from watching them. And it took a few days of frustration and tears, but eventually, Wren could heal her cuts into thin pink lines, and then until the skin was perfectly smooth. Wren often left them as thin lines so they'd turn into scars, but occasionally, like the time she'd been cut on her forehead, she healed the wound completely.

Mim worked with Wren the whole time she was in sword training. In those eight years, Wren learned how to heal with her magics and also with the herbs and flowers around the grounds of the estate. She could brew sleeping droughts, remedies for coughs, salves for sunburns. On her own, she studied more and learned to brew poisons that would cause stomach cramps, aroma salts that caused nose bleeds, an ointment she could slather on the edge of her blades that caused temporary paralysis. She never used them, but they were interesting to know, regardless.

Mim gifted Wren with crystal bottles and vials. Together, they built a small shelf for Wren's room where she could keep her ingredients. One corner of Wren's room was dedicated to her botany. She collected mortar and pestles, oil droppers, and books of edible and poisonous plants. Her last few years at the estate, she didn't use those things much, but she always kept the crystal bottles dust-free, and she treasured the things Mim taught her and the things she learned herself.

The stall under the tree holds an assortment of glass bottles. Some are teardrop shaped, some shaped like stars. Wren picks one up carefully, a circular one with a short neck and flat bottom.

"You've got a funny look on your face, Wren. What are you thinking about?" Ophelia stands next to her, her head tilted to the side, her mouth pulled into a mischievous smile.

Wren sets the bottle back on the wooden surface of the stall's counter. "I used to have a set of bottles like this back in Sudal. Well, mine wasn't really *a set*, but I had shelves of bottles like these. Filled with herbs and dried flowers and pieces of mushrooms." She misses the way those shelves looked. In the summer, the sun would stream through her window, hitting the bottles just right, sending a cascade of rainbows across the ceiling and other wall.

Ophelia picks up a set of bottles rolled up in a thick leather case. "How much for a set?"

"Fifteen crowns," the old woman says. She'd been watching them from her crooked stool, but now she stands. She leans on a cane that looks hand carved.

Wren sighs. "I don't have any money," she says.

"Done." Ophelia puts down the leather roll and reaches into the pocket of her trousers.

"Wait, Ophelia." Wren puts her hand on Ophelia's arm.

Ophelia smiles at her. "You can pay me back. First job you complete. Okay?"

Slowly, Wren removes her hand from Ophelia. She nods. "Okay. Thank you."

Ophelia winks and hands the woman the bills. Then she turns to Wren, handing her the leather roll. Inside, the empty bottles softly clink against each other. "Let's go fill 'em up."

There's a meadow not too far from the market square. It's quiet and cool and a few butterflies flutter by on the breeze. Wren takes in a deep breath, grateful for the smells around her instead of the smell of sweat like at the market. Lavender and thyme and rosemary fill her lungs, awakening a part of her she hadn't known was asleep.

Ophelia had gone to tell Ezra where they were heading, so Wren takes a few minutes to drag her hands along the tops of the long grasses. She pulls her boots off and kneels, pushing her fingertips into a bit of soft mud. She can still hear the bustle of the market a bit, but the surrounding trees create a barrier from the outside world. Insects buzz through the air; a few birds sing high in the trees. The bubble of a stream nearby matches the beating of Wren's heart.

When Ophelia joins her again, Wren unties the leather roll, pushing it open until it lies flat. Inside, thirteen glass bottles are secured with twine around their necks and leather across their bodies. They're not as ornamental as the single ones that had been laid out on the stall's table, or the ones meticulously organized and labeled on Wren's shelves at the estate, but they're beautiful and shine in the sun just like hers did when she would refill them in the garden.

On the days she had no sword training, Wren would walk around the grounds with Mim and harvest herbs and roots and flowers. They always replaced what they took by planting seeds, seedlings, or bulbs. Some things, like lavender and thyme, were propagated in little glass bottles and then planted outside the window of Mim's cottage once roots started to grow.

"Where do you want to start?" Ophelia asks, her arms hanging loosely at her sides.

Wren carefully unties the twine and unclasps the leather from two circular flat bottles. She hands them to Ophelia and points across the meadow. "You start with rosemary and thyme." She takes another identical bottle from the roll, along with a cylindrical vial secured only in a leather pocket. "I'll do lavender and strip some bark from these trees."

They work, the bees and butterflies floating around them. Occasionally, Ophelia will call to Wren, who makes her way over to see what Ophelia has found. There's a cluster of lovage, the same herb on the altar for Anrena and Iros, at the base of a tree. Ophelia ties an extra bit of twine around the stalks and cuts them at the base. Then she strips the flowers from the stems and places them inside a bottle Wren hands to her.

The sun climbs higher in the sky and then sinks back toward the horizon. By the time they need to head back to *The Altean*, all but one bottle is filled.

Ophelia mentions a mushroom and shows the fungus to Wren, who carefully cuts and collects it and places it into the final bottle.

The glass bottles clink softly together as Wren rolls and reties the leather pouch. She places it gently into her satchel, pulls on her boots, and she and Ophelia start making their way back to the market square. Wren lets the long grasses run between her fingers.

As they're boarding the ship, Ezra ahead of them with a paper bag clutched in his arms, Wren keeps her hand placed on top of her satchel. The flowers and herbs inside are a piece of Sudal she can carry with her, like her cloak, and having them at her side brings comfort she didn't know she needed.

Grace greets them as they come up the gangplank and excitedly tells them she helped Arden make dinner.

"Oh good, I'm *starving*," Ophelia says as she ruffles her fingers through Grace's hair.

Wren goes down below and hangs her satchel back on its nail by her hammock and scrubs the dirt from her hands and the knees of her trousers. She opens the flap of the satchel before going back up to the deck and runs her fingers over the leather roll, smiling at this small piece of home.

Arden and Grace bring out the food on platters and Lex brings out a stack of plates and a basket of napkins and cutlery. They all sit in a circle on a deck as they eat.

"This is delicious, Grace," Ezra says, his mouth stuffed full of rice and roasted duck.

Grace beams at Ezra, and Arden and Jez look at the girl with pride in their eyes. Grace is only twelve and has been with *The Altean* for a little over a year. No one had mentioned her family, or what had made her decide to join a ship's crew, but Wren can't bring herself to ask. She knows Clare isn't Grace's mother and didn't pretend to be, but otherwise, Wren doesn't know.

As Wren shovels another forkful of rice into her mouth, she says a silent prayer up to Adreus to thank him for saving Eli and Kiara. If it hadn't been for them, where would this ragtag group of people be? Where would she be? A wife, stashed somewhere in a small house, while her husband trains to be a judge. She sets her fork in her bowl and runs her fingers along the boards under her and presses her palm into the deck. If *The Altean* is alive, and if she hid Wren until just the right time, she should thank the ship, too. She can't be sure she's not imagining the slight vibration in the tips of her fingers.

When they've all had their fill of duck and rice and vegetables, Wren helps Lex clean up and do the dishes. The sun has set completely when they rejoin the others on deck. Ezra goes around lighting the lanterns.

Wren and Lex join Clare at the bow where they sit and pass a flask of a sweet fizzy lemon drink around. A breeze picks up and puts the fire in their lantern out.

"Dang. Hey, Ez!" Lex calls, picking up the lantern.

Ezra makes his way over to them. "Sorry about that. Must've forgotten to close the door."

"It's all right. I have matches," Wren says, plunging her hand into her pocket.

Lex laughs. "It's okay, Ezra's got it."

Wren holds the book of matches in her hand and looks at Ezra, standing over them.

He shrugs. "I'll go do the others, then."

Ezra turns and leaves and Wren strikes the match against the deck. When the fire blooms at the end, she holds it to the lantern wick until it catches. Lex makes a big show of closing the door.

"That's how you do it, Ezra!" they yell across the deck to where Ezra stands with another lantern in his hand.

Ezra pulls his hand from the lantern's wick and holds up his middle finger toward Lex.

Wren and Clare fall into each other, laughing as Lex flounders. "That's rude!" they say.

Ezra laughs, hangs the lantern on a hook by Eli and Kiara's door, and moves to where Ophelia sits with Penelope on the steps to the quarterdeck.

"He's so rude," Lex says again as they turn back to Clare and Wren.

"Don't goad him, then, Lex," Clare says as she tips the flask to her lips before handing it to Wren.

Wren takes another swallow. "Yeah, you kind of brought that on yourself."

Lex snatches the flask from Wren's hand, tips it up and chugs the rest of it. "Well, you two are no fun. You're supposed to stick up for me."

"Not in my job description." Clare leans back on her palms and stretches her long legs out in front of her.

Lex looks at Wren, who shakes her head. "Mine, either," she says, scrunching her nose.

"Well, fine." Lex stands and leaves them. They turn and say, "I'm going to find Arden and see what he made for dessert."

"See you," Clare says, leaning her head back and closing her eyes.

Wren watches as Lex disappears down below and then laughs. She's glad for Lex. She's glad for Ezra. She's glad for Grace and Arden and Clare. Wren always imagined this is what it would be like to have a big family. Teasing and silly disputes and eating picnic style in a circle. Sure, she never imagined it would be on a boat, but she's grateful for *The Altean*, too. It's turned into more of a safe haven than she expected when she stowed away on it nearly a month ago.

She runs her fingers over the boards again as she lies back on the deck, clasping her hands under her head. She watches the stars overhead. They're the same constellations she'd see out her window, or when she lay in the grass in the garden, but they feel different here. She feels different here. Free and wild and safe. She again sends a silent prayer to Adreus thanking him for his gift.

That night, after everyone has gone to sleep, Wren pulls the roll from her satchel and runs her fingers over the necks of the bottles inside. The glass is cool under her fingers and she can vaguely smell the lavender and thyme and lovage. Her room had smelled the same at the estate.

She rolls the leather again and clutches it to her chest as she turns on her side and closes her eyes.

SIX

A FEW DAYS LATER, *The Altean* is on open water when the sun is suddenly blocked out by thick grey clouds.

"It's not rain," Eli says. "Must be the changing of the season." She looks over at Wren and winks, but the captain's shoulders have tensed.

Wren knows it's not. It was barely spring when she ran from Sudal. She also knows it's not rain. The clouds are dark but not heavy; the air doesn't smell like rain.

The Altean continues forward as fog envelopes them. Wren pulls her cloak tighter around her shoulders. Her bones seem to hum with anxiety.

"Captain?" Kiara stands from her bench and leans on the rail, her hands flat on its surface, looking out toward the front of the ship.

"Keep an eye out," is all Eli says, but the rest of the crew stops what they're doing and starts watching the sea around them.

A whistle rings out and Wren turns to see Jez motioning to Grace, who runs to him. They disappear below deck together, Penelope following close behind.

The sea is calm, though the fog continues to grow thicker around the ship. Wren glances around them, swiveling in her spot on the quarterdeck, her fingers tangled in the fabric of her cloak.

"Anything?" Eli calls, making rounds on the deck, her eyes trained on the horizon as she walks.

"Nothing starboard," Ezra calls back.

"Nothing port, either," Lex returns.

Kiara joins Wren on the quarterdeck. "What are we looking for?" Wren asks her, still looking out over the water.

Kiara is quiet. Then she points to the front of the ship. "That."

Through the fog cuts another ship. It's too far out for Wren to see it clearly and the fog obscures it even further, but it seems like the fog is leaking from the sails and boards of the hull, creating a cover.

"Ophelia, the flag!" Eli yells, standing near the stairs.

"On it!" Ophelia moves from her spot at the bow and climbs up the mast, her hands and feet finding holds in the wood. In seconds, their green flag is exchanged for a white one.

We surrender, it says.

Wren stands, still on the quarterdeck, one hand holding her purple cloak tight around her shoulders. She watches the other ship approach, her heart thudding against her ribs. Her eyes are trained on the approaching ship. Their sails are grey and patched, the rotting hull congested with barnacles. At the top of their mast, a black flag with a crown of twigs flaps lazily in the wind.

The Altean and her crew seem to hold a collective breath as the other ship advances. As it passes, Wren locks eyes with one of the people on deck and her chest constricts. He looks like he's been painted with watercolors where the world around him has been done with acrylics. His pale skin and eyes are stark against the darkened wood of the ship. His dark hair, light at the roots, is dull. The only bright thing about him is his mouth, a harsh slash of red against his pallid face. When his eyes meet hers, he lifts his chin a little, one corner of his mouth twitching up.

Once the ship has passed, *The Altean* comes back to life. Ophelia shimmies back down the mast and stands with Ezra and Eli.

"Wren!" Fingers wrap around her wrist and pull her back. She turns and Kiara is there, her eyes wide.

Wren comes back to life herself, forcing her thoughts from the receding ship and the ghost aboard it. She realizes she had walked all the way to the railing and leaned far forward, one knee raised to rest on the bench. "Sorry," she says, her voice barely above a whisper. "I'm fine." Absent-mindedly, she rubs her fingers hard into her sternum.

Kiara hesitantly removes her fingers from Wren's wrist. When Wren looks back at the receding ship, the man has moved closer to the rail and is looking at her, the smirk still on his face. She watches for a few more moments until he turns away from her.

She hadn't recognized the flag from her lessons. It didn't belong to any government, to any known crime ring, to any prevalent pirates roaming the sea. She had no guesses to who that could be. Still, he had intrigued her. She'd felt pulled to him, as if an invisible string were connecting them. She's sure she's never seen him before, so why had she felt some kind of recognition? Maybe he had a rare and powerful magics, something like a siren, pulling vulnerable and naïve people closer until he could devour them.

Wren shakes her head. If someone had been born with that kind of magics, it wouldn't be a secret. He has to be older than her, at least by a few years. There's no way he would have slipped by undetected.

Still, as the ship becomes a dot on the horizon and the fog and dark clouds above them dissipate, she wonders. What remote parts of the world had magics that were unregistered?

That night, after *The Altean*'s flag has once again been switched to green, and the crew has eaten their fill of freshly caught fish and preserved apples, Wren lies awake in her hammock, swaying with the waves against the ship, listening to the snores of her crewmates.

She dreams of home. The lush gardens she ran through barefoot, the training grounds where her instructor taught her sword fighting, the bedroom she slept in for nearly twenty years with the big window that looked out over the gardens. In her dream, a little boy with light hair and dark eyes follows her. She recognizes him; he's the son of her papa's head counselor. Jakob. Her best friend.

As she runs through the gardens and through the marble halls of the estate, Jakob changes. At first, he's a little boy, just how he was when they first met. But as they go on, finding hidden corners in hallways and empty rooms with sheet-covered furniture, he changes into a lanky boy, then to a well-fought swordsman, and then into a sailor with strong arms and hair shorn close to his scalp. Wren changes, too. A little girl with skinny ankles, an herbalist's student with dirt under her fingernails, a young woman with long orange hair and a pocket full of paintbrushes.

They stand at the dock in Sudal, Jakob in his navy uniform, Wren in a purple dress, her hair pulled back into a braid running down her back. They say goodbye, then Jakob steps into a small boat. As it pulls away from the dock, he turns and waves at her, a smile crinkling the corners of his eyes. As the boat gets further from her, waves build behind it, getting taller and stronger, rocking against the sides of Jakob's boat, causing him to stumble. He looks at her, eyes wide, gripping the spot on his jacket over his heart. Terror builds in Wren's chest until it rips from her ribcage and her throat turns raw from screaming. A final wave crashes over the boat, pushing it under the surface. Pieces of wood pop up from the water, creating an outline against the bright horizon. Jakob never surfaces.

Wren wakes with a start, her heart jackrabbiting. Around her, the cabin is dark, filled with the soft sighing of her fellow crewmates in slumber. She lies in her hammock for a while, but when it's clear she won't be able to sleep again, she swings her legs over the side and sets her bare feet on the floor. Sleeping bodies fill the other hammocks and bunks around her. Except for one, tucked into the corner, heavy canvas draped from the walls to keep the light out.

On deck, the Star Child sits straight-backed in a chair near the ship's wheel. Their bright white hair falls loosely down their back, their chin tilted up slightly toward the stars.

The moon is full, and Wren is able to see the deck well enough to make her way up to the quarterdeck. She remembers the ghostly ship, the man standing aboard. A pull in her chest makes her turn toward the back of the ship, to where she was standing when the ship finally disappeared on the horizon. She shakes her head, clearing the ship and the people on its deck from her mind, and sits near the Star Child, leaning against the railing.

In Sudal, Wren had only ever heard stories of Star Children. There were pictures in books of people that were all light except for their eyes, which were inky black pools flecked with bits of white, making them look like the night sky. Her books made it clear that Star Children didn't have magics the same way that light or water users did, but were born with different abilities. There were theories that they'd been blessed by Ekris, god of dark and the moon, and were the embodiment of his gift.

There was little work for Star Children at the estate, where guards were posted around the clock. Because of their ability to see in the dark, they were often employed on ships to keep watch at night, when it would be impossible for people with typical vision to see past the railings of ships.

The Star Child on board *The Altean* had smiled kindly and bowed their head when they'd met Wren, though they only speak to Eli or Kiara. Wren has never heard their voice, never seen their mouth move at all, except to eat. All she knows is this Star Child is the reason for many safe nights and saved lives.

Wren watches them as they scan the horizon. The moonlight illuminates them, making their hair and skin appear to glow. Their eyes look empty in the dark, like Wren is looking right through their skull into the night sky.

The Star Child keeps their eyes on the water, their hands flat on their thighs. Wren almost speaks, but it seems a crime to shatter the early morning quiet.

Eli joins them on deck just as the horizon pinks. The Star Child stands when Eli climbs the steps. They nod once at the captain, then turn and nod to Wren before walking down the steps to the main deck and disappearing below.

"Couldn't sleep?" Eli helps Wren to her feet.

"I...I had a dream." Wren hasn't shared Jakob with anyone yet, and she's not sure she wants to. She hasn't thought about him much since joining Eli's crew, and just the thought of mentioning him now causes a lump to form in her throat and her chest to constrict. Though she's healed and come to terms with his death, it's still hard to talk about him with people that never knew him. It would be like sharing a piece of someone else's secret. She likes to hold him close to her. If he's with her, he can't be hurt.

Eli hums and surveys the horizon. It's still dark enough that Wren can't see the look on her face from where she stands. "Did you recognize that ship? From yesterday?"

Wren snaps her head up. The captain is still looking out over the sea. The water stretched before them is calm, splashing gently against the sides of the ship. "No," she says. "Why?"

"Their captain. His name is Aris." Eli turns around and leans against the railing, her arms propped up beside her. She worries the inside of her cheek. "He's been trailing us for a year or so. He hasn't done much, but we always fly the white flag, just in case."

Though Eli hasn't specified, Wren knows the one she saw yesterday—the ghost with odd hair and red mouth—is their captain.

"What do you mean, he's been trailing you?"

Eli sighs. "His parents hired us to deliver him to an island two years ago. He's the banished Prince of Breton and we were told to drop him off and leave. It was," she pauses, takes a breath, "not a nice place to be left. Small and swampy. There wasn't much for him to cling to." She turns back to the sea, her eyes unfocused. "We thought he would die. That's what his parents intended, anyway. Then, a few months later, we noticed a ship following us that would make a brief appearance and then disappear into the fog. One night, they got close, and we thought we were being haunted.

Then he blew a hole in our side and disappeared. Yesterday was the first time we've seen him in months."

The banished prince. Wren remembers her father telling her that the Breton prince had been executed for crimes against his family and country. She assumed he'd been hung, not abandoned on an island.

"How did he survive?" Wren traces the whorls in the wooden railing with her nail.

It takes a few moments for Eli to answer. "I don't know," she finally says. "When we saw him again, we thought it was his ghost because he looked so different. When he was with us, he had life. His face was flushed and full, his skin pink from the sun. But now he looks...well, you saw him." Eli looks over at Wren, her green eyes troubled.

She nods. He looked hollow, like a strong breeze could blow him away. Like the sun had bleached all color from him.

"You never met him, did you? Not at any dinners or gatherings as the duke's daughter?"

Wren shakes her head. "I only met the royal family from the kingdom of Kornas. The Breton queen and king never visited Sudal, and we never visited them." She thinks about telling Eli about the pull she felt to Aris. She's sure Kiara would have told Eli how close she had come to jumping overboard.

But Wren says nothing and Eli doesn't ask, so they stand at the rail and watch the sun turn the sky from pink to orange to purple and then blue. The final stars disappear as the sun fully rises.

SEVEN

THAT NIGHT, WREN DREAMS again of the estate. The lights on the walls illuminate her way down the hallway leading to her room. Through her door, the light is watery, like when it rains in spring. Her bare feet make no noise on the carpeted floor.

When she enters, her room is much like she left it the day she would have been married—a pair of shoes tossed into the corner, a nightgown draped over the backside of a chair, there's an indent on the bedspread from where she was sitting before being called to leave for the church.

But something is different about this. She had been alone that morning, apart from the handmaidens that had done her hair, but now, Aris stands near her desk, his long white fingers tracing a knot in the wood.

She hesitates, watching Aris take in the crystal bottles of dried herbs and flower petals. He turns toward her when the door closes with a click. His eyes land on hers and the corner of his mouth tugs up in not quite a smile.

"Wren," he says. His voice is coarse, deeper than she imagined it would be.

She steps further into the room. "Aris."

He does smile then. "You know me."

She swallows. "Enough. How do you know me?" Rain patters against the windowpanes.

Instead of answering, Aris strolls around her room. He moves like a shadow, his shoulders barely dipping with each step. He trails his fingers along the bookshelves on her wall, the posts of her bed, the frame around the portrait of her and the duke she was given when she turned ten, the edge of a mortar bowl on her desk. "This is the room of a lady," he says. Turning to her, he adds, "Not a pirate."

Wren watches him, tracking his movements as he walks around her room. "I'm not a pirate," she says.

He laughs soundlessly. "Then what are you doing with Captain Eleanor Crowley?"

Wren pauses. Despite the pull in her chest suggesting otherwise, this is a stranger. Aris keeps his light eyes on her, waiting.

In the end, she decides to say, "Running away." After all, this is only a dream, no matter how real it might feel.

Aris chuffs. "From this?" He spreads his arms out. "Why would you run from this? Why give up a life of luxury for a hammock on a damp ship?"

Again, she hesitates. But again, she speaks. "My papa tried to sell me," she says. It's not entirely untrue. Her marriage to the judge's son would have come with new alliances and things to add to the duke's home. It's what she felt he was doing.

Aris clicks his tongue. He continues moving around the room, touching book spines and crystal bottles.

"Why are you here?" she asks. She had moved to the window seat and sat there, her feet flat against the floor. Aris obviously wasn't in her room that day, so why would he suddenly show up in what would otherwise be a memory Wren has only of herself?

He turns to her, clasps his hands behind his back. Taking slow steps toward her, he says, "You've never been walked upon, I take it?"

Her breath hitches in her throat. She wishes she could take back her admittances. This is a dream, but it's not a figment of Aris here. It's his physical presence. Aris is a dream walker.

Dream walking is a rare gift and Wren has only known one other dream walker. Jakob. After he'd gone to serve in the Kornesian Navy, he visited her regularly. They had a schedule of visits, and he never left Wren waiting. When he didn't show up one night, her chest grew heavy. And when he didn't visit the night after, she knew he was gone. She knew before Jakob's father and the duke that he'd died.

"I have. Though I admit it's been a while." Her hands wring together in her lap.

Aris's steps are quiet on the carpet. This close, she can see how pale his skin is, can see the thin blue lines of his veins, the shadows under his eyes. His left eyebrow has a vertical scar through it.

"When was the last time?" he asks, his voice low.

Her heart stutters. "Five years ago."

He holds out his hand and steps ever closer, ghosting his fingers over her jawline. "Perhaps we can make this a frequent affair?" Aris's fingers are cold against her skin and the places he's touched feel empty when he drops his hand.

A shuddering breath leaves her chest. She doesn't know why, but she nods and Aris's smile tugs at the corners of his mouth.

"Until next time then"—he bows his head—"my lady." Then he's gone.

The room feels too big with him gone. She lies down on the window seat and curls her legs to her chest. As she lies there, her eyes find the gold plaque on the frame around the portrait of her and the duke. "Duke Lionel of Sudal, and his daughter, Lady Wren," it reads.

She closes her eyes and when she opens them again, she's back on *The Altean*.

"Didn't think you had that much whiskey last night, Wren."

She and Lex sit on the deck in the shade of the mainsail. Wren has a flask of water in her hand, half empty for the third time that morning.

Shaking the flask a bit, she says, "I guess so." The water is cool against her tongue, but does little to clear her head.

It's not the whiskey, she knows. When Jakob would visit her before his death, she'd wake up feeling hungover and parched, a side effect of being visited. She'd stay in bed all day with the curtains closed and a revolving door of servants bringing her cold water. She had quenched her thirst earlier, but her head is still fuzzy and the sun makes her eyes ache if she looks up too long from the ship's deck.

Lex bumps her shoulder. "Arden swears that a raw egg will cure a hangover." They prop their arms on their knees. "I think the captain keeps a secret stash in her cabin. Wanna make a heist?" They waggle their eyebrows at Wren.

She laughs. "Thanks, but I'll be fine." She holds the flask up again before tipping her head back and draining it. "A heist does sound fun, though. Maybe we'll have to stage one sometime."

For a while, they sit in the shade, listening to the waves against the hull and Eli and Kiara's laughs from where they sit. Penelope joins them, lying at their feet in the sun.

She'd lied awake in her hammock that morning after waking from her visit with Aris, wondering why he'd chosen *her* to visit. Surely there was someone else he could fill his time with. Had he felt the same pull in his chest as she did? Like there was some link connecting them that neither knew about until her dark eyes met his light? It made no sense. She'd never met him, never known his name until Eli told her the day before. What was she to him that he made time out of his day to invade her dreams?

She shivers, despite the warmth of the sun overhead. She can't shake the feeling of his fingers on her jaw, how cold they were dragging across her skin, the way she felt empty when he pulled away. How she still feels that emptiness now.

Wren stands and refills her flask for the fifth time since she woke. When she rejoins Lex at the mast, she asks, "How often do Aris and his ship come by?"

Lex had closed their eyes a little while before, their head leaned against the mast. Now, they lift their head and open their eyes, taking a deep breath through their nose. "Not too often. Once every few months or so." Lex shakes their head. "He's only engaged with us once. Usually, he just sails by, staring at us."

"Do you know what happened? Why his parents sent him away?"

"No," they say. "Eli wasn't told what happened and, as far as I know, we didn't ask. There were rumors, of course. People from Jinsimbia and the far west in Maia and the southernmost part of Kornas had ideas. Arson, treason, murder. But I'm not sure anyone but Aris and his family know." They look over at Wren. "You don't have any inside information, living in the duke's house, do you?"

Wren gives them a small smile and lets out a quiet laugh. The time before Aris was banished would have been the same time she was grieving Jakob's death. Even if there had been talks of him and his crimes, she wouldn't have cared enough to listen. "Nope," she says. "Didn't even know his name until yesterday."

Lex hums. "And I thought nothing could go down in the world of royalty without everyone knowing about it."

Wren laughs. "I guess not being born into royalty has its disadvantages."

"Yeah. Don't know why you were invited to join our crew. You're useless." Lex bumps Wren's shoulder with theirs again.

Wren drinks from the flask again. "Incredibly. Just throw me overboard now."

Lex laughs and lifts their hand, shading the sun from their eyes when they look up. "I would, but I'm too lazy. I'll dunk you in the sea next time we're at port."

"Deal."

Ezra and Ophelia join them a little while later and ask Wren to help them take inventory in the hold. She stands and stretches, her legs and shoulders sore from sitting on the deck all morning.

The hold is cool and crowded with empty barrels and crates. Their water stores, though not in danger of running out, are getting low and their food stores need to be consolidated. Wren and Ophelia start moving the empty containers to one side while Ezra pulls a piece of parchment from his pocket with the list of supplies and starts making tick marks next to the things they have plenty of. He marks off salt, a few small crates of sugar, barrels of gunpowder.

"I don't know how you know what's in them without looking inside," Wren says, knocking her knuckles against the top of a crate.

Ezra laughs and makes another mark on his parchment. "They're coordinated by metal," he says. He taps his pen on a metal band around a barrel. "Iron for gunpowder, silver-plated for water." Then he taps the top of a crate. "Gold plated for sugar, bronze for meat, steel for weapons." As he talks, he makes marks on the parchment. "It was started to prevent theft from ships carrying high-end goods, but changed to standard practice for loading and unloading at ports."

"Good thing they changed it," Ophelia calls from the other side of the hold. "Having every ship use the same system didn't prevent theft, it just made it happen quicker."

Ezra makes a few final marks and tucks the parchment and pen into his pocket. "Nothing makes sense on the sea, Ophelia. Haven't you learned that yet?"

"Evidently not, Ezra." She rolls another empty barrel to the pile she and Wren had made and makes her way over to Ezra. Standing on her tiptoes, she kisses his cheek. "That's why I'm in love with you and not Eli."

Ezra shrugs. "Everyone is in love with Eli, so I mean, no one would be surprised if you were in love with both of us."

EIGHT

IT'S HARD TO MISS the blackened stone buildings and piles of burnt lumber in the streets when they dock a week later in Staptonbury to replenish their supplies. As Wren and Lex walk down the dock and into the small town, they notice makeshift neighborhoods made up of tents. Many of the people they see have bandages over their hands; some have arms in slings or are using crutches.

Rubble has been piled up to form an altar base, where candles burn and tributes of toasted bread and vegetables wither in the sun. A sign carved into a broken piece of wood reads, "Adreus welcome us."

The market has a handful of threadbare stalls run by haggard citizens. The wares laid out on their counters are well worn or scorched. The food is a few days past peak freshness.

"What happened here?" Lex asks, dropping a handful of coins into the hand of a woman with her hair pulled back in a loose bun.

Her fingers are bandaged, and she winces a bit as the coins hit her palm. She shoves the coins into the pocket of her patched apron and starts putting apples from a wooden crate into a paper bag. "We were hit a week ago."

"Hit?" Lex echoes.

The woman nods, weary. "I take it you haven't been to land in a little while?"

Lex and Wren shake their heads.

The woman sighs. "Just after sunset, it got foggy. The next morning, we noticed a ship docked, but thought nothing of it. That night, my family and I were eating supper and," she pauses, shakes her head. "I'm not sure, really. It all happened so fast. There were explosions, fires. They barely missed our home."

Lex reaches their ringed hand across the stall counter and places it palm down. "I'm sorry that happened. Is your family all right?"

The woman nods first, then shakes her head, her hand fluttering at her chest. "We're intact," she says, her voice wobbly. "My husband ran out to help, and he pulled a woman and her son from under a beam. But it fell and hit his ankle. We think the bone is shattered."

Lex flicks their eyes at Wren and raises their dark eyebrows an almost imperceptible amount.

Wren takes in a sharp breath, flexing her fingers against her trousers. She's never healed a shattered bone before. On the training fields, she'd done a few broken ribs, a finger or toe, but the shattered ones had always gone to the medics. Still, she nods. She has to try.

Lex turns their attention back to the woman. "My friend Wren is a healer. Maybe we can help?"

The woman looks at Wren. There are streaks in the dirt over the deep brown skin of her cheeks. Her dark eyes take in Wren's face and then she takes a deep breath. "All right," she says.

Lex and Wren follow the woman—Aida—into a narrow alleyway behind a pub. She was right in saying the fires barely missed her home. The pub's front is streaked with black, the windows broken. But when Wren and Lex peak inside, it's mostly untouched.

Down the alleyway, a few doors before they enter Aida's home, is an empty door frame. A window in one of the walls lets in sunlight, showing that this place wasn't as lucky as the pub. Black soot smears the walls, and a beam lies across the floor, a streak of blood under it where it looks like a body has been pulled.

Aida opens the door to her home and they walk inside. It's furnished simply, a few faux leather chairs, a table made of light wood, a blue patterned rug. Through another door, they come to a man laid out on a bed. His left foot is propped up on a stack of multicolored cushions, a bandage wrapped around his ankle.

"Khari?" she starts. When the man opens his eyes, she continues, "This is Wren and Lex. Wren's a healer. She's going to try to fix your ankle." She touches her husband's forehead with the tips of her fingers and then steps aside, motioning for Wren to kneel at the end of the bed.

Wren doesn't wait for Khari to respond. When his wife had finished speaking, he'd nodded and thrown his arm over his eyes. He must know that healing doesn't feel like healing until it's over.

Unwrapping the bandage, Wren's fingers trail over his skin. The swelling is more than Wren's ever worked with, but she can feel the pulse of his blood under her fingers. She closes her eyes and maps the bones in Khari's leg and down into his foot.

The bones in his ankle are shattered as they'd feared and once she's confident with their placement, she says to Khari, "Do you want me to warn you before I do anything, or just go for it?"

He mumbles something, but Wren can't make it out, so she looks to Aida. "Just do it," she says. "He won't tense as much."

Wren nods. She prefers working that way. In training, when people she healed were warned, they had the tendency to hold their breath or tense their muscles. It wasn't impossible to heal them that way, but it was much easier when they were relaxed.

Her fingers hover over Khari's ankle, brushing his skin over the part she chooses as her starting point. She lets her fingers heat slightly and presses them into his swollen skin. His bones shift and a hiss escapes through Khari's teeth. Wren knows how it feels; intense burning, like a fire has been lit under the skin. She's never had a broken bone, but she's felt them scrape together under her fingertips and she can't imagine that it's comfortable.

Khari's leg relaxes, and he lets out a small breath. Her work is nowhere near done, but this tiny shift must be enough to bring some relief.

She smiles. She's always liked healing people. She never knew how to make people feel better when they were sad, but wounds were easier. Wounds she could fix.

The first time she healed someone other than herself, she was twelve. She had been healing herself for years before, but after failing to heal her mother's lungs, she was too afraid to attempt healing anyone else.

Jakob blocked a blade from a sparring opponent, but it had caught on his sleeve and cut into his forearm. It wasn't a deep cut, and he was happy to bandage it so he could get back to sparring, but Wren insisted.

"Are you sure you know what you're doing?" he asked, watching as Wren wiped her hands on a cloth hanging by the bucket of water she'd washed her hands in. He held his arm up, a cloth pressed to the cut to stanch the bleeding, sitting on a bench in the shade of a big oak tree.

Wren sat next to him. "I've healed myself plenty of times. How different could it be on another person?" She wasn't sure she totally believed it would be the same, but she wanted to prove to Jakob and herself that she could.

Jakob laughed. "I'm sure it's plenty different, Wren."

"Well, I guess we'll find out, won't we?" She wrapped her fingers around Jakob's wrist and pulled it into her lap. She took a deep breath, carefully removed the cloth, and ran her fingers over the skin surrounding the wound.

The cut was clean, shallow, barely the length of her index finger. Jakob took a deep breath as she ran her finger over the edge of the cut. "This is going to be unpleasant," she warned, looking at him from under her eyelashes.

"Yes, I've been healed before," he bit back through gritted teeth.

Seeing Jakob just as nervous as she felt gave Wren a jolt of confidence. She grinned and let her fingers heat. Starting at one end of the cut, she pressed her finger down, and dragged it along the cut, feeling Jakob's skin stitch back together. When she was finished, the cut had sealed, and only a thin pink line remained. The only evidence that it wasn't an old wound was the smeared blood still on his skin.

Jakob ran his fingers over his arm. "Wow, Wren." He met her eye, the corner of his mouth twitching up. "You're a healer."

She stood, wiped her palms on her trousers, and offered a hand to Jakob. "That's what I've been telling you."

He took her hand and let her haul him up. "Want to spar?"

They raced off to the training ground, laughing.

Now, as the swelling in Khari's ankle lessens, and the number of bone shards grows less, Wren finds her forehead breaking out in a thin sheen of sweat. The room they're in has a window where the sun shines through right on her back. It doesn't help that she has to heat up her hands every time she uses her magics.

"Wren," Lex says. When she turns, they're holding out a canteen. "Take a drink," they say.

She does, greedily. She'd been kneeling at Khari's ankle for nearly half an hour and she hadn't realized how dry her throat had become.

Lex takes the empty canteen and Wren turns back to Khari's ankle. After looking away and coming back, she notices how different his foot looks compared to when they came in. The swelling has definitely decreased, the purple bruises have faded. He even starts moving his toes a bit when Wren presses her fingers into his skin.

Another half an hour passes before Aida helps him stand. He's a little wobbly, but in no pain. He winces when he puts weight on the foot, and Wren worries she's set a bone wrong or fused the wrong pieces, but he laughs nervously. "After a few days of lying around, my body is a bit stiff."

His steps through the house get steadier until he's no longer leaning on his wife. He's still stiff, but he's making jokes and raiding the cabinets for food.

Wren watches him to make sure he's able to move normally, to make sure there's no drag to his toes or pinch when he puts his heel down. Lex bumps her shoulder and winks when she looks at them. She looks down to suppress a smile. There had been plenty of minor injuries on *The Altean* that she's healed, but nothing like this. She's never healed anything like this. She can't help but wonder if Mim would be proud.

Aida insists on sending them away with some fresh baked bread and a small lavender cake. They put their goodies into a paper bag and tuck them away in Lex's shoulder bag.

As they leave, Aida clutches Lex and Wren's hands, tears hanging on her bottom lashes, and says, "Thank you. I was afraid we would have to try to convince a doctor to come see him here."

Lex squeezes her hand back. "We are more than happy to help. It's what we do."

As they walk back to the market square, they share the lavender cake between them.

"It's too small to share with everyone. What they don't know won't hurt them," Lex says, their mouth full.

The cake is dense, moist, and sweet. The earthy taste of the lavender reminds Wren of the tea she'd drink in the garden at the estate. A wave of grief washes over her. She's never been away from Sudal for this long. Lex must feel her change of mood because they slip their hand into hers and give her fingers a squeeze. They smile at her when she looks over, a smear of frosting on their top lip.

As they walk, they see Arden and Ezra helping townspeople pile wood and bring in wheelbarrows. Ophelia is kneeling in front of a small child with a pouf of hair, holding out a wooden doll, probably carved from a piece of wood she'd found on the ground. The child takes it and smiles widely. They make a motion with their hands and Ophelia nods, signing back. She stands when the child turns and disappears down an alley.

Popping the last pieces of cake into their mouths, Wren and Lex join Ophelia. She pulls another half-carved doll out of her back pocket and starts shaving away more wood.

"Have you been carving those all day?" Lex says, nodding to the doll.

Ophelia smiles. "Yeah, passing 'em out all day, too. There were so many homes that were lost. There are a lot of children with no toys. Everyone else is helping with clean-up already." She lifts the doll a bit to squint at the grain. "I wanted to help with something a little different."

"You have a bigger heart than this world deserves," Lex says. Wren nods in agreement.

Ophelia continues to carve toys and pass them out. A young boy asks her for a cat and it takes a few minutes of searching, but finally another child runs up to Ophelia with a sizable piece in their hands, a smile wide across their face.

Ophelia takes the wood and examines it, turning it over in her hands a few times. "This will work magnificently," she says, winking at the child and touching the end of their nose with her finger. She sits on some steps leading to a shop front that's been burned and starts carving. The children gather around her, hanging on her shoulders or sitting by her feet. When she hands them out, the children hug them to their chests.

Lex joins Arden and Ezra, piling bricks. The three of them, along with a few other townspeople, make quick work of unblocking a street. A few children stack the bricks into houses or shops and play with their carved dolls.

Wren walks around for a little while, helping where she's needed. She visits the altar and runs her fingers over the names of people painted over the rocks. Twine and frayed ribbon tie up small bouquets of bluebell flowers and fennel.

A stuffed lamb with a burned ear has fallen to the ground. Wren kneels and picks it up, dusting off the worn wool and setting it on an empty spot on the altar. She props it up, making sure it won't fall off again.

"Heard you healed a shattered ankle," Clare says, stepping up beside Wren.

Wren stands, wiping her palms on her trousers. "Yeah." Her voice is small. "Not sure it means anything. There are so many names."

Clare puts her hand on Wren's shoulder and squeezes. "It made a difference for that family. We can't change what's already happened, Wren, but we can help *now*."

Wren nods, her eyes trained on the lamb. "They gave us cake," she laughs. "Lex and I ate it before anyone else could see."

"Good," Clare says. She has a blanket draped over her arm. "Honestly, I'm surprised they shared with you at all." She links her arm with Wren's and starts walking her toward town.

They lay the blanket in the shade of a tree and sit, their legs stretched out in front of them. Penelope joins them, rubbing against their arms before settling down between them, her paws tucked in.

As people pass with injuries she can see, Wren offers her healing abilities. Clare cleans dirt from faces, brushes tangles from hair. She braids one girl's hair down her spine, weaving dandelions in the strands. Penelope is happy to let people pet her or pull her into their laps as Wren mends their injuries. She sits patiently as children pull the yellow dandelion heads and place them on her head and down the length of her body.

Wren thinks of the lamb, ear burned and flopped on the ground. The people that stop have burned faces, scraped palms, sprained ankles. Most of them sit with heaviness, the corners of their mouths pulled down. But when they leave, new pink skin over their cheeks or hair free from knots, they're smiling and laughing.

Wren and Clare listen as they work, trying to piece together people's stories of the attacks.

Fog blanketed the city one evening. It was unusual—Staptonbury has a warm climate year-round and not used to fog in the summer—but not worrying. A ship arrived in the night, quiet and seemingly empty. No one unboarded during the day and any attempts at contact went unanswered. The fog stuck around, hugging the buildings and pulling at people's clothes, but business continued as usual.

That evening, just after sunset, when the market had closed and most people had gone home for the night, there was an explosion in the bakery. More had come in neighboring businesses and when people went to help put out the fires or find survivors, a group of people swept through the town, attacking people and taking anything of value.

More fires started, in homes and alleyways, high in the trees. There were a few magics users in town and they'd been able to put the fires out by working together to pull the sea water over the docks. It had taken until morning, but finally the worst of the blazes had been extinguished and they were able to assess the damages. It hadn't been until the fires were out and the smoke and fog cleared that they'd realized the ship and its inhabitants had disappeared with no one noticing.

Most people made it out alive, but there were some that were killed in the explosions or the attacks that followed. A few died in the fires, or from injuries due to them. Even now, a week later, there were still people missing.

Wren has to take a break in the mid-afternoon. She stands, stretches, shakes out her hands. Clare had braided her hair into a loose crown on top of her head and she's glad for the cool breeze on her neck.

A woman she'd healed earlier comes by, carrying a paper bag. She hands it to Wren and says, "I wanted to thank you again. I can't pay you, but I hope this will suffice."

Wren takes the bag and sets it down on the blanket. "You don't need to give me anything," she reassures the woman, "but it's very appreciated. Thank you."

"You've helped so many here. All of you have. You don't know how appreciative we are." The woman smiles at Wren and then calls to a child standing at Ophelia's feet. They give Ophelia a quick hug and run off with the woman.

Wren sits again, watching the woman's retreating back. Her fingers itch with the use of her magics, her blood and bones and soul humming. Clare was right that there were a lot of people they couldn't help. The names of the people on the rocks, the owner of the little lamb. But there were also a lot of people they could help—Khari, the children Ophelia's carving toys for, the people whose hair Clare managed to untangle. And while the lost people would be mourned, it would be the living that grieved.

Inside the bag are cucumber sandwiches on fresh bread, two apples, and a small bar of chocolate. Wren gives a sandwich and an apple to Clare and sets the chocolate aside.

Clean-up continues around them. Jez and Lex work together to sweep and pick up broken glass, Grace and Kiara bring bundles of clothes and food to people. Eli walks around the marketplace, talking to people and offering sweets from her pocket to anyone that looks in need of a pick me up.

A fire breaks out under a pile of lumber Ezra and Arden are moving just as Wren finishes her apple. She quickly sets the core aside and stands to help, but her foot is asleep and she stumbles.

Clare reaches out to steady her and they laugh until Wren is confident in her steps. She starts to make her way to the fire, but when she looks up, the flames are already gone. Ezra flexes his fingers and wipes his palms on his trousers as Arden claps him on the shoulder.

Before she and Clare get back to work, they share the chocolate. It's melted a little in the warm air and sticks to their fingertips. Placing it on her tongue, Wren has to bite back a moan. The chocolate is dusted with tiny chili flakes that set a fire in the back of Wren's throat.

She continues to heal and Clare continues to comb hair and wash faces and Penelope continues to allow people to pet her. Just as the sun sets behind the buildings of Staptonbury, a whistle comes from the deck of *The Altean*.

The crew finishes what they're doing and say their goodbyes to the friends they've made. A small group of children hug Ophelia's legs and yell her name as they follow the crew to the docks. Penelope rubs herself along the legs of a few people waving after them and trots to catch up to Wren and Clare.

As everyone reboards the ship, Eli meets them, her hands clasped behind her back. Kiara is sitting on the bench, mending a blue shirt. Penelope hops up on the bench and bumps her head against Kiara's arm.

"Good work today, crew. We didn't plan a detour this long, but you helped a lot of people." She smiles at each of them, then locks her green eyes on Wren. "Wren, I heard you were responsible for healing a lot of people. I'm grateful you're here with us and I know many people in town are, too."

Wren smiles as Ezra whoops and bumps his shoulder against hers. "Thank you, Captain."

Eli nods at her, then turns to the rest of the crew. "Now, did anyone learn anything about what happened?"

Clare recounts what she and Wren were told, and Eli's face grows graver and graver as she goes on.

"Thank you, Clare. Anyone else?"

"Kilkea was hit two weeks ago," Ezra says. "Then Staptonbury a week later. Then Bodenceton three days ago."

Eli raises her eyebrows. "Same story?"

Ezra nods. "Bodenceton was almost completely destroyed. The people that survived came here."

Kiara joins the group, putting her hand on Eli's back. "Captain?"

Eli nods, her lips pressed into a thin line, and takes a deep breath through her nose. "We believe we know who is behind these attacks."

Wren holds her breath and worries the inside of her lip. She thinks she knows who Eli will accuse, though she's not sure when she figured it out. The fog, maybe, or how no one she'd spoken to had been able to describe their attackers with any clarity.

"It's Aris," she says, her voice quiet, her chest growing heavy.

Eli's eyes snap to Wren's face. "Yes," she says slowly. She looks away and continues, "We don't know why. Perhaps *why* doesn't matter. The only thing that matters is how we stop him."

PART II

NINE

THE NEXT SIX WEEKS are spent traveling from port town to port town, helping clean up and rebuild. Wren and Clare find a spot in every town and lay out a blanket or find a bench where they heal people's wounds or just sit and listen. Penelope joins them in most places, curling up next to them on the blanket or finding a sunny spot nearby. She purrs and allows people all the time they need when they approach her. She's happy to take offerings of chicken or fish if anyone offers.

The casualties in each town aren't always as bad as they were in Staptonbury or Bodenceton. Sometimes no one was killed, or just a few in the attacks during the looting. None of the other towns have altars for Adreus and their dead. Some have tribute piles on the docks, but most have spent their time rebuilding the lives that are left.

The story is always the same. Fog rolls in one evening, then the town wakes the next morning to a strange and empty ship at the docks. The night begins with explosions, then attacks and looting and fires. The intruders and ship always vanish without notice.

Some of the crew describe Aris to the people they speak with, hoping to get confirmation of their suspicions. But no one has seen him. When asked about the people that attack, the citizens describe what the crew can only say look like ghosts.

"They're quick," they say. "They wore masks and shrouds. They came from nowhere, then disappeared."

Eli points out one night that only port towns with no naval activity or defenses get attacked. She uses a map Kiara buys in Kilkea to mark which ports get attacked and which get overlooked. Aris and the crew of *The Basilisk* don't seem to be following the trade routes, as sometimes a port town will be skipped and then hit a few days later, after the next one on the route is attacked.

Aris doesn't dream walk on Wren often. And when he does, there aren't many words exchanged between them. She's angry and tries to ignore him, but as the weeks wear on and the attacks become more frequent and violent and Wren heals wounds that a healer with only basic training has no business even attempting, she finds herself relaxing into the quiet moments she and Aris share. Despite knowing he's behind the attacks, despite seeing the people he's hurt and the homes he's destroyed, being with him brings her a calm she hasn't felt in five years, since she was with Jakob.

It's hard to admit to herself that she's feeling this way. When she realizes she's leaning against his shoulder or running her fingers over the tall grasses as they walk, her heart drops and she squeezes her eyes closed until she wakes back on *The Altean*. Her cheeks heat with shame when someone mentions the bags under her eyes or when she has to sneak back to the water barrel to refill her flask.

After one particularly long and hard day where Wren attempts—and fails—to heal an infected arm and makes it back to the ship just before dawn the next morning, Aris is waiting for her in a meadow. Wren is barefoot, walking through the wildflowers. Aris is standing a little way from her, and she makes her way to him, stopping to pluck a flower. He stares out over a lake, its glassy surface barely moving.

She steps up beside him and the scene around her changes. It takes a few moments for her eyes to adjust to the sudden darkness, but when they do, she realizes they're in the interior of a ship. At first, she thinks it's Eli's quarters on *The Altean* but it's too dark and cold and damp. She looks around. Aris is sitting at a desk, his hands clasped on the top, his pale blue eyes set on her.

"Is this your ship?" she asks. There are things stacked haphazardly on the shelves lining the wall. Books and broken trinkets, all covered in a thick layer of dust.

Aris nods once. "Yes. *The Basilisk* isn't half as nice as *The Altean*, but I do hope you'll enjoy your stay."

Wren takes her eyes off a broken hourglass on the shelf and looks at Aris. "Stay?" She rubs the flower from the meadow between her fingers. It's a bluebell, the same flower on the altar in Staptonbury.

He lets out a huff of breath. "Well, *visit*. I thought I'd change the scenery. I've grown tired of meadows and gardens."

Wren is still barefoot, and the hard floor is cold under her feet. Aris motions to a chair in front of the desk and she sits, her hands folded in her lap around the flower, her spine straight. It's the posture of a duke's daughter, of a lady, not the posture of someone that lives on a boat.

It's quiet between them for a while. Aris busies himself with papers over his desk; Wren looks around the room, tracking the dust motes dancing in the weak sunlight through the windows.

Her eyes drift to him, watching his long fingers as he pushes papers from one side of the desk to the other. Something in the shake of his head reminds her of the lambs in the grassy fields in Sudal. She almost smiles, until she remembers the lamb on the ground in front of the altar, burnt and left behind.

"Aris."

"Hmm?"

"Eli thinks you're the one attacking port towns."

He laughs, once. "Does she?" He moves two papers to the side. "And what do you think? Do you think it's me?"

"I know it's you," she says.

Aris pauses. It's only a fraction of a second and Wren only notices because she's watching him. "Hmm," he says.

She waits for him to say something else, but he only continues shuffling papers. She lets out a huff of breath. "What are you doing?"

Aris sits back in his chair and waves his hand through the air. The papers dissolve. Wren takes in a sharp breath through her nose; she'd almost forgotten this is a dream.

He leans forward again, placing his elbows on the desk. "Are you going to ask me to stop?"

Wren presses her lips into a thin line. She'd hoped it was someone else, though she knew it was unlikely. The fog and disappearing ship could be no one else. Still, his confession has her cheeks heating with shame. She'd spent so much time with him in her dreams. She tried to fight, tried to resist her feelings. But she was weak, relaxing and relishing the moments beside him, the ocean beating against the shore or grasses drifting in the breeze. She's seen the horrors he's orchestrated, helped clean them up, healed his victims. She's seen firsthand the chaos he'd sown.

Aris looks at her, his pale eyes boring into hers. "Are you going to ask me to stop?" he asks again pointedly.

"I'm not sure asking will do any good."

The smile he gives her almost reaches his eyes. "You're right, Wren. It wouldn't."

Eli's words echo in her head.

"When we catch *The Basilisk*, and we *will* catch them, we destroy their ship." She'd been standing at the mast, her hands behind her back.

"What if we see them docked and not at sea?" Ezra asked.

"We dock next to them and remain vigilant until they unboard. Then we protect the town."

There was a block of ice in Wren's chest. She knew it was Aris behind the attacks. She knew Eli would be working to stop him, that her ultimate goal would be to put an end to his attacks. But she hoped they could reason with him. Convince him somehow to stop. She didn't want it to end in violence. What would be the difference between *The Altean* and *The Basilisk* then?

"Aren't we supposed to save people? Not..." she trailed off.

Eli gave her a sympathetic smile. "Yes. And if we can stop Aris, think of how many people we'll save, Wren. Sometimes, one must be sacrificed in favor of many."

Wren plays with a loose thread on the cuff of her sleeve, the bluebell, forgotten, falling to the floor at her feet. "Eli said that we'd kill you if given the chance. She wants you dead, Aris."

His smile does reach his eyes now. "She's been wanting me dead since she picked me up in Mythshade. Her wanting me dead now neither surprises nor intimidates me."

"Aris, she's trying to track you down." Wren pauses, pinches the inside of her lip with her teeth. "She knows where you're going next and we're on our way there now," she lies.

Aris raises his left eyebrow. She notices again that it's split in two by a vertical scar.

"And where does Captain Eleanor Crowley think I'm going next?"

Wren squeezes her fingers into a fist. "I don't know. She—she didn't tell me."

He smiles again, leaning back in his chair. "She doesn't trust you." It's not a question. "Have you told her about us?"

Wren feels a heat creep up her neck and into her cheeks, but she ignores the way his question makes her heart jump. "She hasn't told anyone." Even if Eli does know where he's going—and Wren can't be sure she doesn't—why would she tell the crew? Wren's sure she doesn't tell the crew everything. The only person who would know everything Eli knows would be Kiara.

Aris hums, an amused smile on his face. "What would you have me do, Wren?"

They watch each other, her breathing coming rapidly, an amused look on his face.

"Stop," she says finally, even knowing he won't. "Stop attacking towns and stealing from those people. What good does it do you? What do you get out of it?"

He lifts a shoulder. "I got your attention."

Wren scoffs. "You've been visiting me for *weeks*, Aris. What makes you think you didn't have my attention?"

He sits forward again. "I wanted you to know who I am and what I can do."

"And what's that?"

"You've seen how strong I am and seen that I can give power to those who want it." He looks around his quarters, at the disheveled books, broken things, and dust. He waves his hand, and the broken trinkets and messy books straighten or fix themselves;

the dust turns to mist and disappears. The light doesn't change, it stays dim and cold inside his quarters. "Before I became captain of this dump they call a ship, the old man that lived in this room drank all day and let his crew run wild. Now, they work as a team, doing things they never thought they could." He lifts a shoulder. "I had to replace a few of them, but that comes with the territory, I suppose."

Wren pulls her eyes from the tidy shelves that seconds before had been in disarray. "Why would you need my attention for that? I don't need power or whatever it is you think you can give me."

Aris laughs, haughty and proud. "You're wrong, Wren. You *do* want power. You want a *place*. You want your father's seat as the Duchess of Sulesia."

Wren jerks her chin back and stares at him. "What? What gives you that idea?" Taking the duke's place had never been a thought in her mind. Even when she was still living in Sudal, she never thought about it. She didn't relish the idea of her papa dying, in taking his spot. She hadn't been raised to take over after him.

"I saw the way you looked in your room that night. The first time I visited you. You miss it, the stability of a home. You hate being on that boat."

"You're wrong," she says. It's true that she does miss the estate, but *The Altean* has become her home. It's as stable as her home in Sudal had been.

"Maybe so," Aris says. He taps the top of the desk with his hands and stands. He holds his hand to Wren.

Slowly, she takes it and allows him to pull her up. He leads her to the door and opens it. She doesn't see what's on the other side, but she hears him say, "Or maybe I'm not."

TEN

WREN LAYS IN HER hammock for a little while after she wakes up. She can tell Ezra and Ophelia are still asleep by their soft snores. The curtain had been closed when she made it back to the ship and Wren was worried she'd fall asleep to their quiet noises, but Ezra's rumbling snores proved her wrong.

It's darker in the belly of the ship than it should be, but the patter of rain on the deck above her explains the lack of sunlight filtering through the portholes near the ceiling.

She knows she should get up and make her way to Eli's quarters. Tell her that Aris visited her. That he's *been* visiting her. But she can't stop thinking about what he said.

You do want power. You want a place. You want your father's seat as the Duchess of Sulesia.

Does she? She has to admit, having a place of power is enthralling. But to get that power, she'd have to take it from the duke—her papa, the man that raised her after her parents died.

And, despite her anger and grief, he's the closest thing left she has of a family.

Next to her, Ezra snorts in his sleep and Ophelia groans. Even without seeing them, Wren knows Ophelia shoves Ezra's shoulder and turns away from him.

No, the duke isn't her only family. She's got family here on *The Altean*, too.

She pushes Aris's words from her mind. *He's wrong*, she thinks. *I don't need power. I have everything I need right here.*

Finally, it's the pounding in her head that makes her swing her legs over the side of her hammock. She has to steady herself against the pole her cloak hangs from before she straightens. After exerting herself for so long the day before and Aris's visit, she's exhausted. The flask of water tucked into her satchel is full and she drains it, barely stopping to breathe.

Once it's empty, she tiptoes past the other cots, filled with sleeping bodies. One of Grace's stuffed animals has fallen from her grasp and Wren stoops to pick it up and tuck it back under Grace's arm. She watches the rise and fall of Grace's chest for a few moments before making her way to the deck, stopping on the way to refill her flask.

Kiara is on deck, staring out at the horizon. The water is calm, ripples from the raindrops scattering on the surface. She turns as Wren approaches.

"Good afternoon, Wren."

"Hello. Is it afternoon?"

Kiara smiles and lets out a small laugh. "Yes. It's after two. Most everyone is still asleep." She nods to the quarterdeck, where Lex is sitting, an embroidery hoop in one hand. Their other hand pulls a needle through the fabric.

Kiara and Wren watch the water for a little while. She heard Eli giving the order to leave the docks a few minutes after she made it back to the ship that morning. "Are we headed to another port town?" Wren asks.

Kiara takes a breath. "Yes. But not one that's been attacked. We haven't heard of an attack in a few days. The town we helped yesterday was the last as far as we know."

Hopefully, it will be the last, Wren thinks, though she doesn't have much confidence in that. She almost tells Kiara about her visits, but she bites her tongue. Now doesn't feel like the time.

She drains her flask again, tipping her head back and dumping water down her throat. After she refills it, she joins Lex and sits down next to them.

"Embroidering in the rain?" The water in her flask does little to wet her tongue.

Lex huffs. "Well, I keep having to pull the fabric taut again, which is annoying, but there's no light anywhere else."

"Are we out of oil?" During the day, oil lamps are hung in the crew's quarters and are easily accessible in the storage rooms and other places in the belly of the ship.

"Gods, no. We've got barrels of it. But I didn't want to wake anyone in the bunks, and the storage room is lonely." They look up at Wren from under their long eyelashes. "At least up here, I have the sea. And Kiara." They smile in Kiara's direction.

Wren looks at the design on the fabric. "Are they flowers?"

Lex holds the hoop away from them. "They're supposed to be trees." They pull it back and put the needle through the fabric. "It's a gift for Arden. His name means forest. Or, at least, he claims it does. I wanted to make an apron for him for his birthday."

The stitches don't look like trees. But Wren knows that sometimes embroidery doesn't start out looking like what it's supposed to be. Once, she had started a project and it looked like a blob of blue gravy dropped on the floor. In the end, it turned into a jellyfish she'd seen an illustration of in one of her tutor's books. She'd ripped the page out and tacked it to her wall. She was so proud of it once the stitching was finished that she hung it over her desk, rather than stuffing it in a drawer like most of her other finished hoops.

She puts her hand on Lex's shoulder. "It's going to turn out great. And Arden is going to love it."

An hour later, Eli joins them on deck. Ezra and Ophelia had joined shortly after Wren sat with Lex, and Arden and Grace brought up bowls of stew. Lex shoved their project into their shoulder bag, looking sheepish, when Arden climbed the steps. The rain has stopped, though the clouds are still dark grey and heavy in the sky.

"Crew!" Eli calls out, standing from the bench where Kiara does her mending. Penelope gives an irritated meow and turns over, curling her tail over her nose. Apparently Wren isn't the only one who'd had a late night.

Everyone quiets their conversations. Eli turns toward them, her hands clasped behind her back. Wren thinks they should all be stood at attention, like Jakob was during his drills. Instead, Ezra and Ophelia are draped across each other, Lex is on their back, eyes closed, foot bouncing. Arden stands off to the side, his big arms crossed over his equally big chest, leaning against the railing. Clare watches a game between Jez and Grace, a pad of paper balanced on her knee and pen in hand to keep score.

"It's been a rough couple of weeks. Unfortunately, I'm not sure our work is done." The crew lets out a collective groan. Eli gives a small laugh. "*However*, we are going to Therma to spend a few days. It's a university and tourist city, so there are a lot of things to do there, and we'll all be able to relax."

Lex gives a whoop from their spot on deck, punching their fist into the air. Arden laughs quietly and shakes his head.

"It's not all fun," Eli warns. "While there, we'll restock our stores. And I want you all to find out if there are any port towns in Kornas that have been attacked, and if there have been any sightings of Aris or *The Basilisk*."

"How long will we be staying?" Wren asks. Her papa's ties to the kingdom were long woven into the history of Kornas as well as Sulesia, and that meant she was, too. She'd been to Therma before and, though it wasn't for long, she was welcomed warmly. She'd gone around with her papa meeting important people—the dean of the university, owners of popular businesses, well-known and well-to-do citizens. She was only sixteen at the time, but she can't help feeling she'll be recognized. That someone will report to the duke where she is.

"Not long," Eli says pointedly, as if she knows Wren's fears. Maybe she does. "Only long enough to get refreshed and find out any worthwhile gossip."

ELEVEN

The trip to Therma takes a week and a half. The last town they'd helped, Kakos, sits on the south-western shores of Nestad so *The Altean* follows the coast of Sulesia east to Kornas and then around a peninsula to the university town. Wren ties her hair up into a purple scarf and traces a kohl pencil around her eyes. She's about to walk up the stairwell to the deck when Ophelia stops her.

"Whoa, hey." She puts her hands on Wren's shoulders and holds her out at arm's length. She's standing on the second stair and can look Wren in the eye. "Did you do this in a mirror?"

Wren pulls her chin back. "Yes. Is it not even?"

Ophelia laughs. "It's definitely even, but it's too polished." She looks at Wren's worn and patched trousers with leather knee patches and visibly mended shirt. "I'll help." She licks her thumb and before Wren can stop her, she rubs the line of black on Wren's upper lid.

"Hey!" Wren pulls away from Ophelia. She'd worked hard to get the lines straight and precise.

"*Here.*" Ophelia's thumb has a smudge of black on it when she pulls out a small gilded folding mirror from her trouser pocket and holds it out to Wren.

Wren takes it and opens it, looking at Ophelia, her lips pursed. She can see the difference between her line work and Ophelia's smudge work. But she has to admit, she can see how the one Ophelia had done is an improvement. The kohl is still dark at the base of her eyelashes, but it's smoked out to look worn in. The line Ophelia hadn't touched looks too clean, too sharp, in comparison.

She snaps the mirror shut and holds it back out to Ophelia in the palm of her hand. "Fine," she relents.

"Do you want me to do the other one?" Ophelia asks, mouth pulled up in a smirk.

Quietly, Wren huffs out, "Yes."

Ophelia laughs, licks her other thumb, and rubs Wren's eyelid. There are a few touch ups with a handkerchief but, eventually, they're walking down the gangplank arm in arm to the pier.

Ezra is waiting for them, his bare feet dangling over the water, and when he sees them, he bounces up from where he sits. "Finally!" he says, grabbing his boots from the dock and pulling them on. "What took so long?"

"I had to give our newbie pirate a makeup lesson," Ophelia says, bumping her shoulder against Wren's.

"Are we pirates?" Wren asks as Ezra takes her other arm.

"Are we not pirates?" Ezra says.

"I've never heard of any pirates that *clean up* towns rather than destroy them."

Ezra and Ophelia laugh. "Well, then I guess we're more like privateers," Ophelia says.

"Are we working under a government?"

Ezra scoffs. "Leave it to a *lady* to know the difference between pirates and privateers." He rolls his eyes.

"I think the god of life and death surpasses any governing body, anyway, don't you think?" Ophelia skips a few steps, her arm still looped through Wren's.

Wren can't argue that.

Just as they make it to the end of the pier, a call makes them turn back toward the ship.

Eli has disembarked and jogs her way to them, her green coat flowing out behind her. She nods to Ezra and Ophelia when she catches up and says, "I was hoping to speak with Wren for a moment."

Ophelia and Ezra let Wren's arms drop. "Of course, Captain." Ophelia turns to Wren. "I'm sure we won't be hard to find."

Wren smiles after them, then follows Eli back aboard *The Altean*, where she's led to the captain's quarters. Kiara is pouring tea into two floral printed cups and setting out tiny pink cakes on a white plate.

When they've sat, Eli turns to Kiara, "Dear?"

"Yes, heart?"

"Would you please go make sure our crew is staying on task?" Eli had told the crew that they were welcome to do as they wished in Therma, as long as they asked around about Aris and his attacks.

Kiara stands and dips her chin toward her chest. "Of course."

"Thank you, my darling."

As Kiara leaves, she pats her palm against her thigh and gives a low whistle. Penelope jumps from the bed behind the curtains with a curt meow and follows Kiara out.

Eli waits until the door is closed behind them before she says, "Wren."

Wren automatically straightens her spine and places her hands flat on top of her thighs. Though Eli's voice is nonchalant, the way she says Wren's name makes her feel like a child.

"Are you being visited by a dream walker?"

Wren's breathing quickens and her heart picks up its pace. "Yes," she says, fighting to keep her voice even.

Eli picks up a pink cake and turns it over in her fingers. "Who is visiting you?"

She knows. Eli knows Wren is being visited by Aris. She knows he's been invading her every thought, her every breath. She knows, and she's going to punish Wren by forcing her back to Sudal. She knows and—

"My friend Jakob," Wren says. She hates lying, especially about Jakob. And she's not sure why she feels the need to lie in the first place. It's not like she's done anything *wrong*. She's not responsible for Aris's actions. Gods, she might be the one responsible for getting him to stop. Still, she can't tell Eli about him. She's not ready for him to not be her secret.

"A friend from Sudal?" Eli's shoulders have relaxed.

Wren nods, slowly. She looks down at her hands. They'd balled into fists on her lap and she forces them to relax, wiping her sweaty palms on her trousers. "Yes. We—we miss each other, that's all."

Eli takes a bite of the cake and chews. "I understand what it's like to miss a friend."

To calm herself and give her hands something to do, Wren reaches up for a cup of tea and dumps a careful spoonful of sugar into the brown liquid. Kiara had set a pot of honey out as well, and Wren ladles a small amount into her cup. She takes her time stirring, scraping the spoon against the bottom of the cup.

"How did you know?"

"Hmm?" Eli had made her own cup of tea, looking at the maps on the top of the desk as she stirred it absentmindedly.

"How did you know I was being visited?"

Eli laughs. "I've been around long enough to know the difference between hangovers and walking sickness."

"Right," Wren says to her tea.

"Hey," Eli says, putting down her teacup on its matching saucer. "Let's go into town and check out the cheese shop."

"The cheese shop?" Wren echoes. "That seems like a niche outing."

"Yes, the cheese shop!" Eli says joyously. "Kiara said she saw a specialty cheese shop when she went into town and got these cute little cakes." She pops one into her mouth.

"Aren't you worried about leaving the ship?" Eli had been in the towns they helped after Aris's attacks, but she seemed to be more comfortable on board, or close to.

Eli takes a few drinks of her tea before she answers. "Leaving *The Altean* always makes me a little nervous. But as captain, I can't ask my crew to do something I wouldn't do. I wouldn't be respected by other captains, or by world leaders, or—most importantly—by my crew." She sets her empty cup down on the saucer.

"Even with the rumors surrounding me and Kiara, I have no reason to believe that someone is trying to hurt us. And I like cheese, and nothing is going to stop me from trying new ones. So," she stands and holds out her hand to Wren, "would you like to join me?"

TWELVE

TAKE IT CHEESY IS nestled between a small coffee shop and a used bookshop. The bookshop has a cart of books outside with a sign that says, "Buy one, get two free! This cart only!"

"We'll have to check that when we come out," Eli says, winking.

Inside the cheese shop, a round woman with heavily pierced ears and light brown skin stands behind a counter, wearing a yellow and white striped apron around her waist, matching the bunting flags hanging from the glass display case. She grabs a silver platter from the top of the case and makes her way over to Eli and Wren.

"Care for a sample?" the woman asks.

Eli takes a cube of a creamy white and purple marbled cheese and pops it into her mouth.

"Good choice," the woman says. "That's one of our most popular. It's goat cheese made with blueberries and honey."

"It's delicious, is what it is." Eli walks further into the shop and looks at the selection of cubes, blobs, and slices of cheeses in various colors on display in the case.

The woman offers the platter to Wren, and she hesitates before picking up a thick slice of hard, pale yellow cheese.

"That one," the woman twirls back to the counter, sets the platter down, and grabs a shallow white dish with sliced fruit, "is best paired with strawberries."

Wren has never eaten cheese with fruit, but she takes the woman's advice and chooses a piece of strawberry, placing it on top of the cheese before placing the whole thing in her mouth. To her surprise, the combination *is* good. The nutty flavor of the cheese and the sweetness of the strawberry make Wren's taste buds explode.

Eli orders a sample plate and soon she and Wren are sitting at a small marble-topped table, the plate of cheeses and a dish of fruits, jams, and crackers between them. Eli buys a cheap bottle of red wine as well and she fills her glass.

"I've heard," she says, swirling the wine around her glass, "that wine pairs well with cheese."

Wren takes a sip of the wine. The hair at the base of her skull tingles, making her cringe. "Do you think it's true?" she asks, the tartness lingering on her tongue.

Eli takes a swig of the liquid. "No," she says decisively, scrunching her nose.

Wren takes another tentative sip from her glass and has to choke it down. "I agree," she manages. She looks up at the captain and they laugh until Eli has to dab the corners of her eyes with the yellow napkin on her lap.

Eli picks up her glass of wine and tips it, looking at the red liquid pooled at the bottom. "How is it I can drink a whole glass of whiskey to myself without wanting to chase it with anything else, but a single sip of wine makes me want to stuff my face with cheese?"

The woman working the shop comes over then and sets down another dish of sliced fruit. "Why else would we suggest wine?" she winks at Eli and Wren before leaving them with their food.

While they eat the cheese and fruit and make sandwiches out of the crackers and jam, Eli asks Wren more about her life growing up. Not at the estate in Sudal with the duke, but in the tiny one-bedroom house she shared with her parents. Her memories there and with her mother and father are fuzzy, but she shares what she remembers.

The neighborhood where she lived was crowded with small clay houses. Every house shared their outside walls with the one next to it and the ones behind it, a cluster of six houses all together. Narrow alleyways separated each cluster from the next, and a wider road in front. Wren and her parents lived in the house right in the middle. The three of them shared the single bedroom in the back, a pile of secondhand blankets and pillows on a hand-sewn mattress stuffed with old clothing. Wren slept at the foot of the bed, where she kept her threadbare stuffed animals and a blanket that was made for her when she was born.

Her mother was tall, with a thick waist and round arms. She was the strongest person Wren knew. She spent her days singing while doing the neighborhood's laundry, bouncing an exhausted mother's baby on her hip while she worked. Despite her busy days, she always had dinner waiting by the time Wren's father came home from work.

Her father worked on the docks. He did whatever was needed. Hauling fishing nets, loading barrels and crates onto ships, scrubbing and waxing decks. He was the second strongest person Wren knew. He came home tired and sore every day, but when Wren would meet him at the end of their street every evening, he'd smile at her and swing her around in a circle. She always held his calloused hand as she skipped home beside him.

"You've got your father's hair," her mother would say as she tried to brush Wren's orange curls at the end of a long day of play. Wren would giggle and squirm until her mother allowed her out of her lap.

Her parents were in love, truly. Her father, who was shorter than her mother, would look up at his wife with such awe in his eyes, as if she hung the stars and held sunlight in her yellow hair. Wren would lay on their old sagging couch watching them dance before falling asleep.

Wren spent her days playing with the neighborhood kids. They kicked around a ball sewn from old leather pieces, playing with dolls made from the dried husks of corn, played dress up with dresses and trousers with holes in the seams and stains on the hems.

She discovered her light magics when she was four, and healing talent the summer after.

When she was six and in the worst winter of her life, a sickness swept through the neighborhood. Her friends' families got sick and died. Her parents stopped their usual jobs and helped take care of the newly orphaned children until they died, too. Wren would sit at the window, watching bodies being carried away in wheelbarrows where they'd be burned in giant pyres twice, then three, then four times a week. Even after her parents fell sick, they still did what they could to help the neighbors that remained.

Then one day, her father didn't get up. He stayed in bed for three days until the sickness finally took him from Wren and her mother.

Wren had gotten sick, of course. How could she not have, being around so many others who were? Before her mother died, she kept Wren warm and hydrated, even if it meant sacrificing herself. Wren pulled through, miraculously unscathed, and when her mother fell into bed one night and not gotten up, Wren decided to try out her healing magics. She did what she'd seen the other healers do, placing her hands on her mother's chest and letting her hands fill with light. But it didn't work, and the next morning her mother didn't wake up.

Wren stayed in their home for a few days, her mother's body draped in blankets so she didn't have to see it. Soon, people knocked on her door and, knowing they were checking to see if the people inside were still alive, she hid in the closet until the men with masks covering their noses and mouths hauled her mother away. She hadn't left the house since her mother's death and, with the only thing keeping her there gone, she wandered the streets, amazed at how empty they were. None of her friends were left. The only people she saw were the duke's masked men that came to get rid of the bodies. Whenever she saw one, she ducked into a dark house or behind a dumpster. She didn't know what they'd do with her when she was found, and she didn't know if she wanted to find out.

That night, she went back home to find it gutted. The duke's men were pulling everything from inside the houses to burn anything that might have been contaminated with the illness. Foolishly, she expected them to wait a few days. Her blankets and stuffies were gone, the mattress that had indents of her tiny body, the pillows that smelled like her mother's shampoo and father's soap were all piled up to be burned.

She huddled in the corner of the bedroom, her legs and arms tucked into the only shirt she owned and fell asleep.

A few hours later, she was shaken awake by a man with dark hair. "Hello," he said. "What's your name?" He wasn't wearing a mask.

Wren tried to melt into the walls. She was so cold and the lantern the man carried was so bright.

"It's all right," the man said. He shrugged out of his coat and draped it around her. "I'm Elliot."

Wren let out a small cough. "I'm Wrennley," she squeaked.

Elliot smiled at her and held his arms out. "Well, Wrennley, I'm afraid you can't stay here, but I can take you somewhere warm and safe. Is that all right?"

She nodded and allowed the man to pick her up. He had to take his jacket off of her to get her situated in his arms and she cried from the cold, but then he wrapped it around her again and stood.

The other men in the streets chastised Elliot, saying he was going to catch whatever had killed the riff. Elliot covered Wren's ears, so she didn't hear what they called her family, her friends. He told the other men he didn't care; he wasn't going to let a child die. She wrapped her thin arms tighter around his neck and buried her nose in his shoulder. She fell asleep.

"Wow," Eli says, a bit of blackberry jam in the corner of her mouth. "You were so young. It must have been hard."

Wren shrugs. "I don't really remember how hard it was," she says. "My mother and father made sure I had an easy life. I never went to bed hungry or cold."

Eli wipes her mouth with her yellow napkin. "I meant losing your parents when you were six."

Wren laughs. Of course that's what Eli meant. But she was six and didn't really understand what death was. She knew her parents were gone and she wouldn't see them again, but her days were full of too many other things to have time to be sad about them. Then, by the time she was able to understand death and grief, her memories of her parents and her old neighborhood were too fuzzy to feel any loss.

When they've finished their cheese platter and licked the dregs of fruit from their fingers dragged along the bottom of the jam bowls, Eli buys a few wax-wrapped chunks of the cheeses they liked best and a jar of blackberry jam.

They say goodbye to the cheese seller and leave the store, stopping at the cart outside the bookshop before going inside.

The shop is crowded with shelves and stacks of books along the floor. Eli looks at spines and flips through pages. She kneels and inspects the dusty corners for hidden gems.

Wren thumbs through a few thin paperbacks with taped-together spines. The covers are all hand drawn couples, the women in silk nightgowns that barely cover their chests, the men with tight leather pants and no shirts. Wren picks up one where the woman on the cover is laid out on a rock as waves crash behind her. Her clothing is inappropriate for her surroundings, Wren thinks. Above her, a man wearing leather pants stands, his hands gripped around the hilt of a sword he's holding above his head. It looks like something Ophelia would enjoy. Wren laughs and places the book back in the bin.

She continues looking around, running her fingers over spines on a set of leather bound encyclopedias. In a corner in the back of the shop is a pink velvet couch where a skinny grey cat is curled on a pillow. Wren sits on the couch and gently places her fingers near the cat's nose until it raises its head and meows at her with a crackly voice.

"Hello to you, too," Wren says, dragging her fingers down the cat's back. The cat nestles back into its pillow and purrs.

Wren stays there on the couch, absentmindedly petting the cat as Eli continues her search through the shop.

After a while, Eli finds Wren on the couch. "I love bookstores, don't you?" she asks Wren, two books tucked under an arm.

Wren nods, then sneezes. "Don't much like the dust."

Eli laughs. "I imagine not. Go on and wait outside. I'll be out in a minute."

Wren gives the cat one last pet before she goes and stands outside the bookshop, holding the paper bag with the cheese and jam. The coffee shop has a few tables outside with people sitting, drinking their coffees from white cups. A few hold open books in their hands or have a newspaper spread out on their table. Some are talking with their tablemates. There's a child dunking their patchwork fabric doll into a cup of water. The adult at their table watches them over the cup they have held to their lips, their eyes wide. They sigh and take a long drink.

When Eli comes out, three books in her hands, she takes the bag from Wren and places her books inside.

On their way back to the pier, they run into Lex and Arden. Lex has a piece of paper clutched in their hand. "Look!" they say, shoving the flyer into Eli's hand.

She smooths it out as best she can on her thigh and reads it. "Interesting," she says.

Wren tries to read over the captain's shoulder but before she can get past 'Attention! To the captain of the ship *The Altean:*' Eli turns to her and says, "I've got to find Kiara and get to work on this. Go find Ezra and Ophelia and enjoy your time here." She's smiling wide as the sky on a clear day. Her steps are quick as she rushes off back to the ship, the paper bag of goodies clutched under her arm.

Wren walks with Arden and Lex in the market square. Lex tells her there's no word about new attacks, and no sightings of Aris since his last attack two weeks before. They find Ophelia and Ezra with Clare at a table in a pub eating greasy food laid out on brown paper.

The three of them join their other crew members and all of them order tall glasses of amber beer that make their laughs louder and their words slur. Eventually they all throw in a handful of coins or bills and their waitress smiles while shaking her head as they leave.

THIRTEEN

 that night. She doesn't even dream. It's the first night in weeks where she wakes feeling refreshed. Well, apart from the headache that is definitely from the alcohol she'd had the night before. It's such a different feeling, this headache that comes from fun instead of intrusion—even if that intrusion was somewhat welcome—that she almost savors it.

Just as she closes her eyes again, Ophelia rips open the curtain between their bunks and dumps a bucket of water on her.

"Excuse me!" Wren jumps up from her hammock and starts wringing out her shirt. It's the same shirt as the day before and she realizes she must have spilled on it, as there's a big brown stain down the front.

Ophelia laughs and drops the bucket on the ground, which makes Wren's head pound. She's starting to regret those four—five glasses of...whatever it was she'd had the night before. "Sorry, sleepyhead," Ophelia says, still laughing. "The captain wants us all up on deck." She turns to leave, then looks back at Wren. "Oh, also, you've got sick all over your shirt. See you on deck!"

Above, in a clean shirt and after draining her water flask twice, Wren stands next to Lex, leaning against the mast. They're still docked at Therma and from where they stand, they can see the citizens of the town walking around the booths set up on the pier. Before they'd made it back to the ship the night before, all of them sat for an artist that exaggerated all of their features. Wren saw it tacked to the wall of their quarters as she'd chosen a shirt from the shared trunk of clothes.

"Crew!" Eli shouts. She stands with Kiara, the flyer from Lex grasped in her hand. "Yesterday, we had a successful day. We learned that Aris has not attacked any more towns since Kakos. This doesn't mean he *won't*, but if we don't learn of any more in the next few days while we're here, then I think it's safe to say that he's stopped, at least for the time being.

"Furthermore," she continues, "Lex and Arden found this flyer." She holds up the paper, then reads, "'Attention! To the captain of the ship *The Altean*: The sisters Dínn of Loksa, Nestad request your assistance in retrieving an asset which has been stolen from us, being held in Erama, Jinsimbia.'" Eli looks at the crew from under her oil black eyelashes. "'Whether or not you decide to undertake this very important job, we request an answer in haste so we can make preparations for your arrival, or other arrangements.'" When she's finished, she looks up at the crew, the smile she wore the day before back on her face.

"Are we going to take it?" Ophelia asks. She sits on the deck, cleaning under her fingernails with a knife.

"Kiara and I have spoken at length about it. And, yes, we sent a messenger hawk this morning saying that we are interested in meeting." She looks over at Kiara, who smiles warmly at the captain. Turning back to the crew, Eli says, "We leave Tuesday morning at dawn. Now, off with the lot of you!"

FOURTEEN

Eli joins Wren in the crew's quarters as she packs her leather bag with a change of clothes.

"How would you feel about adding to our portrait wall?" Eli asks.

"The portraits in your quarters?" Wren had only seen it a few times. She could pick out most of her fellow crewmates, but a few were missing.

Eli nods. "We've been meaning to have Ophelia and Grace sit for portraits in town, but I know you used to paint in Sudal. Would you do them? We'd need one of you as well, of course."

Wren smiles, setting the strap of her satchel on her shoulder. She'd been missing her easel and pots of paints and brushes. "Yes," she says, her smile breaking her face in two. "I don't have supplies, though."

"Not to worry," Eli says, smiling conspiratorially. She reaches into her coat pocket and pulls out a few bills. "Will this be enough?"

Wren fans out the bills, counting. "This will be more than plenty," she says. She takes half of them and offers them back to Eli, but the captain puts her hand over them.

"Keep it for your time."

Wren nods and places the bills in the pocket of her cloak. "Thank you," she says.

Eli shoves her chin in the direction of Ophelia and Ezra, waiting by the stairs for Wren. "Have fun. See you soon."

The only shop selling the supplies Wren needs is small, like a closet has been renovated into a craft store.

Ophelia and Ezra wait outside as Wren shops. As she's looking at the small stock of canvases, a short woman with hair shaved close to her scalp comes over.

"Sorry for the pitiful selection. We don't have many painters in town, so I don't keep stock."

"No need to be sorry," Wren says. She picks up three small canvases. "You've got exactly what I need."

The woman smiles. "Are you the painter, or are these a gift?"

"I used to paint," Wren says. "I used to paint much more, but the need hasn't arisen lately." She yearns for her easel, the collection of bought paints and the ones she'd made herself from crushing berries or dried flower petals.

She follows the woman to a shelf where tubes of paints are hung and a small selection of brushes sit in jars. "Were you any good?" the woman asks as Wren picks up tube after tube to inspect the shade.

Wren shrugs and moves onto the brushes. "I wasn't bad," she admits. "I mostly did landscapes, but I dabbled a bit in portraiture and still life."

"A woman after my own heart."

Once the supplies have been paid for and packaged carefully in brown paper, Wren rejoins Ophelia and Ezra outside. Ophelia loops her arm through Wren's, and they walk to a small park where Clare and Grace are sitting on a blue blanket spread on the grass.

"Got everything you need?" Clare asks, tying a bow with an orange ribbon in Grace's curls.

"Yep," Wren says, sitting down in front of them. To Grace, she asks, "Are you ready?"

Grace nods, practically bouncing up and down where she sits.

The woman at the shop had gifted Wren a ceramic palette, and she starts mixing paints on its surface. After prepping the canvas, she drags the brush across the surface, looking up at Grace occasionally. She'd only worked with a canvas this small once, when she had painted a portrait of herself back before Jakob left on his assignment. What had become of that? Was it in Jakob's pocket when he died? Did it float away in the shipwreck, forever lost to the sea? Wren shakes her head to clear those thoughts and stretches her shoulders to cover.

When she's finished, she turns the canvas to show Grace and her face lights up.

"Wow!" she says. "I've never had my portrait painted before!" She carefully takes the canvas from Wren and holds it up to the sun to see the details. Wren had been meticulous in placing the freckles on her nose, the archer's bow of her lips, the pocked scar on her cheek, the delicate curls framing her face. The orange of the silk ribbon had been a challenge to get right, but Grace runs her fingers over the already dry paint of it and smiles.

"It looks just like you," Clare says to Grace, looking over the girl's shoulder at the painting.

"I look like my mum," Grace says and Wren's heart lurches.

Before she can say anything, Ophelia says, "Okay, my turn! I've never had my portrait painted either."

"A shame. They should hang portraits of you in museums," Ezra says, moving a strand of hair over Ophelia's forehead.

Ophelia smiles at him and then turns to Wren. "You hear that? This will end up in a museum someday, so don't make any mistakes. No pressure." She winks.

"No pressure," Wren echoes as she wipes the palette clean.

Ophelia is a little easier to paint. Because Wren spends most of her time with Ophelia, she doesn't have to look up as often. Her paintbrush glides over the canvas, leaving behind the curve of Ophelia's nose, the arch of her eyebrows, the slightly pointed tops of her ears. Wren paints her with a mischievous grin, the corners of her mouth pinched in and a slight smile on her lips.

When the last of Ophelia's freckles have been placed, Wren looks up at Ophelia and then back down at the canvas. "Can I borrow a knife?"

Ophelia raises her eyebrows. "A knife? For the portrait?"

Wren lets out a laugh. "Yes," she insists. "You have one, right?" Her eyes dart down to the knives strapped across Ophelia's chest.

Ophelia pulls a short-bladed knife from its place and scoffs. "Of course I have one."

Wren smiles and uses it to scrape away a bit of paint on the portrait, leaving behind a thin scar on Ophelia's throat. Wren holds the canvas up next to her friend's face and smiles. Ezra comes over and gives a low whistle.

"This really does belong in a museum," he says. "Nice work, Wren."

Ophelia takes it and looks at it, gasping. "This is the best I've ever looked." She turns to Grace and Clare and holds the canvas in front of her face. "Can't tell the difference, can you?"

Grace giggles and points at the canvas. "If your head was really that small, I would be concerned."

Ophelia puts the canvas down and rolls her eyes. "Well, let's thank the gods that my head isn't this small, then." She ruffles Grace's curls, disheveling the orange ribbon.

"All right, Wren. Your turn." They turn to Jez, who had joined them around the time Wren was painting Ophelia's eyes. He's holding the last canvas and has a paintbrush tucked behind each of his ears.

They all laugh. "Can you paint?" Wren asks.

Jez turns the canvas around where he's painted a smiley face in wobbly black lines.

"Well, I think it looks just like you," Ezra says.

Wren throws a tube of paint at him.

Jez hands the canvas to Wren. "I hope I didn't ruin it?"

Wren shakes her head and smiles at him. "Not at all. This paint is very layerable."

They watch her as she works, cleaning the palette and then squeezing more paint to mix. As with the portrait she gave to Jakob and Grace's orange ribbon, she can't quite get the color of her hair right, but she's able to mix a close enough shade. She borrows the small compact mirror from Ophelia and gets started on her self-portrait.

She hasn't changed much since living in Sudal. Her eyes are the same brown, her freckles and eyebrows the same. Her hair is the same, though maybe a little longer. In the portrait she'd painted before, she'd left her mouth neutral, as if she was sitting on the window seat in her room looking out over the gardens. But in this one, the one that will be hung in Eli and Kiara's quarters on *The Altean*, she paints herself smiling, like she's sitting on the deck with Lex, listening to an exaggerated story Ezra is telling. She paints herself with slightly pinked skin, like she's been lounging in the sun with Penelope all day. She paints herself free.

When she's finished, there's still a slight shadow of Jez's smile visible under her.

FIFTEEN

EZRA, OPHELIA, LEX, ARDEN, and Wren rent rooms at an inn a few blocks from the market square. Ezra and Ophelia's and Wren's rooms are connected by a door and Lex and Arden get a room across the hall. On their first night, they order room service and use the extra bed in Wren's room as a picnic place. They pile the food in the center and sit around it. Wren, Lex, and Ophelia fit on the bed and Ezra and Arden pull up chairs, propping their feet up on the bed, using their legs as tables.

After dinner, they order dessert and after dessert, once the dishes are taken by the attendant, Ezra and Arden pile onto the bed as well. While they talk amongst themselves, Ophelia braids Wren's hair, Ezra draws on Lex's hand with a pen, Arden mends a hole in the trousers Ophelia is still wearing. They stay in a pile until Lex complains about how hot they are, and Ophelia says she needs to use the toilet. Then, they all say good night and go to their rooms, leaving Wren on her own for the first time since she joined the crew four months ago.

She lies back on the bed, arms and legs spread out like a starfish. She pushes her trousers off her hips and tosses them into a pile near where her boots landed earlier. It's warm in her room and she doesn't bother crawling under the sheets before she falls asleep.

Over the next few days, Wren explores the city with Ophelia and Ezra or Arden and Lex. Grace, Jez, and Clare join them during the day, and they eat at cafés and pubs and street carts.

Clare joins them at the inn on their third night and Wren has to clear the spare bed of discarded clothes and food wrappers.

"Sorry," she says, dumping the clothes into a chair. "I'm not used to sharing a room like this."

Clare laughs and kicks her boots off into a corner. "No worries," she says. "My kids were terrible at keeping their room clean." She lies back on the bed, crossing her arms behind her head.

Wren straightens slowly from picking up a stray wrapper. She turns to Clare. "You have kids?"

Clare lets out a small laugh. "I did, yeah. Two sons." Wren waits, but Clare doesn't elaborate.

"What happened?"

"They died," Clare says, her voice quiet. She sits up and touches her fingertips to the scar running down her face and disappearing into her shirt. "In a fire. I couldn't save them."

Wren sits on the edge of her bed, her hands cupped lightly in her lap. "I'm sorry. I had no idea."

Clare looks at her, her clear blue eyes bright with tears. "I've forgiven myself for it. It hasn't been easy, but Eli and Grace have helped a lot." She smiles at Wren and then says, "Do you have any siblings?"

"No, it's just me," Wren says. Her parents never had a chance to have more children, and the duke never adopted another.

Clare pulls her feet up on the bed and crosses her legs. "Then that means you've never had a sibling spa day."

"A what?"

Clare jumps up off the bed and knocks on the door between their room and Ezra and Ophelia's. It opens a minute later, and Ophelia and Clare exchange a few quiet words between them before Ophelia disappears with a squeal. Clare steps back and crosses her arms loosely over her chest.

Ophelia arrives a few seconds later, holding two washcloths in her hand. "Ready?" she says to Wren.

Wren glances between Clare and Ophelia. "For what?"

Ophelia giggles and closes the door leading to her room.

They stay up well past midnight, sitting on the beds in their underclothes, passing around a bottle of cheap wine Ophelia had bought and eating chocolate cookies from a tin Clare had pulled from her bag.

As Ophelia puts Clare's long blonde hair into two braids down her back, Wren digs through a zippered bag from Clare's luggage with bottles of nail varnish. There are a lot of shades to choose from, but eventually, she settles on a deep green color that reminds her of the gardens at the estate. Ophelia paints Wren's nails while Clare braids her hair into a loose crown on top of her head.

Once all nail varnish has dried and all hair has been braided—Clare even managed to get a few in Ophelia's short hair—their conversation switches to the job they'll be taking in Nestad.

"Maybe we'll be retrieving a treasure chest of rare candies," Ophelia says, turning a cookie over in her hand.

"We'll have to watch Lex like a hawk if that's the case," Clare says, laughing. She hums. "Maybe it's something really rare, like a first edition printing of *The History of the Maian Empire*."

They turn to Wren. "What do you think?" Ophelia asks.

Wren rolls over onto her stomach and reaches off the edge of the bed for the tin of cookies. Ophelia nudges it closer with her foot.

"Maybe it's something living. Like a person or exotic pet." She examines the cookie she'd picked up. They have chocolate dipped bottoms and more chocolate drizzled over the top. She used to get ones just like this in Sudal. "Or maybe it's nothing exciting at all and they just said *asset* to entice us." She pops the whole cookie in her mouth.

Ophelia lets out a bark of laughter. "Wouldn't that be something?"

Finally, after the cake they'd ordered when they finished the cookies has been reduced to crumbs, and the bottle of wine is empty, Clare yawns and goes into the bathroom to brush her teeth. Wren and Ophelia sit on Wren's bed, their legs stretched out in front of them.

"If it is a person, and they ran from something, we'll just be taking them back somewhere they don't want to be," Ophelia says, tracing the lines on Wren's palm.

Wren had thought about that. Her first thought after hearing "asset" was a runaway bride like herself.

"Yeah, I know," she says, her voice quiet.

"What will you do if it is?"

The shower turns on in the bathroom and they hear Clare's voice through the wall, her singing clear and honeyed.

Wren shakes her head. "I don't know," she admits. "I don't think there would be much I could do."

Ophelia lays her head on Wren's shoulder. "I hope you're right. That it's just some ploy to get our attention and when we show up, it's, I don't know, a barrel of apples or something."

Wren looks at her, smiling. "Wouldn't that be something?"

When the shower water turns off, Ophelia climbs off of Wren's bed and walks over to the door between Wren's room and the one Ophelia shares with Ezra. "See you in the morning?"

Wren lies on her side over the rumpled covers of her bed. "I'll be here," she says.

"Good night, Wren."

"Good night, Ophelia."

The door closes behind Wren's first friend since Jakob with a click.

Their last day in Therma comes all too soon, in Wren's opinion. But they make the most of it. Ezra, Ophelia, Clare, and Wren surprise Arden and Lex with breakfast in bed for Arden's birthday. The donuts are a day old, and the coffee is cheap and bitter from the lobby, but they feast on them, scalding their tongues on the coffee. For lunch, they meet up with Jez and Grace at a pub near the inn and they all give Arden his gifts. Clare, Wren, and Ophelia put money together for a new set of knives. Ezra gifts him a new bottle of whiskey. Wren watches Lex as Arden opens his other gifts. With each one, Lex's shoulders tense a little more. She nudges them under the table with the toe of her boot and when their eyes lock, she gives a small smile.

"He'll love it," she mouths.

Lex smiles and pulls a paper package from their shoulder bag. They hand it to Arden and smile sheepishly. "It's, um. Well." They shrug.

Arden makes sure Lex sees his smile and kisses their forehead before ripping the paper and twine bow off and pulling out a dark green piece of fabric. He unfolds it and holds it up. "An apron," he says, the smile obvious in his voice.

"They're supposed to be trees," Lex says, gesturing to the embroidery on the pockets.

Arden sets the apron on the table and smooths it out, tracing the stitching with a big thumb. "I th-think they look just like t-trees." He looks at Lex and puts his arm around their shoulders, pressing another kiss to their temple. "Thank you, bee."

Arden carefully folds the apron, and Lex puts it in their shoulder bag, along with the other things Arden has been gifted. Grace says she has a gift, too, but it'll have to wait until they're all back on the ship.

After lunch, they stop at the currency exchange booth outside the market so everyone can get more money. It's one of Wren's favorite things about new towns, seeing the different bills and coins, although Kornas crowns are not foreign to her. She always keeps one bill or coin from each country—Maian *freza* coins in different metals; green Jinsimbian *grotze* bills and silver coins; Nestadian chips, bills in different colors based on their denominations; Breton crowns, coins in gold and silver and orange bills. Her small collection and the bulk of her money she keeps tucked away in a small, worn leather wallet she'd bought at a secondhand store in

Kamba. Her spending money is kept in a purple cloth bag that cinches at the top with a thin strip of cord.

She joins Lex and Arden after she's finished at the booth. Despite not being hired, the people of the towns they'd helped insisted they pay the crew of *The Altean*. And Eli and Kiara made sure the crew was paid for their work, regardless of whether the townspeople gave real money or food or only their thanks.

Eventually, the rest of the crew finishes at the exchange booth, and they spend the rest of the day hanging out in the market. Wren and Arden get their faces painted with Grace and they come away with glitter on their cheeks that Wren is sure will take weeks of scrubbing to get rid of. Ezra and Lex each lose twenty Kornas crowns to Jez in a game of dice. Ophelia and Clare get their fortunes read by a woman in pink and purple skirts, with glitter dabbled across her nose and cheeks.

"Long life," she promises them both. "You'll be very happy together."

"I think she was confused when we told her we were friends," Ophelia says.

Clare laughs. "No kidding," she says.

That night, all gathered on deck, Grace goes to Ezra and whispers something in his ear. He gives her a conspiratorial smile and then stands and follows her to the galley.

When they come back out, Grace is carrying a white frosted cake with multicolored lit candles stuck in the top. "Happy birthday," she says to Arden, her face broken in two by a smile.

Arden mirrors her smile, thanks her, then blows out the candles. Grace sets the cake on the deck; Ezra sets plates and forks down next to it. Arden slices into the cake with one of his new knives, then serves pieces to each crew member.

"To Arden," Eli says, holding up her flask, her plate balanced on her knee.

"To Arden," they echo in a shout, their own flasks or cups held up. They tap them twice on the deck, then tip their heads back and drink.

SIXTEEN

The Nestadian sky is grey overhead, and frothy waves rock *The Altean* lazily as they dock at the small watery town at the southern tip of the country. Loksa is still asleep beyond the docks.

Eli asked Wren the night before if she would join her and Kiara to meet with the Sisters Dínn so she could see how they conduct negotiations. Wren was sure that someone else might like to go, but Ophelia laughed and waved her worries aside with a flick of her wrist.

"We've all seen it," she said. "It's not nearly as exciting as you might think."

Wren rose that morning and tied back her hair with a piece of leather and dug through the shared trunk to find the least worn clothes that fit her.

Then she meets in Eli's quarters, listening to Eli talk about rules and expectations while breakfasting.

"Look unimpressed, no matter what you see." The captain stands in front of the mirror and straightens the collar of her green coat, pulls on her sleeves. "Don't make conversation. You are not who they are negotiating with." She pulls the tie from her locs and reties it with a new strip of leather. Then she turns to Wren. "Are you ready?"

Wren stands and nods, putting her napkin on the desktop. "Yes. Do we know what the job is?"

"All we know is that it's an asset retrieval." She leads Wren and Kiara out onto the dock. "We'll know more after this meeting." She throws a wink over her shoulder at Wren before turning to the rest of the crew gathered on deck.

"Crew!" she calls out. When they've all turned to her, she continues, "Wren, Kiara, and myself will be meeting with the Sisters Dínn to discuss the job they've commissioned us for. I expect us to be gone for a few hours. Please stay on board until we return." She turns to Arden. "If we're gone past lunch, you and Clare come to the warehouse and ask after us."

Arden nods and locks eyes with Clare across the deck before turning back to Eli.

The captain flashes them all a big smile. "All right. We'll see you soon."

The dock at Loksa is all but deserted. Only one other ship is docked, the people on deck loading and unloading unmarked barrels. They don't look at Eli, Kiara, and Wren as they pass. Wren follows Eli alongside Kiara, her arms hanging at her side as she looks around.

They have to stop at customs where she shows her passport and magics registration. She had to reapply for her documents at the first major port town she'd been to after becoming a crew member of *The Altean*. She was afraid they'd ask for documentation that she was allowed to leave Sudal, but they'd only asked for her name and birthday and a witness's signature before issuing her new paperwork. Ophelia served as her witness, saying she and Wren were friends since they were young, although they only knew each other for a few days at that point.

"They don't care too much if your magics aren't rare," Ophelia said, thumbing through Wren's new passport. It didn't have the noble seal of Sulesia or Kornas on it, the way her other one did. But she knew claiming to be the duke's daughter would raise flags, and she didn't want to explain what she was doing outside of Sulesia. Her magics registration was under her birth name anyway, not under the duke's name. And that's what she'd given when the registrar asked.

When the customs agent has stamped her passport with a black Nestadian emblem, she tucks it into her trouser pocket and steps back so Kiara can get hers.

"Your book is white," Wren says when Kiara rejoins her and Eli. "I thought only magics users had white passports."

Kiara shrugs and puts her book away in her skirts. "I've had this passport for a hundred years," she says. "Things change more often than you think. Come on, we have to be at the warehouse in a few minutes."

The warehouse sits on the edge of the sea, sitting halfway in the water and half on the crumbling concrete foundation on the sand.

Wren expects the warehouse to be decorated in banners and flags, but there are no indications that this is anything other than an abandoned building being reclaimed by the sea.

Wren and Kiara stand back as their captain knocks on the warehouse door. After a few long minutes, the door cracks open and a short girl, probably not much older than Grace, pops her head out.

"Are you the captain of *The Altean*?" the girl asks, her voice raspy and thick.

"Yes," Eli says. "I'm Eleanor Crowley, and this is Kiara and Wren." She indicates each of them and the girl nods before turning back to Eli.

"Please, come in. Apologies for the floor." She opens the door the rest of the way.

Inside is worse than outside. Only the outside walls and skeleton of the structure remain intact. The wooden floor is rotted where the water has leaked in and the salt eaten away at the beams. It's chillier, too, and Wren wishes she'd brought her cloak.

The girl, wearing a thick woolen blanket over her shoulders, leads them into the only room with standing walls. It's still mostly underwater, but a makeshift floor has been constructed from broken tiles and sea-smoothed planks of wood.

The other half of the room is sand and rotten wood. To Wren's surprise, there are many people here. A group of people, all female-presenting, ages ranging from the girl that greeted them to wrinkled and old, sit or lounge out of the water on large rocks. There are a few seals, too, poking their heads above the surface.

One of the women stands. Her thick curly hair falls below her waist. "Thank you for joining us, Captain."

Eli nods once. "Thank you for inviting us. How can we help?"

The one who had stood steps forward. She's barefoot and thick waisted. The meager light from outside shines off the water and reflects off her pale skin. "Our sister has been taken from us." Her voice is raspy, just like the younger one. "She was captured and is being held by a merchant named Van Zellar. I assume you've heard of him?"

Eli takes a deep breath through her nose. "Yes, I have heard of Mr. Van Zellar." She shakes her head. "We've never had the misfortune of running into him, but it was only a matter of time before we were brought together."

The woman nods. "Will you help us?" There's more than just what she's asking in her voice. There's desperation there, too.

Wren doesn't have siblings. She's never had any reason to know what that kind of relationship is like. But the sisters gathered here, with their different skin tones, different eyes, different hair, probably aren't all related either. And Wren knows what that feels like. Friends that have become family. If Ophelia or Lex or Kiara had been taken, Wren would do whatever it took to get them back. She knows that desperation. She had been desperate when Jakob died, too, though she knew there was no way to get him back. Adreus didn't barter with the already departed.

"We'll do what we can," Eli assures her.

The woman's shoulders relax, and a collective breath is let out by her sisters behind her. They murmur among themselves, grasping hands and touching fingers to cheeks.

After a few moments, Eli asks how the sisters heard of her and *The Altean.*

"We've been watching you," the woman says. "We've seen the way you help others. We admire it. When we saw you sailing toward Therma, we created the flyer and tacked it to the board. We were elated that you responded so quickly."

Eli bows her head. "We are happy to help." She lifts her head and looks at the others gathered on the rocks. "Tell us about your sister."

The girl who had led them in sits up straighter. "Her name is Aedi."

"Yes," the woman says. "We believe she's being held at the Van Zellar estate in Erama. What do you know of Van Zellar?"

Eli takes a breath before saying, "Not much. As I said, we've never had any contact with him. But there are talks that he trades in unusual creatures."

Wren's eyes drift around the sisters. All of them have a dark, heavy blanket draped across their shoulders. A shiver runs down her back as she realizes what the Sisters Dínn are. The wool shrouds aren't blankets, they're seal skins. The sisters are selkies. And their sister Aedi has been stolen to be sold; not as a bride, but as a pet or meat delicacy.

"That's correct," the woman says. "We fear for our sister and pray she hasn't already been hurt."

"You said Erama," Eli says. "Do you have any other information?"

The woman nods. She holds out one of her thick arms and Eli steps forward to a small table sitting away from the water. There are maps and papers scattered across it.

As she and Kiara talk with the woman and a few of the other sisters over at the table, Wren sits and talks with the young girl they'd first met. Her name is Lin.

"How long have you been with Eleanor?" she asks.

"A little over four months," Wren says. "How long have you been with your sisters?"

Lin smiles, showing off her trident-shaped teeth. "Forty years," she says. She laughs, low and crackly, at the surprise on Wren's face. "Selkies age differently than humans. In your years, I'd be about twelve."

"Have you been with them your whole life?"

Lin nods. "Selkie family harems aren't all related. My mother is in a different harem, my blood sisters in others. Our families aren't bonded by blood, but by shared experiences."

"Sounds like *The Altean*," Wren says, her voice quiet.

"Then you understand our desire to bring Aedi home," Lin says, watching her older sisters and Eli and Kiara at the table.

Wren puts her hand on Lin's shoulder. "Yes," she says. "And we'll do everything we can to bring her home safe."

The next morning, Kiara goes into Loksa to send a message to a contact in Jinsimbia to ask for blueprints of homes similar to Van Zellar's. Eli tells Wren that many of the estates are similar in Erama, built to withstand siege, storms, and aid in survival.

Kiara comes back shortly and gives Eli a nod. "The message has been sent, Captain."

"Thank you, heart."

The rest of the crew was excited to hear of the job. Lex grabbed Wren's arm and shaken it excitedly. "We get to have our heist!"

As they pull away from the Loksa dock, Wren sits with them and Arden, Ezra, Ophelia, and Clare, all of them leaning against the railing at the bow.

Ezra and Lex talk animatedly, sitting across from each other. Lex mimics punching and mentions Ezra may have to fight. Ezra laughs, loud and bright, throwing his head back.

"I think it's going to be great," Ophelia says. "Having something to do rather than clean up after a spoiled prince." She's sitting cross-legged, rocking from side to side.

Clare sits across from Wren, looking out over the surface of the water as they cut through the waves. Wren stretches her leg out and nudges Clare with the toe of her boot. "What are you thinking?" she asks when Clare turns to her.

Clare takes a breath. "What if she's already been sold? Or she's hurt? Or killed? What do we tell her sisters? What do *we* do?"

Wren opens her mouth to say something, but Arden says, "We do our best to take her home. Even if the only thing left is her in memory."

SEVENTEEN

THEY DON'T STOP ON the way to Erama. It's only ten days' journey, and they were able to refill their stocks the evening after meeting with the Sisters. A few days out, a hawk with a leather case strapped to its back lands on the railing. It's waiting for them in the morning when Wren and Ophelia make it on deck. Wren goes and stands near it while Ophelia knocks on the captain's door and lets Eli and Kiara know of its arrival. It looks at Wren with black eyes, cocking its head and surveying her.

Eli steps up next to Wren and lets out a contented sigh when she sees the bird. "This is from our contact in Jinsimbia," she says, stepping up to the hawk. She pulls a piece of dried meat from her pocket and offers it to the bird. When it takes the meat, Eli eases the top off the leather case and pulls out a rolled piece of yellowed paper. She unrolls it to check its contents, and a smile breaks over her face.

"What is it?" Ophelia asks, standing next to Wren.

"The blueprints we asked for," Eli says, rolling the paper up again. The bird nips at her hand and Eli laughs and pulls out another piece of meat, giving it to the hawk. It swallows the treat and lets out a sharp call. Eli closes the case again and runs her finger along the bird's head. "Off you go, girl. Thank you."

After a moment of looking at Eli, then Ophelia, then Wren, the bird opens her wings and pushes off from the railing. The wind catches her, and she sails away from the ship.

"After breakfast, we'll all meet up and go over these together," the captain says. "For now, I'll speak with Kiara and draw up a plan."

The sun is high when they gather around the unrolled blueprints on the quarterdeck. Everyone sits cross-legged as Eli kneels in front of them and Kiara stands at the rail. It reminds Wren of the few tutoring classes she had with other children. All that's missing is the fireplace to her right and the worn carpet under her.

"Based on what her sisters told us, we believe Aedi will be in the sub-basement. It's accessible through a tunnel that leads off-grounds." Eli points to a spot on the blueprints labeled SUB and drags her fingers over a long, narrow hallway. She taps her finger at the end. "There will be a gate here," she says. "It will likely be locked and guarded."

She turns to each of the crew as she assigns jobs. "Ophelia, you'll go ahead and scout any obstacles or guards. Ezra, Lex, and Arden will follow. You three are the best with short-range weapons. Wren and I will bring up the back. Clare will stay at the gate, watching for patrols." She points to a small thatch of vegetation labeled TREES. "Kiara will wait here and will be ready to alert Clare if the need arises."

"Are these the blueprints for the Van Zellar estate?" Ezra asks. Eli told them she wasn't sure if her contact could get those specific ones, and there's no indication either way on the papers.

"Unfortunately, no. But estates in Erama were all built to withstand the same things." She looks at Wren expectantly.

"Siege, storm, and survival," Wren recites.

"Exactly. Still, keep in mind the Van Zellar estate may mirror this, or even be completely different. Either way, our goal is the same. We get Aedi and return her safely to her sisters."

The crew nods and waits for their captain to continue.

"Jez, you, the Star Child, and Grace will stay on the ship." She turns to Grace and says with a smile, "Stay below deck and get us ready for celebration when we return." Then she turns back to Jez. "You and the Star Child will be here, on deck and ready to set sail. We'll signal if we need backup."

She sits back on her heels. "Any questions?"

The dock of Erama, a large warehouse city on the southernmost coast of Jinsimbia, is crowded with workers loading and unloading cargo ships. The sun beats down on Wren's head, making her scalp tingle.

Eli said they'd be in town for a few days before the rescue so as not to draw suspicion. After pulling *The Altean* into port, Wren, Ezra, Ophelia, and Arden go into town and eat at a restaurant with a sign outside that reads, "Nice drinks and food!" Below is an arrow pointing further down the road and the message, "Dunno, maybe nice drinks and food. But why risk it?"

Inside, the tables are set under gas lamps, and all the chairs are mismatched. The bar at the front of the room is carved from a single tree trunk, as wide as Arden is tall.

They choose a table away from the windows and the hot sun streaming through. They're barely settled when Ezra challenges Arden to a drinking contest—whoever gets drunk first loses.

Wren and Ophelia look at each other over their glasses of orange juice. Ezra crosses his arms over his half-as-wide-as-Arden's chest and leans back in his chair, a smug look on his face.

Arden lifts his mug of beer. "You're on," he says.

They're both three mugs in by the time the food comes, and Ezra can barely sit up straight in his chair.

"Maybe you should stop, Ez," Ophelia says, her sandwich halfway to her mouth.

"I'm fine," Ezra slurs as he knocks back another drink, sloshing part of it down the front of his shirt.

Arden chuckles and takes another drink from his cup.

After two more mugs each, Ezra puts his back on the table with a loud thunk. "Are you even feeling it?" he asks Arden.

Arden thinks for a moment before moving his hand in a so-so motion. Ezra groans and picks up his glass again.

They finish eating and Ezra leans against Ophelia and Wren as they walk out onto the dusty road.

"We should get you back to the ship," Ophelia says as his head nods forward.

"I'm fine," Ezra says.

"You're not," Wren says.

Arden laughs and takes Ezra from Ophelia's shoulder, saying he'll take Ezra back. Wren carefully disentangles Ezra's arm from around her neck, and she stands with Ophelia, watching them walk back toward the dock, Ezra's feet a few steps behind Arden.

They walk for a while, side by side, their steps in sync, until they come across an inside market. The stalls inside are close together and crowded with shoppers, but it's a cool reprieve from the sun outside. They spot wind magics users spread throughout, moving their arms in slow movements to swirl the air inside.

Wren and Ophelia stroll through the aisles, looking lazily at the wares in the booths. Wren buys a small bottle of lavender oil, dabbing a few drops on her wrists as they walk away from the booth. She flips through a basket of old ordering catalogs while Ophelia looks at an assortment of antique knives until a green cover catches her eye. On the cover is an illustrated picture of a large tree, a face carved into the trunk. A girl in a white dress lounges in the shade, staring up into the leaves. In gilded letters, the title *Sulesian Tales for Children* is stamped across the top. She recognizes it as the cover of the same book of fairy tales that the duke used to read to her on those infrequent nights he put her to bed. She runs her finger over the title, over the face in the tree trunk, but her chest pulls, and she decides to buy it. When Ophelia points to it, Wren tucks it under her arm and says, "It's for Grace."

Ezra is still asleep when Wren and Ophelia leave for their patrol that night. As Wren changes into a black linen shirt, she hears Ophelia whisper goodbye to Ezra.

They walk along the road the Van Zellar estate sits on, shuffling their feet in the dirt and dragging their fingers along the iron fencing and the long grasses on the other side of the road. Eli told them to make it seem like they belonged, just two girls taking a stroll at dusk. They pass a few other people on the road, and they smile and nod at them, tell them good evening, or offer a short hello. It's possible that some of them are on patrol for Van Zellar, but Wren doesn't make notes of them yet in the notebook Eli gave her.

After dark, they sit in the thatch of trees that was marked on the blueprints. As they walked past other estates, they noted that some of them had patches of flowers, a tiny meadow, or the sawed-off trunks where trees once stood. When they saw the trees where they'd be hunkered down for the night, they looked at each other with relief, glad to have the cover.

It's easy to tell the patrols from the pedestrians based on who carries a torch and who stops near the gate. Wren writes everything in the notebook, using a small glow of light held in her palm after each patrol disappears around the estate's corner.

Ophelia stands two hours after they settle and disappears, winking at Wren. Wren watches the grass sway as Ophelia makes her way out of the copse of trees to check the gate across the road. She's gone for only a short time and when she reappears beside Wren, flopping back down onto the grass, Wren startles. Ophelia chuckles and tells Wren about the lock—wrought iron and a bit rusted but easily picked. The ground around the gate is trimmed and clear of debris, likely used more often than not. Ophelia picks long pieces of grass as she talks, and Wren writes all of her observations in the notebook.

Throughout the night, Ophelia times each of the patrols with a watch and Wren writes that in the notebook as well. Ophelia weaves the long stalks of grass she'd picked using the light from Wren's hands.

At dawn, they pick their way out of the trees between patrols and walk along the road again, grass crowns sitting on their brows. They don't pass anyone on the road and are surprised at the lack of work on the docks. Wren notes that as well.

Eli and Kiara meet them at the top of the gangway, and they breakfast in the captain's quarters while Ophelia and Wren tell them of their observations. Eli takes the notebook and tucks it away in a drawer in her desk.

The captain and her first mate thank Wren and Ophelia, and they head to bed, exhausted after a long night of no sleep. Wren doesn't change clothes, just kicks off her boots and strips off her trousers before climbing into her hammock.

Ezra welcomes Ophelia back and then he rolls over, immediately starting to snore again.

The sun is high when Wren wakes. Ophelia is just starting to move next to her.

"I am starving," Ophelia groans, her eyes still pinched tight.

The ship is empty, apart from the Star Child sleeping in their corner, and Kiara and Penelope on deck.

"The others went into town for lunch," she tells them.

After a quick hello to Penelope, Wren and Ophelia walk into town and find their crewmates at the park, picnicking in the shade under a big oak tree.

Ophelia plops down between Ezra and Lex, and Wren sits next to Clare.

The food is nearly gone, but Ophelia and Wren find enough to fill their plates. As they eat, Ezra tries to goad information out of them about the Van Zellar estate and the guard patrols.

"Is it the same guard every time? How many times did they walk by in an hour? What kind of things did they look at?" He fires off question after question without waiting for an answer, looking between Ophelia and Wren, his honey eyes sparkling.

Ophelia mimes zipping her lips and locking them, then throws Wren the key. Wren catches it and does the same thing, dragging her fingers along her lips and twisting. Then she throws the key into a small patch of long grass and flowers.

"Oh, come on!" Ezra says. "You've gotta tell us something!"

"Ez, you will find out for yourself in, like, eight hours," Ophelia says around a mouthful of food.

Ezra lets out an exasperated sigh. "*Fine,*" he says, sitting back on his hands and pushing his bottom lip out.

Ophelia rolls her eyes, laughing, and stuffs more food in her mouth.

They stroll the town a bit more before heading back to the ship. When the sun gets close to the horizon, Ezra and Lex meet with the captain and Kiara on the quarterdeck. Wren watches them from where she leans against the mast, sure she's never seen either of them so focused or serious.

When they're finished, they walk down to the main deck and the rest of the crew stands at the rails to see them off. Ezra presses one kiss to Ophelia's mouth and another to her forehead before waving at Wren. She waves back and watches his dark head disappear down the gangplank.

Arden and Lex are on the dock, their foreheads pressed together. Arden says something Wren can't hear and Lex laughs, looking up at Arden through their eyelashes.

"Bye, Ezra! Bye, Lex!" Grace yells, leaning over the railing and waving her arm furiously.

Ezra and Lex both laugh and wave to her before turning their backs to *The Altean* and disappearing into the city.

Ophelia and Wren stay on deck well after the rest of the crew heads to bed. The light coming from under the captain's door flickers and then disappears as the moon rises higher.

The girls spread a blanket out in the middle of the deck and lie down, their arms crossed under their heads, their elbows overlapping. The Star Child sits in a chair near them, their eyes trained out at the water. Penelope curls up between them, her head on Wren's knee, her tail draped across Ophelia's shin.

Ophelia points out a few constellations to Wren: the pitcher, the scales, the sea serpent. Wren knows them all and the stories that go with them. Goddess Anrena's pitcher, which was used to pour out the sea, so travel would be easier between the continents. The scales, signifying the twins Ekris, god of dark, and Etris, goddess of light. And the sea serpent said to patrol the Isles of the Damned, swallowing sailors and trespassers with no remorse.

Ophelia switches the conversation to Evey. Wren doesn't mind. The sound of Ophelia's voice and the waves against the hull are comforting. Ophelia taps her fingers against the deck, in a rhythm Wren doesn't recognize, but Ophelia keeps up, even through her talking. Wren starts to drift off, closing her eyes against the dark of the sky.

Around midnight, Ophelia shakes Wren awake and they walk together down to the belly of the ship, Penelope trailing behind. In the dim light of a lantern near Grace's cot, Wren sees the book of Sulesian fairytales open across her stomach. Wren makes her way over to her and takes the book, closes it, and places it in the bin of other books by the cot. She pulls the blanket further up Grace's body and smooths the curls off her forehead.

Wren waits until Ophelia lies down before turning the lantern down the rest of the way. She slowly makes her way to her hammock, lighting the floor at her feet with a soft glow from her hands.

EIGHTEEN

Ezra and Lex return while Wren and Arden have breakfast on the steps of the quarterdeck. Lex sends a warm smile to Arden before they and Ezra knock on the captain's door and enter.

After a little while, they return to deck, closing the door behind them. Ezra waves to Wren and Arden before going down to the crew's quarters. Lex lopes over to where they sit and Arden stands, plunging his hand into the pocket of his trousers.

"I saved this for you," Arden says.

Lex smiles, their face split in two, and they take the bundle from Arden's palm. They open the napkin and pull out an apple turnover, slightly smushed, and let out an excited squeal. They sink their teeth into it and their eyes roll back in what Wren knows is not an exaggeration. "Thank you," they say around the bite, looking up into Arden's face.

Arden nods and leans down, planting a kiss on Lex's forehead. "Go sleep," he says. "I'll see you in a little while."

Lex bounces off, their shoulders dancing as they disappear down the steps.

The rest of the morning, Wren and Grace help Arden in the kitchen while Clare, Jez, and Ophelia run errands in town. Wren peels potatoes and Grace boils vegetable scraps for broth. Arden had bought a few chickens in town the day before and butchered them that morning before breakfast. He plucks them, sitting on a wooden three-legged stool while Wren dumps the potato peels into Grace's broth pot. Another pot full of water boils next to her and when Arden starts on another chicken carcass, he stands from the stool and dunks the body into the water, swirling it around for a minute. As he works, he explains the process to Grace, who watches aptly as she stirs.

"The boiling water helps loosen the feathers, so they release from the skin and meat easier," he says. Once he pulls the bird from the pot, he tests the temperature with his fingers before offering it to Grace. She pulls a few feathers from the wing.

"Do you think it's ready?" Arden asks her.

She nods and returns to her stock pot. "I think so," she says, her curls bouncing as she nods.

Arden sits on his wooden stool, an empty bucket in front of him and he begins pulling feathers, dropping them into the bucket when he's got a handful.

Wren had seen animals being butchered at the estate, but she always found an excuse to leave when it started. She'd feign a headache, or an assignment from one of her tutors. When she was little, before she knew what it entailed, she offered to help butcher the chickens. The cook warned her that she wouldn't like it, but she insisted. So, she stood, holding the bucket where the body would be cast after the head was cut off, and when the axe met the stump, successfully severing the head, she screamed. She dropped the bucket and ran to her papa's office, where he was meeting with some foreign dignitary.

He was a bit cross with her, but after she calmed enough to explain what had happened, the duke explained what was happening, and why it needed to. She was upset and, though it took a while for her to eat meat again, she understood why it was necessary. Though, until she was well into her teens, she always said a small prayer to Lathos, god of harvest, and Adreus. Jakob always made fun of her, but she ignored him and bowed her head.

Lex and Ezra wake early in the afternoon. Lex feigns starvation and sits in the kitchen on the wooden counter, plucking raw vegetables from Wren's cutting board.

"Would you stop that?" She swats at their hand, but they manage to grab a carrot chunk and pop it in their mouth, grinning.

Dinner is light that evening. Roasted chicken and noodles cooked in the vegetable broth Grace made.

When the crew has eaten their fill and the dishes have been piled to take down to the kitchen, Eli and Kiara stand, and the captain clears her throat to get their attention.

"We feel confident in the information we've gathered," she nods at Wren and Ophelia, Ezra and Lex, "and with the information from our sources in town. We intend for the rescue to happen in two nights, at sundown."

She tells the crew that the next few days will be for gathering supplies and making preparations. "Keep in mind your assigned position and only buy things *you* will need." As Eli talks, Kiara walks around the deck and gives each member a few bills from a stack she pulls from the pocket in her skirt. Once Kiara rejoins the captain, Eli says, "Kiara and I will be available until midnight for any questions or concerns you may have. Until then, get some rest." She gives them all a wide grin. "We'll meet back here on deck in two days at three o'clock."

The next day, Wren trails behind Arden in the market square as he picks up tin after tin of gunpowder. Wren has seen the long-barreled shotgun and small pistol he kept locked up in the kitchen but has never seen him take them out.

When he's decided which tin is the best, he passes the shopkeeper a few bills and tucks the tin into his pocket, thanking them and turning to Wren. "Ready to go to the apothecary?"

Wren smiles and nods and takes the lead, walking the rest of the way into town.

The main street is noisy, and they have to dodge shoulders and flipped hair to make it to the apothecary shop. The windows tower above her, and she squints against the reflection of the sun, a smile breaking out over her face. Wooden boxes sit underneath the windows, full of herbs and medicinal flowers. Wren runs her fingers over the lavender as she pushes the door open.

A small bell rings as they walk over the threshold. The bustle of the street disappears as the door closes behind them and the smell of dirt and herbs and flowers envelopes them. A man with dark skin and a piercing through the bridge of his nose stands from a stool and sets down the book he's reading pages first on the counter.

"Welcome in." He smiles, revealing another piercing between his upper lip and teeth. "Is there something I can help you find?"

Wren returns his smile, bouncing on the balls of her feet. "Thank you," she says. "I'm looking for some jonquil."

The man's eyes widen, but his smile doesn't falter. "Ah," he says. "How much are you looking for?"

"Enough to make oil and sap."

The shopkeeper's eyebrows raise. "Is it for medicinal purposes?"

The corner of Wren's mouth twitches and she shrugs a shoulder. "Not strictly."

He nods and disappears behind a curtain hung behind the counter. He returns a moment later, holding a plain wooden box. He sets it carefully on the counter and nods for Wren to step closer. "I don't have any jonquil, but I do have this. Similar properties and side effects, but different name."

The lid lifts easily off the box and makes a light *thunk* as the shopkeeper sets it on the counter. The flowers inside aren't exactly what she wanted, but the cuttings here will work just fine for what Wren needs. They're freshly cut, some fully bloomed, and some buds just barely opened.

"They're perfect," she says.

The shopkeeper bags the plant cuttings carefully for her, wrapped in thick cloth and then paper before being placed in a paper bag. Wren pays for the cuttings and two glass dropper bottles with all the money Eli and Kiara gave her, plus a few bills from her own wallet. It would have been infinitely cheaper if she'd gone foraging herself—and she would have preferred that to buying—but it's too late in the year for the flowers to have been growing wild. These must have been cultivated specifically for the shop.

Wren carefully tucks the bundle into her leather bag and thanks the shopkeeper before bidding him goodbye.

He waves after them as they step back onto the street.

Ophelia bounces up to them, Ezra and Lex on her heels. "Got what you need?" she asks.

Wren nods and pats her satchel. "All set," she says. "You?"

Ophelia looks at Ezra and Lex, grinning. "Yep!"

"Onward?" Wren offers her elbow to her friend and together they walk arm in arm in front of the others, making their way back to *The Altean*.

Ophelia lounges next to Wren on the deck as Wren spreads out the things she'd gotten in town, plus a jar of olive oil from Arden, a pair of scissors, and a marble mortar and pestle she'd found tucked away on a dusty shelf in the storage room.

Carefully, she takes out the paper bag from her satchel and unrolls the packaging.

"Daffodils?" Ophelia asks, sitting up. "What are those for?"

Wren starts cutting the blooms from the stalks, dropping the flower in the mortar. "I'm making oil," Wren says, cutting off another yellow flower. She sets aside the stem and leaves. "And extracting the sap. Daffodil sap is good for inducing gastrointestinal issues."

"Huh," Ophelia replies. "And, um, what are you going to use it for to get the selkie back?"

Wren smiles, dropping the last stem onto the paper she'd unwrapped them from. "If there are stationary guards in the basement, this can be dropped into their food or drink, and they'll have to leave to find a toilet." She picks up the mortar and starts gently pressing the petals and buds.

Ophelia picks up a stem and twirls it between her fingers. "How are you going to get close enough to give it to them?"

Wren smiles and looks up at her. "That's your job."

Ophelia smiles back. "Oh!" She lets out a laugh. "I like this side of you."

Wren winks and then drops the bruised buds and petals into the jar of oil. She screws on the lid and shakes the jar, watching the petals and flower buds swirl around inside.

"In twenty-four hours," she says, "we'll have a poison worth giving a shit over."

Ophelia groans, but then they lock eyes and fall into each other, laughing.

NINETEEN

THE NEXT DAY AT sunset, after reviewing the blueprints and the plan, the crew leaves in pairs and makes their way to the thicket of trees outside the Van Zellar estate. Wren walks with Lex, her fingers wrapped around the glass dropper bottle of daffodil sap in her pocket.

The oil would have been more potent if left to steep longer, but it was adequate. The sap, though, was perfect. Wren wasn't willing to test it, and she wasn't going to ask any of her friends to, but it was sticky between her fingers and thick in the bottle. It was a challenge extracting the sap from the stem and leaves and only filled the bottle a quarter of the way. She'd hoped for more, even though this was enough sap to put a man larger than Arden down for a few hours.

When they reach the trees, Lex first picks their way into the shadows and then Wren, carefully stepping over the fallen branches. They wait a few more minutes for Ezra and Arden, and then Eli clears her throat.

"Remember that this is a rescue mission, but our number one priority is safety. If it comes to saving Aedi, or one of us, the choice will be us." She looks at each of them, carefully holding their gaze for a moment before moving on. "Our first patrol will be passing in a few minutes. Ophelia, are you ready?"

Ophelia looks at Wren, who passes her the bottle of sap. Then she turns back to Eli and nods. "Yes, Captain."

"Good. As soon as the patrol passes the gate, start picking the lock. You know what to do once you're through."

Ophelia nods and then looks at Wren and then to Ezra, winks, and disappears. If Wren didn't know it was Ophelia's steps moving the grasses, she'd have no reason to believe it wasn't the wind.

A few minutes later, a sound like an owl hooting echoes in the night.

Two more guards pass them before Eli sends Ezra, Lex, and Arden out of the trees.

A moment later, another owl hoot.

Eli looks at Wren. "Ready?"

The hinges of the gate are quiet as Eli and Wren open and walk through it. Inside, water puddles along the walls, and dim amber lights reflect off the damp floor. Wren and Eli don't talk, just walk steadily down the tunnel.

Wren startles at every sound, every whistle from the crew ahead, every scuffle of her boots along the floor. Her heart is beating so fast she's afraid it's going to give them away.

After a while, Wren realizes they're walking at a downgrade. It's not steep, but it's enough for her calves to burn.

Half an hour later, Eli and Wren meet up with Ezra, Lex, and Arden. They wait for a few minutes in the dark, the only sound between them the dripping of water and their steadying breaths. Wren startles when Ophelia appears beside her and Ophelia chuckles before turning to Eli.

"I found the selkie," she says, her voice louder than Wren thinks it should be. "She's being held in a cell downstairs. There's no guard outside the cell, but there are revolving patrols every twenty minutes." She takes a deep breath. "There's one more thing. It's not just Aedi in the cell. There's also a siren in a tank."

"That complicates things," Eli says. "But our mission is the same. We rescue Aedi and reunite her with her sisters."

Eli sends Ophelia back down the stairs and tells her to signal when the next patrol passes.

It comes two minutes later, a soft hooting that causes a stir through the crew members waiting in the darkness.

They go down quietly, one after another, led by Eli and Arden bringing up the back.

The stairs lead to an open chamber, the same amber lights hung at intervals reflecting off the water on the floor. There are three cells, one left, one forward, and one right. The left and right cells are empty, but standing in the middle of the forward cell is a short girl with a round face and a dark blanket draped over her shoulders. No, not a blanket—her seal skin, just like her sisters'. Next to her is a glass tank, the lid secured with bolted leather straps.

Eli approaches the cell, motioning for the rest of the crew to sink back into the shadows. When she arrives at the door, the girl steps up and puts her hand on the bar. Wren strains to hear what they're saying, but all she can make out is the low rumble of conversation.

They talk for a few minutes, and then Ezra's head snaps up. "I hear footsteps."

Lex and Wren try to get the captain's attention without making any noise, but she doesn't turn toward them. The steps get closer, echoing off the stone walls.

Wren's breathing quickens as Ophelia grips her hand and squeezes before she disappears from Wren's side.

She reappears next to Eli, who turns to Ophelia and gives a curt nod. Ophelia puts her hand on the captain's arm, and they disappear just as the guard walks through the right doorway.

The selkie has to compose herself and shrink back into the cell as the guard passes. He pauses and looks into the cell before hitting his baton on the bars, which causes her to flinch and something inside the tank to shift. He laughs as he withdraws through the left doorway.

Eli and Ophelia reappear and Eli motions for the rest of the crew to join her and Ophelia.

Arden immediately kneels and gets started on picking the lock to the cell. Eli makes quick introductions. The selkie is, as they know, Aedi, and the siren was picked up and brought here just a few days prior. The cell is bare, with a tipped bucket in the corner and an old tray that might have once brought food. Wren looks around for a cot or someplace where Aedi might have slept, but then she notices how dirty her arms and face are, and she realizes it must have been the floor.

"We will get you out," Eli assures the selkie. "We'll get you back to your sisters. You have my word."

"Thank you," Aedi responds, her voice rough, like waves on a stone beach.

Arden stands then, and nods at Eli.

Eli returns the nod and then turns to Aedi. "The door is un-locked, but we're going to wait until the next guard passes to give us as much time as possible to get out. We'll be right up the stairs, waiting."

Aedi nods, her lips pressed into a thin line, then looks at the tank next to her. This close, Wren can see something moving inside. A hand-like shape presses against the glass.

Eli leads the crew back up the stairs, leaving Ophelia at the bottom to let them know when the next patrol has passed.

"Captain?" Arden says, his voice quiet in the dark.

"Hmm?"

"What about the siren?"

It's quiet for a moment. Then Eli says, "We leave her. Our mis-sion is to get Aedi out and back to her sisters. The siren isn't part of that."

"But we have time to get both of them out," Ezra says. "We shouldn't leave it."

"Ezra—" Eli starts.

"I agree with him," Lex interjects. "We've got time. We can carry it. We have to take it, too."

Wren steps away from the group, their discussion fading as she steps closer to the stairwell. She creeps down and looks ahead, where Aedi and the siren are. Aedi appears young, though Wren knows she's older than she might think. She thinks of Lin, ap-pearing the same age as Grace, but being older than most of *The Altean*'s crew. Still, Aedi looks vulnerable, scared, as she swivels her head from side to side, wringing her hands together as she waits for the next guard to pass.

Ophelia comes and sits next to Wren. "What are they on about?" she asks, jerking her head toward the rest of the crew.

"If we should take the siren or leave it here."

"What are they saying?"

"Eli says to leave it, Ezra and Lex say to bring it." It's dim in the stairwell, but Wren can just make out Ophelia sitting next to her.

"I think we should take it, too. It might not be part of *this* mission, but it's part of our mission all the same." Ophelia stands and moves back down the stairs, already invisible again.

It would be hard, Wren thinks, to save the siren, too. It would take longer as they would have to carry the tank, rather than just walk swiftly back up the tunnel. But Ezra and Lex are right, they'd have enough time, if they hurry. And Ophelia is right, too. Adreus never specified what lives should be saved, just all that ask. And while the siren might not ask in as many words, Wren knows no one would want to be left down here, in the damp and dark, not knowing when or if they'd ever get out.

Wren's chest warms with the knowledge that her friends really are as good as she thinks. She stands and goes back to the crew, who are still quietly arguing the fate of the siren.

Just as she's about to say something, Ophelia hoots. Eli leaves them and goes down the steps hurriedly. Aedi is already there when the others arrive, standing outside her cell with Ophelia. Eli starts to close the door when Ezra puts his hand out and stops it.

"We have to take the siren."

"We have to hurry," Ophelia says, bouncing on the balls of her feet.

Wren looks in the tank, where the siren lays. It's not a very large tank; probably only big enough for Ophelia and Grace to lie down side by side, and neither of them have a tail.

She looks at Eli, who finally lets out a sigh. "Adreus tasked us with saving as many as we could. We'll take the siren with us."

Ezra visibly relaxes and he and Arden enter the cell.

"It'll be too heavy with the water," Eli says. "We have to drain some."

Ophelia takes two knives from the strap across her chest and hands one to Lex. The two of them slash the leather holding the lid on the tank and then step back to make room for Ezra and Arden. They look hesitant to lift the lid.

"Let me," Aedi says. She walks to the tank and puts her hand on the glass. The siren shifts inside and lashes her tail against it. Aedi doesn't flinch. She talks in a scratchy language, unlike the one Wren heard the selkie harem speaking. After a moment, she stands, steps back, and nods. "You can let out the water. She'll be okay for a little while."

Ezra and Arden look at each other before lifting the lid and tipping the tank. Water sloshes out over all of their boots and Aedi's bare feet. The siren's skeletal hands grip the edge of the tank, holding herself inside. When they're finished, they replace the lid and pick up the tank with the litter poles it sits on. Wren can see the strain on their faces as they settle into their new positions.

"Let's go," Eli says. If she regrets her decision, she doesn't show it, though her mouth pinches at the corners.

They go up the stairs and don't hesitate as they make their way back up the tunnel. Ophelia stays behind, giving Wren's face a short caress. "Take care of him," she says.

Wren nods and follows the rest of the crew.

Their hurried steps bounce off the walls. Wren and Lex take over the task of carrying the siren half way up, though they're not strong enough to keep up as long as Arden and Ezra. They have to switch back after only a few hundred yards.

Finally, they make it to the gate. Clare is just inside. Her eyes go wide at the siren's tank, but she doesn't stop to ask about it. She tells them a guard has just passed by with no indication they suspect the selkie or siren are missing. Clare pushes the gate open and takes over the litter from Ezra. Once the siren is through, Eli takes over from Arden.

Footsteps ring down the tunnel and Wren's heart jackrabbits against her ribs. She and Ezra wait as the footsteps get closer. The amber light doesn't reach this close to the road and Wren can't tell who it is. She flexes her fingers against her trousers, ready to heat her hands to burn the eyes out of the guard as they appear, but just as she lifts her hands and shines light at them, Ophelia pops out of the darkness.

"Whoa!" she says. "It's only me. But the guards are coming to check the gate. We need to go."

Ophelia and Wren run through the gate and pause, waiting for Ezra. He plunges his hand into his trouser pocket and whispers, "Go. I'll catch up."

The girls don't wait. But instead of running down the road after the rest of their crew, Ophelia pulls Wren into the copse of trees. Kiara has already left back to the ship.

They watch the spot where Ezra must be standing, the night silent except for the gentle chirp of crickets.

Then the night breaks apart. An explosion in the mouth of the tunnel lights up the night and Wren flinches away from the blast. She sees Ezra's silhouette, his hands in front of him, thrown up in front of his face. He's knocked down, and Wren doesn't see him move as the fire in the tunnel dies. If she wasn't already kneeling, she would fall to her knees.

It takes a minute, but she realizes that Ophelia hasn't moved. Hasn't made a sound. Wren puts her hand on Ophelia's shoulder. "O..." she starts.

Ophelia looks at her, grinning, then confusion takes over instead. "What?"

Wren shakes her head. "Ezra. He—"

Ezra pops up in front of them, his hair windblown and smelling like smoke. He smiles when he looks at them. "Ready to go?"

The others are already on board when Wren gets back to the ship with Ophelia and Ezra. As soon as they run up the gangplank, Arden and Lex pull it in, and they push off from the dock. Ezra and Ophelia start on bringing up buckets of water and refilling the tank the siren is in. Clare helps Jez and Grace pass out small flutes of champagne in celebration of a successful rescue.

Wren wants to ask Ezra about the explosion. She didn't know that was part of the plan. And if it wasn't part of the plan, why did he do it? What did he use? She doesn't remember him carrying a pack into the tunnel. Did he plant something when he was on watch with Lex? Did Eli know about it? Wren looks for the captain, but she's not on deck. Wren remembers seeing her when she, Ezra, and Ophelia got back. She barked orders until the ship pulled away from the docks, then... Wren can't remember. She was busy healing the ripped calluses on Lex's palms, rubbing peppermint oil into Clare's forearms. She turns to find Ezra, but he's disappeared now, too.

Aedi sits on the stairs to the quarterdeck, Kiara sitting next to her. The selkie holds a cup of tea in her hands and Kiara uses a washrag to wipe the dirt from Aedi's face. The siren's tank sits against the wall by the captain's quarters. It's easier now to see the coils of the creature's tail behind the glass. Her skeletal fingers ghost against her confines.

Wren joins Kiara and Aedi and asks if Aedi has any wounds she'd like healed. Aedi puts down the teacup and shows her wrists, scabbed and flaked with dried blood.

As Wren cleans the dried blood with the washcloth she takes from Kiara, Eli walks up. She's taken her green coat off and wrapped her locs into a bun on the top of her head. "How are you doing?" she asks Aedi.

Aedi gives a small smile and Wren notices her teeth. Sharp incisors, while the others are almost trident-shaped, the same as Lin's. "I'm okay," she answers. "Glad to be out of that cage."

Eli nods. "We'll get you back to your sisters. I've already sent word to them to expect us."

"Thank you," Aedi says. She looks toward the tank where the siren is curled in on itself. "What about her?"

Eli raises her eyebrows and follows Aedi's gaze. "It would be dangerous to release her this close to land," she says, running a hand over the back of her neck. "I'm not sure where the best place to take her would be."

Aedi takes one of her hands from Wren's, her wrist free of blood and scabs. She tests the movement and nods at Wren in thanks. Turning back to Eli, she says, "I know a spot that would be safe to release her. I can take you there."

Eli nods and smiles down at the selkie. "That would be very appreciated, Aedi, thank you. And please, let me know if there's anything else you need."

Aedi thanks the captain and then Eli leaves, calling to Arden and Ezra, who has reappeared on deck.

Wren finishes healing Aedi's other wrist and then looks at her. "Anything else?"

Aedi runs a finger over her wrist, shaking her head. "No," she says, as if her mind is somewhere else. "Thank you."

Kiara stands then, touching her fingertips to Aedi's shoulder and Wren takes her places on the steps. "There's a bruise on your temple," she says.

Aedi lifts her hand and touches her head gently. "It's all right, it doesn't hurt." She turns to face Wren. "Will you sit with me for a while?"

Wren nods. "As long as you'd like."

They watch as Arden and Ezra move the siren's tank down the stairs. They struggle more this time, now that the tank is full and their arms have been given time to relax. She wonders where the tank will sit until the creature can be let free. The storage room? The kitchen? The crew's quarters?

"What do you know about them?" Aedi says as they disappear below decks.

Wren shakes her head. "Not much," she admits. The duke told her stories of sirens, of course. Stories that painted them as monsters, murderous and unrelenting. It was the opposite of the stories of selkies and mermaids. Creatures that would help humans, rather than luring them to their deaths. "I didn't even truly believe they existed until now. Or that selkies did, either," she adds, turning to Aedi.

Aedi gives her a sideways smile. "There are many more creatures in the sea that you'll never know about, then there are creatures on land and sky that you do."

TWENTY

Wren goes to bed when the sun comes up, after Kiara and invites Aedi to sleep in the captain's quarters. Most everyone else is still asleep, but Grace is up, reading the fairytale book Wren gave her by lantern light.

"How do you like it?" Wren asks, kneeling by her cot. She pulls the blanket up on Grace's legs.

Grace gives her a wide grin. "I really like it," she says. "There are some that are similar to ones I heard in Breton, but I like these better."

Wren smooths the hair down over Grace's forehead and touches her finger to the end of Grace's nose. She stands. "Good night, Grace."

"Good morning, Wren."

That evening, Wren sits with Ezra and Ophelia, their dinner spread before them on a blanket.

Wren woke up to Arden and Lex in the storage room, gathering old barrel rings and rods. Arden carried everything to where the siren lies curled in her tank; Lex carried coils of rope over their shoulders. They made a makeshift cage around the siren's tank, hoping the iron could negate some of her influence on the crew. Aedi watched them, her arms crossed over her chest, saying that the iron wouldn't negate her pull, but might help some.

The siren beats her tail against the glass, making the crew's dinner feel less celebratory and more like they're being held hostage.

Wren tries not to think of the cage around the tank as a prison, even though she knows the creature would rather be swimming in the open ocean than stuck inside a too-small tank. She can empathize with that, at least.

Despite the thumping below their feet, the crew tries to relax, tries to treat this as any other dinner. Lex and Arden lean against the railing, sharing a bowl of stew. Arden has the apron from Lex tied around his waist and he keeps running his thumb over the trees stitched in the fabric. Kiara and Eli share a small loaf of bread, ripping off chunks and dipping it into their own bowls, occasionally giving a piece to Penelope, who sits at their feet, her tail wrapped neatly around her paws. Clare sits at the railing, watching the horizon and ripping off pieces of dried meat with her teeth. Jez and Grace are at her feet, tossing a pair of dice made of marble they bought in Therma. Occasionally, one of them will punch the air and take a handful of green candy discs from a leather satchel.

Aedi isn't with them. After the cage had been set up, she'd disappeared. Wren sets her bowl aside and starts to stand to find Aedi, to ask about the siren and wherever it is she's guiding them to release her, but Kiara joins them. Eli stands on the quarterdeck, smoothing out something on the railing and studying it.

Ophelia taps her foot to a tune only she can hear. She stops when Kiara sits between Ezra and Wren, tucking her legs under her skirt.

"So," she starts, "what do you think of our new crewmates?"

Ophelia shrugs and dunks her bread in her stew. "It's a surprise that we have two now. But I'm glad we didn't leave the siren behind. It would have felt wrong."

"I do wish it had been something different we'd found or had to retrieve. Like a chest of gold, maybe," Ezra says.

"Or a barrel of apples?" Wren adds, and Ophelia shoots her a knowing look, smirking.

"Is anyone worried about having a siren on board?" Kiara asks. Her voice is light, but Wren has the suspicion she's been sent around by Eli to see what the crew *really* thinks.

"I can't say I'm excited about having her on board, but it won't be long, so," Ophelia says around a mouthful of food, shrugging again.

"What do you think, Wren?"

Wren turns a bread roll over in her hands, the siren punctuating the silence between them with slow, melodic thumps. "Papa used to tell me that sirens could reveal what you really wanted. That's how they lure their victims."

"Are you worried?"

Wren thinks for a moment, then shakes her head. "Aedi said she could keep us safe." And she's not worried, not really. She trusts Eli wouldn't have allowed the siren on board if she thought it was dangerous for her crew, and she trusts that Aedi can keep her promise to keep everyone safe.

"What would a siren reveal to me?" Ezra taps his finger against his chin. "What would be what I *really* wanted?"

"Mine is that you would stop snoring," Ophelia says.

"I don't snore!"

"You do," Ophelia and Wren say in unison. Kiara snorts.

"Okay, well, maybe I do *a little*." Ezra holds his thumb and index finger close together.

Kiara stands and touches her fingers to Wren's shoulder briefly. "I can't promise that the siren won't try to tempt you, but I can promise that she won't be able to hurt you." She smiles at them and then turns and walks toward Clare, Jez, and Grace.

Ophelia nudges Wren with the toe of her boot. "What would she show you, do you think?"

Aris's words come rushing into her mind. She's caught off guard and tries to hide it by taking a bite of the roll. *You want power.* She tries to push the words from her mind, but they stay. Aris's voice is sure, echoing in her ears. *You want a place.* She hasn't thought of them in days. *You want your dear papa's seat as the Duchess of Sulesia.*

She forces the bite of bread down her throat, pasting a smile on her face. "For real, or are we still picking on Ezra?"

"We're always picking on Ezra. But for real."

Wren takes a deep breath through her nose. She's thought about it before. When her papa first told her about the creatures, she wondered. If she was younger, before she was adopted, it would be a bigger house, a little brother or sister. Then, it would be for Jakob to come back, then for the duke to leave her be as she was. Now, though, she's not sure what it would be, just what it wouldn't be. "I don't know," she confesses.

Ophelia nods. "Mine would be for Evey's indenture to be paid off, so we could find a piece of land somewhere in central Maia and live on a farm." She laughs when Wren raises an eyebrow. "We'd have pigs and goats and a duck pond. Evey would sell eggs and goat's milk in the village. Ezra and I could get married and adopt a horde of children and raise them as champion swine riders."

"I thought we were being serious," Ezra says, cocking his head.

"I am being serious."

"Oh, well, in that case." Ezra takes a breath, his lips pursed. "Mine would be that I could get rid of these." He places a flat palm against his chest, right where the binding is under his shirt. "Then I could choose a piece of farmland and raise a horde of champion swine riders with Ophelia."

Wren looks away. Moments like this, where Ezra and Ophelia gaze at each other like no one else in the world exists, are hard. There's a pang in her chest, almost like jealousy, but not really. They've been like this plenty of times, off on their own, as if each of them had an idea of exactly what they wanted, and they were looking at it right in front of them. And, like all those other times, Wren wonders what that's like.

There's never been any desire for her to have someone like that. She'd rather learn to sword fight, or read a book in a day, or walk along the beach and collect different colored shells. The only time she felt like that might be part of her story was with Jakob, when they were eighteen. He had been her first kiss only a few days before he was shipped off. But then he left and died, and they'd never gotten the chance to see if what they'd thought might be there was there at all.

Watching Ezra and Ophelia out of the corner of her eye, she realizes all she really wanted was someone she could call her own. Not in the same way as the two of them, but to always have someone that was *there*. Someone she could have silly dreams with and whisper secret jokes with late at night. There were few opportunities for that in Sudal.

She leans back on her hands and lets herself imagine it happening on *The Altean*. Maybe she'd be invited to join Ezra and Ophelia and Evey on their farm in Maia, or maybe she'd become a godmother to Lex and Arden's seven cats, or maybe Eli and Kiara would allow her to stay on board and welcome new crew members. Here, she could be someone's Ophelia, lying in the hammock with them, Penelope curled up in their laps, telling them about her childhood to help them feel at home on *The Altean*. Let them know they're not alone.

After all, that night, when Ophelia told her about the man she'd killed and her running with her sister, is when Wren started knowing Sudal was never meant to be her forever home. After Jakob died, Sudal was too big, too stifling. Maybe a city isn't what Wren was made for. Maybe she was made to sail the sea and make friends in port towns. Maybe she was made to pet Penelope on the quarterdeck while the ship sailed toward the setting sun. Maybe she was meant to be relentless and powerful like the sea.

From a tiny voice in the back of her head, she hears, *Maybe you were meant to rule.*

PART III

TWENTY-ONE

THE DAYS SEEM TO drag on the further from Erama they sail. The water around the hull feels thicker, like cutting cold butter with a dull knife. The crew gets up every morning, exhausted from a night of little sleep. Despite the iron around the siren's tank, her power over them is strong.

Arden's steps are heavy on the deck as he makes his way to the bow carrying mugs of tea. Jez, Lex, and Ophelia are below, trying to catch up on sleep. Grace and Clare are with the captain and first mate in their quarters. Aedi sits on the quarterdeck, starying out at the ocean waves, her seal-skin clutched tightly around her shoulders. Ezra and Wren sit at the front of the ship, their backs against the railing.

"It's cold," Arden says. "I didn't trust myself with the stove." He runs his hand across his face and through his uncombed beard. His stutter is stronger, and he has to start his sentence over a few times before he makes it through.

Aedi warned them that even the most minuscule things could turn into temptations. Wren has had to force herself away from the railings a few times, her white-knuckled fingers gripping so tightly to it so she wouldn't jump overboard. The siren could easily make something terrible—like drowning or burning your hand on a hot stove top—seem appealing.

She watches Arden as he takes careful sips from his beat-up cup, as if the tea is hot and he might burn his tongue. He's strong, physically and otherwise, but even the strongest of the crew isn't immune to the siren's calls.

Wren doesn't mind the cold tea he's poured into her cup, but Ezra shivers when he tips his cup to his lips.

Wren rubs her eyes, feeling the sting of exhaustion behind them. Aris has visited since they'd pulled out of Erama, but his visits were still short and wordless. She tried talking with him, but he only looked at her, an eyebrow raised just slightly, or his lips quirked at the corners. Even though he doesn't speak, his words echo in her head.

You want power.

He's wrong.

You want a place.

She has a place.

You want your dear papa's seat as the Duchess of Sulesia.

No. Aris is wrong, Wren thinks. She doesn't want the seat, she doesn't want the responsibility.

Even when she was at the estate, she never thought of herself as the heir to the duchy. The duke had no other children, no close family, so it would make sense that it would fall to her when the time came, but she was never trained, hadn't been brought up to believe the title would be hers.

What would she even do as a duchess? She couldn't make laws or change the way things were run. She would be expected to raise a child. She would have to make sure Sulesia was in good economic order but would have no say in how to fix it if it wasn't.

She would have influence with the Kornesian king though. And he's old, with his oldest son only a few years Wren's senior. She thinks she could sway them to change things, if necessary.

What, though, would she change?

The first thought comes crashing with surety at her question.

Outlaw arranged marriage. No more selling children—or any-one—to rich men.

She takes another sip of her cold tea. It's bitter. No sugar or honey could dissolve in the water. Arden's hands are wrapped around his cup as he watches the horizon, like the cup is a lifeline he's holding onto. It's cloudy, and the sun is in a losing fight to get through. She turns to Ezra to see him breath in the steam off the top of his cup before he drains it in one gulp.

You want power.

Maybe he's right.

You want a place.

A place next to the king.

You want your dear papa's seat as the Duchess of Sulesia.

Maybe she does.

She tips the cup to her lips and drains her cold tea.

TWENTY-TWO

Even with Aedi on board, the crew can feel themselves succumbing to the pull of the siren. They complain to Eli, begging her to let the siren go. She refuses, but the dark circles under her eyes and the downwards pull at the corner of her lips show that she's not immune either.

Aedi talks to the siren in that husky language that comes from her throat. When she's finished, Aedi shakes her head at Eli. "I tried to reason with her. I'm not sure what good it will do."

Wren finds herself daydreaming about the seat she could have next to the king. She tries to force the thoughts away, to think of anything else. She busies herself by tidying—the crew's quarters had become messy since the siren was brought on board, everyone using their time to catch up on sleep or stare out over the water, lost in their thoughts.

She works quietly to not wake the others, putting the clothes that are scattered across the floor and heaped in piles into canvas bags to be taken into town for washing. She takes any dishes into the kitchen and piles them in the sink, throwing old food into the trash bins as she passes. There are piles of maps stacked up near the bed Lex and Arden share, forgotten since Eli loaned them out. Wren gathers them up and turns to leave.

Grace, asleep in her cot and curled into herself, clutches a faded purple bunny with one ear. Wren tucks the blankets around her and pushes the hair from her forehead. "It will be over soon," Wren promises.

On the journey from Nestad to Erama, Ophelia and Wren sat at Grace's cot, playing with her and her many stuffies. Ophelia was great at it, giving each animal their own voice and mannerisms. Wren was unsure, not having played like this except on her own and was instead braiding a plush doll's yarn hair.

Somehow, by either Ophelia's interference or the purple bunny's, a pillow fight broke out. Wren was happily unknotting a ribbon around a yellow octopus's neck when a velvet pillow hit her square in the chest.

She looked up to see Ophelia and Grace and the bunny staring blankly at her, each pointing a finger—or paw in the bunny's case—at the other.

Wren sat the octopus aside and picked up the pillow, smoothing the fabric with her hands and saying, "You know, if you wanted a pillow fight, all you had to do was say so." She sat up on her knees and threw the pillow back at Ophelia.

"Hey!" Ophelia shouted and Grace fell backward, clutching her middle and laughing, a clear, bright sound that echoed off the boards. "It wasn't me!" Ophelia insisted.

"I'm sure," Wren said slyly, sending a wink at Grace, which caused more peals of laughter.

"All right, *princess*," Ophelia said, righting herself and picking up another cushion from Grace's cot.

"Actually," Wren said, reaching behind her and taking a pillow from Clare's cot, "my title would be *lady*, not princess." She raised the pillow above her head and brought it down on Ophelia.

Ophelia rolled sideways, effectively dodging the blow before jumping up, letting out a cry, and diving for Wren.

It continued, for what felt like hours, Wren against Ophelia, Ophelia against Grace, Grace and the bunny against Wren.

Finally, exhausted and their chests heaving, they sat together on Grace's now bare cot, their backs against the wall. Grace leaned against Wren, sat between her and Ophelia, her purple bunny clutched in her arms, and fell asleep.

Ophelia ran her fingers gently through Grace's curls and gave a sad smile. "This poor girl has been through so much," she said quietly.

"What happened?" Wren asked, rubbing an elephant's ear between her finger and thumb.

Ophelia took a deep breath before starting. "She grew up in Mythshade, in Breton. Her family was pretty religious and went to church like, every night or something." She let out a huffed laugh and checked to make sure Grace was really asleep before continuing, "Grace was sick one day and was staying with the neighbors during a service and a fire started at the church. The doors had been locked and the hinges fused so no one could get out once they discovered the fire." Ophelia's light eyes met Wren's over the top of Grace's head. "Have you ever been to Breton?"

Wren shook her head.

"The churches there only have windows at the top of the walls, which are something like twenty feet high. I'm not sure why. Maybe that's how they've always been built. But it meant that no one could get out. Every single person that was in the church died."

Ophelia stared straight ahead, her eyes unfocused. "Grace was only nine when she lost her family."

Wren reached across the girl and took Ophelia's hand in hers. "She found a new one."

Ophelia shook her head. "It's not the same. She still wakes with nightmares sometimes."

It was quiet for a minute. Then Wren asked a question she thought she already knew the answer to. "Did they ever find out who started the fire?"

Ophelia didn't hesitate. "Aris."

Wren pulls the blanket over Grace's shoulders and smooths her limp curls again before taking the maps back to Eli's quarters.

She places them into a drawer in the desk and straightens, her eyes catching on a lemon cake on top, next to a forgotten cup of tea. Her fingers itch with the urge to snatch it up and shove it in the pocket of her trousers, and her mouth waters at how she imagines the cake to taste. Sweet, a tiny bit tart, silky smooth cream.

As soon as the drawer slides into place, she turns and forces herself from the room, closing the door behind her and leaning against it. She knows the iron around the siren's cage keeps her power muted. What would they be like if the iron wasn't there?

On deck, Ezra lounges on his back in the sun, his arms crossed behind his head. He'd had a rough night; Wren lay awake, listening to Ophelia begging him to stop his search for her knives.

"I just want them gone," he sobbed.

"I know, Ez," Ophelia soothed. "Soon, I promise. But we have to be safe."

He cried himself to sleep, his sobs muffled in the pillows or Ophelia's chest. Ophelia sat up all night, pushing the hair from his face, rubbing circles on his back.

There are dark circles under his eyes now, his eyebrows knit together as his foot taps nonsensically on the deck.

Wren joins Kiara on the quarterdeck, deciding her tidying of the crew's quarters is done for now. Kiara leans on the railing, watching the water as it ripples away from the ship. "I'm not sure how long the crew can stand her being on board," Kiara says. "I've talked to Eli. She won't let her go here, not where anyone can pass by and get hurt. She says we have to go where Aedi is guiding us."

Wren stands next to her, her cloak pulled tight around her shoulders, despite the sun beating down. "Where is she guiding us?"

Kiara shakes her head, pressing her lips tightly together. "I don't know. She only gives us directions." She looks at Wren. "We've had worse jobs, you know."

"Worse than this?" Their crewmates are barely sleeping, eating cold food and drinking cold tea. Knives are hidden and sweets are locked away. This isn't even a job, just a side quest on the way to reunite Aedi with her sisters—the job they were hired for.

Kiara lets out a huff that Wren suspects is supposed to be a laugh. "Yeah, three hundred years of doing this and this is hardly the worst."

Wren knows she shouldn't ask, but curiosity gets the better of her. "What was the worst job?"

Kiara shrugs. Her hair has started to come loose from its normally near-perfect braid. Wisps of it float around her face in the breeze. "I think it depends on who you ask. Eli would say the time we transported six families from Akros to Sudford just to learn a few days later they'd been killed, anyway. Lex would say it was the time we helped an elderly woman transport her only child's body home so he could be properly buried. Clare might say it was the time we were asked to bring a stock of gunpowder to a village to help protect them from pirates, only to arrive after the invasion. She ran inside a burning building to save a child."

Wren remembers Clare's sons, killed in a fire. "Her scar," she says, her voice barely above a whisper.

"Yes," Kiara says. "Clare lost her family in a house fire. She couldn't bear the thought of another mother losing her baby."

Wren bites the inside of her cheek before asking, "Did she save them? The child?"

Kiara smiles. "Yes. They both came out with major burns, but the child is all right. They still keep in touch."

"What about you?" Wren asks. "What do you think was the worst job you've done?"

Kiara is quiet. Wren doesn't think she's going to answer, but then she says, "When we picked up Aris and promised to leave him to die."

TWENTY-THREE

FOR THE FIRST NIGHT since Aedi and the siren came aboard, the ship is quiet. Wren lies awake, staring at the ceiling, while her crewmates sleep around her.

Just after midnight, after tossing and turning for the last few hours, Wren swings her legs over the side of her hammock and makes her way up to the deck. The Star Child sits in their chair on the quarterdeck, their hands in fists on the top of their thighs.

The boards under her bare feet seem to hum in welcome as she settles against the mainmast, her head tilted up to the stars. As she traces the constellations, her mind keeps wandering to Aris, which is not unlike every other night, but instead of thinking of him now, she thinks of him how he might have been.

She imagines a little boy running through the halls of the Breton castle where he grew up, clutching a threadbare stuffed toy in his fist. The sun shines off his dark hair as he runs past thick glass windows. His bare feet slap the stone floors and the noise echoes off the walls.

He hides in alcoves and ducks under hall tables. He plunges his free hand into his pocket and pulls out a yellow candy disc. It sits on his tongue for a second before he closes his mouth and moves the disc to his cheek.

It's hard to picture this small child growing up to burn a church full of people. Or destroy port towns, homes, businesses, families. She sees herself in him, small and running alone through a home that's too big.

But Aris *had* grown up to do those things. What was the reason? Could there be a good enough reason? And what was the reason for his banishment? Surely it couldn't just be the church.

There had been no rumors from Breton about what he'd done to warrant a death sentence. Not that she would have been privy to any information if any had come, anyway. She was still piecing herself back together after Jakob's death and was most focused on getting to the next day.

Wren's hands bunch into fists. Her papa always attended any executions he sentenced as *judge* was just as much a part of his title as *duke*, and Wren had only known him to issue a hanging or firing squad a few times in the eighteen years she lived at the estate. Once, she asked him why he attended them.

"If I pass the sentence that a person should die, the very least I can do is be there to witness their death. So, I go and I force myself to watch." He tapped the end of Wren's nose. "Death should not be taken lightly, Wrennley. And telling someone they should die should be taken less so."

Aris's parents were too cowardly to even watch their sentence be carried out. What had they hoped would happen by hiring *The Altean* crew to do it for them? And why had they thought the Isles of the Damned were a better option than an execution in Breton?

A noise on the deck next to her pulls Wren from her thoughts. Penelope sits there, the moon reflected off her eyes. She mews at Wren and flicks the crooked end of her tail.

"Hi, Penelope," Wren says, lifting her hand and scratching the top of the cat's head. Penelope leans into her touch and starts purring. "You wanna go to bed? There's plenty of room in my hammock."

Penelope waits as Wren stands and then lopes down the steps in front of her, looking back to make sure Wren is following.

Wren gets back into her hammock and pats her thigh, inviting Penelope up. When they're settled, Wren lies back against her pillow, hoping that when she's finally able to sleep, Aris will visit and they can talk.

He does visit that night, but when she asks him about what he did to warrant a death sentence, sitting on a bench in the gardens beneath her window in Sudal, he's quiet. When she looks over to where he sits, he's gone.

TWENTY-FOUR

A WEEK AFTER LEAVING Erama, *The Altean* docks in an eastern Nestadian port town called Stanes. Eli and Kiara had been exchanging letters via messenger hawk with their contact in Erama and, as far as they could tell, and despite the explosion at the gate, the Van Zellar estate was oddly quiet and there was no reason to believe *The Altean* was involved in anything. Even so, they tell the crew to keep eyes and ears open for mentions of Aedi and the siren.

"This is where Kiara and I met," Eli announces, her arm draped across Kiara's shoulders. Kiara smiles up at the captain, her hand tangled with Eli's on her shoulder. "If you'd like to see a part of our history, you can eat at a little pub called Falcon's. We carved our initials at a table there for our two hundredth birthdays."

They set off for Falcon's in a rush, happy to get away from the heaviness on board. Jez and Grace peel away from the others to sort through bins of dice and stacks of illustrated cards in a little game shop.

At the nearly empty pub, they go around and look on each tabletop for a carving. Ophelia finds it and whistles, calling them over. On top of a table tucked into the corner near the bar is a little worn carving, EC + KT. It's old and almost lost in the smoothing that comes from a hundred and fifty years of hands and plates, but the dirt that's stuck in the grooves could read as nothing else. They gather enough seats for them all, pulling chairs from other empty tables, their knees and elbows crowding together. Ezra and Ophelia, Arden and Lex, Wren and Clare, all gathered around a small table that's really only meant for two. Ezra orders a round of ales, and they toast to their captain and first mate. "To soulbinds," Ezra says.

"To soulbinds," the rest of them echo. Their clinks send drops of ale onto the table.

They order fried balls of cheese, fried pickles, and fried corn flower squares with a bowl of melted cheese to dip them in.

"Is everything fried?" Wren asks, dipping a cheese ball into the red tomato sauce they come with.

"Of course, it's a pub," Ophelia says, dipping a finger into the melted cheese and licking it off.

On their third round of ales, Wren realizes she doesn't know the reason that all of them joined *The Altean*'s crew. She mentions this to the others who immediately quiet.

Clare sets down her glass and volunteers to go first. She's been with Eli the longest, besides Jez. After her family died in the fire and she lost everything else in her life, she wandered the ports hoping to find work in the pleasure houses or on the barges that floated just off the shore. Kiara found her and invited her to dinner. Clare assumed Kiara was the captain's errand runner that was sent to retrieve a pleasure girl and accepted the invite. When she boarded, she was surprised—and grateful—to find Eli instead of a haggard old sea captain. Eli asked about her story, and she was welcome to join the crew.

Arden and Lex were next, a few months after Clare. Arden had been hired by a family friend to deliver a trunk of clothes to their daughter in Alder, Jinsimbia. He met Lex there, and they became friends, then more after a few nights together. They decided to stay in Alder for a little while until they made enough money to travel. Lex found work in a bookshop and Arden started as the head cook at a restaurant. It was there that he heard a rumor about an immortal pirate captain. They traveled to the nearest port town and then played cool when they met Eli and Kiara, but it didn't take long for Lex to spill the real reason why they'd requested an audience with her.

"Eli *laughed*," Lex says. "She didn't lie, though. She told us it was true, though she insisted they were *not* pirates. And then she asked if we wanted to join her."

"Lex asked if they would be immortal if we joined, but unfortunately, that's not how it works," Arden adds.

Lex dips their finger into the cheese. "You win some, you lose some."

Ezra tells how he was looking for work and a flyer was pinned to the message board in the marketplace in Kosnas advertising for a deckhand on a cargo ship. He ripped the flyer down and made his way to the port.

"It wasn't a cargo ship, obviously. I thought it was a joke, but I went and met Eli. She said she never put up a flyer, hadn't been to Kosnas in years, but the ship must have thought they needed me because otherwise where would the flier have come from? I was dumbfounded, of course—"

"Of course, Ophelia butts in.

Ezra pulls his eyebrows together and scoffs at her. "*Anyway*," he says. "Why would a ship *think*? And why would it think it needed *me*? But I joined because who was I to say no to a magic ship?"

Everyone around the table laughs while Ezra takes a drink of ale and waggles his eyebrows at Wren.

She does know Ophelia's story, but so does everyone else, and Ophelia tells it anyway. Ezra props his elbows on the table and watches her as she tells it. Ezra and Wren squeeze her hands as she recounts her sister entering into an indentured contract. "I just hope Evey's doing okay," she finishes.

Arden reaches over and hands her a handkerchief embroidered with a lopsided honeybee. Ophelia takes it and wipes her eyes. "Thanks," she says, letting out a watery laugh.

Then everyone looks at Wren.

"Don't you know the story?" she asks.

"Well, yeah, but." Clare shrugs and stacks the now-empty dishes into a pile in the middle of the table, pushing them off-center to not cover up the carving of their captain and first mate's initials. "We want to hear you tell it."

Wren starts, a little shaky at first. She tells them how her papa—the duke, she corrects herself—arranged a marriage for her and how she had no choice in whether to go through with it or not. "I could do it on my own, or he'd force my hand," she says. The duke said nothing of children, or a family at all. She wasn't sure exactly what he expected of her, and she certainly didn't want that for herself. He was afraid she'd become too free, she heard him say to Jakob's father. She was too wild in her own life. He was worried she'd never settle.

"So, I ran. The morning of the wedding, they left me in the dressing room at the church to have a moment alone before my life changed. There was a window, and I climbed out." She traces her fingernail in a gouge on the table. "I ran as fast as I could and hid in the first place I saw. Which was *The Altean*. I was there for three days before Lex found me and Eli said she could take me somewhere. Somewhere to start a new life, if I wanted, in Maia or Breton or Jinsimbia." She smiles at everyone around the table, her eyes landing on Ophelia. "But she also said I could stay. And here I am."

The smiles that return to her warm her more than any fire in her grate in Sudal ever did. She's grateful now, for those cold days in the belly of the ship, with no food or water. She's almost grateful for the duke forcing his hand and arranging a marriage for her. If he hadn't, where would she be? Back in Sudal, in the estate built for the duke's family generations before she was born. She wasn't even his real daughter. She belonged to the riff in the clay neighborhoods.

She entered the duke's household knowing basic mathematics and how to read and write well enough. She wasn't in school in her neighborhood because it was too expensive. Instead, her mother or her friends' parents taught her and other kids whatever they thought necessary.

When she was adopted, the duke hired tutors for her. They pushed her and she absorbed whatever she could. The duke asked her if she wanted to join a private academy where she could learn with other kids. He explained that she would go every day, she'd have to wear a uniform, and after school she may have extra work that needed done before the next day.

"I don't think I want that, Papa," she said with a laugh. She started calling him papa a year after he adopted her. It felt weird at first—for both of them—but it didn't take long before it was second nature.

"Why not, little bird?" He smoothed her hair back from her forehead. He was usually too busy to tuck her into bed, but that night he made sure he was the one to settle the blankets under her chin and turn out her light.

She thought about what her family was called that night Elliot found her. *The riff.* She'd heard it before, from the duke's men patrolling the streets where she played. It didn't bother her then, when everyone around her was riff, but now, here in the duke's household, she was the only one. Even the servants had come from generations of servants before them, born and raised under the duke's roof.

"I won't fit in," she said, small in her big bed, the pillows and blankets fluffy like clouds around her.

He laughed, and it stung. "Everywhere you go, you will find places you don't fit in. If you were made to fit in, you wouldn't be your own person." He leaned down and pressed a kiss to her forehead. "But if you don't want to go to school, that's up to you." He stood, said goodnight, turned down her lamp, and left, pulling her door closed behind him.

From that day forward, he let her make most of her own decisions. At ten, when she wanted to learn sword fighting instead of cursive, he commissioned a steel blade with a hilt encrusted with purple jewels. At sixteen, after her sword training was over and her apprenticeship with Mim had come to a natural end, she decided to replace swords with paintbrushes, and the duke bought her an easel made from white wood. The first time he stood his ground was when she was twenty-four and she was being forced into a marriage she didn't want.

With the crew of *The Altean,* she found that she did fit in. Her fingers and palm fit perfectly in Ophelia's. Her sense of humor fits perfectly with Lex and Ezra. Her taste for rich and sweet foods alike fits perfectly with Arden and Grace. Her love of quiet and savoring the sun fits perfectly with Jez and Clare and Penelope. Eli and Kiara had welcomed her from the very beginning. All of them accepted her with no questions. It was so easy to incorporate herself into the crew, it seemed like fate she'd made it here.

She lifts her glass, and the others click theirs against hers, spilling more ale onto the top of the table.

TWENTY-FIVE

That night, after they've stumbled back to the ship, their arms draped around each other's shoulders, Eli and Kiara tell them that Aedi had the idea of finding a sheet with iron stitched in to drape over the siren's tank. They had a hard time finding one, but after going on a chase all day, Eli and Kiara had returned with a heavy piece of sail with iron threaded through.

The merchant at the shop told them the sail belonged to an old ship that transported sirens a few hundred years ago, when it was legal to sell them as pets or hunt them for delicacies. When they'd asked what Eli and Kiara needed the sail for, Eli told them it was for a collection they were helping build.

"He gave us a very odd look but didn't refuse us," she says.

The next few days sailing are near-easy compared to the last week. The siren is not happy in her newly iron-covered tank, but the crew is less haggard every morning. Ophelia doesn't have to hide her knives, Arden doesn't have to hide the paper sacks of sugar from Lex, and he can cook with the stove again. Wren sleeps well enough. Aris doesn't visit her, and that helps her get more restful sleep, but she wakes in the mornings wondering if he's okay. She worries her question scared him off.

The next time they dock, it's at a port town in Sulesia. Aedi says the best spot for releasing the siren is on the north side of Nestad, in a channel shared with Jinsimbia called the passage of death. Normally, if that was the destination, they'd stick to the coast of Nestad, but Eli wants to stay more in open water and Sulesia is closer than Nestad when their stores get low.

Wren decides to stay on the boat, though they're far enough from Sudal that she's unlikely to be immediately recognized.

"You go have fun," she tells Ophelia and Ezra. "You'll have a better time in a Sulesian market than with me on board."

"Can we bring you anything?" Ezra asks. He steps into a pair of trousers and rolls the cuffs to his knees.

Wren shrugs from where she lies in her hammock, one leg dangling over the side. "If you see a cart with round blue candies, bring me a whole boatload, please." The duke always made sure to have a stock of the candies. Wren would eat the honey and vanilla candies until they turned her tongue the same color as the bluebirds outside her window. She's never gone so long without them and it's one of the things she misses most about Sudal.

"Sure." Ezra winks at her and Ophelia gives her a quick hug before the two of them bounce up the stairs, their hands tangled between them.

She swings in her hammock for a little while until the hunger pains in her stomach convince her to get up. She finds a few leftover pastries in a box on the table in the galley and picks one out, biting into it and taking the stairs up to the deck.

"Oh, Wren, I didn't know you stayed behind." Kiara sits on the bench, a pair of pants draped over her lap. "All okay?"

Wren nods, joining her on the bench. "Worried about being recognized, I guess."

Kiara smiles and touches her fingertips to Wren's arm briefly. "Glad to have your company."

Wren digs through the pile of clothes that need mending and finds a shirt with a hole in the bodice. She threads a needle and starts a crosshatch stitch to fill the hole. Penelope hops up on the bench beside her and swats at the string, trying to bite the end and catch it whenever Wren pulls the needle through.

"Stop it," Wren scolds. "You are going to stab yourself and then get mad at me." Penelope responds with a petulant meow. "Yeah, yeah. Here." Wren picks up a near empty spool of green thread and tosses it across the deck.

"That girl has a hundred toys stashed all over the ship, and she's more interested in an empty spool of thread than any of them." Kiara watches the cat bat and jump on her new plaything.

Wren's fingers hurt by the time she's finished with the small hole. "I don't know how you do this all day, Kiara."

Kiara waggles her fingers. "Three hundred and fifty years of calluses will do wonders. And three hundred and fifty years of taking care of everyone on board doesn't hurt either." She winks.

Wren asks if Kiara knows of any other tasks she can do around the ship and Kiara gives her a few ideas. Which is how she ends up sweeping the galley, oiling the ship's wheel, and reorganizing the trunk of clothes the crew all shares. She brings up a small pile of them that need mending and smiles shyly at Kiara as she sets them on the bench.

"My work here is never done," Kiara says with a sigh. But she smiles up at Wren and so she knows Kiara doesn't really.

Shortly after, Eli and Kiara leave the ship to find lunch. They invite Wren, but she shoos them away. Then she finds herself alone.

The siren, Aedi, and the Star Child are on board, of course, but Wren knows the siren and Aedi aren't much for company and how much of a conversationalist the Star Child isn't. So, she finds Penelope and brings her down to her hammock and they nap.

Her dreams take her to a port city in Breton, one that she visited just weeks after joining *The Altean*'s crew. She peruses the stalls for a while, running her fingers over bolts of fabrics and leather goods. People move in blurs around her, their words muffled and jumbled in her ears.

She turns a corner and the other patrons disappear, leaving her standing between a booth with pots of dye and another with little metal trinkets. Aris stands at the end of the aisle, his hands clasped behind his back.

"Aris," she says, almost too enthusiastically.

He nods at her. "Wren." His voice is even, neutral, but there's a small quirk up at the corner of his mouth. His steps are even on their way to her.

"Where did you go?" She matches his gait as he walks by her, back the way she'd come. She can't remember the exact name of this town and wonders how far it is from Mythshade.

"I was thinking," he says. They walk without purpose, wandering between stalls shoulder to shoulder. "About what you asked me."

Wren's steps falter for a second. "You had to think about it?" She thought the answer to his banishment would be easy, even if not easily given.

"I had to decide on whether or not to tell you. No one but I and my *family*"—he spits out the word—"know what happened. I wasn't sure I was ready for *you* to know." He puts emphasis on *you* and softens his voice.

Wren picks up a string of lopsided pearls from a table they pass and rubs them between her fingers. "Is it bad?" she asks.

Aris's shoulders rise from the breath he takes. "I think it depends on whose side you were on."

She waits, a knot of anxiety and anticipation forming in her stomach.

"Do you know that I have a younger sister?" He turns to face her. The circles under his eyes stand out against his pale skin. When she shakes her head, Aris continues, "Her name is Josephine. We call her Josie. I was six when she was born. She became the favorite, very quickly." He laughs, but the sound is sad.

As they walk, he talks.

Josie was loved throughout their kingdom. All of Breton celebrated her birth and as she grew, it became obvious she was favored for the throne after Queen Lily abdicated or died. Aris realized he was not the choice and, because the crown went to the oldest living heir, Aris would either have to give up his title as prince willingly or be dead.

He became afraid. His parents, seemingly oblivious to the rumors of Josie inheriting the kingdom, didn't listen to him when he went to them with concerns. He started finding people in the kingdom and in his house who were on his side. People that wouldn't allow a spare to take the crown. He doubled, tripled his guards. But it didn't matter.

Council members and well-known families in Mythshade still sent people after him. Assassins and mercenaries, sometimes citizens themselves, would attack Aris in the streets or climb into his bedroom, hoping to get rid of the rightful heir so their favorite royal child could take over.

Aris had no choice but to fight back. He found out the names of his sister's biggest supporters and confronted them. Some submitted and vowed to support whoever was on the throne. Others refused, saying Josie was the better choice. He killed those people before they got the chance to do the same to him.

"The queen and king found out and had me arrested. I was held in a cell for days without any explanation as to why. When I was finally allowed out, my mother only asked me why.

"I told her it was because I had no choice. They would do nothing to quell the conspiracies and attempts to end my life. So, I did it myself. They didn't believe me. They sentenced me to die."

Aris sounds defeated. And why shouldn't he be? In the end, it was his parents that caused him to lose his title. Not the people, not an untimely meeting with death, not his own choice. The two people that were supposed to keep him safe were the ones that decided his life wasn't worth protecting. His early death would rid them of the responsibility and ensure their favored child would take the throne when the time came.

There's one part of the story he's left out. And though she doesn't know if she wants to hear the answer, she asks anyway. "What about the fire at the church?"

Aris stops walking. His light eyes search her face, his lips pinched at the corners. "How do you know about that?" His voice has gone hoarse, like he isn't used to talking this much.

"The little girl on *The Altean*. Grace. Her family died in the fire."

Aris nods, averting his eyes to the darkening horizon. "I didn't know there was anyone in there," he says quietly. He shakes his head. "I burned it because it's the place Josie was baptized. I wanted it to be a symbol of sorts, I guess. Burning her beginning so that she doesn't get to the end."

Wren looks at him, wide eyed, her heart stuttering in her chest. "You wanted her dead?" He never alluded to that in his story, didn't force her name out like it pained him the way he did with his parents and her supporters.

"No," Aris admits. "I hated her, yes. But she's still my sister. She didn't choose what happened to me. I didn't want her to have the throne, but I never wanted her dead."

Wren nods and they continue walking, their arms brushing.

"I thought I'd be hanged," he continues. "But the queen and king were too cowardly to watch my life end. Instead, they hired a crew to take me to the Isles of the Damned and leave me there." He snorts. "And look how that ended up."

TWENTY-SIX

WREN WAKES, HER TONGUE like sandpaper, her thoughts murky. She's never felt so out of sorts after a visit. The water she gulps from her flask does little to quench her thirst.

The sun is heavy when she makes it back to the deck, just behind Penelope. Kiara and Eli lean against the railing, looking out over the little port town. Wren joins them, her flask filled from the barrel of water below.

Eli smiles and nods to the flask. "Having a good day, Wren?"

"Definitely, Captain." Her voice is hoarse. She clears her throat. "It's just water."

Eli laughs and plunges her hand into the pocket of her green coat, pulling out a white mesh bag. "Here," she says, holding out the bag to Wren.

Inside are a handful of blue candies. "Oh, my gods, you found them!" Wren digs into the bag and pops one of the candies into her mouth. She leans against the railing, letting out a small moan as it melts on her tongue. She's immediately twelve years old again, sitting in her papa's meeting room, flipping through the heavy book of maps he kept on the table.

"Ezra and Ophelia have more for you, but they gave me a small bag to give you before they got back. We weren't expecting you to be asleep," Eli says, pulling Wren from her thoughts. She reaches across Kiara and plucks two candies from Wren's bag, dropping one into her mouth. She offers the other to Kiara.

Kiara takes it gratefully. "These are very good," she says. "Lex would probably go nuts for them." Penelope hops up on the rail and Kiara pets her, scratching under her chin.

"I'm going to have to hide them," Wren says.

Another memory comes as she puts another candy in her mouth. She was younger, maybe nine, and it was one of the rare nights she was able to spend with the duke. She crawled into his bed, and they shared a bowl of the candies as he told her stories of mermaids and pirates and a privateer with flying ships.

"Those aren't real!" she said.

"Oh, privateers are very real. And this one is a *legend*," he said, touching his finger to the end of her nose.

"No, Papa, the ships! The *flying ships* aren't real!"

"I don't know." He shrugged. "If they're always above the clouds, how would you know they're not real?"

She didn't have a good answer. And she didn't know how ships or flying things worked. So, she snuggled into his blankets next to him and listened to stories of the legendary privateer and his flying ships.

Eli, Kiara, and Wren stand on the quarterdeck for a while as the sun continues to sink. Penelope takes turns with each of them, letting them pet her or scratch behind her ear. Now she sits in front of Wren, and they laugh as the cat meows and Wren just looks at her, her arms crossed on the railing. Penelope lifts one black and white paw and touches it to Wren's chin, giving another pert meow, which makes Wren surrender and run her hand down the cat's back.

Eventually, Penelope tires of their antics and hops down to lie in a patch of sun on the deck. The three women share the bag of candies and when it's emptied, Wren shoves it into the pocket of her trousers.

The others make their way back just after sunset. Ophelia and Ezra make a big show of giving Wren a canvas sack of the blue candies.

"The confectioner claimed he was the creator of them," Ophelia says.

"They also claimed that the duke used to order massive batches of them for his daughter," Ezra adds, stealing a sweet and popping it into his mouth.

"The duke's daughter has good taste." Wren closes the sack and ties a loopy bow with the drawstring.

Arden and Grace bring back a few boxes of roasted fish and fried rice and the whole crew sits in a circle on the deck and passes them around. Wren had placed the majority of the candies in her satchel hanging by her hammock, carefully sliding the leather roll of glass bottles next to it, but she'd refilled the little mesh bag, and they pass that around, too.

By the time the food is cleaned up and the others are getting ready for bed, Wren's eyelids are getting heavy. She lies in her hammock, her cloak tucked around her legs, and is asleep before Ezra puts out the lantern.

TWENTY-SEVEN

ARIS VISITS HER AGAIN that night. And the next night. And the
night after that.

He starts asking about her life, before *The Altean*. She's shared
some, her adoption and running away, but now, after hearing his
own story, she doesn't hold much back.

He listens aptly as she tells him about her parents and the clay
neighborhood. About her tutoring at the estate and how she loved
to read stories about dragons and knights and princesses trapped
in towers. About her sword fighting lessons and how she learned
to heal and use plants as medicine. They sit in the garden under her
window as she tells him about the birds she would feed looking out
over them. She tells him how much she loved to paint, especially
the view of the garden and ocean from her bedroom. She doesn't
specifically tell him about Jakob, but he's there, woven throughout
her childhood and adolescence, brush strokes broad and bold even
now that he's gone.

"I've been to your room," he says. They're sitting on a bench overlooking a bay where a pod of dolphins flip and jump out of the water. Behind them are rolling green hills, dotted with snapdragon flowers. Wren had plucked one when they sat down, running her fingers over the delicate bell-shaped blooms. They're the same flowers embroidered on the hem of her cloak. The same flowers that she would pick with Mim and place in a clay vase with a narrow neck.

Wren laughs. Their thighs press together, the coolness of his skin seeping through the fabric of his trousers. "You have."

"It's rather intimate, don't you think? Sharing your bedroom with someone else?" He picks up a curl of her hair and rubs it between his fingers.

Before he left, Jakob was in her room many times. They played there as children, studied together. He read to her while she painted. The window seat was where they had their first—and only—kiss.

"Yes," she agrees. "It's too bad I won't get to see yours."

"You've seen my quarters."

"That's not what I mean."

Aris drops the strand of her hair and straightens his spine. His light eyes train on the bright line of the horizon. "Would you like to see my bedroom?"

Wren stills but for the breeze through her hair. "What are you asking?"

He lets out a breath that sounds vaguely like a laugh. He turns to her. "A duchess should get to know her allies, should she not?"

Slowly, Wren replies, "She should."

"Then it's settled." He turns back to the water. "Once you become duchess, I'll send for you to visit me in Breton."

"Once I become duchess," Wren echoes, her voice quiet.

Aris turns again to look at her. "Yes," he says. "If I have any say about it, and I *will*, you will be Duchess of Sulesia."

She forces herself to turn and look at him. His eyes, so light they're nearly as white as the beach sand in Sudal, are soft, but unreadable. He places his hand against the side of her neck, ghosting his fingers along the skin behind her ear. A shiver runs down her spine and it's not only because of how cold his skin is. Her breath hitches as he brings his head closer to her. He waits, and she nods, almost imperceptibly.

Just before his lips touch hers, she wakes up.

TWENTY-EIGHT

EVEN WITH THE OLD sail over the siren's tank, some days are harder than others. Today feels heavier than others and Wren can't be sure it's because of her visit with Aris the night before.

Ezra taps his fingers unrhythmically against the rail, watching the water split in front of them. Ophelia has to cover his hands with hers to get him to stop fidgeting.

Lex has started carrying a short piece of rope in their pocket. Wren watches them pull it out occasionally, make a knot, untie it, and stuff the rope back in their pocket.

Arden keeps his hands busy, too. He takes over the mending from Kiara, helps scrub the deck, checks and double checks the rigging. Eli and Kiara watch him, their hands up to shade the sun from their eyes.

Grace and Jez stay busy with their dice game. They offer to teach the others, but no one can seem to sit still long enough to listen to the rules.

Wren sits against the mainmast, one of her glass bottles in her hand. She uncorks it, smells the lavender inside, and replaces the top. She hasn't stopped thinking about Aris's declaration of *once* she becomes duchess. Not *if*.

Could she really do it? Be duchess of a whole nation? She watched her papa do it, sitting at his feet or standing by his side, but he was raised for the job. Taught from the time he was able to walk what his role would be. His family has been friends with the king's family for hundreds of years. Wren hasn't even been part of it for twenty.

Maybe, though, with Aris's help, she could. She's confident she would be a good ruler. She was only a little girl when she was adopted, but she remembers enough of growing up in the clay neighborhood to be sure she could do right by the people living there. Perhaps she could use that to her advantage. All of her friends and their parents died from the sickness, but there were plenty of other neighborhoods just like hers. If she could convince them she was still one of them, she could get their support, and other's fealty would follow.

Duchess Wrennley Newbury, only daughter of Duke Lionel Newbury and the first of her name.

She has to admit she likes the sound of it.

She leans her head back against the mast and closes her eyes. Down below, the siren beats her tail against her tank.

TWENTY-NINE

T HAT NIGHT, AFTER LYING in her hammock for hours, listening to the siren thumping against the sides of her tank, Wren finally falls asleep.

Aris doesn't visit her.

She dreams of Sudal. The estate she was adopted into. The hallways were wide, with tall ceilings and plenty of hiding spots for her and Jakob to duck into. The kitchen and common rooms were all on the first floor. She would sneak into the kitchen, stealing cookies and apples, giggling when the cook would swat at her hands with a towel. The dining room wasn't used often, and when it was, it was rarely only her and the duke. He would have guests, the King of Kornas and his council, or a judge from the smaller cities of Sulesia. Sometimes, it was her and the duke, and Jakob and his father.

On those nights, the duke would sit next to his daughter, and Jakob and his father would sit across from them. She and Jakob would toss their peas at each other, or flick water from their fingers across the table. Their fathers would laugh, the beer in their cups warming their bellies.

After dinner, she and Jakob would go upstairs to her bedroom, their pockets stuffed with rolls.

She had her own wing on the third floor. West, so she could see the sunset from her window seat. There was a second bedroom across from hers. It was unoccupied, and she and Jakob liked to hide under the bedsheets, swapping stories and the vanilla and honey candies she loved so much.

On days the duke had other business to attend to, away from the estate, she would stay behind, running through the hallways and empty rooms barefoot. The duke didn't have a throne room, of course, but he had a study where he would take his most important meetings.

The room was on the second floor. It was large, with a table for meeting with the king, or other visiting well-to-dos. There were couches, used for after the meetings were over, where the duke and his guests would sit and drink. He kept a small trunk of old toys for when she would play in the office while he was sitting behind his desk.

The desk was solid, carved from a single trunk of a tree taken from Adreus's sacred forest in Kornas. She would run her fingers over the carvings of mermaids and sea serpents, imagining what the creatures were really like. Sometimes, she sat in the chair, her feet dangling over the carpet, and placed her small hands palm down on the top of the desk, where she could swear she felt it hum beneath her fingers.

Along the back wall, behind the desk and surrounding the window overlooking the training grounds, stood bookshelves, heavy with leather and cloth-bound books. She pulled one down once and flopped it onto the desktop, opening it to a random page. The words were in a language she didn't understand, so she left it there, still open, when she hopped down.

When the duke returned that night, he found the book in his office. He smiled, knowing his daughter's hands had been the one to pull the book down and page through it. He closed it, eased it back into its place on the shelf, and took the stairs up to the third floor.

She was already asleep—it was well after midnight—but he opened her door and peeked inside. She looked so small in her bed, curled up in the very center, the blankets pulled up tight to her chin. When he turned, the floorboards under his feet creaked and he watched as she sat up, turning toward him.

"Papa?"

"Yes, little bird. It's me."

"You're home." She was smiling.

"I'm home." He was smiling, too.

"Will you tuck me in again?"

How could he not? He pushed the door open the rest of the way and made his way over to her. He placed his hand on her head, smoothing the hair from her face. Her red curls had relaxed a bit in the two years since she'd joined his home.

"Where were you?" she asked him, her lids and voice heavy with sleep.

He sat on the edge of her bed. "I was meeting with the privateer with flying ships."

She laughed. "No, you weren't."

He laughed, too. "No, I wasn't."

She was quiet for a moment. He thought she'd fallen asleep. But then, he heard her say, "Is being a duke hard?"

"Not so hard," he said. "It is a lot of work, but I'm happy to do it. Do you think you'd want to be duchess some day?"

She hummed. "No, I don't think so. I like running through the halls and playing with Jakob best."

"Then that's what you should do," he said.

He kissed her head and stayed with her until she fell asleep again.

When he got up from the bed, careful not to disturb his daughter in her sleep, he whispered, "Good night, little bird."

As he eased the door back into its jamb, he heard her whisper back, "Good night, Papa."

THIRTY

WREN'S BARE FEET MAKE no noise on the way down the stairs. She pauses at the bottom, listening for anyone else in the room, but the only sound is a soft swish of a tail through water. She steps the rest of the way into the darkness.

The sail over the siren's tank is heavy. Wren lets out a quiet grunt as she shoves it aside. The creature's tank had been placed on top of empty crates to keep her off of the bare floor. Wren is grateful she doesn't have to crouch.

The siren, awake as if waiting for her, watches Wren with quiet eyes, colorless and deep. She opens her mouth as if to speak.

Wren braces herself, hands clenched into fists at her sides. She doesn't know how this works. Does the siren just...show her what she wants? Does she have to ask, have to voice her request? The stories only told of sailors diving into the sea, of men and women being dragged by their ankles or wrists, of sirens devouring bodies whole.

"I'm here for," Wren pauses, "a favor. No, not a favor. I just have a question."

The siren's mouth curls into a smile. She leans her shoulders back, crossing her arms over her thin chest. She tilts her head as if to say, "Go on."

Suddenly, Wren feels silly. What is she doing with this creature? A creature that has no more clue of Wren's life than a stranger in Nestad. Still, she doesn't know what else to do. Her chest aches and her voice hitches when she asks, "What do I want?"

The siren floats in her tank for a minute. Then she rushes the glass in an explosion of bubbles and hits her fist against the only thing keeping her contained. Wren flinches, but she doesn't step away. The corner of the siren's mouth quirks up, impressed. Then she places her palms against the glass and nods at them, indicating for Wren to mirror her position.

The glass is cool under Wren's palms. She takes a shuddering breath and when the siren closes her eyes, does the same, leaning her forehead against the glass.

Immediately, she sees a face. It's pale and has no definition, but so is everything else in this vision. A flash of a smile, a hand around her wrist. There's a laugh, not unlike the ones she's heard on *The Altean*. In her ear, she hears a whisper. "Come with me," it says.

She pulls away from the glass, breathing hard, and stares at the creature floating in the dark water.

The siren tilts her head. "Well?" she seems to say. "How did I do?"

Wren's chest tightens. "Thanks," she says. Then, without thinking, she pulls the sheet back over the siren's tank. Somewhere, she acknowledges the scratching of the siren's nails on the glass, but her brain is too fuzzy with what she saw, what she heard, that she doesn't register it. She turns and walks back up the stairs, back to her bunk. She crawls into the hammock, pulls her cloak up to her chin.

She almost hopes Aris doesn't visit her.

Almost.

THIRTY-ONE

WREN GETS NO VISITS from Aris for the next few days. She doesn't sleep well, though.

They dock at one last port town before releasing the siren. Lex and Arden go into town under the guise of restocking the kitchen, but everyone knows it's an excuse to get away from the ship. Away from the call of the siren.

Wren doesn't feel up to going into town and after she eats a meager breakfast, she lies back in her hammock, her cloak wrapped tightly around her.

Ophelia's laugh filters down the stairs, her footsteps quiet on the steps. She quiets when she sees Grace and Jez asleep on their cots. Her voice is quiet when she invites Wren to town with her and Clare. Wren objects, saying she wants to nap, but Ophelia wraps her fingers around her wrist and says, "Come with me. Please?"

Wren tries to ignore the way her heart stutters.

"Sure," she says, swinging her legs over the side of her hammock.

They invite Ezra but he shoos them away. "Go," he says, smiling. He sits on the dock, his trousers rolled over his calves, his bare feet dangling over the water.

Wren and Ophelia walk up the pier and into town with their hands clasped together. Clare's arm is looped through Wren's on her other side.

There's a shop nestled between two bakeries. The gilded letters on the window are peeling, the paint on the wall faded. Through the windows, there are tables and curio cabinets crowded with things. It looks like it smells musty.

"Let's go in," Wren says, her forehead pressed against the glass.

Ophelia lets out a laugh and pushes the door open. A bell chimes.

The shop does smell musty. It reminds Wren of the way the basement smelled at the estate, crowded with old things that she and Jakob were told not to play with.

She trails her fingertips over the things on the tables, the wood of the curio cabinets. There's one cabinet full of labeled animal skulls and jars of tiny pink skeletons. There are shelves crowded with dusty leather books. Another cabinet has pink and green and blue crystals. There are racks with old lace and silk clothes that have frayed hems and moth-eaten seams. Wren rubs a faded yellow nightgown between her fingers.

"That would look good on you," Ophelia says, leaning up against an overstuffed bookshelf.

Wren pulls the hanger from the rack and holds up the nightgown. "It's too small." She pulls the fabric a bit to see if there's any stretch. There isn't. "I don't think I could get it past my thighs."

Ophelia takes the hanger from her. "It would be like a tent on me." She holds the nightgown against her. The bottom hem drags on the floor.

Clare takes the hanger next. "I think it would fit me," she says. "Too bad yellow clashes with my hair."

They laugh and replace the nightgown to the rack and continue walking through the aisles. There are oil lamps and old purses and a mannequin wearing two plastic tiaras, three masquerade masks, and a leather contraption strapped across its hips that Wren can't make sense of, but Ophelia sees and says, "Ooh, that's nice."

"What is it?" Wren asks, her head tilted slightly to the side.

Ophelia and Clare laugh.

"I'll tell you when you're older," Clare says, her hand on Wren's shoulder.

They continue on. There are booths stuffed with toys. Some are made of wood, and others are made of metal with keys that turn and produce a sound or turn the wheels or move the horse's legs. A few in a locked case are made of blown glass with gold decorations in the shapes of flowers and scalloped bands. A placard claims they're from Sulesia, but Wren has never seen anything like them.

The shop seems to go on forever, with booths full of things neither Wren nor Ophelia nor Clare can make sense of. The last one they stop at has a locked cabinet full of blades. Knives and swords, all laid out on glass shelves, their blades sharpened and polished. Most are plain, used simply for defense, but a few, just as sharp as the others, have ornamental handles. Jewels inlaid in silver or gold, hand painted scenes of ships on the water, of waterfalls, of grass meadows.

Wren continues to look at them while Ophelia goes off to find someone to unlock the cabinet and Clare goes back to the booth of old toys.

When Ophelia returns, an older man with thinning grey hair and an eyepatch over one eye follows her, carrying a ring of jingling keys that must weigh at least half as much as Ophelia.

The man steps back after unlocking the cabinet and allows them to take out one knife each. The one Ophelia has chosen sinks in on itself, hiding the blade inside the hilt, which is made of four brass rings. She slips the rings over her fingers and, with the press of a button with her thumb, the blade shoots out. Her face breaks out in a grin.

Wren's is more ornamental. The hilt and sheath are hand painted with purple and white petunias. The blade is about as long as her hand and is sharp enough to take the hair off her arm.

While Wren stands aside, admiring the blade and its hilt, Ophelia keeps looking at the weapons in the case. "How much are these?" she asks the old man, three other knives in her hands.

The man chuckles, deep and hearty. "Five for a hundred chips, or thirty each."

Ophelia looks at the ones in her hand, the brass ringed one she'd sat on a case next to her, and the one in Wren's hands. "Deal," she says, smiling.

They follow the man to the front of the shop and see Clare there, a stuffed camel on the counter in front of her.

"I get a new one for Grace every town we stop in," Clare tells Wren when she raises her eyebrows at the toy.

"I thought her cot was getting more crowded," Wren jests.

"Can't help myself," Clare says, picking up the camel and shrugging. "They're just so darn cute."

After they pay for their new things, and the blades are safely tucked away on their person, Wren, Ophelia, and Clare stop at a bakery and share a piece of berry cake.

"This is so good," Ophelia says, her pale eyelashes fluttering.

They spend the rest of the day walking in the market, picking out fruit to take back to the ship, and people watching on a bench under the shade of a big tree. Ophelia leans her head on Wren's shoulder, and Wren puts her head on Ophelia's.

"I'm glad you joined us," Ophelia says.

"I am, too," Wren replies. She means it.

THIRTY-TWO

THE NEXT FEW NIGHTS, Wren's dreams are muddy, as if they've been drawn in ink and water splashed over them. Only a few things show up with clarity—sails on a boat, a black coat, a large snake.

When she wakes, it's still dark. She lies in her hammock for a while, listening to the breathing and soft snores coming from her crewmates. Sometime during the night, Penelope had hopped up with her and now she lay curled at Wren's side, her head resting on Wren's stomach. When Wren touches her fur, Penelope lets out a tiny squeak and starts purring. Wren closes her eyes and tries to let the cat's purring and the breathing of those around her lull her back to sleep.

It doesn't work, and one loud snore from Ezra startles Penelope from her dreaming. She lets out an exasperated meow and hops down from Wren's hammock. Her paws are soundless on the floor.

Wren follows Penelope's lead and rises from her bed. She doesn't pull on her boots, but she drapes her cloak around her shoulders, clasping it at her throat, and slowly makes her way to the steps leading to deck.

The Star Child is sitting in a chair on the quarterdeck, their eyes on the horizon. Wren goes the opposite way, heading to the bow of the ship. She leans against the railing, closing her eyes against the breeze off the sea. It's chilly, but her cloak keeps her warm. The only part of her she needs to warm are her feet.

Her thoughts turn to Aris, as they are apt to do in the silence. Especially now, especially since the siren came aboard. Aedi had done her best, but the creature's call is strong. It invades every thought, every waking moment. Even Wren's dreams aren't safe.

She imagines Aris standing next to her, the breeze running through his strangely colored hair.

"I don't want to be duchess," she'd say.

"Are you sure?" he would counter. His voice would be smooth, a hint of a smile on his lips.

"Yes. It's too much. I like it here."

"You liked Sudal, too. The steadiness. The security."

He wouldn't be wrong. She did like those things. But the loneliness, the tedium, the politics. She didn't—and wouldn't—like those.

But, he'd counter, even with him an ocean away, she wouldn't be completely alone. And she'd have Ophelia and Clare, too. She could throw parties and invite Eli and the rest of *The Altean*'s crew, using the ballroom at the estate that rarely gets any use.

As duchess, she could host them, and they could relax in the great halls as long as they liked. They could visit whenever they wanted, and perhaps she could travel with them, too.

She shakes her head against the sea wind, dispersing the image of Aris next to her.

No, she thinks. I like being just Wren.

She hears Aris's voice as if he really is standing right next to her. "I think *Duchess* is better than *just*."

Wren doesn't get any more sleep until that night. She goes to bed early, exhausted from her early morning and working on deck all day with Ezra and Lex. They wanted to keep their hands busy, and Wren decided that might be helpful for her, too.

When she falls asleep, it's more of the same muddy dreams. They have no clarity, no defining lines or shapes. And then, slowly, the dream fades away.

She wakes long enough to pull the cloak back over her legs and readjust the pillow. Around her, the rest of the crew has made it to bed, and the lantern has been put out.

Her next dream is clear. The garden outside her window in Sudal. The sun shines through the leaves of a tree, dappling the grass beneath it. Bees and butterflies float on a breeze that brings the smell of dirt and lavender. Wren is sitting on a blanket, her legs stretched out in front of her. She leans back on her hands and lifts her face toward the sky, closing her eyes.

Something against the back of her hand makes her look to her side. Aris sits there, in a black coat and trousers. His fingers are cool against her wrist.

"Thought I might find you here," he says. He looks up at the estate's walls, the white brick shining in the sun. There are ghosts of ivy running up toward the window of Wren's room. "It's beautiful."

Wren nods. "You've seen it before."

"Yes," he agrees. Sun peeking through the leaves highlights the pale skin across his cheekbones. "This is what your home would look like if you were duchess."

Wren looks at the building. It looks the same to her. The grass may be a bit more overgrown near the bottom, but there are no significant differences.

"It looks the same," she says.

Aris shrugs. "From the outside, sure. But, oh, the inside. It's lively and full of music and dancing. You host parties and dinners. People from all over the country come to dwell in your presence."

Wren's chest hurts looking at him. She realizes how badly she wants what he's saying to be true. She can almost hear the music and laughter, almost feel the pounding of feet on the ballroom floor. Her cheeks ache at all the smiles she'll have.

Aris puts his hand back on hers. "Come with me," he says, quietly, breathlessly.

Her chest heaves and her lips part. She can't speak. She only nods.

The corners of his mouth quirk up. "Go on deck," he says, then he's gone.

She wakes, enveloped in darkness. Her heart rattles against her ribcage as she rises from her hammock. She can hear Ezra and Ophelia snoring on their mattress. She watches them for a few moments, in the moonlight filtering through the windows. Then she turns, grabbing her satchel and cloak, her boots from the floor. She slips on her boots, adjusts the satchel so it sits against her without a lump when she puts on her cloak. She fastens the gold clasp at her throat and walks up the steps leading to the deck.

The Star Child is in the same spot as the night before, watching the horizon. Wren looks toward the bow, then makes her way up to the quarterdeck. She leans against the railing, willing her breathing to slow, her heart to calm. When the Star Child looks at her quizzically, Wren gives them a small smile and says, "If you'd like, I can take over. I can't sleep, anyway."

There's a moment of quiet, the only sound the waves against the hull, the creaking of the rigging above them. "Thank you," the Star Child says. Their voice is deeper than Wren thought it would be. She waits to see if they say anything else, but when they stand and disappear below decks, Wren knows all those stories the duke had told her of Star Children being able to see the future are untrue.

PART IV

THIRTY-THREE

In the distance, a pinprick of light appears on the dark horizon. Wren stands facing it, her hands flat on the railing. As the light gets closer, the pull in her chest tightens. Her fingers itch to sign documents as duchess, her feet long to dance across the ballroom floor with Ophelia and her other invited guests.

She sees Aris's silhouette as the ship gets closer. And when it pulls up beside *The Altean*, he stands at the railing across from her. The pull in Wren's chest makes her almost want to jump the gap onto *The Basilisk*'s deck. But she waits. It takes a few tries, especially since there's no one but her to guide the gangplank down.

She climbs aboard it, using the railing on *The Altean* as a step up. Her cloak catches on something as she hoists herself up, and she tugs it free, then walks swiftly across. Aris reaches out his hand and she takes it, allowing him to guide her onto the deck.

"Welcome aboard," he says, dropping her hand.

The rest of his crew has already started pulling the gangplank back and started to sail away from *The Altean*. Wren watches it until it's swallowed in the darkness.

Wren looks at him, conceding that she won't see *The Altean* or the people on board until she's back in Sudal as duchess. She offers Aris a small smile. "Thank you, Captain."

He smiles back. "No need for that. Come, let's get you changed."

Wren has seen Aris's cabin before, but it looks different to how it was when she'd been here during one of his visits a few months ago. It's dusty still, but the things on the shelves are lined up meticulously. The books are arranged by size and thickness. Along the walls not inhabited by shelves are pieces of framed art leaning against each other. The bits and pieces of them that Wren can see are coastlines and mountains, a depiction of Adreus, a castle cloaked in mist and trees.

There's a shrine set up for Iros and Anrena, but the silks on the table are faded, the edges frayed. The dried flowers scattered on the top look like they might turn to dust if anyone looks at them for too long. The bowl of salt is like ash, the candles melted to shells, matted in dust and the wicks long and curled.

Aris crosses the floor and digs into a trunk tucked behind the desk. He pulls out a folded cloak. "Here," he says, walking back to Wren and holding the bundle out to her.

Wren reaches for it but stops before she takes it from him. "I have a cloak," she says.

Aris smiles. "Yes. One that was given to you by the man that was buying your hand in marriage, correct?"

Wren nods slowly. It had been given to her by the judge's son. When he arrived in Sudal from Nestad, he stepped off the boat and, after greeting the duke, gave Wren a package. He insisted she open it there on the dock. It was their first interaction and though she wasn't eager to seem excited, she gladly took the package and opened it. When she pulled the cloak out, she gave the one she was wearing to her handmaiden and allowed her future husband to drape the new one over her shoulders.

It was the only thing she took with her when she left Sudal, except for the wedding dress Arden had cut into rags. She wasn't even wearing any shoes.

Eli offered her another cloak when she joined *The Altean*'s crew, one with embroidered mermaids along the bottom and a pearl clasp, but Wren turned it down. The one she wore was warm, with snapdragon and gladiolus flowers embroidered along the bottom hem and a golden fastener that clasped at the base of her throat. The lining was sage green silk, which, paired with the purple wool on the outside, showed the joining of the duke's house with the Nestadian judge's. It fit her perfectly and she wondered if the judge's son had gotten her measurements from the duke's tailor before purchase. Her cloak, though it had come from a stranger and wasn't from Sudal, was the only thing she had for a while that belonged only to her.

Aris pushes the cloak into Wren's hand. "Please, take it," he says. "We can keep yours safe."

She nods, unfastens the golden clasp at her throat, and pulls her purple cloak from her shoulders. She folds it and hands it to Aris, who takes it and places it in the trunk, shutting the lid. The one he'd given her, a brown one with no embroidery along the bottom and a brass clasp, hangs heavily on her shoulders. But she smiles at him. "Thank you," she says.

They go back on deck, and Aris introduces her to a few of his crew members. A tall and broad man named Ramsey is Aris's first mate. He's a head taller than Aris, his dark hair cropped short. One of his eyes is clouded, a scar cutting through it. He nods at her, his huge golden hands clutched around the wheel.

Two others sit at the bottom of the steps to the quarterdeck, passing a mostly empty bottle of whiskey between them. They stand when Aris and Wren step onto the deck beside them. Aris looks down his nose at them and introduces Wren.

A light-haired man with green eyes and no teeth whom Aris says is their wind magics user. Wren remembers him standing at the sails as they left *The Altean* behind, his arms lifted above his head.

With him is a woman, wrinkles at the corners of her eyes, her dark hair pulled into a tight bun on the top of her head. Her mouth looks like it would be stuck in a permanent frown.

Each of them nod at Wren, but don't hold her gaze.

The names of the other crew members' names swirl together in her head. They don't seem interested in her, either, barely glancing her way before going back to what they're doing.

Wren and Aris stand on the quarterdeck with Ramsey and the crew stays on the main deck, standing at the bottom of the steps if they ask their captain or the first mate a question. They barely acknowledge Wren, their eyes skipping over her. Aris continues to look down his nose at his crew and waves away questions to Ramsey. He stays by Wren's side until they return to his quarters for dinner.

They eat at the desk, Aris sitting behind it, Wren sitting in a chair in front. When they're finished and the tray has been taken, Aris shrugs off his coat and takes off his boots.

Wren stands, her hands wringing together under the cloak. "Where will I be sleeping?" she asks.

Aris looks up at her, his light eyebrows raised. "In here, with me."

"Not..." she trails off, looking toward the door.

He gives a curt shake of his head. "I won't have you sleeping with the crew. You'll sleep here." He motions to the bed, portioned off behind dark curtains.

She nods. "Thank you," she says.

Wren had brought a nightgown from the shared chest of things on *The Altean* and, after changing, she crawls between the sheets on Aris's bed. He changes too, and crawls in after her. The bed is big enough for there to be space between them and she stays turned away from him.

He blows out the candle by the bed. "Good night, little bird."

She closes her eyes tightly against the darkness. She can hear Aris breathing beside her, can feel the blankets rise with every breath. The only people she'd slept in the same bed with were her parents and the duke. She was much smaller then, and she wishes she could curl up into herself now.

"Good night, Aris."

THIRTY-FOUR

It takes another week of sailing before Aedi says, "This is it."

Ezra and Arden had hauled the siren's tank up to the deck the day before, when Aedi told Eli that they were getting close. Now, they take the lid from the tank and set it on the deck. They lift the tank, and the siren gives Eli one quick glance with wide eyes before backing as far into the tank as she can without breaking the surface of the water.

Lex meets them at the railing and they and Ezra ease one side of the tank over the edge. It takes a few moments for Arden to readjust, but he brings his side to the railing, too, and the three of them start gently pouring the water over the side.

The siren holds on, grasping the edge of the tank with white-knuckled fingers, and lets out a cry as her tail slips free. She dangles there for a long moment, her eyes wild, looking from the ones at the railing to Eli. Then her eyes slide to Aedi, and her mouth forms a snarl. She says something in her raspy, slurring language, her tail falling limp over the side of the ship, and she lets go, dropping into the dark waters below them.

As Ezra, Lex, and Arden lower the tank back onto the deck, Eli turns to the selkie. "What did she say to you?"

Aedi shakes her head, her face gone pale. "I didn't catch it all. Something about my sisters." She waves a hand in the air and clutches her seal-skin cloak tighter around her shoulders. "It doesn't matter. Everyone will be safe with her here." She looks up at Eli.

The captain nods. "Where to next? I'm sure you're ready to be reunited with your sisters again."

Eli sent them a letter when they'd rescued Aedi in Erama and told them about the siren. Rai, the selkie who had spoken to them in the warehouse, wrote back that Aedi would be good for the job. She mentioned that her sisters wanted to swim out to see *The Altean*, to see Aedi, but Rai was worried that Van Zellar would be watching for selkie harems visiting ships in open water. She hoped that Eli would be willing to bring Aedi to them once the siren had been released. Eli wrote back that, yes, they would bring Aedi wherever it is she wanted to go and included the necessary information for the final payment.

Aedi nods, smiling. "Yes," she agrees. "I can't wait to see them again. Would the southern coast of Maia be too far?"

Eli shakes her head. "Of course not. We'll make preparations at once."

The next day, they dock in a small port town to restock their food and water stores. They have a small celebration on deck for the successful release of the siren, but no one is feeling much like celebrating.

During the week, Eli tried distracting herself with every paper in and on her desk, every leather-bound book in the hold. She even allowed herself to open the barrel of aged whiskey from Kornas she kept in her quarters and drank half of it herself, but nothing took her mind off of Wren.

Had she thrown herself into the sea after speaking with the siren? Had she been kidnapped or killed and dumped into the water? She couldn't have just disappeared. In all of Eli's 350 years, she had never known anyone to just vanish. There was always an explanation.

That day, before Eli came to learn Wren wasn't on board, started out the way they always did. As she dressed, she hummed a tune from a song she'd long since forgotten the words to. She tied her hair back with a strip of leather, not bothering to light the lantern hanging by the door. As she shrugged into her green coat, she noticed a small hole in the seam of the sleeve. She looked at Kiara, still asleep in their nest of pillows and blankets, and laughed quietly, pulling the door from its jamb. Her steps were quiet on the deck when she eased the door back into place.

When she climbed the steps to the quarterdeck, she was surprised to be greeted by Ezra and Ophelia instead of the Star Child. It wasn't their normal routine—Ezra is keen on sleeping in—but it happened occasionally that a crew member would relieve the Star Child and they'd be the one to greet the captain in the morning. The change in routine was no cause for alarm. Eli knew the Star Child would never go to bed without speaking with her had they seen anything.

"Good morning," Eli said to Ezra and Ophelia.

They turned to her, surprised as if their minds were preoccupied and they didn't hear her approach. "Morning," Ophelia said, her voice watery.

Eli stopped on her way up the steps. "Is everything all right?"

Ezra and Ophelia looked at each other. That's when Eli saw the small piece of purple fabric in Ophelia's clutched hand. "We can't find Wren," Ezra said.

The rest of the crew was roused and the ship and surrounding waters were searched. Even if they'd found her in the sea, Wren would have been in the water for hours and most likely dead from hypothermia. Even with her warming abilities, there would have been little hope of her surviving in water that cold. Still, they had to check, even if only for their own relief.

Eli spoke with the Star Child as the others searched. They had seen Wren that morning, an hour or so after midnight. There had been no other ships nearby, no one and nothing else on the water with them at all.

Eli returned from talking with the Star Child, worry in her eyes and her lips pinched together at the corners. Aedi, wringing the water out of her hair, must have donned her seal-skin and dove into the waves to search the ocean floor, shook her head when she made eye contact with the captain. The others gathered around Eli.

"Wren took over watch this morning after midnight. That's the last time she was seen." She looked at Aedi. "Will you speak with the siren and find out if she has any information?"

Aedi hesitated, biting her lower lip. Eli knew the siren would be of little help. Though Aedi could resist them, the selkie was not immune to the siren's power completely. If the siren thought that what Aedi wanted most was for Wren to be dead, or in the hold, or back in Sudal, that's what the siren would say, and Aedi would believe it, with no reason to think it was untrue. Finally, she said, "I will try."

The only information Aedi was able to glean was that yes, Wren had spoken to the siren. Eli stood by, watching the siren smile wickedly, baring her sharp teeth, her arms crossed over her thin chest.

The rest of the crew sat on the steps of the quarterdeck. Clare comforted Grace, rubbing her hand in circles on the girl's back. Ophelia tried not to cry, worrying the piece of Wren's cloak between her fingers. Ezra's jaw was clenched as he stared out at the horizon. The others sat silently, hoping and praying their friend would be found.

Eli met with Kiara and Aedi in her quarters. "Why would she have spoken with the siren?"

Kiara spoke up. "She believed the siren could tell her what she truly wanted. Could tell her what her deepest desires were."

Aedi scoffed. "That's not what sirens do. They show what their victims want most at that moment. If Lex wants a lemon cake more than anything, they could be convinced there's one at the bottom of the sea. No amount of pleading would lead them astray. They'd get that lemon cake no matter how hard anyone tried to stop them."

Rai had warned Eli of this. She had thought Aedi's presence on board would protect her crew from succumbing to the siren's calls. She felt foolish for not warning them, for not taking better precautions, for bringing the siren along at all.

Aedi's voice was quiet, strained, when she said, "I've lost so many friends to them. I hope we can find Wren."

"We'll do everything we can," Eli said. She turned to Kiara. "Can you try to find her?"

"Where?"

"Everywhere. Sudal, Stanes, Antsa. Any place you can think of, Kiara."

She nodded, her face grim. "What if we don't find her?"

Eli sat down heavily in the chair at her desk. "We write to the Duke of Sulesia and tell him his daughter has been lost at sea."

Kiara searched every night since. And this morning, her results are no different. They leave the port town and start sailing to Maia, where Aedi will finally be reunited with her sisters.

There were calls for *The Altean*'s help at the port's message board, but Eli and the crew had agreed that finding Wren should be their first priority.

This isn't the first time someone has left the crew without warning. The difference, though, was that they had left while the ship was docked and then left a note on the board for the crew to find. No one had ever vanished from the ship, in the middle of the ocean, overnight.

Eli tries to keep the ship running as normal. Arden makes breakfast and lunch, and Grace helps him pass out bowls and plates. Ezra and Ophelia take stock of their remaining goods, though they had just days prior. Lex organizes things on deck and keeps the crew's quarters clean. Clare and Jez keep the ship moving steadily toward their destination.

When Aedi is reunited with her family, she promises Eli that she'll keep an eye and ear out for anything and will send word as soon as she can. She says her goodbyes to the crew and dives into the water where they can see Lin and Rai's and the rest of the sisters' faces. There's much celebrating and they all wave as *The Altean* sails away.

Kiara stays in bed most of the day, but one evening, an hour before dusk, she joins Eli on the quarterdeck.

"Any thoughts?" Kiara asks.

Eli trails her fingers along the carvings on the ship's wheel. It had been a gift from one of their past guests. An earth magics user who had asked if she could join them from the north of Maia to the Bay of Kornas near the Sacred Forest of Adreus. When they arrived, the woman had carved the wheel from a slice of wood from one of the trees.

"Jakob," Eli says. "I think he's still in Sudal." Wren had never specified where her friend Jakob was, only that they kept in contact through Jakob's ability to dream walk.

Kiara nods. "If I can't find him?"

Eli takes a deep breath through her nose and lets it out through her mouth. "I don't know." She turns to Kiara.

Kiara's hand is warm against Eli's cheek. "We'll find her, heart."

Eli lifts her hand and presses it against Kiara's. She nods. "I know you will."

THIRTY-FIVE

JAKOB AND WREN WERE introduced shortly after Wren was adopted into the duke's household. She was in one of the sitting rooms, playing with a doll with a porcelain head and stuffed body while her nanny, a round woman with a kind face named Freida, sat in a wooden rocking chair knitting a green sweater.

Jakob was dressed in a smaller version of their country's naval uniform: dark grey trousers and red coat, a tailored white shirt. The buttons on his coat were shined so much Wren thought she could see the reflection of the multicolored woven rug on their surface.

The duke and Jakob's father entered with him and the duke motioned for Wren to stand. She did, still clutching one of the doll's hands in hers as she put her hands behind her back.

Jakob's father, a tall man with light hair and dark eyes like his son, put his big hand on the boy's shoulder. "This is my son, Jakob," he said. Wren had seen the man before; he was the duke's most trusted council member, and his best friend.

The boy bent at his waist. "Hello," he said when he stood straight again.

"Hi. I'm Wren." She stuck her free hand out. She had never shaken anyone's hand before, but she remembered seeing her father do it when he started working for a new captain on the docks.

Jakob put his hand in hers and gave it a firm shake, squeezing her fingers. "It's good to meet you, Wren." He smiled at her.

They became fast friends after that. They weren't the only kids at the estate, but Jakob didn't care that she'd been born in the clay neighborhoods like the others did. They spent their days climbing trees and stealing cakes from the kitchen. Sometimes, they hid in the darkest corners of the hallway until a visiting noble or one of the staff came by and they'd jump out, screeching, hoping to get their victim to drop whatever it was they were holding. It was all fun and whoever they startled laughed off their misfortune until one day when the Kornesian king was visiting. His escorts and guards surrounded him and when Wren and Jakob jumped out, his guards assumed it was an attack and detained the children.

They were brought before the duke and Kornesian king, their hands bound in rope. Wren cried, thinking she'd be sent away. Jakob laughed. Not at her, but because he knew his father would get him out of trouble.

And, after they were given a stern talking to, the rope was removed from their wrists and Wren and Jakob were dismissed. Before the doors could close behind them, Wren heard the duke raise his voice at the king. Her heart swelled then, knowing that her papa would protect her, even if it meant he could be at risk of repercussions.

During the summer, the duke opened the estate's grounds to the other council members' children. She had met a few of them before, but they all lived off-grounds. Jakob's father was the only council member that lived among the duke and his household and once his mother died, Jakob joined him year-round.

The other kids would shun Wren, calling her riff and kicking dirt on her clothes. Jakob would stand in front of her, his trousers taking the worst of the dirt. He told the other kids to leave her alone and hand her his embroidered handkerchief to dry her cheeks.

Despite his standing up for her when the other kids were mean, Jakob wasn't always the kindest to Wren. He tugged on her hair and tripped her in the halls. He stole sweets from her pockets and dropped insects down the backs of her dresses. His father and the duke deferred his punishment to their nannies, and they only ever gave him a slap on the wrist. Eventually, Wren stopped telling them. She pulled her hair into buns, made sure to step on his feet instead of tripping over them, put her sweets in hidden folds in her dresses, or replace them with sweets soaked in vinegar. The insects were harder to combat, but in a moment of what 9-year-old Wren would call genius, she placed a snake from the garden between his bedsheets.

The snake bit him on the ankle that night, causing his leg to swell from knee to toe. It was decided that the snake came in through his open window—a set up Wren had planned—and he was sent to bed with hot water packs and a promise that his nanny would always check the bed before he crawled between the sheets.

When she came to visit him a few days after the incident, she said, "What do you think is worse? A snake in your bed, or bugs down your back?"

Jakob's face dropped at the realization of what she had done. He sputtered after her as she left, one of his bowls of chocolate pudding in her hand. He never put anything down her dresses again.

As they got older, Jakob's teasings were less obvious, but still there. He would poke fun at her feelings and use just a little more force than necessary when they sparred.

When they were alone, Jakob was softer with her, pushing her hair behind her ears or pulling her favorite blue candies from his pocket. They studied together, spread out on her bed or on the rug. He read to her while she painted.

When Jakob enrolled in the navy, Wren would go to all of his drills. She watched him from the sidelines as he took aim and shot at the targets. Even without archery or shooting lessons, he was the best in his class. He hit the target every time, whether it was stationary or moving.

When he won a medal for most targets hit, Wren insisted on celebrating with a special cake from the bakery in town.

"It's just for show, Wren. It doesn't mean anything," Jakob said, his new medal pinned to his training uniform shining in the setting sun.

"I don't care," she said, dragging him through the streets toward the shop. "You're finally better than me at something!"

The sun was high over the water and Wren was sitting on the window seat in her room watching the waves when there was a knock at her door. She granted entrance and there stood Jakob, in his naval uniform. Dark trousers, red with silver buttons, a white shirt well suited to his frame.

"Well, look at you!" Wren closed the book that was in her lap and put her feet on the floor. "You look very handsome."

He stepped further into the room, his lips pinched at the corners. "Thank you," he said.

"Are you all right?" Wren straightened. She was in her dressing gown and, to give her hands something to do, she retied the cinch around her waist. He didn't say anything as he sat down on the seat beside her. She knew then that something was wrong. Jakob was rarely quiet.

"I got my orders."

Oh. "And?"

He offered her a small smile. "I leave on Sunday. I'll be gone for two years."

Her heart sank. "That quickly?"

"The letter came this morning."

Wren rubbed the end of the tie of her robe between her thumb and finger. "Where are they sending you?"

Jakob pulled her hand into his, traced her knuckles with his thumb. "The Reidde Sea."

She looked up at him. "You're going to be on a boat for two years?"

He laughed. "It's the navy, Wren." He shook his head. "We won't stay on the ship for the entire two years, but most of our time will be on board, yes."

She readjusted so she was sitting on her knees facing him. "Will you write to me?"

"I'll visit you."

"Every night?"

Jakob's shoulders relaxed, and he leaned back against the windowsill, Wren's hand still clutched in his. "Maybe not every night."

"Three times a week, then."

"Once a week," he countered.

She shook her head. "Twice a week."

Jakob's dark eyes ran over her face. "Fine. Twice a week."

Wren lifted her other hand and traced the scar through his left eyebrow with her thumb. She had given it to him during their first spar when they were eleven when she hit him accidentally with the butt of her sword. One of the medics offered to heal it, but he said he liked the way it looked and would prefer to leave it the way it was. It healed well, but the hair never grew back in.

When her fingers touched him, the small smile on his face fell and he sat up, pushing himself closer to her. Then his hand went to the side of her face, his fingers tracing the curve of her ear.

They looked at each other for a long moment, her breathing quickening. Gently, he pressed his lips to hers.

Wren had grown up hearing the servant girls talk in hushed voices about meet ups with the boys. She saw the results of their trysts in the swelling of bellies and children running around with bare feet. But even with their stories, Wren couldn't have imagined what it would be like to kiss someone.

Jakob was warm. She knew that. After all the afternoons lying together in the sun, their arms pressed against the other's. After the borrowed jackets in the winter garden when she stubbornly refused to wear one, relying only on her still-strengthening warming abilities. After the laughter and secrets they shared while huddled in dark corners. She knew Jakob was warm.

And though she knew what his lips looked like from every angle and every distance, she could never have known how soft they were and the tenderness behind them.

When he pulled away, he leaned his forehead against hers and said, "You know I love you, right?"

She nodded. "Yes." She did. It wasn't the first time he'd said it, but she never thought it was romantic. She never thought they'd be anything more than friends. And she wasn't sure she *wanted* to be more. Jakob knew her better than anyone else. He knew her favorite sweets, her favorite flower, the way she wore her hair, the way her lips curled defiantly at a corny joke. He knew her favorite book and least favorite pair of shoes, how she took her tea, and what cookies she liked after a bad day.

She knew him, too. She knew the way he always took a breath through his nose before pulling the trigger at target practice. She knew he preferred the dark bitterness of coffee over tea, knew how he couldn't sleep with any more than one pillow, how he slept with the window open no matter the weather. She knew he would never admit it, but he liked the flower crowns Wren made.

Their fathers had never expected them to get married. Jakob and Wren were friends. And though neither of them were betrothed to anyone else, the duke and Jakob's father hadn't made an arrangement between their children, either.

They talked about it themselves, though only when they were children.

"Do you think we'll get married one day?" Jakob had asked once when they were eight. He was lying in the grass with his hands behind his head.

"I don't know. I hope not," Wren said. "I don't want to get married." She was weaving yellow-headed weeds together to make a crown.

"Ever?" Jakob opened his eyes, squinting against the sun.

Wren shrugged. "I don't think so." She looked down at him. "I like being by myself." She thought for a second. "Well, except for you. But I don't want to marry you."

Jakob took the chain from her fingers and placed it on his head before closing his eyes again. "I don't want to marry you either."

But then, ten years later, as she looked at him while they sat on her window seat, she thought maybe she could marry him. They were comfortable with each other. And although she knew she wasn't the only girl he'd ever kissed and there had been girls he'd done a lot more with than only kiss, she was okay with that.

In the days leading up to Jakob's departure, they spent as much time as they could together. It was no different from their normal days, though some of their time was spent in his room rather than Wren's.

His room was in a separate wing to hers, near the front of the estate rather than the back gardens. He'd moved bedrooms since the snake incident and now was on the second floor.

She helped him pack, mended clothes he'd wear on his days off in port towns or around the ship. He sat with her while she read or painted. They didn't kiss again, but it didn't feel awkward between them.

On his last day, Wren gave him a small miniature of herself she painted. It wasn't perfect; she couldn't quite get the shade of her hair right. "So you won't forget how pretty I am," she said.

"With how much you've reminded me the last eleven years, how could I ever forget?" But he placed it into his leather satchel next to the wallet of money he'd been saving and his favorite marble shooter. Wren knew those things would be pulled from the satchel and tucked into the pocket of his trousers every morning when he dressed.

The morning he left, Wren and the duke went with Jakob and his father to the docks to see him off. His trunks were loaded earlier that morning, so all he had was his satchel, which Wren had taken and insisted on carrying to the ship. "Don't want to ruin your uniform," she said.

After Jakob said goodbye to his father and shook the duke's hand, he and Wren walked to the end of the gangplank. He took the satchel from her, slung it over his shoulder. "I'll see you soon, yeah?"

Wren reached out and flattened a wrinkle on his shoulder under the strap of his satchel. "Yeah," she said. "I'll see you soon."

He tucked her to his chest, squeezed her shoulders. She had thought he might kiss her again, but he only pressed his lips to her forehead before he turned and walked up the gangplank to the ship. He stopped halfway up and waved down at her. "Goodbye, little bird," he called.

"Goodbye, Jakob!" She waved back, smiling. Then, he turned and disappeared into the ship.

Wren had thought at one point that she and Jakob could be soulbound. They were soulmates, surely, but had their souls become bound together? She looked it up in one of the many books in the duke's library.

The book said soulmates and soulbinds both could be any kind of relationship. Familial, platonic, romantic. It didn't matter how or where the two lived, their souls would find each other. In soulmates, they sometimes lasted a lifetime, but sometimes they fizzled out before either of them died.

Soulbinds, however, would be secured to each other forever. Some said that soulbound people shared a soul, but it had been split in two somehow and ended up in different people. It was believed that if one half of a soulbind died, the other half would become a shell. More often than not, though, the other half would die shortly after the first.

When Jakob died, Wren had been so heavy with grief that she didn't leave her room for months. She thought the hurt in her chest was crushing her lungs and heart to pulp and she'd go to sleep one day and not wake up.

But, of course, she did wake up. Every day she opened her eyes and every day she was reminded that Jakob was never coming back. She kept thinking she'd feel different, hollow or weightless, but as time went on, and the days of crushing grief were easier to manage, she realized she'd been wrong. She and Jakob weren't soulbound, but simply soulmates.

Eventually, as the years passed, her grief, at one point a cloud, became a shadow, then something she could keep in her pocket, then she could drop into a bottle and tuck it into the shelf in her room. Occasionally, it reared its head again, and she was stuck trying to push her way through life. It got easier, though, and she finally was able to think and talk about Jakob without feeling the weight of his death.

It hurt to admit to herself that she and Jakob weren't soulbound, but she was happy that the loss of him hadn't resulted in the loss of herself as well. She saw him in things. The sunset, the forget-me-nots that grew in the garden, the golden eagles that soared overhead. It wasn't always easy, but it grew to be.

She thought of him daily. His light hair in the sun, his deep laughter echoing around the garden, his face hovering over hers when he woke her up on warm summer mornings. He was still with her, even if not physically. She held him in a spot behind her sternum, somewhere close to her heart. He'd stay there until she died.

THIRTY-SIX

THE MEMBERS OF *THE Basilisk* sit near the railing, enraptured in their chores or games. Wren and Aris stand mirroring each other, holding a dull knife in their hands. They stand in the middle of the deck, their feet apart, their knees slightly bent. She had been bored that morning and Aris had suggested they spar. They had no destination and were sailing in open water, the sun high overhead. Wren accepted his offer, growing restless in the week since she'd joined Aris and his crew.

"Attack me," Aris says.

Wren lunges forward, ready to disarm him. But he turns at the last moment, dodging her advance. She turns to him, resets her stance.

"Again."

She lunges and this time, she follows when he turns, expecting his dodge. She hits his forearm with the butt of the knife. She smiles, pleased.

"Good," Aris says. He takes a few steps away from her. "Again."

They go on like this. Wren lunging and Aris dodging. She gets in a few more hits, though she never successfully disarms him.

After an hour, they're both sweaty in the early autumn sun. Aris has taken off his coat and tossed it to the side; Wren has tied up her hair with the piece of purple fabric she'd gotten from Arden and Lex. She pushes the heavy feeling in her chest away when she thinks of them.

"Again."

Wren pushes forward, her fingers tightening around the hilt of the blade. Instead of dodging this time, Aris braces himself, squaring his shoulders, holding up his knife. He's yet to use it against Wren and she's surprised, but she doesn't stop.

She reaches him and they spar for a little while, the blades hitting each other as they turn across the deck. Wren has a fleeting worry for her fingers but pushes it away and continues her dance with Aris. Wren manages to knock the blade from Aris's fingers, and she allows herself a tiny moment to celebrate, but it doesn't last long. Aris reaches up and closes his fingers around her hand. While she's distracted, he loops his leg around hers and pulls her forward, causing her to fall onto her back on the deck. Her knife clatters across the boards.

She clenches her jaw and lets out a hard breath.

Aris straightens and looks down at her for a moment before offering his hand to her. She takes it and allows him to pull her up.

"I thought you said you were trained in combat at the estate?"

"I was," she says, dusting herself off. "More than ten years ago. It's been a while since I've had to spar anyone." She hasn't sparred since before Jakob left on his assignment.

Aris takes a few steps and bends to pick up her knife. "You know," he says, spinning the knife in his fingers. "If you used your magics, it would be easier for you to win."

"What?" Wren asks, perplexed, shaking her head. "I'm a healer." There was the moment in Erama, after Aedi and the siren were taken back to the ship, when she and Ezra stood at the end of the tunnel. Someone was rapidly approaching and Wren was ready to blind them, but then Ophelia was there and she never found out if her light would be useful for defense.

"Yes," he says. "But you can hold light as well, right?"

She could, though she was more likely to use the light like a lantern, to read or take notes by. Healing was what she mostly used her magics for, not light or warming rooms or others. Warming herself didn't require her to use light, just heat from her skin.

"Yes, a little."

"Well." Aris sweeps his hand out, still holding the knife.

Wren stands, her feet shoulder width apart, and holds her cupped hands out. A tiny ball of light forms in her palms, though it's barely visible in the sunlight. Aris watches her, his pale eyes focused on the light in her hands. She looks up at him.

The light goes out.

"You have to hold the light, Wren."

"I can," she says.

"Show me." Aris's voice is stern.

She starts again, holding her hands out. Again, a small ball of light forms between them. She can feel the heat coming off of it, can feel it gaining strength. A yell from one of the crew members distracts her and the light goes out.

Wren shakes out her shoulders, her arms, her hands. She flexes her fingers before trying again.

The combat instructor she had at the estate tried to get her to train with light. He had said the same as Aris; that using her magics would make it easier for her to win. But she didn't train to win, she only wanted to learn. Her instructor thought her silly for only using blades, for training hand-to-hand, but didn't push her. Jakob tried to convince her, too.

But she insisted on only learning what Jakob and the others were. And because magics users in the infantry were trained in their magics somewhere different, she only learned weapons.

This time, the ball of light grows. Even with the sun high above her, she can feel its glow on her face, feel the sweat breaking out on her brow. She watches it grow in her palms, a smile spreading across her face.

Aris's voice breaks into her thoughts. "Good," he says. "Have you ever thought about making light blades?"

The light in Wren's hands sputters and dies again. "Light blades?" She wipes her hands on her trousers and stretches her fingers.

Aris nods once. "I've seen it used one other time, though this was a water magics user. They were able to create weapons out of water. Weapons that they could use like any other. It meant they had an almost endless supply. They could never be disarmed, could never lose their blade." He pulls the knife Wren had been using during their spar out of his pocket. "You would be even better off than he was. His blades were limited to the amount of water around him. Yours would have no such limitations. You *create* light, you don't just wield it."

Wren looks from the knife to her hands. Could she do that? Could she create a weapon out of nothing but light? She looks back up at Aris.

"Perhaps we can try tomorrow?" he offers.

Wren flexes her hands. She nods. "I would like to."

"Good." He looks up at the sky. The sun has reached its apex above them. "Are you hungry? I think it's lunchtime."

THIRTY-SEVEN

THE NEXT DAY, THE crew moves all the crates and barrels to the side or takes them down below to give Aris and Wren as much room as possible. Some of the crew are still in their quarters, sleeping off their drunken stupors from the night before, but Ramsey and a handful of others watch them from the quarterdeck.

Aris stands in front of Wren on the deck, holding a knife in his fist. Wren mirrors him, her fist empty.

"Imagine the blade," Aris says. "The weight, the way the hilt feels beneath your fingers."

Wren closes her eyes, tries to imagine the blade in her hand. She's no stranger to them but imagining something that isn't there proves harder than she's willing to admit.

"Do you feel it?"

She tries, squeezing her fingers so hard, her fingernails leave imprints in her palm. "No," she admits, dropping her hands. She shakes her head, feeling silly. "Why am I doing this?" It sounded like such a good idea yesterday. But now, it feels like a childish game.

Aris lets his arm drop. He jerks his head, motioning for Wren to come closer to him. When she steps up, he takes her hand and presses the knife into her palm. He wraps her fingers around the hilt and holds her hand in both of his, squeezing.

"You won't always have someone to protect you, won't always have a blade for defense. But if you have a weapon that you can create, you will never be caught off guard." He dips his head to meet her eyes. "You will forever be protected against anyone that might see you hurt, anyone that might want you dead. If you can do this, there is nothing that anyone can do to disarm you."

Except cut my arms off, Wren thinks. She decides not to say this.

Aris raises his eyebrows in question. Wren nods. "Okay," she says. "I like the sound of that."

He gives a curt nod and crushes her fingers around the hilt one more time before removing his hands. She lets the knife fall from her grasp. "Do you feel it?"

She closes her fist. The ghost of the hilt is there, and she nods.

"Good, now lift"—Aris raises his hand, the knife again in his grasp—"and bring it down fast. Imagine you're driving it into something." His blade arcs down and reflects the sun as it meets its invisible target.

Wren follows his lead. She has to push aside the foolishness that has crept back in, focusing on the imprint the hilt had left on her flesh. She's trained with knives, knows exactly how it's supposed to feel, knows the satisfying thunk of when the blade is buried to its hilt. She tries to imagine what it looks like from the point of view of the men on the quarterdeck. Like she's a pantomime, an interpretive dancer, a child just learning to fight.

Aris relaxes, and she does, too, rolling her shoulders and squaring her feet.

"Again," Aris says.

They do the same dance, again and again and again, until Wren's forehead is beaded with sweat and her tongue is dry.

"Show me your light," Aris says.

She holds her hands together, forming a cup. Without thinking, a sphere of light forms in her hands. She removes one, letting the light bathe the deck in front of her.

"Brighter."

The light grows until the deck is awash with a warm yellow glow.

"Hone it." Aris walks around her in a circle, his hands clasped behind his back.

She tries, concentrating on the ball until it becomes a small column of light.

"Now close your fingers around it."

Slowly, Wren moves her free hand towards the column of light, hesitating when it flickers. But then her fingers are around it and she can feel it pulsing, feel it thrumming against the pads of her fingers, her palm, her bones. She hears a hum in her head. *This is what power feels like.*

She removes the hand under the column and squeezes until a hilt-like shape forms. Then, she watches in awe as the rest shapes into a blade.

Aris takes in a breath through his nose. "Good," he says. "Now throw it."

Wren whips around to face him, nearly extinguishing the light in her fist. She refocuses on it and lifts her head to look at him. "I thought I was just meant to fight with it."

"Have you never thrown a blade?"

"Of course I have." She nearly spits out the words.

"Well," he nods at the light blade, "then throw it. It's no different."

She wants to laugh. *No different.* No ordinary blade could be wrought from nothing. No ordinary blade felt like this in her fingers. No ordinary blade could burn a hole in the boards of a ship.

She's not sure her light blade could either, but she realizes she wants to know. She wants to watch her creation bore into the wooden side of this ship. She wants to watch the smoke curl into the sky as her blade carves a void into its structure.

So, she leans back, planting her feet, and throws her arm forward, releasing the blade. But, as soon as her hand opens, the light disappears. Small embers fall to the deck at her feet, but they burn out before so much as leaving a mark on the wood. She clenches her jaw against the heat enveloping her face at the laughs from the quarterdeck.

She hears Aris turn behind her. "Enough!" he calls out. The crew immediately quiets. "Let's see you do what Wren has done. Can any of you hold a weapon of light?" No one answers. "Any of you laugh again and you'll lose your tongues."

His hand on Wren's shoulder is cool, and she's grateful for his touch. "Again," he says.

Wren stays on deck for hours, creating light blades and practicing her throws. She never successfully keeps the blade in its shape after it leaves her fingers, but she feels more confident in her ability to create them.

She practices throwing a real knife for a little while, to make sure she has the correct technique burned into her muscle memory. It leaves pock marks in the wall next to Aris's door. Every time she pulls it free, she runs her thumb over the entry mark, longing for the satisfaction of making one with her own blade.

When the sun has sunk below the horizon and turned the space between the sky and the sea pink, she collapses on the steps leading to the quarterdeck. Aris, in a move she wouldn't have expected of him, sits next to her and offers her a flask from the pocket of his jacket.

"Drink," he commands.

Blessedly, it's water. Wren drains the flask, throwing her head back and lifting it to get the last few drips from the brim.

Aris chuckles and takes the flask, tucking it away again in his pocket. "How are your hands?"

Wren holds them in front of her. There are small burns along the skin on her fingers, but nothing she can't heal herself. "Tired," she says. "As am I."

Aris shoves his head toward their shared cabin. "Go rest. I'll bring supper when it's ready."

Wren is grateful for their sun-warmed cabin. After changing and sitting cushioned against a pile of pillows, she looks at her hands. The burns are more like calluses than wounds. Her light blades have heat, and sometimes they singe, but she's able to keep them steady, so they're cool enough to not cause any nasty damage. She thinks about healing them but decides that they're better as calluses. Better to let the skin build up to protect, than to let new skin constantly burn. Once she figures out how to hone and hold her blades without burns, she can heal the calluses. Until then, she puts a topical cream on top of them and lays her head back on the pillows.

When Aris wakes her, the cabin is bathed in warm candle light. The sun has fully gone down and the temperature inside their cabin has lowered.

They share a dinner of hearty vegetable stew and rice. After their tray has been taken, Aris blows out all but the candle by the bed and slips under the sheets next to Wren.

He's facing away from the candle, his face in shadow. "You did well today, Wren." When she doesn't respond, he says. "Tomorrow we'll work on keeping the blade whole."

He turns away from her, blows out the candle, and settles into the sheets.

Over the next week, they work every day. During meals, Wren calls light blades into her hands without thinking. She traces the grain on the ship's railing with the burning tip, carving new lines in its wake.

Her throwing improves slower than she'd hoped. By the end of the third day, the blade stays in its form for a few feet before flickering out. On day five, it reaches the deck railing, but before it can lodge into the wood, the light disappears.

It's frustrating, but Wren tries not to let it show on her face, or in her body language, or in the way she walks across the deck to run her fingers over the tiniest burn on the railing.

Aris has stopped standing over her. He watches her from the quarterdeck, and he no longer tells her "again" or "one more time." When something new happens, she looks at him, and she's glad every time to see his chest puffed out, a tiny smile pulling at the corner of his mouth.

On the seventh day, a week after her first attempt, the light blade manages to stick in the railing. It doesn't last long, and her focus on it has to be strong, but thin wisps of smoke curl from the surrounding wood before it fades and winks out. She reaches out and lets the smoke play over her burnt and callused fingers.

Aris joins her near the burn on his ship. His fingers probe the mark and come back slightly blackened with soot. "Good," he says, rubbing the ash between his fingers and thumb. He turns and, as he strides back to the quarterdeck, he says over his shoulder, "Now do two."

Two is, Wren decides, harder than one. But it takes her less than a week for the blades to stick in the railing. Then, at Aris's request, she keeps adding blades, one at a time, until she's up to five. By the time she's mastered that, the ship's railing has severe burns along its surface and a few holes through which Wren can see the swirling ocean.

"Why do you want me to add so many?" she asks him one night while sharing a bowl of stew and a half loaf of bread.

Aris chews slowly and shrugs a shoulder. "Wouldn't more make you feel more secure?"

Wren shakes her head, saying, "I don't know. I guess? It's just a lot to focus on all at once."

"Well," Aris says. "You don't have to use all five all the time. But it's good to be sufficient in them, anyway."

Aris had said he wanted Wren to be able to protect herself if the need arose. Since joining him, she'd noticed that he always kept a blade close by. On the nightstand by the bed, in a drawer in the desk, stashed behind a barrel on the quarterdeck. She knows he has one strapped to his side, and one in the pocket of his trousers right now.

Had he noticed her lack of weapons? She had the one she'd gotten in that port town with Ophelia and Clare, but it was usually put away in her satchel, slung over the chair she's sitting in.

Is his proactivity the result of the attacks he endured in Breton? How often had he been without a weapon and had to rely only on his hands? Wren's magics weren't used for combat, but they still offered some protection. But Aris's magics only granted power when he was asleep, and only superficial power at that; he couldn't defend himself with dreams.

Sometime during the first week of her light-blade training, while getting ready for bed, Wren looked up from her book to see Aris pull his shirt over his head. The skin over his chest and back was the same as his hands, pale and marbled with blue veins. A few scars littered his shoulders, puckered and dark pink against his ghostly pallor. He turned toward her, reaching for another shirt from the end of the bed and that's when she saw a scar across his belly, the length of her forearm.

"What happened?" she asked.

Aris looked up at her and then down to his stomach, where her eyes were resting on the scar. "I told you, it's not safe to be without protection." He said nothing more, just slipped the shirt over his head and crawled under the sheets next to her, turned out the lantern, and went to sleep.

A few days later, they dock in a town that has a training field and Aris rents it for the day while the railing Wren had burned is repaired by a scraggly old man with thin hair, three missing fingers, and calluses along his remaining ones.

At the field, employees in tan pants and shirts set up dummies in random formations and deflate when the first of many of Wren's light blades set them aflame. She feels guilty, but Aris circles his finger in the air and the dummies are extinguished and replaced.

When he's satisfied with her aim, Aris calls for volunteers so she can have some moving targets. The crew members that joined them are hesitant, but Aris looks at them with a hard stare and slowly a few of them step forward. Wren promises to heal any burns. The ones that had come forward—the wind magics user, Laszlo, and the woman with a tight bun, Collins, among them—make their way onto the field. Aris sends them in zig-zag formations toward her one at a time. If she concentrates, she can make her blades disappear just before they lodge into the flesh of someone's body, leaving them lit just long enough to leave a tiny mark on their shirts where they would have entered if left to burn.

After each crew member—and a few brave employees—have run at her twice, Aris sets them up to run horizontally across the field. Again, Wren lets her blades live just long enough to mark its entrance and then lets the light die.

She only misses the first few runs of each drill. Throughout the weeks since she'd started, she discovered that if she twitched her fingers in the direction she wanted the blade to go, just as it left her hand, the blade would follow that trajectory. She thinks that if she continues working and training, she could simply look at a target and her blades would know the course to take.

Her hands have built up enough calluses, and she's learned to control the temperature of her blades while they're in her hands, so there are no more burns on her fingers. But, even after weeks of throwing, her arms and shoulders are still sore and tired at the end of the day. She stretches before and after each session, and she does so now, while Aris directs the crew and employees where to go. Despite the stretches and the muscle relaxants she takes in the evening, she's still stiff when she first wakes up.

After all but one crew member has left the field and the employees have been dismissed, Aris walks up to her. The sun on land is different from the sun on board *The Basilisk* and Aris's cheeks and nose have turned pink under its rays.

"One more drill," he says. He stands next to Wren and turns, pointing to the man in the middle of the field. He's haggard from life at sea; his skin yellowed, his hair hanging in strings around his wrinkled face. "I want you to put a blade through that man's sternum."

Wren turns to him. "What?"

Aris juts his chin towards the man, not looking at her. "The sternum is the bone that holds the ribs in place over the heart and lungs." He draws a finger down the center of his chest. "It's a strong bone. I want you to put a blade through it."

Wren lets the light blades she's holding die. "I know where the sternum is. Why do you want me to kill him?"

Aris shrugs a shoulder. "I need to know you can protect yourself. And he's of no use to me anymore. He has no money, so it's either a quick death from you or he starves to death on the streets." Finally, he turns to her. "You can give him a quick death, can you not?"

Though she knows what Aris is saying is true, she hesitates. She's never killed anyone. She looks at the rest of the crew, standing off to the side in a few groups. Though Aris had replaced some of *The Basilisk*'s original crew members with younger and stronger people when he became captain, many of the ones here look like they're on their way to looking like the man in the field. Wrinkled around their eyes and mouth, their necks hanging loose like a turkey's. Some of them only have a handful or no teeth at all.

The man in the field hasn't been of any help on board the ship. In all the time she's been on board, she's never seen him do anything other than sleep and tip a bottle to his lips. He's old, most likely on his way out of this world already. The difference between what she'd do now and how he'd die on the street is quickness. Mercy.

"Yes," she says, her voice barely louder than the breeze. "I can make it quick."

The blade is in her hand before she thinks better of it. She steels her mind, her heart, her stance, and throws.

Her blade would have found its mark, but she extinguishes the light before it can bury itself. She can see a tiny smoldering hole in the man's shirt where the tip had touched before dying. It sits right in the center of his chest, right where Aris had indicated.

The man's face is surprised for a fraction of a moment before he falls backwards into the dirt. He scrabbles away from where he'd been standing, his eyes darting from his captain to Wren.

"What are you doing?" Aris turns on her, anger in his voice.

She looks at him, her jaw set, her hands fisted at her sides. "You taught me this so I could protect myself, Aris. *This* is not protection. I won't do your killing. If you want him dead, do it yourself."

She turns on her heel and walks away from him, back toward the dock, toward where *The Basilisk* is being repaired.

If Aris wants her to learn to use her magics to protect herself, fine. She'll happily do that. Happily burn holes in the side of his ship, burn tiny holes in the shirts and trousers of his crew. But she won't kill just because he commands it.

She hears the man scream once behind her, but she doesn't turn to look at what Aris has ordered in her place.

THIRTY-EIGHT

IT'S BEEN A MONTH and a week since Wren joined Aris and the crew of *The Basilisk*. He hasn't brought up her becoming duchess or his becoming king and, if she's honest, she's relieved. Since joining him, being duchess has lost nearly all of its draw. Her body feels heavy when she thinks of it, the papers she'd sign, the dances and parties he'd promised she'd have in the ballroom. But he doesn't bring it up, and neither does she.

Most of her days, she stays in his cabin, summoning light blades and reading the books on his shelves. She eats with him, sometimes at the desk, sometimes in the mess.

On days she's on deck, she stays standing on the quarterdeck, the cloak Aris had given her pulled tightly around her shoulders. She wills her arms and legs to be warm, her hands twisted in the wool of the cloak.

Her home in the clay neighborhood was cold, even with all the blankets on her bed. On a particularly chilly night, she huddled under the blankets and imagined herself warm. She thought of the sun shining on her skin and the way her limbs felt after running around the streets.

And it worked. She was able to get warm and sleep like it was late spring instead of the middle of winter. In the morning, when she told her parents, they exchanged a look and smiled. Her father took the day off work—something he rarely did—and spent a little of the coin they had in savings on a tiny orange cake. It was smaller than her palm and there was barely enough for each of them to have a single bite, but it was a memory Wren would hold in her heart for years afterwards.

Now, though warming herself is second nature and much easier than when she was small, Wren prefers cloaks and blankets. "They're cozier," she'd say if someone asked.

Aside from the first few days on board, she'd never had to warm herself on *The Altean*, but here, on *The Basilisk*, she finds herself doing it more often, even under her cloak and long sleeve shirts. Aris's cabin is nicely insulated, but the hold, galley, and crew's quarters are drafty and damp. The crew and Aris seem to treat *The Basilisk* as simply a vessel to get to their next destination, rather than as a home as *The Altean*'s crew does. When she was on board, Wren felt as if the boat was as much a part of the crew as Ezra or Jez.

Standing on the deck of *The Basilisk*, where the cold breeze never seems to let up, Wren usually has the hood pulled over her hair and her hands stuffed into the pockets of her trousers or tangled in the edges of the cloak.

It doesn't help that summer has officially left, and autumn is in full swing. The spring and summer days at sea were kind. There were cooler days when it rained, and days spent in port towns that were under cloud cover year-round, but autumn is proving harder than Wren had expected.

Aris steps out of his cabin, climbs the stairs, and stands next to her. "Have you eaten?" he asks.

Wren looks at him, her hair floating around her like a halo in the wind coming off the sea. "No," she says.

Aris nods toward the stairs that lead down below deck. "I've been told the stew is ready. Care to join me in the mess?"

Wren isn't particularly hungry, but it's probably warmer below deck and out of the sea breeze. She nods and allows Aris to lead her below.

It is warmer out of the breeze and with the heat coming off the stove. The mess is crowded with other crew members, and when Aris clears his throat, they all move to one of the two tables, leaving the other empty.

Aris sits, and Wren sits across from him. A few moments later, their cook, a short fat man Wren has never seen anywhere but the galley and mess, brings two bowls of stew and sets them in front of Aris and Wren.

"Eat," Aris says, picking up his spoon and dipping it into his bowl.

Wren picks up her spoon and stirs the stew in front of her. It's thick and smells strongly of onions.

They eat for a while, the food warming Wren from the inside. It's what the duke would have called "sticking to the ribs" food.

Despite the lack of breeze and the warm food, Wren still shivers when she pushes her empty bowl away.

"Are you cold?" Aris asks.

She shrugs a shoulder. "I've been warmer."

Aris lets out a breath through his nose. "Do you miss them?" His voice is nonchalant, but his shoulders are tense, his jaw clenched.

She wonders what she might be doing if she were on *The Altean*. Probably having dinner with Ezra and Lex, leaning against the railing. Maybe passing a bottle of whiskey back and forth with Arden. Singing with Ophelia and Clare and Grace. Maybe that night, she'd let Jez teach her a new dice game he'd thought up, a blanket wrapped around her legs, Penelope curled up in her lap.

"Yes," she says, looking into her empty bowl. "Very much."

"Do you want to go back to them?" He looks at her, his elbows leaning on top of the table, his chin resting on his fists.

She shrugs again and pulls the cloak tighter around her. "Not as badly as I want what you can give me." She doesn't quite believe the words as much as she would have when she first left *The Altean*, but there's some truth in them still.

The corner of Aris's mouth lifts and his shoulders relax. "We should get to work on that, shouldn't we?" He stands and offers his vein-marbled hand to her.

She takes it and lets him pull her off the bench. "How?"

"Let me worry about the details. You just sit back, perfecting those light blades and reading my books."

They go back to his cabin. Aris sits behind his desk and Wren shrugs out of the cloak, hanging it by the door. She sits on the side of his bed, takes her boots off, and crawls under the covers. It's still early, not quite time for sleep, so she takes the book she'd been reading from the table and opens it to the page she'd dog-eared that morning.

THIRTY-NINE

Wren knows she's dreaming. The forest around her feels familiar somehow, and it's not until she touches her palm to the bark of a tree that she realizes why. This is Adreus's sacred forest, in the southwestern peninsula of Kornas. Her fingers trail over the patterns in the bark, remembering the way the carvings on the duke's desk felt under her skin. The trees seem to hum around her, vibrating her bones the way *The Altean*'s boards did. Beneath her feet, the ground is littered with leaves and acorns. In the branches above her, birdsong and the chirping of insects mingle into a chorus.

She walks through the trees, her fingers only leaving the bark long enough for her to move her hand to the next. She picks up acorns from the ground and drops them into the pockets of her trousers. After a few minutes of walking, the trees thin, revealing a lake.

As she steps into the clearing, Wren shields her eyes from the light reflecting off the surface of the water. It's small, mirroring the clouds in the sky on its glassy surface. On the other side, someone sits on a blanket spread out in the grass.

Wren makes her way over to them, stooping to trace the cap of a mushroom or pinch a few buds of lavender between her fingers. Her boots sink into the mud at the edge of the water, and she kicks them off, tossing them between trees.

She stops short when she realizes who's sitting on the blanket. "Kiara?"

Kiara turns to Wren, her brown hair falling over her shoulder. Her eyes crinkle at the corner as she smiles. "Hello, Wren."

Wren sits down on the blanket, careful to keep her muddy feet away from the food spread over it. There are little pink cakes and a blue floral printed teapot with matching cups. She hadn't dreamt much while aboard *The Basilisk*. The dreams she has had have been occupied by Jakob, certainly not of *The Altean*'s crew. Around her, the trees shimmer in the light reflected off the lake. "What are you doing here?"

Kiara picks up a cake and takes a bite. "Looking for you," she says.

Wren shakes her head. "I don't understand." She looks around for Aris, wondering if he'd created this scenario, but she and Kiara are alone, apart from the swooping birds and flitting insects.

Kiara licks the frosting from her fingers. "We've been looking for you, Wren. We've all been so worried. Ezra and Ophelia are beside themselves."

As if she hasn't heard Kiara, Wren says, "You're a dream walker."

Kiara smiles again. "Yes," she says. "I've been searching all over, but Eli finally figured it out." She shakes her head and lets out a sad huff of a laugh.

She explains the crew's searching. The day of Wren's disappearance, the crew had nearly turned the ship upside down. Aedi dove into the water and looked for hours, surfacing only long enough to catch her breath before letting the waves swallow her again. Then Eli asked Kiara to dream walk.

"She asked me to try to find your friend Jakob. We weren't sure if he was still in Sudal, but she wanted me to check." Kiara picks up another cake.

Wren's heart heaves at Jakob's name. And, though she already knows the answer, she asks, "Did you find him?"

Kiara lets out a sad laugh. "You know I didn't, Wren." She turns to look at Wren. "Jakob is dead."

"Yes," Wren looks down at her lap, "he is. He died five years ago."

Kiara places her hand on Wren's arm. "I'm sorry."

Wren is quiet for a moment, then asks, "So how did you find me?"

"We went through everything we knew about you. Eli talked to everyone. I told Eli about the first time you saw *The Basilisk*. How I had to pull you away from the edge. And then, when Aris was attacking all those port towns, one day you woke, and we could tell that you had been visited. We realized the attacks stopped after that.

"We wrote to one of our contacts in the Maian Empire and asked if Aris was on the registry as a dream walker. We got their reply quickly and after we read that Aris was registered, Eli asked me to try." She shrugs, her face downcast. "And here I am."

"Why did you come after me?"

Kiara looks confused. "Why wouldn't we? We care about you, Wren. We just wanted to make sure you're okay. Eli thought that if we didn't find you soon, we'd have to write to the duke and tell him you'd been lost at sea."

Wren worries the inside of her lip. Why is she surprised they wanted to find her? There would have been little she wouldn't do if Ophelia or Lex or Jez went missing. It's bittersweet hearing Kiara say it. Wren felt at home on *The Altean*, but the pull to Aris was stronger. She couldn't *not* go with him.

She puts her hand over Kiara's on the blanket. "I'm glad you're here," she says. "I've missed you all more than you can imagine."

Kiara smiles, her eyes brimming with tears. "We've missed you, too. Everyone will be so glad to hear you're all right." She pauses. "You are, right? All right?"

Wren looks down at their hands. She nods. "He's been nothing but kind to me," she says. She doesn't mention the threats he gives his crew, or the man he killed at the training center.

"Is that how he got to you? He was kind?"

Taken aback, Wren asks, "What do you mean?" She pulls her hand back from Kiara's.

"Aris," Kiara says, as if it should be obvious. "How did he get to you on *The Altean*?"

Wren's eyebrows knit together. "He visited me. We talked. He asked me to go with him. And when I said yes, he came for me."

It's Kiara's turn for her eyebrows to knit together. "Why?"

Wren shrugs. *Power*, she wants to say, but that seems silly. Here in Adreus's forest, the duke's seat in Sudal, the throne in Mythshade, they seem so far away, untouchable and childlike. But she doesn't have another answer, so she keeps her eyes on the lake. She's still not even sure if it was the power she wanted, or if that was just an illusion she believed because of the siren.

After a few minutes of silence, Kiara says, "Wren, has Aris told you what caused him to be banished?"

She nods. "Yes."

"Did he tell you what happened on the voyage to the Isles?"

He had. In Mythshade, he was beaten and left bloody and swollen. He was taken to *The Altean* in the middle of the night, hooded and chained. He was confined in the hold, with only an empty bucket and a small flask of water. It seemed harsh, and not at all how Wren would have thought Eli and the rest of the crew to treat someone aboard their ship, even if that someone was a banished prince that had been sentenced to death.

"Yes," Wren says. "Why did you treat him so harshly?"

Kiara had been looking at the clouds lazily floating across the sky. Now she turns her eyes on Wren. "We treated him as well as we could have. I told you, it was hard having him on board. For more reasons than one."

Wren stands, her hands balled into fists at her sides. "I can't imagine what it was like for him," she says, tears pricking the corners of her eyes. "Being stripped of everything he's ever known and sent away to die. And you didn't even stand up for him. You didn't even try to save him."

Kiara looks up at her. "Wren," she starts.

Wren cuts her off. "No, Kiara. Adreus gave you and Eli your lives to *help* people. Not to send them to their deaths."

Kiara sighs and stands. She opens her mouth to say something, but she stops herself. Then, with a sad smile, she says, "Be careful, Wren."

Wren blinks, and Kiara is gone.

FORTY

"Didn't get much sleep last night, huh?" Ramsey stands next to Wren on the quarterdeck, the sun glinting off his golden skin.

"Guess not," she says, tipping the canteen of water she's been carrying around all morning into her mouth.

Ramsey makes a noise. "You best be careful to hide your walking." He lifts his chin and watches Aris on the main deck.

Aris is dressed in plain clothes, shouting orders to members of the crew he didn't bother introducing Wren to. Most of them have scars on their faces, their arms, their backs and chests. They all look older than they are, weather-worn and sunburnt.

"I'm not a walker." She takes another deep pull from the canteen and squints in the sun.

"No, but the captain is. Do you think he won't recognize walking sickness?"

The canteen is empty, and Wren starts walking to refill it in the barrels below decks. "It won't happen again."

Except that it does happen again. Over the next two weeks, Kiara visits every night. She never says anything. She doesn't even look at Wren. They sit in silence. On benches in port towns they visited, on the beach, in forest clearings, in the garden at the estate in Sudal. Once, in a tiny home that Wren doesn't recognize. There are other people there, a small boy with brown hair the same shade as Kiara's, a woman and a man that bump hips playfully as they prepare food in the small kitchen. The people leave her and Kiara alone, moving around them like ghosts. They talk and laugh, but their voices sound as if they're underwater and Wren can't make out what they're saying.

After every visit, Wren wakes with a mild headache and a thirst that's not easily quenched, though she hides her afflictions well enough that Aris doesn't ask her about them.

Throughout these weeks, Aris and his crew dock in port towns in the morning and return in the evening with unmarked barrels and crates. At the next town, they unload their haul from the last and restock with more.

"You're smuggling," Wren says one evening while they're eating a dinner of roast chicken and rice.

"How else do you expect us to make money, Wren?" Aris pushes his half-eaten plate of food away from him on top of the desk.

"Take jobs? You don't have to break the law to make money."

Aris scoffs. "They are jobs, Wren. Just because they're not as virtuous as rescuing a selkie and a siren doesn't mean we're not being hired."

Wren sets her fork down. "I'm not accusing you, Aris. I'm only saying there are other ways."

She leaves him in his quarters, the cloak he'd given her pulled tightly around her shoulders.

The rest of the crew is spread out on the deck. Some are playing cards or tossing dice and whooping or groaning at whatever numbers are rolled. Coins and bills pass from hand to hand as bets are won or lost. Ramsey stays on the quarterdeck, his hands resting on the railing as he gazes at the white horizon line.

Wren joins a group of men tossing dice and nods when they ask if she wants to play. She throws a handful of coins on a pile that's set on a piece of ripped sail. One of the men next to her cuffs her on the shoulder with a wide, scarred hand. He grins at her with a broken smile.

"Didn't think the captain's girl liked us much," he says.

Wren sits up straighter, shrugging his hand off. The nickname has caught her a bit by surprise, and she's not sure how she feels about it, but she doesn't dispute it. Instead, she says, "I don't. Deal me in." She nods at the pile of coins and holds out a hand for the pair of dice.

The man throws his head back and laughs, then claps the mismatched dice in her outstretched hand.

She sits with them until the sun has sunk well below the horizon and a lantern has been lit to keep their game visible. Perhaps if she stays out here until long after her usual bedtime, she'll miss Kiara's visit and get a night's reprieve.

But, after the men she's with have gotten too drunk to keep track of who threw what numbers they need to win, she retires back to Aris's quarters, the pockets of her cloak jingling with coin.

"You won, then?" Aris asks when she steps inside. She had seen him earlier, standing near the ship's wheel, looking down his nose at the crew on the deck.

"You could say that." She didn't win, but she'd been the only one sober and she'd convinced them all that they'd thrown the wrong number and she'd thrown the right one. They didn't question her—whether because they believed her or they were too afraid of their captain to doubt her—just thumped her on the back and swung their flasks and cups toward her, sprinkling her lap and boots with beer or cheap whiskey.

"You know, there are other ways to get coin than by cheating my men."

"Yes," she says, sitting on the edge of the bed they share, pulling her leg up to untie her boot. "But what's the fun in that?"

Every night from then on, Wren joins the crew on deck and throws dice, or plays cards, or bets on who would vomit up their drink first. She rarely wins, but she's good at convincing them that she's thrown the right number or played the right card. Convincing them who had thrown up first proves tricky, but she's resorted to slipping a drop of daffodil sap into a cup and, usually, she can guess correctly after that.

"I don't know how you do it every night, Wren. Are you a witch?" a short and round man with a full mustache and red nose asks her. He's one of the men she'd played with her first night, named Smith.

She had learned many of their names since she'd started playing with them. While most of them had been part of *The Basilisk*'s crew long before Aris took over captaincy, a few of them were Aris's supporters back in Breton. And though none of them will ever feel like family the way the crew of *The Altean* did, she's still grateful for their drunken shanties, candy shared from pockets, and the bottles of whiskey passed between them.

"Not a witch," she assures him. "But I have been known to dabble in herbology." She shows him the little dropper bottle with the sap inside before slipping it into the hidden pocket she had stitched into the cloak.

He gives her a look of shock but then doubles over laughing. "I won't tell them," he says, "as long as you promise not to put any in my cup."

"You've got yourself a deal." She winks at him before going up the steps to the quarterdeck.

Wren wakes late one morning to find the ship docked. She walks out into the sun and pulls the black cloak over her shoulders. She nods to Ramsey on the quarterdeck before walking down the gangplank and onto the dock.

Crew members roll empty barrels from *The Basilisk* down the dock to shore. When they see her, they wish her good morning. When Aris sees her, he raises his eyebrows.

"You're out and about," he says questioningly.

She smiles at him. "It's a nice day. I wanted to peruse the market. Maybe spend some of this money I've won off your crew." She pats the pocket of her trousers.

Aris chuckles. "Be back before nightfall." She starts to walk toward the market just past the docks when Aris calls out, "Little bird." She turns back toward him. "Will you pick something up for dinner?"

She smiles. "Of course," she says.

The only coin Wren ends up spending is on three new pairs of socks to replace the ones she'd brought from *The Altean* that had been mended so much they were more thread than original fabric, lunch at a small café, and food she'd bought at a street cart for her and Aris for dinner. She had enjoyed walking the stalls and running her fingers over bolts of fabric, spines of leather books, dried herbs in bundles, carved wooden toys in the shapes of cats and dolls and elephants. She picks up crystals and watches them shine in the sun, casting rainbows over the cloak.

At one stall, she picks up a knife with a carving of a mermaid on the hilt. For a moment, she forgets herself and turns, getting ready to call out for Ophelia. But at the last moment, she remembers Ophelia isn't here. Her shoulders slump and she places the knife back down on the silk tablecloth.

She turns before the tears run over her cheeks, blinking back quickly and tilting her face up to the sun. Kiara's words echo in the back of her mind. *Ezra and Ophelia are beside themselves.* She hates that she hurt them, hates that they were worried. She should have left a note. Should have woken them up to say goodbye. But if she had, they would have held her back, told her it was crazy to go with Aris.

No matter how they or her other friends on *The Altean* feel, Wren can't shake the feeling that *The Basilisk* is where she's meant to be. With Aris. The pull in her chest had nothing to do with the siren. She would have found her way to him, regardless of if the siren tempted her with his words or not.

The walk back to *The Basilisk* is quiet. She keeps the cloak pulled tightly around her against the breeze that comes off the water. The food is tucked under one arm, her new pairs of socks placed into her satchel.

The crew is still loading barrels onto deck when Wren reboards. Aris supervises, watching as the barrels are rolled across the deck and pushed into a corner. She holds up the paper bag of food in greeting.

Aris nods. When she stands next to him, he says, "If you're hungry, you can start without me. I'll take a bit longer out here."

Wren shrugs and puts the bag back inside the cloak. "I'm all right. I ate not too long ago."

Aris nods again and she moves to the steps leading to the quarterdeck. She sits and places the food next to her, watching the crew move barrel after barrel into place.

She remembers the first time she helped Ezra and Ophelia with the stock. How Ezra told her about all the different metals around the barrels to denote what was in them. How they were meant to deter theft. She laughs. She doesn't have any proof—she'd never looked in the barrels and crates *The Basilisk* carried—but she'd be willing to bet all her won coin on how the metal on these barrels don't abide by that rule.

Once the sun sets, and the last barrel has been loaded, Aris walks to her and offers his hand. "Ready?"

She takes it and stands, picking up the bag, and follows Aris into his cabin, where they close the door behind them.

FORTY-ONE

Kiara visits again that night. Wren had managed to escape her the last few nights, not sleeping until the sun was coming up, but the day docked in town had ruined Wren's routine.

She's waiting on the deck of *The Altean* for Wren. Around her, the rest of the crew works. Wren isn't surprised at how the sight of them makes her heart ache, but she has to grip the railing to keep from falling to her knees. Ophelia and Ezra are standing at the bow, laughing. Arden and Lex have their heads bent toward the other, whispering. Eli stands at the wheel, her green coat billowing behind her in the wind. Jez and Clare sit on the steps to the quarterdeck petting Penelope, who sits between them, her eyes closed and nose turned skyward. The sun is high overhead, but Wren doesn't have to blink against its brightness.

"Hello, Wren," Kiara says. Around her, laughter and gull cries fill the air. It seems like it would be a happy time on board, but Kiara isn't smiling.

In all of Kiara's visits, she'd never brought Wren to *The Altean*, had never shown her any of the other crew members. The only people she'd seen were those in the small house. The boy with Kiara's hair color, the dancing man and woman.

Wren tears her eyes away from Ophelia and Ezra. "Where's Grace?"

"This is before Grace joined us." She motions for Wren to join her.

Wren takes a deep breath and lets go of the railing, walking up to Kiara hesitantly. Though her boots should make sounds on the deck, her steps are silent. "What are we doing?"

Kiara turns and looks out over the side of the ship, toward land that's mountainous. Wren follows her eye line.

They're close enough to shore to see a small gathering of people. A dock sticks out into the bay, hidden from view from the rest of the beach. The sun glitters off of something too small to see.

"I want you to see what happened. All of it."

As they get closer, Wren can see the orange banners of Breton waving in the breeze. Somehow, she knows this is the day *The Altean* picked up Aris.

"How do I know I can trust you? That I can believe what you're showing me is real?"

Kiara gives her a sad look. "When have we ever lied to you?"

"You didn't tell me you have magics. I asked you in Loksa and you didn't tell me. And you're lying now!" Wren shouts. "Aris was picked up in the middle of the night." She points toward the sun.

Kiara sighs. "I didn't tell you in Loksa because I haven't used my magics in years. I'm sorry." She watches Wren and when she doesn't get a response, she says, "I'm sure there will be other parts of this story that don't line up with Aris's. But I promise you that this is how our crew remembers it. How I remember it. When have I ever deceived you?"

Wren can't give an answer. As far as she knows, Kiara hasn't, apart from Loksa. No one on the crew has.

But Aris? She's not sure. She'd like to think he hasn't. He's lied by omission—like not telling her about the smuggling until she confronted him—but outright lying? There's no way she can be sure either way.

And if he is lying, what would she do? Confront him and ask him why? Threaten to leave him if he doesn't tell her the truth? Somehow, she doesn't think either of those would go over well, though the worst he's done to her is raise his voice.

She knows she might regret this, seeing what Kiara is offering to show her. But if she doesn't, curiosity would eat at her.

Her eyes wander over Kiara's face. Then she takes a breath and nods. "Show me."

Kiara holds out her hand.

Eli stepped off the stairs leading to the quarterdeck, her arms swinging freely at her sides. "Crew!" she yelled.

They gathered around her. Overhead, a flock of gulls flew by, squawking.

"This job is not like others we've had. Those jobs were about saving the people we welcomed aboard. This job is about saving the people we're leaving behind." She held up a hand as Ezra started to ask a question. "I don't know the whole story, just that our charge has been accused of high treason, and they have been sentenced to death. We have been hired to deliver them to the Isles of the Damned."

A murmur went through the crew.

"We're to leave them to die?" Ophelia asked. "That's barbaric."

Eli took a breath through her nose. "I did not choose this for them, Ophelia. We've only been tasked to take them there. After that, it's up to fate."

"What about while they're on board? What do we do?" Arden's deep voice stuttered through the sentence. He stood with his arms crossed over his chest, his jaw clenched.

"We are to treat them as well as they deserve. Do not treat them like they're lower than yourself but also do not allow yourself to forget that they have committed crimes." Eli made sure to meet the eyes of each of her crew members.

"Which of us hasn't committed a crime?" Ophelia mumbled.

Eli continued on as if she hadn't heard her. "We will treat them like a guest, unless and until they make it clear they don't deserve that kindness."

She waited a few moments in case the crew had other questions, but they remained quiet. She dismissed them and stood back at the wheel.

When it was time to dock, Eli eased her ship in, and Arden jumped from the railing to help secure her and to guide the gangplank as Ezra and Lex lowered it.

Eli and Kiara walked down the plank and met a guard sent by the queen and king of Breton. They weren't far, just at the other end of the dock, but the guard was sent, anyway. They told Eli that the queen and king would stay long enough to give instructions, then, as the prisoner is being boarded, they'll take their leave back to their home. Eli nodded and thanked the guard.

The prisoner was already waiting for them, a bag over their head and their wrists and ankles in chains. Their spine stayed straight, their feet shoulder width apart. They didn't make any noise and didn't turn to the sound of Eli and Kiara's boots on the dock.

"Queen Lily, King Rufus," Eli said as she approached them. She dipped her chin toward her chest, though she did not bow. A girl stood behind them, her hazel eyes focused on something out to sea, her arms straight at her sides, her hands balled into fists. There were tears gathered on her bottom lashes, her jaw clenched tight. Eli slid her eyes from the girl and looked back at the queen and king.

"Captain," the queen said, the word clipped.

Eli waited, but when no other conversation followed, she prompted, "Your guard said you had instructions?"

The queen's bare hand fluttered at her slender throat. "Yes," she said. "When you take him to the Isles, tie him to a tree. Do not wait for..." her voice trailed off, her gaze on the prisoner. A moment passed before she shook her head, cleared her throat, and met Eli's eyes again. "Leave him there. Then send us a message that you have done so."

Eli nodded once, then looked toward the prisoner. He had a guard near him, but other than that, he was alone on the dock.

"What is his name?" Eli asked, turning back to the queen and king. She waited, but neither of them answered. The girl behind them looked like she wanted to. She met Eli's eyes and opened her mouth, but then closed it again with a shuddering breath, dropping her eyes to her feet.

Eli took a breath and said, "Onto payment, then."

That seemed to pull the king from his thoughts. "Yes," he said. "The agreed upon price is twenty-five thousand *crowns*. Half now and once we receive confirmation that you've upheld your side, the other half will be with a trusted representative in Maia for you to pick up."

Eli stuck out her hand. "All right," she said and, when the queen took Eli's hand in hers, she wasn't surprised when she didn't meet her eyes.

After the queen and king and their guards had retreated to their castle, behind the walls of Mythshade, Arden helped lead the prisoner onto the decks of *The Altean*.

A few other things were loaded onto the ship—barrels of clean water, crates of food and bottled drink and clothes. Then the gangplank was brought in, the ship untied from the dock, and they sailed away, leaving the shores of Breton behind them.

Eli had the prisoner taken to her quarters, where he sat with the bag over his head and chains around his ankles and wrists until the country was behind them.

When the bag was removed, Eli and Kiara took in sharp breaths. This wasn't an ordinary prisoner. He wasn't someone that was caught on the streets of Mythshade. He wasn't a commoner at all. He was the Crown Prince, Aris.

He stared up at them, his eyes light. There was a new bruise under one, a healing cut on his cheek. His dark hair was a mess, sticking up in all directions. It looked as though he was ready to spit at them, and if not for the gag in his mouth, he probably would have.

Kiara looked at Eli and moved to untie the gag.

"Wait," Eli said. Kiara's fingers stilled just as she was about to touch the knot at the base of the prince's skull. "Aris, we're going to take the gag off. But if you attempt to hurt us in any way, we will replace it and the bag. Do you understand?"

Aris made a noise deep in his throat that sounded like a growl, but then he nodded.

Kiara was gentle when she pulled the fabric from his mouth, and Aris watched as she dropped it into a bin by the desk. "Thank you," he said, his teeth gritted.

Eli leaned against the desk and crossed her arms over her chest. "Are you hungry?"

Aris let out a huff of breath. He didn't answer right away. Instead, he looked around the room. The bed was unmade and half hidden behind a swath of green fabric hung from the ceiling. His eyes caught on a collage of miniature paintings hung near the door. He rolled his blue eyes as he looked back at the captain.

"Of course I'm hungry. You think they fed me enough in those dungeons?"

Eli shrugged a shoulder. "I've never been in a dungeon, so I don't know what they do in them." She nodded to Kiara, who hurried to the kitchen. The crew had eaten lunch shortly before docking at Breton and, thankfully, Arden hadn't cleaned up yet. Kiara piled a plate with food and quickly went back to the cabin she shared with Eli.

When she entered, the smell of rice and potatoes filled the cabin. Aris held a tin cup in his still chained hands to his lips, his head tilted back. Water dripped from the corner of his mouth and down his throat. Kiara set the plate down on the desk in front of him and sat behind him on a plush blue chair.

Aris couldn't eat with his hands bound, so his left hand was let free from the fetter, and he was given a spoon to eat with. The potatoes were hot and steam rose from the bed of rice. Brown gravy had been drizzled over the plate and, when he was finished with the food, Aris picked up the plate and licked it clean.

As he ate, Eli explained to him his circumstances. She told him that her ship had been hired to take him to the Isles of the Damned.

He wiped the back of his hand across his mouth and looked up at Eli, who had been standing and watching him eat. She lifted a dark eyebrow.

"Now what?" he asked, his tone bored.

Eli moved around to the back of the desk and placed her hands on top. "Now we can do one of two things. You get to decide which of those two things we'll do. All right?"

Aris gave a grunt of assent.

"Choice one: we lock you in the hold. Water whenever you need it, food on the same schedule as the crew. Your cell will have a cot and blanket. A lantern will be lit for you during the day. In the morning and evening, just after sunrise and just before sunset, you'll get half an hour on deck, your wrists and ankles bound. You'll have a bucket for your business that you'll empty and clean during your time on deck." She paused. "Or, choice two: you're given most of the same privileges as the rest of the crew. You're given chores and you're not bound during the day. At night, you'll get a hammock in the crew's quarters. During the night, you will be bound, but by rope, not chains. Water whenever needed and you get to eat with all of us. For all intents and purposes, you are a part of this crew." She looked at Aris, waiting for his answer. When it didn't come, she said, "Well?"

Aris looked bored; his eyes half closed. He ran his left hand through his dark hair, smoothing it down over the crown of his head. "I can be a prisoner, or I can be a crew member? Those are my two options?" He'd shifted in the seat so he was leaning back, his legs out as far as they could go with the chains still linking him to his right hand.

"Yes," Eli said simply.

"And if I choose to join your crew, what will happen in the end? When you deliver me to the Isles of the Damned? Am I still a crew member, or am I just free labor that you toss out when you tire of me?" Aris leaned forward, resting his elbows on his knees. He looked every bit an arrogant prince, even in his tattered and dirty clothes.

Eli's face never changed. "We were hired to do a job. And it will be done. You may think us cruel, Aris, but I'm only following orders. Your mother—the queen—told us to leave you there, presumably to drown or starve or die of thirst or be eaten by whatever guards those tiny islands. But, when we get there, if you wish, we will give you a merciful death. It's more than your parents are giving you."

Aris scoffed. "So, you're saying I should be grateful?"

"No. But life gives us circumstances that we can't always bargain our way out of. While our fates may be sealed for us, we can decide how we get there. And if you wish to go to your death as a prisoner, so be it. But if you want to live your last weeks as a crew member, with freedoms the people in your parents' dungeons only dream of, we can give you that, too."

They stared at each other, sizing the other up.

Finally, Aris sat back and let his head rest on the back of the chair. "I don't wish to be a prisoner. I don't wish to die either, but I suppose my mother and father have decided that's the best way to deal with their son, so here we are." He didn't sound defeated but resolved.

"Then there's something we must do before we get you on deck and introduce you to the crew," Eli said. She walked around the desk, plunging one hand deep into the pocket of her green coat.

Aris lifted his eyes and watched her.

"Take off these chains."

The first few days with Aris on board passed without incident. He didn't complain about his binds at night, and he was helpful during the day. He was stronger than he looked, and he helped unfurl the sails and restock the ship's supplies on the days they docked. He wasn't allowed in port towns, or to leave the ship at all, of course. But he would make himself busy by cleaning the deck or mending clothes while the others were in town.

After a week, Ophelia noticed one of her knives missing.

She mentioned it to Eli one day while the captain sat with Kiara at the bench on deck. "Maybe you left it somewhere?" Eli suggested.

Ophelia hummed, running her hands over the spot where the knife would settle against her thigh. "I don't think so. It's not one I use often, but I could have sworn I put it back last time I used it."

When it wasn't found in the piles of blankets and pillows she and Ezra shared, or in the supply room, or in the kitchen, she conceded that she'd lost it or given it away and forgotten.

A few days later, Arden told Eli one of his spices was missing. "There wasn't much," he said. "And it's harmless, but…" he trailed off.

"What is it, Arden?"

"It looks like powdered Adelia's Mold." A poison that could cause hallucinations, madness, and death.

Eli ran her hand over the back of her neck. "What is it really?"

Arden shrugged. "Cinnamon. Surprisingly, they smell very similar."

Once a week, Eli, Kiara, and Aris had dinner together. Less as a courtesy and more as a check-in, to make sure Aris was still helpful and behaving.

Their tea was strong that night, spiced and warm. Eli and Kiara excused themselves early, after only a few sips of tea, saying they were feeling more tired than usual. Aris left them, his mouth quirked ever so slightly at the corners.

The morning after, Aris joined the rest of the crew on deck and, when Eli and Kiara stepped from their cabin, they couldn't help but notice the flash of surprise across his face that he tried to hide.

The rest of the day, Aris worked alongside Ezra and Ophelia, checking inventory and taking stock of their remaining supplies. The ship was coming up on a port town and Eli wanted to stock up so they could make as few stops as possible on their way to the Isles.

Kiara and Eli sat in their quarters. Kiara was voicing her concerns about this job. About how wrong it felt to leave someone to die. To have taken this job at all was ridiculous, but Eli waved her hand. She was saying it would be fine in the end. And despite his slip-ups thus far, he was helpful on board. She was about to say something else, but there was a knock at the door.

Ezra walked in, holding Aris, whose wrists were bound in front of him. Ophelia held a handkerchief to her neck, her face pinched and worried.

"While we were checking the dried meat, Ezra left to check stock with Arden in the galley," Ophelia told them once she was sitting. Ezra stood with Aris behind her, his arms crossed over his chest. "I had just put the lid back on the crate I'd been checking when Aris pushed me against the wall." Her voice was quiet as she touched the spot on her throat where Aris pressed the tip of her missing knife. "He threatened to cut my throat."

"Why didn't you call for Ezra?" Eli asked.

Ophelia swallowed. "He's still my prince," Ophelia said. "I don't live in Breton anymore, but I didn't want to risk something happening to Evey if I retaliated."

"What happened next?" Kiara pressed a clean piece of gauze to the cut on Ophelia's throat.

"I hoped that Ezra, or Arden, or Lex, or someone would come down, to need a scoop of sugar, or more thread, or a book. I remembered Ezra's story of a ship needing a new deckhand, and how Eli had said she didn't put up any flyers, but the ship must have decided they needed him. It's silly, but I asked the ship to send someone." She wiped her eyes with the back of her hand. "Ezra returned then." She looked over her shoulder at him.

"He burned me," Aris spat. Ophelia flinched at his outburst.

Eli glanced up at him. "I didn't see any burns. Kiara?"

Kiara gingerly took Aris's wrist in her hands. The skin over his wrists was red from struggling against the rope Ezra had tied around them, but there were no burns. She turned back to the captain and shook her head.

Eli looked back at Ophelia. "Are you all right?"

Ophelia nodded, a new bandage over the cut on her throat.

"Good." Eli's gaze softened, and she said, "You would not have gotten in trouble for standing up for yourself. And nothing would have happened to your sister. I'm sorry that you were hurt."

Ophelia wiped her hand over her face and nodded. "Thank you, Captain."

She left with Ezra, his arm around her shoulders, his head close to hers, whispering comforts in her ear.

Once the door closed behind them, Eli stood and walked to stand in front of the banished prince, her arms folded across her chest. "So," she said.

Aris stared at her, his face blank and eyes heavy-lidded. "So."

"I was really hoping for better from you, Aris." She spoke to him like a mother would talk to her child. As if he was small and all he'd done was steal a cookie, instead of threaten a member of her crew.

"From me?" he asked, genuinely surprised. "That was your first mistake, Captain. Tell me, did dear Mummy and Dad tell you what I did to deserve to die?"

"No," Eli said. "And I don't care. When you were brought onto my ship, you said you'd behave. You said you'd act as crew member. You said you'd do as you were asked. *Tell me*, did someone ask you to attack Ophelia?"

Aris scoffed. "How lucky of me to be part of a crew that will desert one of their own on an island rumored to be inhabited by monsters, left to die."

Eli raised her hand and slapped him. Kiara gasped where she stood, flinching against the sharp sound. Aris's head whipped to the side and when he looked at her again, a red welt was rising on his cheek.

"You..." Aris started, his teeth clenched.

Eli cut him off. "Don't. My crew members are my family. And we were prepared to treat you as such. But family doesn't turn against each other the way you did. Family doesn't hurt each other."

Aris pressed his tongue into the cheek that had been slapped. "Funny. Wasn't it my family that hired you to kill me because they couldn't?"

Eli stared at him, a muscle twitching in her temple. Then she yelled, "Arden!"

The door opened moments later, the tall and wide man silhouetted in the frame. "Captain?"

"Take Aris below. Chain him up. Give him water and nothing else." Her voice was rueful, as if she hated what she was doing to him. As if he hadn't just tried to kill one of the members of her crew. "No deck privileges. Hardtack and dried fruit only, twice a day." She gave Aris one last look as Arden stepped up to him and put his hand on his shoulder. "You know, Aris," she said. "If you'd shown yourself worthy, I would have kept you on as crew. We wouldn't have taken you to the Isles at all."

His eyes were full of fire, but Aris was quiet as he was taken below.

FORTY-TWO

T HE WEEKS FOLLOWING WERE harsh. The weather was unseasonably stormy. The endless rain and crashing waves paired with Aris's screams through the night were enough to drive most of the crew members to madness.

"What do we do?" Kiara asked, as she and Eli ate in their shared quarters. Rain ran down the panes of the windows in rivers. The lantern light swayed as the ship rocked against the waves.

Eli shrugged. "Our job," she said simply. "I'm not sure there's much more we can do." The food Arden had made smelled good, but Kiara could tell how hard it was for the captain to chew, to swallow. Eli put her fork down.

"Do you think he deserves to die?" Kiara ran her spoon around her still-full bowl.

From below their feet, Aris's screams filtered through the boards. It was hard to drown out the sound, no matter which part of the ship they occupied. Kiara felt for the crew, who were much closer to him than she and her captain.

"Not for what he did to Ophelia, no. He doesn't deserve to be part of this crew, but I'm not the one that's been given the right to pass judgment. His parents did, and they must have a reason. *We* are not the ones killing him."

Kiara reached across the small table they sat at and put her hand in Eli's. The captain's fingers were callused from years at sea; pulling ropes, folding and unfurling sails, waxing the deck, from hundreds of years at Kiara's side. Despite them, Kiara knew how soft Eli's touch was against her cheek.

" Are we no better than Aris's parents for abandoning him at the Isles?"

"It's our job, Kiara."

"We have plenty of uncompleted jobs under our belts."

In all their years together, of course there had been disagreements. Disagreements over which cheese to buy, which fabric was softest, disagreements over who should join the crew and disagreements over which jobs to take. But they'd never disagreed over the lives of people. They'd been given their lives—and each other—to save and protect people, not to choose who was worthy enough to be saved.

"Did you mean what you said to him? That you would have offered him a spot on our crew if he'd have earned it?" Kiara dipped her head to meet Eli's eyes, but the captain kept her eyes trained on the table in front of her.

"Yes," she said. Finally, she looked up, her green eyes intense. "I hoped he would make it. Hoped that the rumors out of Breton were false." Eli stood, and Kiara's hand fell to the table.

Kiara pulled her hand back and placed it in her lap, leaving her food untouched on the table. "You know I will go with you no matter what you choose, Eli."

Eli turned to her. They were soulbound, forever. They'd be together until their dying breaths. And, with a little planning, and a lot of luck, that wouldn't be for a very long time. "I know, heart," she said, her green eyes shining.

"What's our course?" Kiara hoped it was something different, something away from the Isles. To Maia, or back to Breton, or to Sulesia.

But Eli said, "Onward, to the Isles."

Kiara wasn't surprised. But her heart hurt, nonetheless.

The day came when they were just a stone's throw from the Isles of the Damned. The grouping of small swampy islands was named for its popularity for abandoning things or people. There were rumors of a sea serpent that guarded the islands, swallowing anything that got too close. Only the damned would travel here, risking getting caught in the swells and whirlpools between the islands, or by the serpent.

The air was thick with fog and some of the crew—Ophelia and Lex and Ezra—watched the water around the hull of the ship, waiting to see if the serpent would show its head.

An hour after the anchor was dropped, Aris was brought out, dark circles under his eyes, wearing the same chains he arrived in, more than a month earlier in Breton.

He walked to Eli, his chin held high in defiance. If he had been able to, he would have looked down his nose at her. "Are you going to offer me that easier death you promised?"

"Would you take it?"

The air seemed to grow heavier around them. "No." He let Arden lead him to the side of the ship where he stepped into the dinghy waiting there and sat, his eyes never leaving the brightening horizon.

Ezra climbed in after Aris, after he'd taken a breath to steel himself. Arden lowered them to the water. Ophelia stood at the railing, watching, a knife clutched in her hand, ready to throw it if Aris moved.

But he didn't, and when Arden climbed the rope ladder down to join Aris and Ezra, Aris lifted his eyes to the sky. His lips moved in silent prayer. Who he was praying to, no one knew. The god of life and death had given life to Aris's executioners. And the only goddess who offered protection was notorious for not answering.

The energy on the ship while Arden and Ezra were gone was buzzing with anxiety. Would the serpent swallow their friends? Would Aris try to tip the boat, causing them to fall into the water and be swept away by the current? Would they get lost in the fog?

Kiara stood by Eli, watching the spot where the little boat had disappeared fifteen minutes before. "Do you think he'll attack them?"

Eli turned to Kiara. "No," she said. "He refused his meals the last few days. He's too weak." It was a logical answer, though the situation they were in was not logical at all. Why had their ship been commissioned to deliver a prince to his death? Why not a prisoner ship or a smuggler's ship? Perhaps Breton's queen and king thought it was less likely *The Altean* would be ambushed.

Another thirty minutes passed before Ezra and Arden made it back to the ship. Eli, who hadn't voiced any worry, let out a breath and relaxed her shoulders when she saw Ezra trailing his fingers in the water.

He and Arden climbed up the rope ladder and together hauled up the boat. As Arden secured it again, he said to Eli, "He didn't fight." He sounded dumbfounded. "He let us tie him to the tree. He didn't even speak."

Eli put her hand on Arden's tattooed arm. She said nothing, just offered comfort with a nod of her head.

FORTY-THREE

Wᴡʀᴇɴ'ꜱ ʜᴇᴀʀᴛ ᴊᴀᴄᴋʀᴀʙʙɪᴛꜱ ᴀɢᴀɪɴꜱᴛ her ribs. She lies awake in the bed, the spot next to her vacant, staring up at the drapes of faded red velvet across the ceiling. Though her head hurts and her tongue is dry, she can't bring herself to reach over and grab the flask of water on the nightstand.

What if Kiara's right? What if what Aris had told her is wrong? She thinks back to his story and compares it to Kiara's. They were similar, but different enough to raise concerns. Opposite sides of the same coin. Mirrored images. She shakes her head.

Why would he lie? What did he have to gain?

Everything, she thinks. Aris had lied to gain her trust, to gain her loyalty. To turn her away from the crew of *The Altean.* To make it so he was the victim, instead of the people he'd killed.

She still isn't sure those people didn't deserve it. The throne was Aris's by birthright, and the threat of his life being lost for his sister to take over was a valid fear. But he shouldn't have lied to her. It wasn't the story she cared about—it was him. She's sure now; her pull to him had nothing to do with the power he was promising her, but to *him*.

She pushes the blankets from her and swings her legs over the side of the bed. The flask on the stand is half empty, and she drains it in two swallows. She knows she needs to confront Aris. Not because of what he lied about, but because he felt the need to lie at all.

The cloak Aris gave her hangs by the door, and she pulls it on, clasping it at her throat. She almost pulls the sheet from the mirror to check her hair, to see how dark the bags under her eyes have grown, but she decides she doesn't care. Aris isn't drawn to her for her looks. She's not sure why he's drawn to her at all, perhaps the power she could have in Sulesia, or the way she left her friends for him. It doesn't matter, she's here now.

Aris and Ramsey stand on the quarterdeck, its boards damp under their feet. One of Ramsey's big hands grips the wheel, and he laughs at something Aris says.

She joins them after refilling her flask from a barrel below decks. It's cooler than most of the water she's had since leaving *The Altean*. She takes a little in her cupped hands and splashes it against her face.

"You look well this morning," Aris says to her.

She knows it's not true. Even without seeing herself in the mirror, she knows her face is pale, her brown irises surrounded by a ring of red. "Thank you," she says. "Has breakfast been served yet?"

Aris declines his head to the main deck, where the cook's assistant, a skinny boy barely older than Grace, is carrying a tray. "Here it comes now."

Wren smiles and turns, the cloak catching in the breeze coming from the sea. "Good. I'll see you inside."

Their breakfast is made up of thick batter cakes with sweet syrup and two pork sausages. The only sound as they eat are their forks and knives on the plate they share. The food helps settle Wren's anxiety, but her head is still pounding and her heart still races.

When the plate has been scraped clean and the tray has been taken away, Wren says, "Kiara visited me last night."

Aris raises his split eyebrow. "That's who've you been seeing?" So, he had noticed she'd been visited, as Ramsay warned he would. "And what did she have to say?"

Wren hadn't taken the cloak off when she'd come back in the room and she pulls it tighter around herself now. "She showed me what happened on *The Altean*. When you were on board."

Aris takes a slow breath through his nose, the only sign that he's heard her. After a moment of quiet, he says, "And?"

Wren feels like her heart is going to leap from her chest. "Why did you lie to me?"

Aris's pale eyes search her face for what feels like ages before he leans forward in his chair and puts his elbows on the top of his desk. "I didn't lie to you."

Wren clenches her teeth together. She wills her heart to slow down. She shakes her head. "You're lying to me now. Aris, you don't have to lie to me. I don't—"

He cuts her off by standing up, knocking the chair over. "I was scared!" he yells. "Is that what you want to hear?"

Wren flinches, but she doesn't back down. "Are you telling me the truth? Or is that a lie, too?"

He stares at her for a moment, his chest heaving with his breaths. There's a splotch of red spreading up his neck. "Ramsey!" he calls.

In moments, the giant is standing in the door frame. "Sir?"

Aris nods in Wren's direction. "Take her below. Use the chains." He turns from them.

Ramsey doesn't hesitate. He grins like he's been waiting for this moment as he yanks Wren from the chair and holds her arms at her sides.

"Wait!" she yells. "Aris, please!"

He doesn't look as she's dragged from the room.

FORTY-FOUR

RAMSEY PULLS WREN BEHIND him across the deck as she screams at the door to Aris's cabin. Any second, she thinks he'll open it and say, "Wait. It was all a joke. Come, have some tea." But Aris isn't one for jokes, and he doesn't start now. And why would he? She's accused him of lying and he's never hidden his cruelties from her before. Except those were always against someone else—a member of his crew, the dock workers in the port towns they stopped in, the people in Breton.

When Aris doesn't appear, she tries calling out to people on deck. They all busy themselves, hurrying down below or up to the quarterdeck. None of them look at her. She shouts at Smith, sure he'll at least look her way. But he only flinches and turns away from her, his shoulders slumping against her calls.

The hold is dark and chilly, with water puddling on the floor. She pleads with Ramsey as he fastens the chains around her wrists, her ankles, and then the pole in the middle of the small room.

"Ramsey, please. Don't leave me down here. I was just—"

He shoves her hands away and spits at her feet. "You're lucky the captain doesn't feed you to the sharks," he says. Then he leaves, slamming the door behind him, causing the lantern on the wall to sway.

The lantern's weak light leaves the room in deep shadow. It's small, no more than a hundred square feet. A bucket sits in the corner, though she's not sure the chains binding her to the post are long enough for her to reach it.

The cloak is still around her shoulders and she's grateful Aris or Ramsey didn't rip it from her before putting her here. It's thick and warm—at least for now—but she knows it won't be of much help once the sun sets and the temperature drops. The water on the floor clings to the bottom and the hem is already heavily wet.

She notices a nail above her head on the post and is glad the chains around her wrists aren't hung from it. She's not sure if that was an oversight or a small mercy on Ramsey's part. She's grateful Aris let her eat both of the sausages at breakfast. Without knowing when she'll eat again, the extra protein he's given her will help keep her strength up.

Above her, she can hear the crew getting on with their chores and games. None of their conversations make sense to her ears, and she's glad she can't hear their speculations about her and her current status. Her cheeks heat as she remembers their faces as she was dragged down here. Not a single glance her way, as if all those weeks playing games with them meant nothing.

And why should they? She wasn't playing with them to gain companionship. She was doing it to avoid Kiara.

As the day goes on, she circles the post until the chains stop her from going further, then she turns around and circles the other way. The water on the cloak creeps up to her knees by midday and she takes it off, hanging it on the nail on the post. She warms her skin just enough to get rid of the chill, but no more. She tries to make a light blade, to cut through the metal of her chains, but the blade doesn't get hot enough to melt it. After a few failed attempts, she gives up. She can't afford to lose her energy so early. Who knows how long she'll be down here, who knows how long Aris's anger will burn.

Once she's run through all the possible ways out and surrenders that she's stuck down here, she leans against the post. As she'd expected, she can't reach the bucket in the corner of the room. Eventually, she pulls the cloak down and tries to use it as leverage to get the bucket closer to her. It works, but the fabric is even wetter than it had been before.

She upturns the bucket, which has a thick layer of an unknown black solid inside, and sits down. *Better the fabric a little more wet now than soaked when I fall over from exhaustion later*, she thinks, wringing out the cloak as best she can.

The pockets of the cloak are empty, except for the little dropper bottle of dandelion sap in the inner pocket. She flips the bottle in her fingers, watching as the sap clings to the sides. Ophelia's voice pushes through her thoughts as she remembers their conversation on the deck in Loksa.

How are you going to get close enough to give it to them?

That's your job.

Oh! I like this side of you.

In twenty-four hours, we'll have a poison worth giving a shit over.

Wren smiles, her throat clenching. The memory of Ophelia's laughter washes over her like a tidal wave. She slips the bottle back in her pocket and leans her head against the pole at her back.

As she expected, the temperature drops significantly in the hold once the sun goes down. She can tell when it does, though there are no windows showing the sea or sky. Above her, the boot falls on deck have all but ceased as the crew gathers into their nightly groups. The rattle of dice on the boards brings her little comfort. The crew's disregard has all but destroyed any of the good memories she has of playing with them. Still, with Aris in his cabin tonight, maybe one of them will take pity on her and bring her something other than the water at her feet.

Those hopes are bashed almost as soon as she thinks it. A pair of booted feet stop right above her.

"Crew!" Aris says. He must be yelling pretty loudly for her to be able to make out his words. "Our guest, the daughter of the Duke of Sulesia, Wrennley Newbury, is no longer a welcome addition to our crew." He pauses to let the crew take in his words. "As of today, she is a prisoner. She will be treated as such until she can learn to behave and respect the authority that has been placed on me as captain. If I hear of anyone trying to help her, in any way, they will be thrown overboard and left to the mercy of the waves." She's been with him long enough to know he's smiling as he delivers the threat.

There are a few calls of agreement, a rumble of laughter, and cheers as Aris's footsteps recede.

A minute later, the door unlocks, and he's standing there, his body silhouetted against the lantern that Ramsey holds.

He saunters into the room, his hands clasped behind his back, and looks around. "This is dismal," he says, though he doesn't address Wren directly. When he looks at her, his eyes are cold. "You can be welcomed back into my bed, you know. It's warmer there. Less," he looks around and kicks a bit of the water toward her, making her flinch when it hits her face, "wet."

Wren stays sitting on the bucket, the cloak pulled around her. "Will you tell me the truth?"

He stops moving and stares down at her. "I did tell you my truth, Wren." It comes out as a growl.

She looks away from him and focuses on a knot in the wood. "Then I don't need your bed."

Aris takes in a sharp breath through his nose. After a moment where she can feel his rage pressing against her skin, he turns and leaves, but not before he says, "Take the lantern."

Ramsey lets his captain pass him and reaches into the room. He unhooks the lantern, closes the door, and locks it behind him. Wren is left in darkness.

FORTY-FIVE

She stays awake that night, a ball of light clutched in her hand, sending a soft yellow glow around her. The light holds no heat, and Wren shivers against the night pressing in around her. As the night wears on, the rattle of dice above her ceases and the crew slowly make their way to their quarters, their drunken laughter floating to her through the ceiling.

The hold where she's kept is down another set of stairs from the crews' quarters, next to the buckets they use as latrines and the storage room where their barrels and crates of smuggled goods are kept. A few people descend the stairs to the toilets, but none of them stop near her door or make any indication they know she's there. One person belches and spills something before they groan and make their way back up the stairs. She calls out to them, but no one answers.

Wren can feel herself succumbing to her exhaustion. How is she more tired sitting in this room than when she was climbing the rigging all day in the sun with Lex? Than when she walked an entire city with Ezra and Ophelia? She takes one last look at the light in her hand before she lets it fade into nothing.

Wren wakes the next morning to her stomach grumbling. She presses her palm to her belly and closes her eyes against the nausea. The room around her is cold, but she's able to warm herself to stave off the chill.

The crew above her starts to stir, plopping their heavy boots on the floor as they stand from their strung hammocks or stand up from their cots. She wonders if Aris is awake, if he'll come to her. Despite herself, her chest aches for him. She tries to push any hope away of his favor, tries to hold on to any scorn she might feel for him, but no matter how much she tries, she can't find any.

Still sitting on the overturned bucket, she rests her elbows on her knees and puts her head in her hands. She calls out to Adreus, to Iros, to the goddess of family, Zatia. Even to Emelia. But no one comes to her rescue.

The days bleed together. The only way to mark time is by the rattle of dice on the boards above her. But once, she falls asleep and misses them, and her days fall over each other like dominoes.

She had been okay for a little while, able to warm her arms and neck and legs with her magics. But now, her body is tired and sore from sitting on the bucket or walking in circles around the post. Her ankles are spared from sores by her boots, but her wrists are raw and red from the rough metal of the fetters rubbing against her skin. She can't gather enough energy to heal them anymore.

Kiara hasn't visited her. Wren had called out to her, prayed for her, every time she felt sleep coming, but neither the gods nor Kiara listened. But of course Kiara hadn't listened. Dream walkers can't hear past their own dreams, their own visitings. Maybe *The Altean* had abandoned her like she abandoned them. It's what she deserved, choosing Aris over them. Choosing cruelty and isolation over family and safety.

It's been days since she had any food. The only water she gets is what seeps through the wall when it rains or when the waves are high. Though the rainy season means cooler temperatures, she's glad she has something to wet her tongue, no matter how little it is.

Aris has visited every day, or every other day, Wren can't be sure. Every time, he invites her back to his bed, his voice like honey, then leaves with the door slamming when all she requests is the truth.

Today, she's barely able to keep her eyes open. Her head is pounding and the shadows swirling in the dark keep reaching their fingers out to graze her skin. Aris stands at the door, a lantern lit behind him.

She reaches for him, as far as the chains around her wrists will allow. "Aris, please. Don't do this. Don't leave me here. Let me...let me come with you." She doesn't ask for the truth. She doesn't care about it. His story and the story Kiara had told her mix in her mind, creating a new one. She's not sure which of the three she believes.

Aris looks down his nose at her. His pale eyes, so full of anger, so full of sorrow. He takes a deep breath through his nose. "No," he says. He turns and leaves, taking the lantern with him. When the door closes behind him, there's no light. Wren closes her eyes against it, against the monsters hiding in the corners, but it doesn't help. They scratch at her anyway, pull at her hair, and blow putrid breath into her face. Aris's boots on the boards above her head do little to scare them away.

He comes again, later. Wren isn't sure how much later. Hours, days, a month maybe. Time hasn't made sense to her in a while. All she can tell down here is when the ocean is angry, beating its waves hard against the hull of *The Basilisk*.

When Aris comes, he leaves a lantern by the door. It's scarcely enough light for him to see by, but even this little bit is too bright for Wren. How much longer would it have been before she went blind?

But, no. It couldn't have been as long as she thought. Aris's hair is the same length, his clothes the same as his last visit. There's still the small oil stain on his white shirt, where some of his breakfast must have dripped.

He kneels before her. "Wren." His voice is soft, as if he's speaking to a baby.

"Aris," she replies, tears gathering on her bottom lashes. She's helpless here, the chains digging into the skin at her wrists. Even her ankles have started to hurt from the constant weight around them. Despite it all, she's happy to see him.

His hand grazes the skin along her jaw, brushes away a tear that has fallen over her cheek. She leans into his touch. "I'm sorry," he says. "I shouldn't have chained you up down here. Would you like to go up to my quarters?"

Something nags at the back of her mind, but she can't quite grasp it. She nods. Her throat is too dry to speak.

"Are you going to behave?"

"Yes," she rasps.

"Do you promise?"

"Anything." She means it.

FORTY-SIX

IT'S WARMER IN ARIS'S cabin. Sun-warmed wood and velvet. Where had he gotten these cotton sheets? Wren doesn't let herself think about it too long. It's too warm, and she's too cold and tired. She'd drunk half a barrel of water when she'd first gotten back on deck. Then she'd promptly vomited it all back up over the side of the ship. Aris had rubbed circles between her shoulder blades, keeping her long hair out of the line of fire. Then, once she'd been changed and bandaged and tucked into his bed, he'd allowed her a few small sips of cool, clean, clear water. It was the sweetest water she'd ever had. She wants to ask for more now, but Aris sits at his desk looking at his maps, scratching his pen across a sheet of paper.

She closes her eyes and drifts off to sleep, dreaming of her garden in Sudal and the towns she had visited with Ezra and Ophelia. It's dangerous, she knows, but her dreams are her own.

At least, they used to be.

The next time she wakes, Aris is sitting in a chair beside the bed. "You're awake," he says.

"How long was I asleep?" Wren reaches for the cup she knows holds water.

Aris picks it up before she can and holds it just out of her reach. She tucks her arm back into the blankets.

"A couple of hours," he says, bringing the cup to her lips. As she drinks, he speaks quietly. "I hated locking you up." He sets the cup back on the side table and pushes the hair back from her forehead. "You never have to go back there again, as long as you don't question me." He looks at her, raises his eyebrows.

She nods, sleepy again. "All right," she promises. "I won't."

Wren stays in the room for a few days, the curtains pulled away from the windows to warm her skin. She eats her meals slowly until her stomach can handle the rich foods again. By the third day, she no longer wakes with a headache from dehydration and is no longer weak from what she learns was only six days in the hold.

Once she's able to stay awake for longer stretches, she realizes how angry she is for being put in the hold. It's not fair what Aris had done, locking her up for nearly a week for a simple question. But, as the days pass, she realizes how much Aris regrets his actions as well. He brings her food and feeds her when she's not strong enough to, gives her sips of water and pushes the hair from her face. He props her up on pillows and reads to her, makes a stop at port specifically to send Smith to get candy disks for her. He changes the bandages at her wrists and ankles until she's strong enough to heal the wounds herself. She was surprised to find her arms and cheeks uninjured; the shadows scratching at her had felt so real. Aris never says as much, but she knows he's sorry, and so he is easy to forgive.

It makes her think of a time with Jakob, when she was thirteen and he tripped her in front of the Kornesian king, causing her to spill her tea all down the front of her dress. Thankfully, it wasn't hot enough to scald, but she was wearing a dress that she and the duke had commissioned specifically for the king's visit. She was so angry, she wanted to shove Jakob down the stairs, but she refrained and bent to pick up the broken pieces of her cup.

She gathered the pieces in her skirts to keep her palms clear of the sharp edges, and as she reached for another piece, she was surprised to find another pair of hands reaching for the pieces, too. She expected it to be a servant, but when she looked up, it was Jakob's dark eyes looking back at her.

They worked in silence, picking up the pieces and then tossing them in the bin in Wren's room. Then, once she was changed, Jakob took the dress she'd been wearing and took it down to the laundry and tried to get the stain out himself.

By dinner that night, Wren wasn't as angry as she was before, and by dessert, she'd forgiven him completely. Like Aris, Jakob never apologized with words, but his actions made it obvious that he was sorry, and he was easily forgiven, too.

"Six days?" Wren asks. "It felt so much longer."

"It felt long to you, but it felt like an eternity to me." They sit across from each other at the desk, tea set up between them.

It's quiet for a few minutes as Aris prepares the cups. When he's finished and the chipped teacups are set in mismatched saucers in front of them, Wren says, "Why didn't you tell me the truth, Aris?" She had remembered the day after she'd been released from the hold what she'd been so adamant about knowing. The nagging hadn't quite left her alone, and after she'd slept and had some food and water, her mind was clear enough to recognize what it was that was pulling at her.

Aris stills. "What do you mean?"

Wren's tea sits on the desk in front of her. She had taken a few sips, but Aris had added too much sugar, and the water wasn't hot enough to dissolve the grains. "Why didn't you tell me the truth? Why did you tell me you were beaten and left without food or water?"

Aris is quiet, taking careful sips of his tea. Wren braces herself for what she knows might be a shout, another order to throw her back into the hold. But she holds her chin high and squares her shoulders, careful to keep the expression on her face soft.

When Aris speaks, it's not a shout, or an order, or even spoken aloud. It's a barely audible, "I was afraid."

This surprises Wren. He'd said as much before, but she assumed it was a farce, a way to gain her sympathy. Aris doesn't seem like the kind of person that would be afraid of something so trivial. "Of what?"

He looks at her, his eyebrows knit together. "In Breton, the people that wanted me dead said that I was weak. They said that's why Josie should have the throne, why I shouldn't." He takes a breath through his nose and looks down into his tea. "I didn't want you to think I was weak, too."

Wren lets out a soft laugh. She shakes her head. "I have seen what you're capable of. I have seen what you and Ramsey and your ship can do. Only a fool would think you weak, Aris. And I am no fool." She stands and circles around to the other side of the desk. The skin over Aris's jaw is cold under her fingers. "You don't need to lie to me, Aris. Just tell me the truth. Please."

Aris lifts his head and looks at her. "They treated me well, your friends. But I was angry. Angry that they'd choose to take someone and abandon them. They were leaving me to die."

Wren nods, tracing his jaw with her fingertips. "Will you tell me what really happened? The whole story?"

Aris shakes his head. "I can't," he says. Then, "But I can show you."

PART V

FORTY-SEVEN

"WHAT DO YOU MEAN?" Wren asks.

Aris nods at the chair she'd been sitting in. "Some dream walkers have the ability to share memories."

"Like Kiara did." She sits again in her chair.

"No," Aris says, shaking his head. "You were asleep for that. She showed you memories like a dream. But you don't have to be asleep for this." He pushes the water kettle and honey and sugar pots to one side of the desk and places his left arm on top, his palm facing up, offering it to Wren.

She takes it, tentative, unsure what to expect.

"Ready?" Aris asks. When she nods, he says, "Close your eyes."

Aris was blindfolded. He'd been arrested in the middle of the night, pulled from his bed by rough hands and shackled in chains in the dungeon of his family's home.

There was a trial, but he didn't have much voice. His parents—the people that were supposed to support him and keep him safe—had decided shortly after his arrest that he was guilty.

He wasn't denying it. He *was* guilty. He'd killed people. He'd hunted people down and killed them in their beds, or in the beds of their lovers, or watched as they choked on the drink that he'd poisoned.

But he'd done it to save himself, to secure his birthright. He loved his sister, doted on her as a baby, and played with her when they were children, but she wasn't the right choice for the throne. She didn't deserve the crown, the responsibility. She was young, and naïve, and soft. Aris should be the one to rule Breton. He should have been the only choice as the oldest child of the queen and king.

After the trial, his mother and father stood in front of the whole kingdom and said that their son was to be put to death. Aris was kept in the dark. He'd been given enough food and water to survive, but when he went to sleep every night, his stomach was growling, and his tongue was dry.

A week later, in the middle of the night, Aris was taken from his chains in the bowels of the castle and placed before his parents. They didn't tell him much, just that a ship was coming for him that day. They didn't answer any of his questions, didn't even react when he shouted at them. He wasn't allowed to see Josie.

Later that day, when the sun was high, Aris was taken to his family's private docks behind their home. A bag was placed over his head; he could only hear the cry of the gulls overhead.

He was loaded on a ship where, after setting sail from the docks, he met the captain, a tall woman named Eleanor, and her first mate, a short, round woman named Kiara. They couldn't have been any older than him. That almost made it worse. By their reaction, they hadn't been made aware the person they were transporting would be the prince.

Because his parents had told him nothing, he hoped that he had been sold to work on the boat. He didn't think he deserved it, but it was better than being hanged.

Eleanor and Kiara didn't let him think that for long. They explained to him he was going to be taken to the Isles of the Damned. There was sorrow and unsaid apologies in Eleanor's voice, but they didn't offer him an alternative. His fate had been sealed by the queen and king of Breton. By his parents.

Aris tried not to show any emotion other than boredom on his face, though the captain's confession surprised him. When he'd first been sentenced, he expected to be hung or shot by firing squad. The Isles of the Damned were the last place he would have wanted to take his final breaths.

Given the choice between seclusion or being part of the crew, Aris chose the only semblance of freedom he had left. He was unchained and given a change of clothes from a large trunk of things in the crew's quarters. He learned then that he was on *The Altean*, the fabled ship with the captain and her first mate that were given immortal life by Adreus. He wasn't sure he believed it—Eleanor and Kiara didn't seem like much. Why would the god of life and death give *them* such a gift?

When he was finished changing, Kiara introduced him to the other members of *The Altean*'s crew. They were all friendly, though apprehensive. He knew none of them knew his crimes,

Eleanor had said as much. He wondered what things they had conjured up to make his death sentence seem warranted.

That night, Aris lay in his hammock, anger turning his vision black. The Isles of the Damned were something every child had grown up to fear. Even in Breton, though the Isles were on the other side of the world, everyone thought of the Isles as a monstrous place, full of monstrous things. It was the worst place anyone could be sent.

A shiver ran down Aris's spine as he thought of the Isles. The Isles were made up of swampy islands, too small to be inhabited, in the northern Reidde Sea. No one that ended up there ever returned. He wondered if it would be exposure to the elements or the sea serpent rumored to guard the islands that would kill him.

He started to think of ways out of his sentence. Eleanor had said he would have more privileges if he promised to do his assigned chores and help out around the ship. And he had agreed. Giving free labor was better than rotting away in the hold.

As he lay in the hammock, the thought of subverting them started to form. He had been so close to usurping his parents. Surely it wouldn't be so hard to do to the captain and her first mate.

He had seen one of the girls—Ophelia, he thinks her name was—with a small armory's worth of knives, strapped to various parts of her body. Perhaps if he took one, he could use it in the night and slit all of their throats, taking the ship for his own.

The chances of that, killing them all before anyone woke, were slim, though. He fell asleep that first night, dreaming of his fingers dripping in blood.

The trip from Breton to the Isles of the Damned was long. Anytime the ship had to dock, Aris was kept on board. He was never chained or hidden, but Arden—a big man with a big chest who rarely talked—was charged with guarding the gangplank to make sure Aris didn't leave. Aris thought it unnecessary, he wasn't going to try to leave, anyway.

The first week was fine. He washed and mended, helped take stock of their goods. He slept in the hammock at night, his hands and ankles bound in rope. This, too, he thought unnecessary, but he didn't complain. At least not aloud. And though he was cooperative with the crew and captain, inside he boiled with rage, and the dream of dripping blood never went away.

One day, as he was cleaning the crew's quarters, he found a dropped knife between some blankets. He looked over his shoulder at the heap of blankets where the ship's Star Child slept, and when he was sure no one was looking, he slipped the knife into his trouser pocket.

Then, a few days later, while helping Ezra and Ophelia with stock by checking Arden's spice supply, he found an unmarked bottle. Its contents were red, and the dust stuck to the sides of the bottle when he shook it. There wasn't much, barely enough for dusting over a cup of tea. He was careful when he unscrewed the lid and gave the contents a sniff. He smiled and slipped the bottle into the other pocket of his trousers.

At the end of the second week, after an unsuccessful attempt on the captain's and first mate's lives, and another on Ophelia's, he was put in the hold. He was given water but was forced to live on hardtack and dried fruit. He screamed most of the night. Not out of fear, or even anger. The crew's quarters were just above him and he knew that his screams would keep them awake. If they were going to make his last weeks miserable, it was the least he could do in return.

A month later, Eleanor told Aris they'd arrive at the Isles the next day. He refused most of his meals the last few days, knowing they were getting close. He was given the choice of a last meal, but he refused that, too, instead choosing to spend his last night hungry.

When they put anchor down at the Isles, Aris was brought on deck. Eleanor and Kiara, Ophelia and Lex were on board, along with his chaperones, Arden and Ezra. The others had stayed below deck, not looking at him when he walked by the crew's quarters. They had to know it was his last day. They had to know even if they didn't actively participate in his abandonment, his death would still be on their hands.

The night before, as he lay on the floor, his hands chained at the wrist, he decided to go to his death with dignity. His parents could think he was a murderer, a traitor, an anarchist, but they'd have to live with the decision to kill their son. He wouldn't give them the satisfaction of saying he was uncooperative in the end.

So, he'd gone with dignity and as much grace as he could muster. And, despite how badly he wanted not to be, he was frightened. These lands were unknown to many, especially to him. The only thing he knew about them was the monster that was said to patrol the waters, swallowing anything that got too near.

Breton was not a powerful country, but his parents were loved. The people revered them, calling them the best rulers in generations. But Aris wasn't. Maybe that was the difference. An unloved first child of the most loved queen and king.

What had he done to deserve this hatred? In recent years, he'd been cruel, but only because his life was in danger. But before then, before there were threats to his life, what had he done to warrant such dislike?

That first day in town, when he was twelve, it was like nothing he'd ever imagined. The people welcomed him, but only out of obligation, not out of love. He'd seen their fake smiles, the way they hid their ambiguity behind their hands. People would never have told him as much, but he could tell he was not the favorite. Josie was asked after everywhere. "How is your sister?" "Is the princess well?" "How does Princess Josie take her tea?" At first, he was happy to answer their questions. Josie was his favorite person in the world. He spoke about her with reverence, like her six-year-old self was a goddess in human form. But by the third place he visited, her name started to taste like vinegar, instead of honey. The picture in his mind of her tarnished, like the silver plate in front of him.

Aris left home promising to tell Josie all about Mythshade and the people he would one day rule over and would return never to speak to her again.

As he stepped into the dinghy with Ezra and was lowered to the surface of the ocean, he thought of Josie, alone in her room, sitting at her window seat, looking down over their city. The water was smooth. The air was still, a thick fog floating over the water. There was no sun to close his eyes against as he lifted his face and prayed. Then he watched Arden climb down the rope ladder over the side of the ship and into the dinghy.

Aris couldn't see *The Altean*, but he stared straight ahead, imagining it becoming a dot on the horizon as he was rowed into the fog.

FORTY-EIGHT

WHEN THEY REACHED AN island with a sizable tree, Aris stepped out and sat against the trunk. He waited as Ezra and Arden tied him to it. Then they got back in the dinghy and looked at him. Ezra looked like he wanted to say something but changed his mind and turned his face from Aris, looking back toward where the ship waited.

Arden, though, watched Aris for a long moment before he asked, "Do you want us to deliver a message to anyone for you?"

Aris always asked the people he killed if they had any last words. Almost all of them did, and most of them were always pleas for their life. There were occasionally the ones that spit in his face and told him he was a monster, a traitor, a coward.

And then there were those that had nothing to say. Some just cried, some screamed, some stared into his eyes as their throat was cut. Aris found himself like the latter, with nothing to say. He thought of his sister and what he might say to her but pushed her from his mind. He just stared at Arden until the giant broke eye contact and started rowing back to *The Altean.*

Aris didn't die immediately, like he'd hoped. He had eaten and drunk just enough on the ship to ensure he wasn't so weak that he'd pass out as soon as the ship left him. The only thing that threatened was the sun. Having burned the fog away, it beat down on him hard. The leaves above him did little to block its rays. He only hoped it would move quickly across the sky and he could be left in the shade of the tree's trunk.

A few days passed and, as he grew closer and closer to death, he started noticing things. At night, he heard something moving through the waves in front of him. He felt things scratching his neck, his arms, his cheeks. But the next day, when the sun rose, he saw nothing on his skin. He prayed endlessly to Emelia, the goddess of protection, asking for her to spare him. He knew she usually didn't respond, and he had no way of making a sacrifice to her, but he prayed anyway.

Nearly a week after being left, Aris closed his eyes, thinking it was the last time he would. But a few hours later, he woke up and was startled to see a man in front of him. He shrunk back against the trunk of the tree, pressing his back so hard into the bark he thought it would slice him through his shirt. He feared this man was one of the clay monsters that were said to guard the beaches north of the mountain ranges in Maia. But this man couldn't be made of clay. His skin wasn't cracked, his movements didn't seem laborious or strained. He looked like a normal man, flesh and blood and breath.

"Hello," the man said. He was handsome, his light hair flopped a little over his forehead; when he smiled, his eyes crinkled at the corners. He had a scar through his left eyebrow, cutting it in half just over his dark iris.

Aris didn't respond. He knew the sun and lack of food and water could cause his brain to make things up. He didn't want to give this any of his energy, knowing how little he had left.

But the man didn't disappear. He stayed with Aris. He brought water and pieces of things to eat. It was never a lot, never enough to build up any strength. But it kept him alive.

The man talked to him. He told Aris about himself. He was in the navy, and his ship had gone down not too far from the Isles. He'd managed to swim to an island. But he'd taken in too much water in his lungs and, without food and fresh water, without a healer, had died.

This took Aris by surprise. But when he looked closer, he could see that the man looked different than a living man should. The beds of his nails and his lips were tinted blue. His eyes were red around his dark irises. His skin was translucent and riddled with burst veins and bruises and scars.

"You're a spirit." It wasn't a question.

The man looked out over the water. "Yes," he said. "I'm fading. I don't remember anything from before my ship sank. I don't know how long I've been here for, but I know I don't have much longer."

Aris knew that feeling. Not the forgetting, but the fading, the not knowing. "Is this what's going to happen to me?"

When the man didn't answer, Aris's heart started beating quickly in his chest. But then the man shook his head. "This happens when you're holding on. There had to be something or someone that I clung to in death. Not physically, there's no other body near mine. But," he trailed off. "I don't know. There's someone out there that I tried to hold on to." The man reached into the pocket of his dark trousers and pulled out a small, square canvas. The water had soiled all but a dark orange splotch where the paint had been so thickly applied, it had seeped into the canvas and stained it.

"A soulbind?" Aris asked. He'd never known anyone soulbound. He wasn't even sure what it meant, other than what it implied: one's soul was bound to another.

The man turned to face Aris. Already, Aris could see him fading further. He could see through the man's skin to the shadows of his bones.

"I don't know," the man says, taking one last look at the canvas before placing it back in his pocket. He looks back over the water. "If that's the case, I hope they're doing okay."

Aris was quiet. Then he asked, "Is there anything you can do?" His mortality was looking him right in the eye. He didn't want to end up like this man, fading and forgotten.

The man's mouth pinched at the corners. He stared at the horizon for a few minutes, dragging his nearly translucent fingertips through the sand. "There might," he paused. He shook his head, then started again. "There might be one thing."

"What is it?" Aris asked. His hands were still bound in chains, the rope still around his middle under his arms.

The man looked at him again. "I've heard stories of spirits tethering themselves to another soul. I would give you whatever is left of my life. It might not matter, you'll probably still die out here." A breath forced itself out through his teeth. "But it might give you long enough for a ship to come by to dump something. They might take pity on you."

Aris didn't hesitate. He pushed up as much as he could, cringing at the pain in his tailbone. "Do it." Even a few extra days would defy his parents, defy the captain and crew of *The Altean*. Even if he died and they never knew of the extra days, it was still a defiance. It was the most rebellious thing he could do.

"It will probably hurt," the man warned, his eyebrows knit together.

"*This* hurts." Aris was pleading with him, begging for those few extra days this might grant. And if the pain killed him, this would be a defiance, too. Making the choice himself rather than it being made for him.

The man stood. "All right." He unlocked the chains around Aris's wrists by shoving his finger into the lock. As soon as his wrists were free, Aris helped untie the rope around his chest.

Then they stood facing each other. Aris was wobbly after sitting for so long, and his feet sank into the soft sand near the water.

"What do I need to do?" Aris asked. His hands hung in tight fists at his sides.

"Stay still." The man reached forward and placed his bony hand against Aris's chest. He pressed forward, his hand disappearing up to his wrist, then his elbow as he took step after step.

It didn't feel like much at first, just a shiver through his ribs. But then the pain hit him, and it felt like lighting had replaced his blood.

His knees made soft thudding sounds as they hit the sand. The man's face contorted, probably because Aris had not stayed still, but he didn't pull away.

It was repulsive, this feeling. The man's breath ghosted over Aris's skin, raising goose pimples on his neck and arms, despite the heat of the air and the way every cell in his body was turning to fire.

The man was half gone now, the features of his face nearly replaced with the hollows and hills of his skull. But still, he pressed forward.

A dam, some kind of impenetrable barrier inside of Aris, burst as the man's spirit combined with his. Aris wanted to say something, wanted to tell the man to stop, but the only sounds that escaped his throat were groans as his body swelled and started to shake. His eyes rolled back into his skull until only the whites of his eyes were visible.

The only thing left of the man were the indents his ghostly shoes left in the sand.

Death was cold, like how Aris had felt the last few days, despite the sun. A cold that sunk into the marrow of his bones, kept a thin layer of ice on his skin. When his eyes finally opened, Aris wasn't cold. The life that had returned to him was warm. Like how he felt every night he'd killed someone and their spurted blood splashed across his face. It was warm, like those days playing on the beach with Josie when they were children. Life was warm like the fire that burned in his blood, his bones, his soul when the man pressed his hand into his chest.

He lay in the sand, letting the water wash over his skin. The sun was high above him and the breeze off the ocean moved his hair, cooling his forehead.

He sat up with a new strength on the shore of his small island. The look of the skin on his hands made him push himself up until he was standing. Then he noticed all of his skin was the same.

Pale, nearly translucent with dark blue veins, the shadows of bones underneath.

He was alone on the island. A pang in his chest surprised him. This spirit—a stranger—had saved him, and Aris hadn't even asked his name.

He waited on the island for a few days, his renewed strength dwindling again. He wasn't brave enough to step into the water and explore the other islands. They were too far, and from the islands he could see from where he stood, he could tell none of them would have anything that would help him.

But, like the spirit had said might happen, a ship floated by. When the crew aboard saw him, they stopped. A boat rowed out to him and a man with golden skin and dark hair stepped onto Aris's little island. One of his eyes was dark, the other light with blindness, a scar running through it from his hairline to his jaw.

"Who are you?" The man's voice was gruff, like he wasn't used to talking.

"Aris."

"Is that all?"

"It's all that matters."

The man snorted. "Why are you out here?"

Aris glanced behind the man and saw the ship he had come from. Its sails were dark, its body unclean and crowded with barnacles. "I tried to kill my parents," Aris said. It wasn't entirely true, but he would have if it had come to it. "I still want to."

"Who are your parents?"

"The queen and king in Breton," Aris said simply.

The man waited for more, looking down his crooked nose at Aris. He was tall, and his chest was at least two and a half times the size of Aris's. When Aris didn't offer more, the man said. "We can take you there. Or wherever it is you need to go."

Aris lifted his chin. "What do you need from me?"

A corner of the man's mouth lifted. "Once you kill them, let us sail under you. Let us do what we like on and off the sea."

Aris smiled. That was an easy ask. "Done. Take me to your captain."

FORTY-NINE

WHEN ARIS IS FINISHED, Wren takes her hand from his and holds it in her lap, sitting back in the chair. The man that had helped Aris, who had given the rest of his spirit so Aris could live…

"It was Jakob." Wren speaks to her hands in her lap, her voice quiet.

Aris raises his eyebrows. "Who?"

Wren stands and turns from him, her arms wrapped around her middle. She feels weird coming out of the memory, as if her body was asleep, but her mind was on overdrive. With Kiara, she was like a ghost, standing in corners and hovering over shoulders. But with this, she was living as Aris and watching through his eyes. She could feel his pain and fear, could somehow hear exactly what he was thinking. Her voice is shaky. Whether from the shock of seeing Jakob again, or from the magics she'd experienced, she isn't sure. "The spirit that saved you. It was Jakob."

"Your friend from Sudal?"

Wren nods, still facing away from him. Her chest hurts, and she has to swallow back tears.

"How do you know?"

She turns to him, angry, with tears in her eyes. "I grew up with him, Aris. We were inseparable from the time we met as children to the time he left on that ship. You think I wouldn't recognize my best friend?" Her eyes flick to the scar in his eyebrow. "Did you have that before?"

Aris stays sitting at the desk, leaned back in the chair. He lifts his hand and runs his fingertips over the scar. "This?" he asks. "No. I noticed it when I got on board *The Basilisk* and was given a chance to clean up."

Jakob had saved Aris. And he'd not only given his life, but a physical piece of him, too.

"Did you notice anything else?" She stays standing in the middle of Aris's cabin, the cloak wrapped tightly around her shoulders. Her breaths come rapidly, and she tries to calm them, digging her fingernails into the palms of her hands.

Aris holds his hand in front of him so the sun shining through the windows lands on his skin. "His skin was like this. I was always pale, but not like this. I thought it was strange when I saw it, but I've come to like it." He traces a blue vein over the back of his hand with a long finger. "He looked washed out except for the dark circles under his eyes." He lifts his hand and runs his fingers through the dark part of his hair. "My hair wasn't always like this. It was always dark. My mother used to say it was like obsidian. Now it looks like this." His hair is no longer obsidian. It's dull and dark grey instead of black. Its roots are pale, almost as pale as his skin. His eyelashes and eyebrows, too.

Is this why she felt a pull in her chest when she'd first seen Aris? Was there some part of her that recognized him? "Did you know

who I was when you first saw me?" If he had physical characteris-
tics from Jakob, perhaps he'd have been given some memories, too.

But Aris says, "No."

Wren sits again, picks up her teacup. She swallows a mouthful,
cringing at the coldness and the way the grains of sugar grate
against her teeth. "How did you become captain?"

Aris reaches his hand toward her and nods to his fingers. She
readily accepts this time, placing her palm against his.

FIFTY

Aris and the man—Ramsey—made it back to the ship in the dinghy and when they climbed aboard, the old captain of the ship confronted them.

"And why have you brought this runt onto my ship?" he asked Ramsey.

Aris thought it was funny to be called a runt. He was at least a foot taller than the captain. "I can promise your ship safe passage anywhere you'd like to go," he said, stepping forward, his hands clasped behind his back.

"Who are you to promise such things?" The captain was weathered. Years of wind and salt air had turned the skin on his face to leather, and he had scarcely any teeth left. One of his eyes was clouded like Ramsey's, but his wasn't an injury, just age. He walked with a limp and was missing three fingers on his right hand.

"I'm Aris, Crown Prince of Breton." He wasn't a crown prince. Not anymore.

And the captain must have known. He laughed, which caused him to choke. "You're not a prince, boy," he said when he'd caught his breath again. "The queen and king of Breton killed their son for arson."

Well, he was half right anyway.

Aris laughed, breathy, almost ghostly. "They didn't kill me." He threw a hand forward and a knife that Ramsey had given him to clean his fingernails hit the captain between the eyes, burying itself in his skull. "And it wasn't arson."

The crew had gathered around them and gasped as their captain fell to the deck, dead before he hit the boards.

Aris tried not to show his surprise. He'd never been a bad shot, but he'd never been particularly good, either. It usually took a few tries to hit the target when he trained. Perhaps it was luck. Perhaps Emelia was looking out for him. He turned and looked at Ramsey over his shoulder. The man nodded once and stepped up to talk to the crew.

"We have a new captain." Ramsey held out his hand like he was presenting a prize. "Aris, prince of Breton and rightful heir to the throne. If we can get him there, he'll let us have our fun on the sea."

The crew was hesitant. Aris watched them, his hands clasped behind his back. Some of them looked at the body of their old captain, still on the boards at their feet. Slowly, they each squared their shoulders and clenched their jaws, and looked up at their new captain.

"What do we need to do?" a rat-faced man with stringy hair asked.

Aris looked around at this crew. They weren't much better off than their captain had been. Many of them were underfed and over-liquored. They were in need of washing and new clothes. Training and fixing and, for some, retiring. The ship, too, was in need of repairs. He assumed there was a lot of upgrading that needed doing. "We fix up this piece of shit you call a ship. Then we fix all of you. We'll train. Then we'll go to Breton. We kill my parents. Perhaps my sister." It didn't bring him joy to threaten Josie, but if it came down to it, there wasn't a line he wouldn't cross.

The crew was silent. Some of them lowered their eyes to the deck. Aris was sure they'd killed before. But, for most of them, probably not their own families.

Aris met Ramsey's eyes and tilted his head at the body in front of him and the puddle of blood that had ceased its spread around the old captain's head. Ramsey pulled the knife from its target with a wet sucking sound. He wiped the blade on his trousers and handed it back to Aris hilt first. Then he picked up the body and tossed it overboard. There was a splash as the body hit the water.

Aris nodded at Ramsey. He cleared his throat to get the attention of the surrounding men again. They raised their eyes to him. "But first. We find *The Altean*." Some of them raised their eyebrows. So, they'd heard of the ship. Probably everyone that lived on sea had. "I'm going to kill Captain Eleanor Crowley."

FIFTY-ONE

"You wanted to kill Eli?"

"No," Aris says. "I *want* to kill her."

She hadn't expected this. Well, that's not true. She *did* expect this. But not now. Not nearly three years later. There had been plenty of time between then and now to hurt Eli. He had even blown a hole in her ship. Why hadn't he done more?

"She didn't do this to you," Wren says. "This isn't her fault."

Aris snorts and stands from the desk. "She still took the job. Still left me on that island. As far as I'm concerned, she's just as guilty as my mother and father. She's just as responsible." Wren can hear the barely contained anger in his voice.

"But you're alive. She didn't kill you. What would killing her do?"

Aris turns from the window he'd been looking out of. Through it, Wren can see a patch of storm clouds coming closer to them from the horizon. They're not dark, but it's likely they'll bring rain.

"It'll make me feel better."

"And that's a good enough reason to kill someone?"

Aris shrugs. "I've killed for less."

Wren lets out a frustrated huff. "Eli didn't make the decision for you to die. She was just the means. If you'd been hung, would you have destroyed the gallows? Or melted the guns that were fired? It's not Eli's fault you were left on that island. *Your parents* hired her to do a job."

"And she took it, Wren. Why is this so hard for you to understand?"

"She took the job because she has a crew that needs to be paid. Just like you do."

He sits. "I don't care about her crew." He waves his hand in the air.

Wren steels herself for his answer. "Would you kill them, too?"

He gives her a long look. "If they get in my way, yes."

Wren knows they would. They wouldn't let their captain go without a fight. All of them, even Grace and Penelope, would go down fighting for Eli and her first mate.

"What if I was on the ship then? Would you kill me, too?"

Aris tilts his head in a way that makes Wren feel like a small child. He stands again and kneels in front of her, putting his hands on her knees. She can feel the coolness of his palms seeping through the fabric of her trousers.

"No," he says. "You wouldn't have left me at the Isles."

She looks at him. She tries to see Jakob in him. In any part of him, other than the scar that had been left in Aris's eyebrow, the light roots of his hair. But she can't. Jakob was broad, strong. Aris is lanky, lean. Jakob's dark eyes were warm, and Wren always knew what he was feeling just by looking at him. Aris's light eyes are, more often than not, cool and unreadable. There's no part of

Jakob that Wren recognizes in Aris's features. Nothing that feels like home.

Her chest aches when she says, "I don't know that I wouldn't have." It scares her to admit. To say these words means that, even though she knows him now, if she had known him then, what would her heart be? What would her feelings toward him be? When Aris was on *The Altean*, it was before Jakob had saved him. Was it Aris she was pulled to? Or the parts of him where Jakob's spirit now resided? Was there a difference or had Aris's soul completely absorbed Jakob's, changing it to fit into his body?

Aris makes a sound in his throat and pushes up from his knees. "If you wouldn't have saved me then, what's keeping you here now?"

When she first joined *The Basilisk*, the answer would have come easily. *Power.* But it's different now. *Power* has no draw to her. *Power* means nothing.

Her previous plan of taking over the duke's seat in Sulesia is null and void now. There's no part of her that wants that. No part of her that wants the responsibility or the authority that it would give her.

No, the reason she stays isn't power. She stays because of Aris. Because of the pain in her chest when she's away from him. He's the reason that even if Eli and Kiara and the rest of *The Altean* crew were to offer her a spot back aboard their ship, she'd turn it down.

Wren stands, places her hand against his chest and says, "Because I know who you are now."

FIFTY-TWO

THEY JOIN THE CREW on deck. Ramsey had been giving orders and keeping the ship running in Aris's place as he watched over Wren during her recovery. But now she's strong and she and Aris stand on the quarterdeck, watching the sea as it splits before the ship.

Wren had never been on the sea before stowing away on *The Altean*. There was once, for her sixteenth birthday, she and Jakob sneaked onto a party barge, but it didn't go far from shore. It stayed in the bay where the docks were less than five hundred feet away. Jakob said if she got too freaked out, she could jump over the side of the barge and swim to shore. She had taken it as a challenge and walked up the gangplank ahead of him, her chin high.

Once they were on board, they joined a group of partiers. They were too drunk to object, and she and Jakob were enthusiastically allowed to stay. They shared a few bottles of sparkling drink and ate the food the others had abandoned on the table in their booth. Young men and women dressed in clothing that was not appropriate for the weather walked around and occasionally took the hands of some of the partiers, leading them down below. They'd come back, their cheeks flushed and shirts hastily buttoned. One of the brothel girls had offered her hand to Jakob, but he declined and draped his arm around Wren's shoulder. It didn't mean anything other than *I don't need your company*, but it made Wren's cheeks flush, anyway. When Jakob pointed it out, she blamed the drink and took another swig from the bottle.

Afterwards, when they left the barge stumbling and slurry-tongued, Jakob held her hair back as she vomited into a bush. It was embarrassing, but Jakob had seen her sick many times before. He made fun of her, of course. He always did. But he also offered his handkerchief and let her take a few sips of water from the flask in his pocket.

That night, the estate was quiet. They sat on a bench in the garden, a green cloak pulled tightly around her shoulders. It was so cold, they could see puffs of their breath in the air. They tried to make shapes. It didn't work, of course, and they laughed, leaning against each other.

Then Jakob led her upstairs and tucked her in. When she woke up in the morning, she was surprised to see Jakob in the chair next to her. His cheeks were flushed, his hair mussed and tangled around his head. He slept with his arms crossed over his chest, one ankle crossed over the other on the end of her bed. At least he'd taken his boots off.

This is different. The motion on the open water is different from a party barge in the bay. It's choppier and, sometimes, Wren wishes the docks were only five hundred feet away, so it would be easy to jump into the waves and swim back home.

But she can't. She's many, many, many miles from home. And besides, Sudal isn't her home anymore. She had always felt that wherever Jakob was, that's where her home would be. And now that she knows Jakob saved Aris, perhaps Aris is where home is supposed to be.

She looks over at him. His hair drifts around his face in the breeze. In the sun, he doesn't look as sallow, but his veins and mouth are still in stark contrast to the milkiness of his skin. He's almost as pale as the Star Child on board, though not nearly as beautiful.

Not that Aris isn't beautiful, but his beauty is a different kind. Star Children were aptly named for the light from the stars on a clear night. Their skin is like a clean sheet of paper, freshly laundered bedclothes, the petals of a white lily. Aris's skin is like fingers of moonlight filtered through the branches of a dead tree in the garden, once brightly colored fabric that's been bleached in the sun, new skin over a scar.

His eyes catch hers and she startles. He lifts his chin and gives her a slight smirk. He holds out his hand to her. She looks down and takes it, lacing her fingers with his. The sun is high and the light warm, but she keeps the cloak he'd given her draped over her shoulders.

"Are you too warm?" he asks her, touching the clasp at her throat.

"No," she says, her voice a bit hoarse. She clears her throat. "I'm all right."

Aris nods and turns back to the front of the boat. "Any word on *The Altean*'s whereabouts?" he asks Ramsey.

Wren's heart stutters. "You're still looking for them?"

Aris turns to her again, his light eyes unreadable. "I never stopped."

Wren takes her hand from his, tucking it into the cloak. "Count me out of it. I don't want any part of your hunting."

She hears Ramsey say something before the door to Aris's cabin closes behind her, but she can't make out his words.

340

FIFTY-THREE

AT EVERY MEAL, EVERY interaction, Wren starts the conversation by trying to convince Aris that Eli is not to blame. That going after her will do no good.

He doesn't listen. He repeats his words to her from their first argument. "She took the job. She's guilty. She's responsible."

Eventually, he stops responding, just watching her over their food or from where they sit on the quarterdeck steps, listening to her.

A week goes by of this. Wren doesn't let up. The only time she does is when she sleeps, or she goes down to relieve herself. When it's obvious Aris won't answer her usual questions, she asks, "Why haven't you tried yet? Why waste two years chasing her without doing what you want?" She means it to antagonize him. Question his motives, and if he really wants what he says he does.

When he doesn't answer immediately, Wren thinks maybe she's gotten somewhere. But then he says, "The story is, she can't be killed while on her boat."

How is it that Aris has heard this story, but she hadn't? The sea has so many more stories and rumors than she would have ever known if she'd stayed in Sudal or gone to Nestad.

She lets out a huff of breath through her nose. "Where did you hear that?" She tries to keep her voice chastising, as if this is the most childish thing she's heard about *The Altean* and her captain, but it doesn't quite come out that way. There's more concern in her voice than she would have liked.

Aris raises his eyebrows, the corners of his mouth lifted slightly. "Heard it in a pub in Maia. Supposedly, they were an old crew member who had left to take care of their mother."

Wren leans back on her elbows. "It's not true," she says, her eyes trained on the horizon.

"No?"

She looks at him, her jaw clenched. "No." She gets up and walks to the front of the boat, leaving Aris smirking behind her.

After that day, Aris avoids Wren. He eats with his crew in the mess, stares out over the water at the bow of the ship, holds meetings with Ramsey in his quarters that quiet when she enters. The only time he's around her is when they sleep, and he only comes in after she's asleep, and leaves before she wakes.

One day, she brings him a cup of tea while he's sitting at one of the mess tables. There are maps laid out in front of him.

When she sets it down, he looks up at her. "Thank you, little bird." Her breath hitches in her chest. They're the first words he's spoken to her in over a week, and they remind her of Jakob.

Jakob had gotten the nickname from the duke. He'd heard the duke call Wren *little bird* once when she was sick. He liked it and adopted it, calling her little bird all the time. Once they were older, he reserved it, using it only in moments of quiet. When she brought him soup when he had the flu. "Thank you, little bird." When she cut her hair and left her bangs a little lopsided, "We can fix it, little bird." When he left on the ship and turned one last time to wave at her, "Goodbye, little bird."

She smiles at Aris and leaves him, her hands clenched together over her stomach as she takes the stairs back to the deck.

Another week passes before she joins Aris and Ramsey on deck. Aris turns to her when she steps up next to them. "Good morning," he says.

"Good morning," she replies, stunned at his initiation. She had almost resigned to not having a conversation with him again.

She had turned twenty-five in the time since Aris had last spoken to her. There was no fanfare, no special cake, no gifts. It was different from her birthdays at the estate, which were almost always a large celebration. She woke up on that day with Aris still standing in the room, buttoning up his shirt. She sat up, swung her legs over the side of the bed. He walked to her, trailing his fingers down her cheek and smiled at her. She took that as her gift rather than something she could hold.

Aris turns to Ramsey. "Where are we headed?"

Ramsey turns to look at them from the wheel. "The Bay of Kornas," he says. "*The Altean* has been spotted in that area lately."

Wren turns sharply to Aris, her breathing coming rapidly. "You're hunting them right now?"

Aris stares ahead for a few moments. Wren almost says something else, but then he takes a deep breath. "I've been thinking. You're right that Eli and the others had nothing to do with my banishment. They were the drones, not the workers." He turns to her. "I want to make a truce with them."

The relief is almost nauseating. Wren steadies herself against the railing. "What do you mean, a truce?"

Aris lets out a long sigh. "I'm tired of hunting, Wren. I want my throne, yes, but I'm done with this useless sailing." He lifts his arm and gestures to the sea around them. "I want to settle, to rule, to live somewhere other than this damned boat."

Wren looks at him. He seems genuine. His weary eyes are framed in dark circles.

"What about me?"

"What about you?"

"What if I...don't want to go to Breton?" She says it quietly, her eyes low. She fights the urge to hug the cloak tighter around her. She hopes he doesn't bring up Sudal, the duke's seat. And she doesn't know where she'd go instead.

He turns to her, runs his fingers down her arm until he laces his fingers with hers. He ducks his head until he meets her eye. "If you don't want to come to Breton, that's up to you. You're welcome, of course. The kingdom will need a queen. But if you prefer to go somewhere else, that's all right, as well."

Her breath catches. "Queen?" she says.

He gives her another smile. "The title is yours, if you want it."

She does want it. She's surprised at the fierceness of how much she wants the title of queen. Not for the power, but for Aris. The title would be a big responsibility, and it's a bit daunting, but with Aris by her side, she could take it.

"Think on it," Aris says when Wren doesn't say anything. "There are a few ways to go about you becoming queen and you taking control of Sulesia. We needn't make any decisions yet."

"I don't want Sulesia," she says. It's the first time she's spoken aloud that her desire isn't the duke's seat. It's relieving and terrifying at once.

Aris smiles again. "As I said, we don't need to make any decisions yet."

Wren wonders how long Aris has been thinking about this. Had he always intended to offer her a spot next to him on the throne? Had this been what he was thinking over in those weeks he was silent?

They watch the waves for a long time, the water cutting through the water like a hawk cuts through air. As the moon rises and the crew takes up their small groups on deck, Wren voices a question she'd been mulling over for the few hours since Aris had mentioned it. "What truce are you going to propose to Eli?"

"I want them to work for me," he says simply. "Eli's ship flies no country's flag. I want them to fly Breton's."

Eli had told Wren that their ship didn't belong to only one country. She wanted it to be a safe haven on the waters where pirates and countries' naval forces worked. That's why their crew came from all over. There was always someone on board that spoke a guest's language. Always someone who knew customs and traditions, food and games and songs of their home. It was easier to trust when someone's idea of home was the same as yours.

"It would be hard for them to work when they're affiliated with one country," Wren says. "Eli likes being tied to no one. I don't know if you could convince her to change."

Aris squeezes Wren's hand. "Oh, little bird, that's why I have you."

FIFTY-FOUR

THE DOCK IN THERMA is crowded with workers and prettily dressed men and women. Wren hadn't seen *The Altean* in any of the ports, but it's the first Monday after the full moon, so she knows she doesn't have the date wrong.

A block up from the docks, where the crowds are thinner and the smell of air is less salt-heavy, sits a small pub with a carving of a dragon curled around the posts on the porch. Wren takes the steps two at a time, the coins in the purse at her hip jangling with every step. Inside, the pub is dimly lit, and it smells like sweat and old oil and spilled whiskey. Underneath a window at the back, Ophelia and Ezra sit. They haven't spotted her yet and Wren watches them from the corner of the bar. Ophelia twirls a knife, the tip of its blade on the table. Ezra has a book open on the table in front of him, but his eyes are trained on a spot out the window. The pub backs up to an alley, so Wren isn't sure what he could be looking at. Her chest is heavy at how much she missed them, at how happy she is to see them.

And when Ophelia finally spots her, the smile that spreads across her face and extends to Ezra's when she touches his wrist and nods in Wren's direction makes it obvious they missed her, too. They're up out of the booth before Wren has made it halfway to them and they meet her on the floor, scooping her up in hugs. Ophelia puts her hands on each side of Wren's face, one of her thumbs wiping away a stray tear on Wren's cheek.

"We missed you," she says, her eyes shining.

Wren nods. "I missed you, too."

They sit back in the booth and Ezra orders a feast of fried foods and warm beer for them to share. Once the bartender brings over the first round, they look at Wren expectantly.

"I don't know what to say," Wren admits. She knows she's there to offer the truce, to lay out the barest terms for them to take back to *The Altean* and recount to Eli, who will—hopefully—accept and agree to meet with Aris to hash out any last-minute details before the papers are signed. But she can't start there. Too much time has passed, and she hasn't seen Ophelia and Ezra—her *friends*—in months. She wants to talk about more than work.

Ophelia laughs and reaches across the table to take Wren's hand. "What happened? How did Aris get to you?"

It's the same question Kiara had asked. And that means Eli and Kiara didn't tell the crew that Wren went willingly.

"Aris didn't take me," she says, cautious. She's not sure how they'll react to learning they were told lies by omission from their captain, or how they'll react to being betrayed by their friend. "I chose to go with him."

Ophelia pulls her fingers from Wren's and Ezra sits back. "You what?" Ophelia says. She shakes her head. "I don't understand."

"Aris is a dream walker," Wren starts. "He started visiting me shortly before we started helping in those port towns."

"The port towns that *he* destroyed, you mean." Ezra crosses his arms over his chest.

Wren nods and traces a gouge in the tabletop with her fingernail. "Yes," she says. "He led me to believe you were cruel to him. That he was wrongfully sent to his death."

"And you believed him." Ophelia's voice is thick with unshed tears.

Wren keeps her eyes on the table. "I'm sorry," she says. "I shouldn't have believed it. It sounded nothing like you." Wren isn't sure if they know about Kiara's walking abilities. So instead of explaining it all, she says, "I confronted him about it. Asked for the truth. He threw me in the hold, but eventually, he did."

She doesn't say this to gain their sympathy. She knows she's not owed that, but to tell them that she knows Aris is cruel. That she's not immune to it. But when Ezra and Ophelia's faces soften, Wren can't help but feel relief.

Ophelia leans forward, but she doesn't reach for Wren's hand again. "And now?" she asks, her voice gentler than it had been moments before.

"Aris has sent me to petition for a truce between his crew and Eli's. He sends his sincerest apologies for any hurt or fear he caused." Wren slides the envelope sealed in black wax across the table and taps it before pulling her hand back.

Ophelia picks up the envelope and runs her fingers along the edges. "Do you know he tried to kill me?" She lifts her fingers, and they press into the small scar on her throat where the knife had pressed into her skin, the same scar Wren had added so carefully into Ophelia's portrait.

"Yes, and I'm so sorry, O. It was wrong of him to hold you accountable." She doesn't want to give excuses for Aris. He can do that himself.

Ophelia sighs. "The worst part is, I don't blame him for it. I know he was scared." She lifts her eyes to Wren and gives her a small, sad smile. "I've been in his position, and I did the same. Except I succeeded."

Wren thinks of Ophelia and her sister Evey, scared and huddled in an alley when a man tried to attack them. Thinking only of their lives, Ophelia fought back. They got away, but the man didn't survive. It's not quite the same as Aris—he wouldn't have gotten away had Ophelia died—but their fear, their fight, was similar.

Wren wants to wrap her arms around Ophelia, but the food comes then, though none of them has much of an appetite anymore. They pick at the fried potato sticks and fried onions. It tastes delicious, but it turns to paste in Wren's mouth.

After a drink of beer that has gone lukewarm, Wren says, "Do you think we could still be friends?"

Ophelia and Ezra look at her as if she's grown a second head. "Of course, Wren," Ezra says. "Why wouldn't we?"

Wren shrugs and slumps a little in her seat. "I left," she says. "I didn't say goodbye. I went with someone that wanted you dead. I believed his lies about you."

Ophelia stuffs a potato stick in her mouth. "We all make mistakes," she says, taking Wren's hand again and squeezing her fingers. She doesn't pull away. "Luckily, most are easy to forgive."

The sun has sunk close to the horizon by the time they leave the pub. Ophelia and Ezra each have a paper bag weighed down by the food they didn't finish, carefully packed away in cardboard containers. "Clare is going to die for these onions," Ezra had said, careful to place the little cup of white sauce into the container with them.

Wren sees Ramsey leaned against the wall of the building across the street from the pub, his big arms crossed over his equally big chest.

"We'll deliver this to Eli," Ophelia tells Wren after one last hug, holding the envelope in her hand. "Then we'll leave a message on the board at the docks tomorrow morning."

Wren nods. She watches as her closest friends since leaving Sudal walk down the dusty road toward the docks. She still doesn't see *The Altean* among the many ships, but she doesn't wait to see what boat Ezra and Ophelia climb onto.

Instead, she turns and walks further into the city, following Ramsey a few steps behind. A few stalls are open along the road, and she stops to buy a small bag of chocolate candies. The inn that Aris had rented rooms at sits at the top of the road, looking down over the lower town and the dock, its windows shining in the sun's last rays. It's the same inn that she had stayed in with Ophelia, Ezra, Lex, Arden, and Clare when they were in Therma the summer before.

Inside, the lobby has tall ceilings and windows with cushioned benches in front. Couches and stuffed chairs sit around polished wood tables. A fire burns warmly in the hearth across from the check-in desk. Ramsey leads her to a tiny elevator and Wren has to squeeze her eyes shut to fight the nausea from the machine's rickety engineering. Ramsey smirks and lets out a huff of air through his nostrils at her when they step out onto the faded blue carpet. She and Aris will share a room, but Ramsey and Smith are in an adjoining room and the door between the two is propped open when they enter.

Aris is waiting for her, standing with his hands behind his back, the window behind him. He gives Ramsey a curt nod and the muscular man disappears into the adjoining room and closes the door between them.

The room they're in is bigger than Aris's quarters on *The Basilisk*. There are two beds, each with crisp white sheets and a blue bedspread. One is covered in papers and maps and an ink pen that's leaking onto the blanket. The other is empty, apart from the cloak Wren had tossed onto it when she came into the room.

The walls are bare, but for one painting over the table between the beds. Wren recognizes the building in it. It's the castle in Akros, Kornas's capital city. She'd been there plenty of times as a child and young teenager. It looks the same in the painting as she remembers it in her mind. All tall towers and arching entryways. The stained glass windows show the history of Kornas and the largest one, the one depicting the god Adreus placing long stemmed roses twisted into a crown on the country's first queen's head, is the one which the king's private meeting rooms lie behind. Wren had played there as a child, with her dolls and stuffed toys gifted to her by the king, while her papa and the king drank red wine and made empty conversation about their country's livelihoods. Wren was young then, making up stories in her head with her toys.

"How did it go?" Aris asks. His chin is lifted a little, his shoulders tense.

Wren sits on the bed with the maps and papers strewn over its duvet, careful not to actually sit on any of the contents. "Fine," she answers. "Eli and Kiara didn't tell the rest of the crew that I came to you on my own. Ezra and Ophelia were not glad to hear it. But they were glad to hear that you don't want to fight Eli anymore."

Aris's shoulders relax and he gives her a slight smile, his eyes remaining neutral. He walks to her and smooths the hair on the crown of her head. "Good." He pauses a moment, his eyes searching her face. For what, Wren can't guess. "Do you miss them? The crew of that ship?"

Suddenly, there's an ache at the back of Wren's throat. She had been anxious to see her friends again and had been overwhelmed at realizing how much she'd missed them. She swallows and nods, looking away from Aris.

"You will see them again soon enough."

FIFTY-FIVE

THE FOLLOWING MORNING, WREN rises early and dresses, careful not to disturb Aris as she climbs out of the bed they share. She can hear Ramsey's snores from the next room, and she tiptoes out to the hallway and then takes the stairs to the first floor. She follows the smell of sausage and batter cakes to the inn's dining room, where breakfast is being served.

There aren't many other travelers in the room yet. An old man and woman, their hair grey; a pot-bellied man with one arm; a small barefooted child clutching a tattered doll in one grubby hand.

Once Wren is seated with her plate full of food, the child comes up to her. They don't say anything, but Wren can tell they're hungry by the way they eye her plate.

She had grabbed an extra fork for this purpose. She's grateful at this moment that the duke took her in. She would have died if she'd been left in her little neighborhood. She wraps one sausage in a batter cake and secures it closed by stabbing the fork through. She holds it out to the child and offers them a smile.

The child's eyes go wide, and they suck in a breath through their nose. They hesitate before reaching for the fork, their eyes darting around the room, looking for the owner or an employee that might shoo them out. When they decide the coast is clear, they snatch the food from Wren and bolt out a side door leading to the street.

Slowly, the tables in the dining room fill up with other travelers and guests. Ramsey and Smith come down after the sun has risen and eat sitting across from each other near Wren. When Aris comes down, he takes a bowl of grain and a cup of orange juice Wren had seen being made and sits next to her.

"Have you eaten?" he asks.

"Yes," she says. "I've been down here for a little while." She had enjoyed watching the sun stream through the windows and seeing the child she'd given food to play in the streets with other kids. A dog had joined them and now they throw a ratty ball to each other, trying to keep it from the animal.

Aris sees her watching them. "Do you want them?"

His question catches her off guard. "What?"

"Children," he clarifies, taking a bite of his breakfast. "Do you want children?"

Wren's answer comes easy. "No. I've never wanted children."

There's amusement in his voice when he asks, "And do you think the king and queen can get away with not having children?"

"I think the king and queen can get away with whatever they please."

Wren knows their relationship isn't typical. They're not intimate, they're not romantic or flirty. Aris will never bring her flowers, and she'll never give him a child. Their relationship isn't built on love, but something else. Power, in Aris's case. Comfort and familiarity, in Wren's. It wasn't what she'd imagined for herself, but it's the fate she's been given, and she's content with the hand she's been dealt.

After breakfast, Wren and Aris take a walk down to the message board near the docks. An envelope is tacked up, sealed in green wax. Aris's name is scrawled across the front in thin and swooping cursive.

Aris unseals the envelope and pulls out a single piece of paper. It only takes a moment for him to read what's written on it. And when he's finished, his fingers curl around the paper and he lets out an angry grunt through his teeth. Wren puts her hand on his arm to calm him. He presses the paper to her chest and walks back the way they'd come, his hands clenched into fists at his sides.

Wren looks at the paper. Written in the same handwriting as Aris's name across the front of the envelope, reads a simple and eloquently written *No*.

FIFTY-SIX

Aris slaps his hand down on top of the desk. They're back in their room at the inn, Wren sitting on the edge of the bed, one knee crossed over the other, her hands flat on the bedspread and supporting her as she leans back. She had expected this. Her meeting with Ophelia and Ezra had gone well, and she felt secure knowing they didn't harbor any resentment toward her. But she knew Eli and Kiara would not agree to meet.

She had thought of telling Aris this, and had even attempted to, but he wouldn't listen, sure that he could convince them through only a letter. She didn't want to argue, so she did what he asked and wrote Ophelia a letter that was delivered via messenger hawk shortly after Aris let her know of his plan. Ophelia's response came quickly, and they agreed to meet in Therma, which was only a few days' journey from where *The Basilisk* was.

Once they were docked, Aris asked Wren to deliver his letter to Ophelia and Ezra. She had given them the bare minimum of what Aris intended: an opportunity to live and work in the world, under

Breton's banner and getting orders from Aris. Eli couldn't go against Aris or the crew of *The Basilisk* and Aris and *The Basilisk* couldn't work against Eli and *The Altean*. But Wren knew Eli wouldn't like it, and likely wouldn't agree. Eli would have her own set of stipulations. If *The Altean* and *The Basilisk* were to work separately with no interventions from the other, Eli would have to know that people would be safe. And Wren wasn't sure Aris would make that promise.

"I don't understand why she said no." Aris has the page with Eli's answer clutched in his fist. There's a splattering of red across the top of his cheeks and Wren can't decide if it's from his anger or the sun.

Wren stands from the bed, pausing to smooth her trousers, and walks to him. She takes his fist in her hands and eases the paper from his fingers. "She just needs a little reassurance, Aris. That's all."

Aris turns to her, his eyes hard. "Reassurance?"

Wren leans against the desk, folding her arms across her chest loosely. "Eli isn't going to look the other way while people need help. People that could get hurt if *The Basilisk* is left to its own devices."

A muscle twitches in Aris's jaw. "Why would she care? They're just people."

Wren almost laughs. "You're asking why Eli would care about people?" Then she remembers that, while there are rumors about their immortality, Eli and Kiara have managed to keep rumors about their gift from Adreus mostly at bay. Aris hasn't asked specifics yet, and Wren thinks he either doesn't know there's more to the story or doesn't care. "Eli is one of the most caring people I've ever met. She's not going to agree to work with you if she thinks even one person might get hurt."

Aris takes a deep breath through his nose, lets it out slowly through his mouth. "I've told you. I don't plan on hurting anyone." He rubs his temples. "I was angry then—"

"You're angry now."

He casts a sideways glance at her. "Not like I was. I'm angry that she doesn't believe I've changed."

Wren lays a hand on Aris's arm. "You've given her no reason to believe you have."

When he looks at her, Wren is surprised to see a scared boy. She realizes that he's just a boy running from a country that hated him. All he ever wanted from his home was love and acceptance, to feel like he belonged. And that security had been taken from him at such a young age. She wants to help him, just like she helped that child at breakfast. Of course, Aris wants a throne and country, not a sausage and batter cake.

"I don't know how," he admits.

Wren nods and looks down at her hand on his arm. "I'll help you," she says, looking up at him again. "I'll go to *The Altean* and talk to Eli myself. And we'll go from there."

Aris lifts a hand and touches the tips of his icy fingers against her cheek. "You're going to make a good queen."

Wren smiles. "I know."

FIFTY-SEVEN

The Altean is familiar to Wren as she walks up to where it waits at the dock. She had no trouble seeing it this morning, sitting in a berth not far from the center dock, its sails tied up, an unlit lantern swaying from the mainmast. The hull had gotten a fresh coat of wax, and a new figurehead was fixed to the bow. Wren smiles as she recognizes it has Kiara's face, one hand reaching forward to split the air, the other placed delicately near her waist. Wren wonders if it was a gift to commemorate her and the captain's three hundred and fiftieth birthdays.

She knew from Ezra and Ophelia that not much had changed since she left, but this morning Wren had worried the ship would feel foreign to her. But it's almost as if the ship is welcoming her, like outstretched arms waiting for a hug.

Arden is on the dock, checking his knots when she walks up. A smile breaks his face in two when he sees her. Before she can say anything, her breath is knocked out of her as his big arms wrap around her, and then he's swinging her in a circle on the docks.

She laughs as he sets her down. "It's good to see you, too, Arden."

He walks with her up the gangplank and she turns and waves at Ramsey to let him know he can go back to the inn. Someone must have seen her and Arden on their way up—Wren suspects Lex, they could never let Arden work on the docks without ogling him from the side of the ship—because when they make it to the deck, everyone is there to see her. Ophelia and Ezra hang back a little to allow the others to say hello. Grace holds Wren's hand and asks if she was hurt, Clare touches her hair, Lex refuses to leave her side. Penelope rubs against Wren's legs and meows loudly until Wren scoops her up and nuzzles her nose into the cat's neck. From their reactions, she's unsure if Ophelia and Ezra told the others that she went with Aris willingly. She's not sure what she'd rather. But she's glad for this happy reunion, whether they know or not.

Finally, after hugs and many reassurances that, yes, she's okay, Eli makes her way to Wren. Wren's stomach had been in knots all night, anticipating seeing Eli and Kiara again, but then the captain is in front of her and she's smiling and she claps Wren on the shoulder before pulling her into a crushing hug.

Wren's eyes fill with tears when Eli's arms go around her. She had known how much they meant to her, how hard it was to leave them, but she hadn't realized the opposite was the same. How much she meant to them, how much they missed her.

When Eli releases her, she holds Wren at arm's length, her hands still on Wren's shoulders. "And what do we owe the pleasure of your visit?" She's smiling, the corners of her green eyes crinkled.

"I've come to invite you to dinner." Technically, the dinner would only be held if Eli agreed to Aris's terms and the truce. But Wren decides that a dinner invitation sounds better than "I've come to convince you the man you left to die almost three years ago, who wanted you dead and has attacked and destroyed count-less port towns, wants to apologize and I'm here to tell you that he's changed now."

Eli's smile falters, but not enough for the others around them to notice. "Let's go talk menu, then." She removes her hands from Wren's shoulders and sweeps her arm out. "After you."

The cabin Eli and Kiara share is set up in a very similar way to Aris's cabin on *The Basilisk*. However, Eli and Kiara's bed is much more rumpled, and their clothes litter the floor and are draped over the backs of chairs. Eli's desk is cleared but for the open letter from Aris, as if she'd been sitting there reading it over and over when someone had knocked on her door and informed her that Wren had come for a visit. The altars behind the desk are clean, the candle wicks are trimmed and the salt in the dish for Anrena is clean and fresh.

Eli waits until Wren has slung her bag over the back of a chair before she says, "This is quite an interesting letter." She picks it up, holding it between two fingers. "Is it a ruse?"

Wren had read the letter before it was sealed and tucked into Wren's bag. She sat with Aris as he drafted it twice, four, seven, ten times before she nodded and he got to work writing it on letterhead with his name. Why he had letterhead with his name, and where he'd gotten it, she didn't know. How many letters was Aris writing and sending? She didn't guess very many; it didn't look like hardly any of the paper had been used.

"It's not a ruse. Aris has decided that he's tired of chasing. He wants his throne, and that's all."

"That's all?"

"Well," Wren shrugs, "that and your loyalty."

"To the crown?"

"To the crown."

Kiara comes in then, followed by Penelope, carrying a tray of sandwiches cut into triangles. She takes the teapot from over the stove and brings it over to the desk, setting it down. She smiles at Wren and pulls her in for a hug. They had said hello when Wren had first gotten to the ship, but she'd hurried off to the galley. She must have known Eli and Wren would be talking.

"I'm not sure, Wren." Eli shakes her head. "If there's one thing I've learned over the last few centuries, if it sounds too good to be true, it probably is." She leans against the desk, her ankles and arms crossed.

"I thought that, too," Wren admits. "But I believe him. He's weary, Eli. He misses Breton."

Eli sighs and looks at the letter again. Then she looks up at Kiara and they have one of their unspoken conversations. All Wren sees is Kiara lifting one shoulder slightly while she takes a drink of her tea.

"You trust him? Truly, I mean. Not just because he's said you can." The way Eli looks at Wren reminds her of when she and Jakob were fourteen and asked the duke if they could go for a walk down the beach after dark.

"Will you be careful?" he asked. "You'll watch out for the other?"

"Yes, Papa. We'll stick together and watch each other's backs. I promise." Wren had been standing in front of him in her nightgown, her dressing robe tied haphazardly in a bow around her waist. Her boots were untied, and her hair was a mess.

The duke looked at Jakob. "And you?"

Jakob nodded, his arms hung loosely at his sides. "Yes, sir. We'll be careful. Nothing will happen to her."

The duke relented, and Wren and Jakob ran down the beach, splashing each other in the waves and tossing each other's shoes too far up the sand.

"Yes, I do," Wren says. "And I believe you can, too."

"He won't hurt anyone else?"

It was silly to hope Eli wouldn't ask this particular question; Wren knew she would. "I can't promise he won't," Wren says. "People always get hurt when a throne changes hands. But he won't do anything that would knowingly put others in harm's way." That wasn't entirely true. She knew the people of Breton would not take kindly to Aris overthrowing not only his parents, but his sister as well. His reentry into the country to claim to the throne alone would put people in danger.

And though Eli must know this, too, she says, "Can we have time to think about it?"

Wren tries to not let her face break into a smile, but she's unsuccessful. "Yes," she says. "You can take as much time as you need." When Eli raises an eyebrow, Wren amends, "Well, maybe a day or so. I know Aris is anxious to get home."

Eli nods, a smile coming over her face. She reaches for the cup of tea that Kiara had prepared for her. A third cup sits ready for Wren, steam swirling over the top of it.

"You know, Wren," Eli starts, "you are always welcome on this ship. You are still a part of this crew." She takes a drink of her tea and sets it back on its saucer. "You can come with us. No truce needed."

Wren admits it sounds tempting. She had packed her meager things into the leather satchel that she'd brought with her. She'd even stopped at *The Basilisk* and gotten her purple flower-embroidered cloak from Aris's quarters before coming here. Ramsey hadn't been keen on the detour, but he'd waited outside his captain's quarters as Wren gathered her things. She knew he would go back and tell Aris, but she wanted her things, and Aris's annoyance at her wasn't a good enough reason to not have them.

But ard*The Altean* could never give her what she truly wanted, only one person could. As much as she wants these people, as much as she wants to be part of their family again, being with Aris is what she wants most. And it's hard for her to admit that, especially now that she's here.

Instead of giving a direct yes or no, she nods. "Thank you."

She had told Aris she planned on staying late on *The Altean*, and likely wouldn't be back to the inn until the next day. She'd been away from her friends for so long and she wanted to make up for lost time, at least a little. Aris hadn't been thrilled, but he said he understood. Still, he wanted her back before dinner the next day, preferably with an answer.

Wren stays in Eli and Kiara's cabin for a little while, drinking tea and eating the sandwiches Kiara had prepared. But eventually, a knock at the door brings Lex and Arden, Ophelia and Ezra, Grace and Clare and Jez. They pull Wren onto the deck, and they dance to music they can hear drifting to their ship from another docked nearby.

They dance for what feels like hours as the sun climbs higher and higher into the sky. At one point, Wren slides down the mast until she's sitting on the deck, breaths coming quickly, her forehead and neck sticky with sweat. She pulls her hair up and holds it, letting the sea breeze cool her. She'd kicked off her shoes earlier and now she wiggles her toes, stretching her legs and feet.

Ophelia drops on one side of her and Lex on the other. Each of them leans their heads on Wren's shoulders.

"We missed you," Lex says.

Ophelia grabs Wren's hand and traces a small circle on the back of it. "A lot," she agrees.

Wren tilts her head and touches her cheek to Lex's head. "I've missed you all, too."

They sit there, watching the others. Penelope takes turns in each of their laps, purring and pushing her nose into their hands. Ezra tries to teach Arden, Jez, and Grace a dance from his small village in Maia. There's a lot of toe tapping, a lot of spins. Arden is heavy on his feet, but Wren can tell by the smile on his face that he's enjoying it.

By the time the sun has sunk below the horizon and the stars are fully out, everyone has decided it's time for dinner. Arden disappears below decks with Grace and when they return, they're carrying trays.

The crew sits in a circle on the deck, lanterns lit around them. The Star Child joins them, clutching Wren's hand and saying they're glad she's all right before they sit between Clare and Kiara.

Wren watches them. They aren't as rigid as the Star Child on *The Basilisk*. The one here didn't join them often for meals, or outings, but occasionally they'd step out into the sun, a hood pulled over their hair, and sit on the deck, or mosey around a shop. Until Wren had taken over watch her last night on *The Altean*, she'd never heard them speak, but now she can hear quiet words exchanged between them and Clare, or Kiara, or Grace. They smile at things Grace says and thank her when she hands them a plate.

The trays of food are set in the middle, along with bowls and plates and silverware. Grace pulls a lid off a tray and a roast the size of Arden's leg sits cradled in a bed of roasted carrots, onions, and red potatoes. Another lid is lifted revealing white rice with herbs and sliced lemons garnished on top.

"After dinner, we have a surprise for dessert!" Grace says, plunking down next to Clare. "I made it myself."

Arden chuckles and smiles at her. "She's quite the baker," he says and the smile that breaks Grace's face in two could light up the dark.

Something pulls in Wren's chest at her smile. She remembers what Ophelia had said, how Grace's entire family was in the church that Aris burned down. He claimed he didn't know there was anyone in it and seemed genuinely distraught about the people inside whose lives had been lost.

Where would Grace be if it hadn't happened? Would she be at home with her parents and three siblings, eating dinner? Would she be at church with them, singing and praying? How different would her life be if Aris hadn't taken out his anger on the church?

Jez puts a slice of the roast on Wren's plate, pulling her out of her thoughts.

"Thank you," she says.

Jez smiles at her. "I know you've heard it a thousand times already, but we missed you so much," he says. He motions at Grace. "Especially Grace. She asked about you almost every day."

Wren nods and looks down at her plate. She has to blink back tears to keep them from rolling over her cheeks.

The rest of the food is self-serve, and everyone heaps piles of vegetables and rice on their plates. The meat is tender enough that they don't need knives. Wren takes a fork, but when she sits back with her food, she notices everyone else eating with their fingers.

Ezra shrugs. "Easy cleanup," he says.

Wren hesitates, but she puts her fork back in the middle and pinches a clutch of rice between her fingers. It's more delicious than anything she's eaten on *The Basilisk,* and she has to bite the inside of her cheek to keep from making a sound. It tastes like home.

Not Sudal. Sudal tastes like blue candies and fresh rain water and lavender. And once, a year ago when Wren first left Sudal, home would have tasted like that, too.

Now, home tastes like cream and roasted vegetables and citrus rice. Home tastes like tea with honey, and strawberries sneaked from the barrels in the galley at two in the morning. It feels like sunshine and salt air and a warm hammock. Home and *The Altean* taste the same.

But there's home with Aris, too. Aris, who feels like cool breezes and candlelight and hands wrapped around a beat-up metal bowl filled with warm stew.

As she eats, watching the others as they laugh and tell jokes and steal bites from each other's plates, she realizes that she's lucky. Many people are fortunate to have one home—a place where they grow up and learn and have a family and grow old. But few people are lucky enough to have two homes.

For a while after her adoption, Wren had a hard time switching where "home" was. She had lived in the same place, slept and played and grown there for six years. That's what she thought of when she thought of home. But she didn't live there anymore and never would again. Slowly, over the course of many months and growth spurts and falling asleep with silk pillows, home became the estate. There was an in-between time where home could be either or both. Maybe this was like that. Aris is home. *The Altean* is home. Both, and.

After dinner, Grace hurries to clear up the dirty plates and now-empty trays. Arden is slow-moving until Grace grabs his hand and pulls him down the stairs.

"Come on, Arden! I want them to have the surprise!" she says.

Arden laughs and winks at the rest of the crew, still sitting in a circle on the deck. Ophelia has her eyes closed, her hands linked over her stomach, leaning against Wren's side.

When they return, Grace is carrying a knife and a stack of clean plates. Arden carries another tray.

On it sits a white cake. The frosting is smooth, with little green and purple flowers dotting the sides. Another purple flower sits on top in the center.

"That looks beautiful, Grace," Eli says, smiling at her.

"And delicious," Lex says.

Grace passes out a plate and fork to each person while Arden sets the cake on the deck and starts cutting pieces.

It is delicious. The cake itself is moist and sweet, the frosting creamy and just a little tart.

"If anyone doesn't want their frosting," Lex says, "I will gladly take it off your hands."

Ophelia laughs and passes her plate to Lex. She had eaten the cake and a bit of the frosting, but they had all gotten at least a few flowers on the sides of their pieces, along with some of the large flower on top. Lex scrapes their fork along Ophelia's plate and shoves the small mountain of green, purple, and white frosting into their mouth. Their eyes roll back in their head, and they let out a muffled moan.

"It's so good," they say to Grace around the frosting in their mouth.

"Thanks, Lex." Grace beams.

Wren helps clean up after they've finished with the cake. There wasn't anything left, except for a few crumbs and a purple smear that Lex swiped off the tray with their finger. They follow Wren down into the galley, the cake tray and a few forks in their hands.

"Grace sure knows her way around cake, huh?" Lex says when they put the dirty dishes into the sink. Their mouth is stained purple.

Wren laughs. "She does indeed."

Wren washes while Lex dries and puts away the dishes. When they're finished, Lex reaches behind a heavily mended cookbook and pulls out a bottle with a faded label.

"Want to try some bootleg whiskey?"

Wren doesn't hesitate. "Absolutely."

It's strong, stronger than any whiskey Wren has ever had, and that includes the well-aged stuff she'd stumbled upon in the duke's cellars in the estate. She takes a drink and coughs after she swallows.

"That is..."

"Amazing, right?" Lex takes another swig and screws the lid back on, carefully tucking it behind the book again. "Arden and I break it out on special occasions." They mock whisper, "Don't tell anyone else." They wink.

Wren laughs and hits her fist against her chest. "I won't. You've got my vow."

Lex hangs their arm around Wren's shoulders, and they walk up the stairs back to the deck. "I knew I could count on you."

That night, Wren chooses a nightgown from the shared trunk and straightens to see the charicature drawing they'd sat for. The artist drew them all with exaggerated features—Ophelia's pointed ears, Arden's bushy beard, Clare's large eyes. It was silly and they all laughed until they cried when it was over.

After changing, Wren sleeps in her old hammock. She hangs the leather satchel on the nail it hung on so many months ago. She had picked up her shoes from the spot where they'd landed when she kicked them off earlier and she sets them under the bag. All her pillows and blankets are still there, a shirt she'd hung from the hook attaching the hammock to the pole at her feet is still there. It's as if nothing has changed. As if she never left the ship, as if she never joined Aris's crew. As if she never realized how badly she wanted to be with him.

She falls asleep there, her arm draped over the side of her hammock, her fingers tangled with Ophelia's, gently swaying with the motion of the water against the sides of the ship.

FIFTY-EIGHT

IN THE MORNING, ARDEN makes batter cakes and strawberry syrup. The crew sprawls out on the deck, their cakes rolled into cylinders and dipped in little cups. Lex finds Wren and Ophelia and hands Ophelia a chipped teacup.

"Here," they say. "Try 'em with this." They sit between the girls and stuff a cake into their mouth.

"What is it?" Ophelia scrunches her nose and peers into the cup. A thick brown liquid sits at the bottom.

"Just try it, O," Lex says around the food in their mouth.

Ophelia hesitates, but Wren reaches over and dips the end of her rolled cake in the cup. It holds syrup, though it's thicker than the strawberry. It's sticky, and when Wren pulls the cake from the cup, it's stringy and drips over the side onto Ophelia's hand.

Ophelia yells out in protest of the syrup on her fingers and Wren shrugs at her, taking a bite.

The syrup melts on Wren's tongue, and she lets out a noise in ecstasy. "Oh, my gods, Lex, what is this?" She dips her cake in the teacup again and Ophelia yells again when the syrup drips on her trousers.

Lex laughs. "It's a bourbon syrup Arden made," they say, winking at Wren. "He was saving it for something else, but I sneaked some away." They waggle their eyebrows.

"So, Arden gave some to you when you asked?"

"Semantics," Lex says, dipping another rolled cake into the cup.

Ophelia shoves the teacup into Lex's chest. "Okay, if you two are going to be disrespectful about this damn sticky mess, you get to take care of it." She licks her fingers. "Though I admit it's a delicious sticky mess, I still don't want it all over my clothes."

"Sorry, O," Lex says. They take a flask and a folded handkerchief from their pocket. They dump a little water from the flask onto the cloth and hand it to Ophelia. She uses it to wipe her fingers and the spots on her trousers. "Nothing a little seawater can't fix."

Wren spends the rest of the morning lounging on the sun-warmed deck and feeling the breeze in her hair. She plays games with Jez and Grace, helps Arden peel potatoes in the galley, reorganizes Kiara's mending kit after she accidentally knocks it from the bench, sending thimbles and spools of thread across the deck. She laughs with Ezra and Ophelia, rolls lengths of rope with Clare, uses her hair to tease Penelope while basking in the sun. An hour before she needs to leave, she stands on the quarterdeck with Eli and Lex, looking out toward the horizon.

From the corner of her eye, Wren sees Eli touch Lex's arm and look toward the stairs leading down to the main deck. Lex nods and leaves, hopping down the steps two at a time. They join Ezra and Ophelia by the bow.

Eli steps up close to Wren, her hands clasped behind her back. "Kiara and I talked over Aris's offer last night."

Wren's heart stutters. She forces a slow breath in and out before she says, "And?"

Eli is quiet for a long second. "We don't love the idea of being tied to a specific nation. The draw of *The Altean* is that we're welcoming to everyone. We don't follow a political law. We have a diverse crew." She looks out at them, a smile on her face. She turns back to Wren. "Do you know what the word *altean* means?"

Wren shakes her head. It had never occurred to her that the ship's name might have a meaning.

"It means *safe harbor* in Ancient Kornesian. When we won the ship, we changed her name and chose *The Altean* because we wanted this ship—our home—to be a safe place for anyone that needed it. Having a tie to a country could hurt what Kiara and I have worked to build."

Wren gives a small nod.

The Altean had been a safe place for her. When she'd first stowed away, she had been running from the only place she'd been able to call home since her parents died. And it didn't take long for her to call the ship home instead. She was grateful then, and she's grateful now for the ship, for the people she can call family, for giving her a safe place. There's a pull in her heart, and a tiny voice that says she could stay here. Stay with Eli and Kiara, the family they created. Stay on *The Altean* and sail away from Aris and *The Basilisk*. She could give up everything Aris had promised her and instead be happy with a hammock, with syrup dipped from chipped teacups, with shared clothes and tight living quarters.

She almost says, "I want to stay with you." But then she thinks of the things she could have if she doesn't stay. A crown. A title. Aris. She could still have this family, still sail with them from time to time. She wouldn't really be giving anything up forever.

So, she says, "Are you turning down his offer?"

Eli laughs. "I didn't say that. But if we accept, we have our own conditions."

FIFTY-NINE

WREN TAKES A SEALED envelope with Eli and Kiara's counteroffer back to the inn that afternoon. Ramsey was supposed to meet her at the dock, but she had left earlier than anticipated, and now she's free to walk the streets alone. She stops at a few of the stalls but doesn't linger too long. She knows Aris will be angry if he finds out she was walking in the city alone. It doesn't stop her from browsing the cart of books outside a bookshop or from accepting a sample of lotion from a woman with a wrinkled face.

She's not afraid of Aris's anger. She hasn't been since she was thrown in the hold.

When she gets to the inn, she nods at the concierge and takes the stairs to their floor. It's a long trip up, but she doesn't trust the elevator enough to take it. Though she knows she doesn't need to, she knocks when she gets to the room. Aris opens it, his face neutral until he sees her. His shoulders tense.

"Wren," he says, surprised. "Did Ramsey meet you at the dock? I didn't hear him leave." His eyes fall to the purple cloak around her shoulders, his lips pinching at the corners.

Wren steps into the room and unclasps her cloak from around her neck. Her fingers drag along the purple fabric when she hangs it on a hook by the bathroom. Ophelia had kept the piece that was ripped off when she left, and Kiara mended it for her the night before. She rubs her thumb over the stitches before she turns to Aris. "No, I walked back alone."

His demeanor shifts. "You what?"

She turns away from him and walks further into the room. "Damn your anger, Aris. I'm not a child."

"No. You're only the duke's missing daughter," he spits. "If you're found here, what do you think the duke will do to get you back? Who do you think will take the fall for your actions, Wren?"

"I will." She crosses her arms over her chest. "The duke, at this point, has to know that I haven't been kidnapped. There have been no ransom demands—"

"That you know of."

Wren scoffs. "Are you sending the duke ransom letters? Have you put a price on my head? What am I worth to you, Aris?"

A vein at his temple throbs. But then his jaw relaxes, and he walks closer to her. His fingers, icy against her skin, push a few strands of her hair behind her shoulder.

"You are worth more to me than anything, Wren. You know that."

Wren stares at his face. "Worth more than your throne?"

He pulls his chin back. "That's not fair."

"A simple question, Aris. If I were to ask you to give up your throne for me, would you?"

"You would not ask me to."

He's right, but she asks, "And how can you be sure?"

"Because you want me to have the throne just as much as I want it myself."

She sighs.

Wren still wonders what the throne is really worth to Aris. She knows he's entitled to it, by his birthright, but what role does she play in him claiming it? What would he do to her to ensure he was given what he believed he was rightfully owed? When he says nothing, she almost asks, but decides his answer would make no difference. She will go with him because that's what she wants to do.

She thinks back to standing on the quarterdeck with Eli. How close she had come to staying on *The Altean* and going with them, watching as Therma and the coast of Kornas disappeared behind them. She had been so close to giving everything up again. But the ache behind her sternum kept her here, with Aris.

His fingers find the curve of her jaw and he drags them down her neck and then her arm. His fingers find hers and he squeezes. "Little bird?"

"Eli and Kiara heard your proposal," she says. She had placed her hand on his chest when he'd gotten close to her and now, she drops it and takes a few steps to where her leather satchel hangs. "They send their thanks. And they've sent me back with a response." She pulls the envelope sealed with green wax from her bag and hands it to Aris. She doesn't know what's in the letter. Eli hadn't told her.

After her conversation with Eli on the quarterdeck, the captain had handed Wren the envelope. "Please give your captain our sincerest thanks," Eli had said.

Wren put the envelope in the pocket of her trousers. "I will," she said, giving Eli a hug. When they pulled away, Wren added, "And Aris isn't my captain."

Eli had given her a sad smile. "He is when you're in his command, Wren." She placed her palm against Wren's face and drew her thumb across her cheekbone. "You're always welcome here." Then she dismissed herself to her quarters, leaving Wren on the deck with an ache in her throat.

"What is it?" Aris asks, taking the envelope and tearing into it.

She doesn't think he's asking for her to explain, but she says, "Eli said they had their own terms. She didn't explain them to me, but I assume that's what's in her letter."

Aris tosses the envelope aside and reads the letter quickly, his light eyes moving quickly across the paper. The corner of his mouth tugs upward slightly.

"Good news?" Wren asks. She had bent to pick up the envelope where it had fallen. Her hand was in her satchel as she walked up the steps back to the room, rubbing her thumb along the seal as she climbed. She almost plucks it from the envelope to tuck it in her pocket but decides not to. There will be plenty of correspondence between *The Altean*'s captain and the king and queen of Breton.

"Well, not bad anyway." Aris hands her the letter and sits at the desk, already drafting a response.

Wren reads over it. In clear terms, Eli says that *The Altean* and her captain are ready to accept Aris's offer, but only after he agrees to a few things. No raids on towns that were not an immediate threat, no people would be harmed by *The Altean* and her crew—and that included the transport of known criminals to their deaths. They could veto any jobs, or abandon them if another, higher-priority job came about. And, though it would be known that *The Altean* worked *with* Breton and its king, they would not work solely *for* the king. They would still be free to help where they saw fit, even if that meant helping the country's enemies. They would work as an in-between but would prioritize jobs from

Breton and for its citizens and ruling entity. They would allow *The Basilisk* to work its own jobs but would intervene if they heard that people were being hurt by those jobs.

Wren knows this isn't the ideal arrangement. She knows Aris would rather have complete control over *The Altean*, but she also knows that it would be better to have them on his side, even in only half the amount he desires.

She dozes a little as he works, his pen scratching the paper on the desk. Eventually, she can tell he's finished when the chair scrapes against the floor. She opens her eyes and sits up.

It's dark in the room, the only light from a lamp by the desk that Aris must have turned on.

He comes and sits next to her on the bed. "Will you read this?" he asks, holding out a paper to her. There are ink stains on his fingers. A faint smear of black across his forehead.

"Of course." She takes the letter from him and reads it silently after turning on a lamp near the bed. Aris has written that he agrees to all of Eli's terms and wants to meet for a celebratory dinner in three days' time. There, they'll finalize their terms, sign contracts, and eat together to celebrate their new alliance.

Wren is surprised at his willingness to give into Eli's terms, but she doesn't question him. Perhaps the throne is worth the compromise.

"I think it's perfect," she says. "Shall I deliver it?" It's late, she knows. It's not likely that anyone but the Star Child and Ezra and Ophelia are awake, but she's sneaked onto the ship before. She can do it again.

Aris takes the letter from her and sets it on the nightstand between the beds. "Tomorrow," he says. "Tonight, we rest." He kicks off his boots and tosses them into the corner where Wren had placed hers earlier. Aris turns off the light near them and they lie together on the bed, her back pressed to his chest. "In the coming days, we will have much work to do."

SIXTY

WHILE WALKING THROUGH THE town the next day, Ramsey at her side, Wren runs into Lex and Ezra. They're at a stall not far from the docks, their heavy-laden canvas bags hanging off their shoulders.

Wren skips over to them and says, "Hey!"

They jump and spin around.

"Gods, Wren," Lex says, clutching the strap of their satchel. After they recover, they ask, "What are you up to?"

Wren shoves her head behind her toward where she knows Ramsey is waiting, his arms crossed over his chest. "On our way to meet with Eli."

Ezra looks from her to Ramsey and back. "Aris sent you with a bodyguard?"

Wren lets out a bark of laughter. "More like a babysitter." She tosses her hair over her shoulder.

Ramsey takes the short silence between the three as an opportunity to yell over, "Let's go, Wren. Aris wants us back for dinner."

"See?" she says, turning back to Ezra and Lex. "Babysitter."

Lex laughs and puts down the wares they'd been holding back onto the stall's counter. They nod to the merchant. To Wren, they say, "We'll walk with you. I think we've got all we came for."

Ezra nods and offers his arm to Wren. "Shall we?"

Wren smiles and turns to Ramsey. "See you there."

The three of them walk together down the road and to the docks, their arms looped together.

Wren stands in front of Eli's desk as the captain reads the letter from Aris. Her lips are pursed and pinched at the corners, but when she finishes, Eli looks up at Wren and smiles. "Well," she says. "It seems as if we've reached an agreement."

Wren bounces on the balls of her feet. "It seems so."

Eli stands and holds her hand out to Wren. "To working together, to friends, and to having the rightful person on the Breton throne."

Wren puts her hand in Eli's, and they shake. "To all of those things and more."

When she's finished writing her reply and sealing the envelope it had been tucked into, Eli walks Wren out to the deck and nods at Kiara. Based on the smile that breaks over Kiara's face, Wren guesses she had been worried over the deliberations that Eli had sent back to Aris.

"Will you stay for dinner?" Eli asks. "Your," she pauses, "*babysitter* is welcome, too."

Wren laughs. "No," she says. "I have to get back. Thank you. But I'll see you at dinner in a few days?"

Eli smiles and nods. "Of course. The letter didn't say where, however."

"Aris wanted to hear your answer before any arrangements were made. We'll send word as soon as they are."

"Then I look forward to your correspondence. Until next time." She offers her hand for another shake and Wren accepts. Eli might have been her captain at one point—and in some ways, she always would be—but they're closer to coworkers than crewmates now.

As she walks down the gangplank after saying goodbye to the others, she thinks it'll be good to have Eli and *The Altean*'s crew on her side when Aris takes the throne.

And on hers, when she becomes queen.

SIXTY-ONE

THE WALK BACK TO the inn through town is slow-going, but only because Wren keeps stopping to look at the stalls and shops along the main road. With every pause and bell announcing her arrival in another store, Wren can feel Ramsey's one good eye boring a hole in her back. She shrugs at him, sometimes offering a look that says "sorry" but she's not and she knows he knows it.

She doesn't have much money, but she has enough to buy a few unusually shaped crystal bottles from an old woman with half her head shaved, a dried flower bunch from a girl with no shoes, and a tarnished silver compact mirror with a purple glass stone set in the center of a magnolia flower from a woman with one baby strapped to her front and another to her back.

"The sun is going down, Wren. We need to get back to the inn." Ramsey puts his hand on her shoulder just before she enters the shop with the cart of books out front.

Without thinking, a light blade forms in her fist under her cloak. She almost runs the tip along Ramsey's arm, but instead, she sighs and lets the blade die. "Fine. I'm out of money, anyway." She holds out the hand that had the light blade in it just moments before and says, "Lead on."

He does, at a quicker pace than she had anticipated, but she follows along behind him, rubbing her thumb against the purple stone in the compact, tucked into the inner pocket in her cloak.

Aris is waiting in the lobby of the inn when they make it back. His jaw is clenched.

"You were supposed to be back an hour ago," he says. He's keeping his voice low to not draw attention of the other guests in the lobby.

"I tried, but she," Ramsey shoves his thumb at Wren, "decided to look at every piece of garbage in that market."

Aris looks at Wren, but his anger is directed at Ramsey. "That's why I sent you with her. *You* were supposed to keep her on task. *You* were meant to bring her back here on time." It looks like he wants to shove his cold finger into Ramsey's chest, but Wren knows he won't. Not here. Aris is cruel, but he won't draw attention from strangers. He'll wait until they're back aboard *The Basilisk* sailing to Breton before he punishes Ramsey.

Aris takes a breath and holds out his hand to Wren. "Come, Wren. Our dinner is waiting in our room."

He gives Ramsey one last withering glare before the elevator doors close.

The food has gone cold in the wait for Wren and Aris, but they eat it still. Aris lounges on the bed, leaned against the headboard, his plate balanced in one hand. Wren sits on the floor, her back against the other bed. She eats directly out of the containers with her fingers.

"Why did you delay your return?" Aris asks. He doesn't look at her.

Wren shrugs a shoulder and puts more food in her mouth. "I wasn't delaying. I just wanted to look at the market."

"I was worried," he admits. "Worried you'd decided not to come back."

"Aris, I was gone for less than four hours."

He looks down at her, his light eyes meeting hers. "Still. I know you miss them."

Wren nods. She takes another piece of beef from the takeout box and says, "They offered for me to stay."

"And you didn't." It's not a question, but there's curiosity there, nonetheless.

The Altean had almost everything. A community, friendship, a sense of family she'd never had. It was worth a lot, and Wren would have happily accepted it a year ago. Even a few months ago, before she'd gotten to know Aris better. And, though Aris isn't the image of a perfect partner, she can't imagine her life not at his side.

"No. You can offer me more."

His mouth pulls at the corner. He focuses back on his plate. "It's not just an offer. It's a vow."

The next day, Aris goes into town with Ramsey while Wren stays in the room at the inn. She debates going downstairs and sitting in the lobby, but instead she orders an absurd amount of food from the kitchen and gorges herself on delicacies and desserts made with cream and chicken and some of that fancy cheese she'd eaten with Eli the last time she was in Therma. With every new food cart, the inn worker tries to peek into the room, probably to see the other people inside, but Wren only opens the door enough to thank them and then watches as they walk down the hallway before she opens the door and pulls the cart in.

There's nothing to hide, especially not a crowd of people with whom she's sharing all the food, but Aris had let no one, even Ramsey or Smith, into the room since the first day, so Wren keeps his habit.

Other than eating, there isn't much to do. She pulls the desk chair to the window and peers down into the street and little market stalls below. She opens the window and a breeze that smells like salt and fried potatoes drifts in. She can see the children from a few days prior playing with their patched ball. The dog that was playing with them before sleeps in the shade. She could go down and look at the stalls, but Aris hadn't left her any money. She'd charged all the food she'd ordered to the room.

Aris and Ramsey are gone most of the day. Other than people watching from the window, Wren naps, bathes, and reads the small book from the drawer of the table between the two beds.

Finally, just before sunset, the door opens and Aris walks through, closing the door behind him.

Wren bounces up from the chair at the window. "You're back," she says. She feels silly being excited. But who wouldn't be, knowing a feast with their friends is only days away?

Aris shrugs out of his coat and hangs it by the door. "It smells like fried potatoes in here," he says.

Wren goes to the icebox and pulls out a box. "I couldn't eat anymore, so I saved the rest for you."

He opens the lid, takes a potato from the box, and takes a bite. "Thank you," he says. He looks around the room. The beds are unmade, the papers that had been scattered across the top of the desk have been pushed aside to make room for Wren to eat, and the towel she had used to dry her hair after her bath is draped over the back of the chair. "Did you have a good day?"

She shrugs and falls back into the chair, tucking her legs under her. "It was all right. I enjoyed the time to myself." Aris doesn't say anything else, so she prompts, "What about you? Did you find a place to host us?"

Aris leans against the low dresser. "Yes. A pub not far from the town center. We have an event hall booked."

A smile breaks over Wren's face. "Has Eli been informed?"

"Yes. She was glad to hear."

SIXTY-TWO

THE NEXT FEW DAYS are busy, with Wren insisting on being consulted about all aspects of the celebration. She approves food choices and convinces Aris to get a baker to make a cake for them. One is hired on very short notice to bake a cake with two wooden ships at the top that's delivered the day of the event.

"It looks like we're hosting a wedding of two ships," Ramsey says, his arms crossed over his chest.

"We kind of are," Wren says unconvincingly. She adjusts the dark ship that represents *The Basilisk* and steps back, her hands on her hips. She shrugs and then turns and busies herself elsewhere in the event hall. She can feel Ramsey roll his eyes before following her.

Aris is out, finalizing things he won't tell Wren about, so Ramsey is once again her bodyguard. After the incident walking back from *The Altean* alone earlier in the week, he doesn't get more than ten feet from her. Wren finds herself drinking more water to have an excuse to leave him for the quiet and solitary sanctuary of the toilets.

Just after lunch, Wren goes back to the inn and bathes. She ties up her hair into two braids and wraps them around her head in a makeshift crown. Aris gave her money to buy a new outfit for the evening—dark leather trousers with matching belt, a white shirt with lace along the collar and cuffs, and a purple velvet vest with light metal buttons shaped like gladiolus blooms. Looking in the full-length mirror on the back of the washroom door, she can see the changes made in her since she left Sulesia. She can also see the ways in which she'll change if she agrees to be the queen of Breton. The crown atop her head wouldn't be made with her own red hair, but with silver and jewels and pearls. Her clothes will be replaced with garments made of fine fabrics and hemmed with stitches that won't wear quickly. Her boots will be made new, just for her, not a pair that her feet happen to fit.

She bounces on her heels before leaving the washroom and going back into the main room.

Aris is there, a package clutched in his hands.

"Wren," he says, seemingly surprised. His eyes glance down at her outfit. He smiles, holding out the bundle to her. "I picked this up for you. I'd hoped you'd wear it."

Wren takes the package and sits on the bed, her legs crossed. She unties the twine bow and pulls out a black cloak. The clasp at the neck is made of silver—real silver, Wren realizes—and is shaped like leaves. She holds it up and notices the embroidery. Down the center hems and around the bottom are magnolia blossoms and the same leaves as the clasp in silver thread. Wren runs her fingers over them.

"They're from the alder tree," Aris says. "There are a lot of them in Breton."

She hums, her voice quiet.

Aris sits next to her on the bed. "The title is yours, Wren. All you need to do is accept."

Wren drops her hands, the black fabric of her new cloak gathering in her lap. She looks at him.

"You don't need to say anything now," he says, reaching into his pocket. "I want you next to me in Breton, but I know your heart may not lie in the same place as mine." He pulls his hand out of his pocket. He takes her hand and places his fist in her palm. "I want you to say yes." He opens his hand, pulling away and leaving a thin silver circle in Wren's palm, "but I will not force it on you."

Wren gingerly picks up the ring and looks at it. It's simple, braided silver with tiny purple stones. It's beautiful. "A ring for a queen," she says simply.

She looks at him. She has to tell him she doesn't want the throne. At least not for the reasons he wants it. "I don't want it," she says before she can stop herself. Aris pulls his chin back, and she corrects, "The throne, I mean. But not because of the power. I don't care about that." She lifts her other hand and runs her finger along Aris's split eyebrow, down the side of his face. "I just want to be with you. Wherever you are, that's where I want to be."

Aris takes a breath through his nose and lets it out slowly. Then he picks up the ring and slips it on her finger. "Long may we reign," he says.

SIXTY-THREE

WREN IS GLAD FOR her new cloak that evening. Though it's spring and the days are warm enough without any cover, the nights are still cool and, with the windows open, the event hall is a bit chilly. She could easily use her magics to warm herself, but the black cloak is heavy on her shoulders and brings her comfort in more than just warmth. She's also grateful she can hide her hand inside. The ring on her finger looks out of place to her, and she knows Lex and Ophelia would see it immediately.

She doesn't intend to keep it a secret, but she doesn't want the rest of the evening to be overshadowed by her and Aris's...*engagement* seems like too heavy a word. She's not sure what else it would be called, though.

The crew of *The Altean* arrives in one big group. Wren can hear when they arrive. Their laughter and footfalls coming up the stairs will forever be familiar and comforting to her. She stands and she and Aris make their way to the door that leads from the stairway to the event hall. Many of *The Basilisk* crew are already inside the room, drinking red wine from crystal glasses.

Eli and Kiara are the first up the stairs, Lex and Arden are next. Clare, Ophelia, and Ezra follow close behind, their arms linked together. Jez must have stayed behind on the ship with Grace. The Star Child, also, is not with them.

Wren welcomes them all with hugs. Aris is cordial, shaking all of their hands and thanking them for coming. Wren has never seen him smile so much. There's no hesitancy, no malice or barely contained hate between Aris and her friends. Perhaps this evening will go as well as she hopes. Perhaps a new alliance can be forged. Perhaps she really can get Aris and her friends all at once.

When everyone has been served their drink of choice—Aris and Ramsey exchange a short look when Wren and Ophelia switch drinks, gagging at their first choices—they sit at a long table. Aris sits at the head, Wren to his right and *The Basilisk* crew down the table next to her, and Eli and Kiara to his left, *The Altean* crew down the table next to them.

Wren raises her glass in her right hand and offers a toast. "To new acquaintances and fast friends," she says.

Everyone around the table lifts their glasses in unison.

"And to you, little bird, who has been invaluable in creating this alliance," Aris says. His hand touches her arm briefly as he lifts his glass a second time.

"To Wren," Eli says, her smile so big, her eyes crinkle at the corners. Then everyone around the table is toasting Wren.

Her chest swells and they drink.

The feast is brought out in courses. A soup made with bone broth, chunks of carrots and celery and onion floating in it; a salad with sliced beets and strawberries; a whole side of beef, roasted and juicy on a bed of roasted potatoes, leeks, zucchini, and purple carrots.

When the plates are cleared after the beef and vegetables, Aris lifts his glass again and touches his silver fork to it, a chime that grabs everyone's attention. He sets his glass and silverware down. "Wren and I," he starts, causing her heart to stutter, "have some news to share." He turns to her and nods toward her lap, where her left hand has been sitting throughout dinner.

She bites the inside of her cheek as she lifts her hand and moves her fingers slightly, allowing the light from the chandelier to catch on the purple stones.

The crew of *The Altean* let out a small collective gasp. Wren doesn't think she imagines the clench in Lex's jaw, or the hitched breath in Ophelia's chest.

If Aris notices their reactions, he doesn't respond. "When we return to Breton, we will be married, and Breton shall have a new queen."

Eli is the first to speak. "Congratulations," she says. She hides her surprise well, but Wren can see the way her lips pinch at the corners, can hear the slight tightness in her voice.

"Thank you," Wren says. "It was unexpected but not unwelcome." That's not true. Aris had all but proposed long before he'd given her a ring.

Ophelia, recovered from her momentary shock, leans forward and says in a mock whisper, "Well, we better be invited, at the very least."

Wren laughs. "I'm going to need a maid of honor."

Ophelia lifts her chin and smiles. "I accept."

Dessert is brought out then. In fine porcelain dishes, chocolate pudding is served with berries and syrup. They're also given a grilled peach half and a scoop of frozen vanilla cream. Jars of fresh honey follow, with warm cow's milk to stir into.

The feast ends with pots of tea and mingling in the dining room. Each crew mostly stays in their own group, but Eli and Aris both make a point of saying hello to everyone. Wren stands alone for a moment, pouring tea into a cup and dumping three cubes of sugar in after.

"Careful, you'll start taking after Lex." Ophelia slides up to her and pops a sugar cube in her mouth.

Wren turns around and leans against the table the pots of tea and mix-ins are sitting on. "They've got some good habits," she says. "Wonder what else they could teach me."

Ophelia chuckles. Then she juts her chin toward Ramsey, who leans against the back wall, a slight scowl on his face as he talks with Laszlo. "Does he ever stand in a different position?"

His arms are crossed over his chest, his chin lifted slightly. His eyes follow Aris as he walks around the room.

Wren shakes her head. "I don't think so. Maybe when he sleeps?"

"Doubtful. He probably sleeps standing up."

Wren laughs. "He might have to with the way his snores could trigger an earthquake."

"Ah, so that's why he works on a ship. Not much to shake when the ocean is your competition."

They watch their friends and the crew of *The Basilisk* quietly for a little while before Ophelia says, "So, you're engaged."

Wren holds out her hand and looks at her ring. "Yeah. I am."

"It's pretty," Ophelia offers.

Wren drops her hand. "You don't like it."

"Oh, no, I love the ring. I just," she lets out a breath. "I just want to make sure you're not doing it because *he* wants you to. It should be because it's what *you* want."

Wren looks at Ophelia for a minute before saying, "It is. I don't know how to explain it, O. But I feel less when I'm not with him."

Ophelia takes her hand and squeezes her fingers. "You are not less without anyone. You are perfect the way you are." Then she looks at Ezra, who is busy trying to balance an empty teacup on the tip of his finger while Lex and Clare egg him on. "I do understand what you mean, though." She looks back at Wren. "And if you're happy, I am too." Wren knows she's telling the truth.

Now Wren squeezes Ophelia's fingers. "What I said is true. I do want you there. And I do want you as my maid of honor."

Ophelia runs her thumb over Wren's. "I know," she says, a hint of pride in her voice. Her blue eyes are shining when she looks at Wren. "And I meant that I accept, too."

As the night winds down, some of *The Basilisk* crew excuse themselves back to the ship. Ophelia and Ezra say goodnight as well and offer their congratulations before heading down the hallway, hand in hand. Each person in Eli's crew is given a small wrapped cake, as thanks for attending the party.

"I am happy for you, Wren," Eli says, her hands holding Wren's. "Know that your spot on my crew is always open for you, no matter your title." She smiles and touches her fingers to Wren's cheek briefly.

"Thank you, Captain. I'm grateful for your companionship." Wren leans her head into Eli's touch and smiles as the captain steps aside to make room for Kiara.

"If you need help with your dress, you know where to find me," she says, winking.

Wren laughs. "I'll remember that. As soon as a date is set, I'll send word to you. I won't have my wedding without you two there." She ignores the way her heart stutters at the word *wedding*.

Wren watches as Eli, Kiara, Arden, Lex, and Clare make their way down the hallway. She laughs and waves to Lex one last time when they turn and waggle their fingers at Wren.

When the last of their guests have gone, Wren sags against the table, exhausted.

"If just one feast leaves you feeling like this, how do you expect to be queen?" Aris asks, leaning against the table. Wren knows he's joking by the slight upturn of his lips.

"It wasn't the dinner that has me exhausted. It was more the anticipation of how they'd react to this." She waves her left hand in the air.

"Ah," Aris says. Then he straightens. "We should get you back to the inn where you can rest."

They leave the rest of *The Basilisk* crew behind at the pub to clean up. Ramsey doesn't look happy as Wren and Aris descend the steps, but he doesn't object.

The streets are mostly empty on their way back to the inn. A few people huddle in doorways, cloaks pulled tight around their faces, mugs of tea clutched in their hands. Aris nods at all of them as they pass.

Wren immediately strips off her boots once inside the room. She rubs the bottoms of her feet and stretches her toes and calves.

"If you're feeling up to it, I have one last surprise," Aris says.

She puts on a pair of slippers and lets Aris lead her up a flight of stairs before he pushes a door open. A rush of cool air hits Wren, and she gulps in the clear salty breeze as she steps onto the roof of the pub. Wren looks up and takes in the stars, the waning moon still rising in the east.

"It's beautiful up here," she breathes.

"Yes," Aris says, "it is." He holds out his hand to her. "Come."

She puts her hand in his, allowing him to lead her to the edge of the roof. She looks out over the town and, off in the distance, can just make out the docks. There are a few lanterns hanging on masts, and dark shadows of ships bob in the water.

"Is this your surprise?" She'd be lying if she said it wasn't a bit disappointing. After the evening with her friends, a clear sky and the ships in the distance are small joys.

Aris lets out a breathy chuckle. "No." He points out to the docks. "Keep watching."

A few seconds later, a loud pop sounds, and then a whistle as a firework is launched into the sky. It's followed by another, then another and another. Blue and purple, pink and green. The starbursts are bright, and Wren's face lights up with wonder at them. She'd been a little girl the last time she saw fireworks. The duke had banned them in Sudal when a local shop had burned down by a stray during a winter solstice celebration.

They stand on the roof and watch the show until it's finished. It's chilly in the open, but Wren's cloak is heavy on her shoulders, and her heart is full.

She'd secured Aris and her friends all in one evening.

Once they're back in their room, sleep comes easily. She doesn't bother washing the kohl from her eyes or brushing out the braids around her head. Aris takes the cloak from her shoulders and drapes it across the back of the chair at the desk, and she unbuttons the vest, letting it fall to the floor. The last thing she sees before sleep overcomes her is Aris pulling the curtains closed.

PART VI

SIXTY-FOUR

THE DOCK LEADING TO *The Altean* is empty. After the celebration at the pub, Eli and Kiara had sent their crew ahead of them back to the ship as they walked down the quiet streets of Therma, hand in hand.

A quiet tune drifts down from one of the other docked ships and Kiara twirls in front of Eli, her skirts fanning out around her.

Eli watches her, smiling. Kiara laughs and dances across the dock, her arms spread out. Eli joins her and they dance, Kiara's skirts hiked up to her knees, Eli's jacket tossed to the ground. They touch ankles, wrists, elbows, before joining hands and spinning under the stars.

A few loud bangs and their faces are lit with color as fireworks burst above them.

"Did you do this?" Kiara asks, her smile wide, gesturing to the sky with a spin of her finger.

"No!" Eli says, still dancing with her first mate. "Celebrations all around!"

They're laughing, their foreheads pressed together, when another bang rings out. Eli falls forward, her head resting against Kiara's shoulder, and Kiara laughs until Eli's knees buckle and she drops to the dock.

All at once, Kiara's laughter dies on her lips and is replaced by a scream. Eli lies in front of her, a hole in her chest, blood pooling around her and soaking her shirt.

"No, no, no, no, no," Kiara says, her hands fluttering over Eli's arms and face.

A small trickle of blood leaks from the corner of Eli's mouth. She raises her hand and places it against Kiara's cheek, leaving a red smear across her freckled skin.

Kiara looks down the dock, where *The Altean* waits, a dimly lit lantern hanging from the mast. "We have to get you on board," she says to Eli. "It's right there, I'll drag you."

"Heart," Eli manages. Her voice has gone quiet, her skin already getting cold. "It's all right."

Above them, more fireworks burst, sending out flashes of color across the dock and Eli's face.

"Eli, please," Kiara pleads. The makeup she had so delicately dusted on runs down her face. "We can make it."

"No, Love, we can't." Eli juts her chin toward her ship. "Go," she says. "Take care of them, okay?"

"Eli," Kiara says again, begging.

Just as another firework explodes overhead, Kiara falls backward. Her chest goes numb and when she looks down, a blossom of red has spread over the top of her dress. She lets out a sob, but not of anguish. She's grateful. She won't be without Eli, after all.

Before the world goes dark, she drags herself beside Eli and places her cheek in Eli's palm.

They smile, one last time, before their ship at the end of the dock goes up in flame.

SIXTY-FIVE

The dining room is empty the next morning apart from Wren, Aris, the other crew members of *The Basilisk*, and a few inn employees. While Wren is gathering her plate and silverware, she notices that the streets outside are crowded. Loud shouts and voices come through the windows. People run down the street. She asks the woman serving the batter cakes what all the fuss is about.

"There was a fire at the docks last night," she says. She places a few batter cakes onto Wren's plate. "It was quite a loss."

"Is everyone okay?" Wren picks up the carafe of syrup and pours a thin stream onto her plate over the cakes.

The woman shakes her head and puts a stack of batter cakes onto Ramsey's plate. "No," she says. "*The Altean* captain and her first mate..."

The woman's words fade as Wren's stomach drops and her heart stutters. There's a sound of breaking glass and something warm splashes onto her legs.

She doesn't realize she's started to run until someone's arms are around her. She beats their forearms as they pick her up. She realizes the screams she hears are tearing from her throat.

She's turned around and her feet are set on the stone floor again. Ramsey's big hands stay on her shoulders.

Aris sets down his plate and silverware and starts walking toward Wren, his hands behind his back. His jaw is set, his face harder than she's seen in over a month. Since he left her in the darkness in the hold.

Her heart drops further into her stomach. "What did you do?" she breathes out, tears brimming on her bottom lashes.

Aris looks at the woman that served her batter cakes just moments before and shoves his head in the direction of the door. She lifts her arm, snaps her fingers once, and the other employees follow her out, closing the door behind them.

"Put those away, Wren," Aris says, looking at her hands.

She hadn't realized she'd done it, but in each of her hands, she holds a light blade. She thinks about shoving her arm backward into Ramsey's stomach. Thinks about lifting the other and throwing it into Aris's skull. But instead, she lets them die.

"Why?" Wren has stopped struggling against Ramsey's hold. Her hands hang at her sides, balled into empty fists.

Aris flicks his eyes at the wall and Ramsey steps away. He leans against the wall behind Wren.

When Aris gets within an arm's reach, Wren slaps him, so hard his head turns to the side. When he looks at her, his fingers touch his cheek gently. The red left on his skin is stark in comparison to the rest of him.

"Why?" Wren asks again. Tears stream down her face, smearing the kohl left from the night before.

"They were a liability, Wren."

"A *liability*?"

Aris walks around her in a slow circle. "You know they were, Wren. You heard Eleanor's terms. She wanted veto power on any jobs we gave her."

"You *agreed* to them, Aris. Why did you agree if you didn't intend to follow through?"

Aris lets out a shallow laugh. "Everyone has heard of the immortal captain and her nearly invulnerable first mate. With your help, I learned the story I'd heard in Maia was true. Why it was so rare for them to leave their ship." He steps in front of Wren and looks down his nose. "I thought about poisoning the food, but decided it was too much work to keep track of which plates they were eating on. Then I thought about their drinks. Lucky I didn't though, since you and Ophelia swapped cups before dinner."

Wren didn't think it was possible for her heart to sink any further. "Ophelia," she breathes out. "Did you kill all of them?"

Aris starts to pace in front of her, two steps to her left, two steps past her to the right. "Multiple bodies were recovered. Only those of Captain Eleanor Crowley and her first mate were able to be identified. The others were burned beyond recognition."

Wren lets out a choked sob. Her vision blurs and the floor rushes up to meet her.

SIXTY-SIX

WREN WAKES TO THE sway of the waves against the hull of *The Basilisk*. The cabin is dark, except for a single lantern casting dim yellow light across the threadbare carpet. The curtains are drawn, and Wren suspects that if she tries the door leading to deck, it'll be locked.

The black cloak Aris had given her in Therma hangs by the door, and she almost pulls it on, but then she notices her purple cloak. She's surprised it's here, that it wasn't left behind at the inn. She picks it up from where it's been draped over the back of the chair at the desk, and she pulls it over her shoulders, fastening the clasp at her throat as she slowly walks across the floor. The brass knob is warm in her hand as she tests the lock. To her surprise, the door swings open.

Sea breeze hits her face, and she squints against the sun. Aris and Ramsey stand at the wheel, staring out at the horizon.

Wren stands in the doorway, her left hand clutched around the clasp of the cloak. She watches Aris. His hands are linked behind his back, his hair moving in the breeze. He looks, as always, like a lost prince, like a character out of a fairy tale. But Wren knows better now than to think he's a lost child trying to get home. He's a monstrous boy that will sacrifice anything in pursuit of his own goals. Whatever was left inside of him that belonged to Jakob is gone.

She could kill him. It would be easy. The light blade is already formed in the hand she keeps hidden inside the cloak. She can feel it thrumming against the pads of her fingers, her bones, her soul, begging to be released. Begging to tear a hole through Aris's chest.

She steps up next to him and pushes the hair from her face with both hands. "Where are we going?"

Aris turns to her; a look of surprise flashes across his face, but it quickly disappears. "Breton," he says. "We're to take our thrones, if you'll still have it."

Wren holds out her left hand, letting the stones in her ring catch in the sun.

Aris has shown her he can be a monster. He knows nothing of her monstrous side.

"Onward, then."

SIXTY-SEVEN

OPHELIA CLIMBS INTO THE dingy as Ezra gently lowers it down into the water. Once it's floating safely on the surface, Ezra climbs down the ropes and settles into it.

"Ready?" Ophelia asks.

Ezra puts his hand on hers. The last few days—watching *The Altean* burn, seeing the bodies of their friends laid out on the docks, most beyond recognition, hiring and convincing the captain and crew of a fishing boat they need to get to Breton immediately, the arduous journey of tracking down *The Basilisk* and its crew—had been challenging and there had been little sleep.

"Yeah," he says wearily. "Let's end it."

The clouds in the sky obscure the moon's reflection on the surface of the sea. Ezra and Ophelia take turns rowing toward Aris's ship.

As they get closer, Ezra's heart races faster and faster in his chest. He can feel Ophelia in front of him, in the dark. She'd pressed herself against the wall of the boat, a knife clutched in each of her hands. Her knee presses into his boot.

"Switch?" Ezra says.

"Okay." Ophelia sheaths her knife and takes Ezra's place on the seat.

Suddenly, a shot rings through the night, and she topples over onto Ezra.

He screams her name, presses his hand to the wound on her back. It's deep, he can tell. And he knows she won't live. They're too far from, well, anywhere.

Another shot rings out and Ezra presses himself to the bottom of the boat.

"Ez," Ophelia manages. "You have to keep going."

He drags his fingers down her cheek. It feels like his chest is caving in. He can't see her face in the dark. "How?" he asks.

"I'll hide you."

The Star Child on board *The Basilisk* watches the dinghy as it approaches. There had been no movement other than it floating closer and closer to the ship. Now, the Star Child sees only one body inside. She's bloody, with red streaks down her cheek. Her chest still rises and falls, but she'll be dead soon enough, so the Star Child holsters her gun and turns from the railing.

Then a knife cuts across her throat, burning her skin and turning it from alabaster to scarlet. She's dead before she has a chance to scream.

SIXTY-EIGHT

WREN AND ARIS WAKE to their door swinging open and banging against the wall. Ramsey stands there, his mouth open to say something, but then he falls forward, a black-handled knife stuck through the back of his skull.

Behind him, someone stands in the frame, silhouetted in the flames burning on the deck. They hold more flames in their hands, illuminating the sharp angles of their face.

"Ezra?" Wren's breath catches in her chest and tears spring to her eyes. At least one of her friends is alive. She gets out of bed and pulls on her purple cloak. "What are you doing?"

The look on his face and his words stop her where she stands. "Destroying you. Like you destroyed us. Eli never should have let you join our crew." Fire spreads up his arms and across his chest, down his torso and legs. As the flames lick up his tear-stained face, he says, "I hope Adreus is half as cruel to you as we were kind." Then, the fire explodes from him and the ship bursts apart around them.

Wren manages to find a piece of the wheel to cling to. The water is cold, and she wills heat into her limbs and fingers to keep her afloat and clutch the wood. The scrapes and burns over her face ache in the salty sea breeze.

A body floats past her and she grabs it, turning it over. It's a crew member whose name she never bothered to learn. She pushes them away.

A dinghy floats close, unharmed by flame. She starts to pull herself over the side, but the person inside makes her limbs go numb as her concentration slips.

Ophelia lies at the bottom, her skin still warm, her chest unmoving. Wren's fingers itch to try to restart her heart, but she knows that's not how her healing magics work. Ophelia's heart could restart, but she wouldn't be the same. Especially without Ezra.

Wren reaches into the dinghy, closing Ophelia's eyes and whispering a small prayer to Adreus. Her fingers brush down Ophelia's chest where her knives are secured.

Somehow, Aris finds her after Wren has pushed Ophelia's dinghy away. They clutch the wheel together. Aris's pale skin has turned blue in the cold, his mouth going from deep red to purple and bruised. Even with her magics, Wren knows they can't hold on much longer.

"Come with me," he says, closing his fingers around her wrist. "Please. Come with me."

Her friends are dead. Most everyone she's ever cared about has had their screams snatched by the wind. Why not her, too? So, she nods, letting the warmth fade from her arms and fingers.

Aris moves to wrap his arms around her, and she lets go of the wheel. Then the sea swallows them, and they're gone.

EPILOGUE

THERE'S A KNOCK ON the Duke of Sulesia's bed-chamber door.

"Come in," he calls wearily.

It's been over a year since his daughter's disappearance. They'd searched for her for months after. He had sent out countless parties to search the port towns and cities she'd been spotted in. They'd all come up empty. Then, all news of her ceased. It was as if she'd fallen from the earth. The duke refused to believe her dead.

"I shouldn't have been so harsh on her," he'd told his most trusted councilman, his best friend, and the father of his daughter's best friend, the morning after she'd run. "I shouldn't have forced that marriage on her." It was his biggest regret. He'd made himself sick with worry and guilt.

Now, he spends most of his days locked in his rooms, doing the least amount of work he can to keep his little country afloat. He signs things put in front of him, approves loans and grants for schools and military buildings. The Kornesian king had sent many correspondences that went unanswered.

"Sir," the man at the door says.

The duke lifts his dark eyes to him. The man's red coat and gun strapped across his back mark him as an infantry soldier in Sulesia's military. He has a piece of paper gripped in his hands. The duke can see the broken orange seal on the page.

"She's been found. Off the coast of Breton, near Mythshade." The man is out of breath, his face nearly as red as his coat. He'd run here, from wherever it was the letter had been delivered.

"Is she alive?" Despite himself, the duke can't help but feel a little hopeful. There was a chance his daughter could come home, that he could apologize, that things could go back to the way they were before. If she was dead, well, at least her body could come home. He could bury her in the back garden, under a patch of lavender.

The man looks at the letter in his hand again, his eyes roaming over the page to double check the information he's about to give.

"Yes."

END OF BOOK ONE

TURN THE PAGE FOR
A BONUS CHAPTER

THERE'S A SMALL ISLAND half a day's journey from the bay of Kornas. They have to anchor at sea and then take the dinghies to the island. Wren rides with Ophelia, Kiara, Clare, and Grace, and when they make it to the sandy beach, Arden meets them to pull the little boat onto land. He ties it off at a stake where the other dinghy is already anchored.

They follow Arden down a pathway that leads to a clearing walled in by mountains. A waterfall from high on a cliff feeds into a swimming hole ringed by grass and boulders warming in the sun.

The rest of the crew has wasted no time. Ezra sits topless on a blanket he's spread out in the sun. There's a large oak tree up a short hill and Lex swings naked from a rope tied to a branch hanging over the water. Jez watches from a rock, pulling dice and cards from the satchel he'd brought. Grace runs over to him, the pigtails high on her head bouncing with every step.

Eli walks over to Kiara, Wren, Ophelia, and Clare. Penelope trots along behind the captain, her paws popping over the long grass.

"This is one of our favorite places to relax," Eli says, draping her arm around Kiara's bare shoulders. She looks to Wren. "Have any places like this in Sulesia?"

Wren lets out a laugh as she looks around. Flowers and wild grasses hug the trunks of trees. Butterflies flit over the sun-sparkled water and bees float lazily from flower to flower. Lex lets go of the rope and whoops before cannon balling into the water. They surface and wipe the water from their eyes before trudging out and making their way back to the tree.

"No," Wren says, another laugh passing through her lips. "We have nothing like this in Sulesia."

Ophelia joins Ezra and Arden on the blanket and Kiara and Eli find their own spot on the grass to sunbathe. Clare and Wren sit on a rock near Jez and Grace and pass a bottle of warm beer between them.

"I'm really glad you joined us," Clare says, wrapping her lips around the mouth of the bottle.

Wren's chest warms, and it has nothing to do with the beer or the sun. "Me too," she says.

Clare smiles and passes the bottle to her. She nods her head and her whole body seems to follow. She turns to Wren. "You ever hear of the phrase three's a crowd?"

Wren nods and swallows the beer in her mouth. She'd felt it plenty going around towns with Ezra and Ophelia. They never made her feel like a third wheel, or like she was in the way, but when they held hands walking through markets or whispered behind their hands at pub tables, it was hard not to notice the emptiness at her side.

Clare shrugs a shoulder. "There's been enough of us to pair off for a few years now. And there always seemed to be someone that wasn't part of a pair." She looks at Wren and winks, bumping her shoulder into Wren's. "But now there is."

Wren takes another swig from the bottle and passes it to Clare. "So, you're only glad because now you're not alone?" She smirks.

Clare laughs. "No. But it is a perk."

Wren is glad she's not alone, too. Since Jakob died, she hasn't had anyone besides the duke, and he wasn't her idea of friendship. It's been nice to always have someone by her side. Lex telling jokes while they wash the dishes, holding hands with Ophelia over the side of her hammock as they sleep, Grace offering an extra slice of cake after dinner, Arden stoic as they peel potatoes and carrots for stew, Kiara beside her on the bench mending clothes. The companionship was the best part of joining the crew of *The Altean*.

"There's always Penelope," Wren jokes, jutting her chin in the direction of the cat, laid out on her back near Eli and Kiara.

Clare throws back her head and laughs and it bounces off the trees and cliffs surrounding them. "Sure," she agrees, "if your idea of a good day is sitting in the sun and eating fish."

"Isn't that what we do on deck, anyway?"

"Oh," Clare says. She tilts her head. "I didn't think of it that way."

They finish the beer, and Clare asks if Wren wants to get in the water. After taking off their outer layer, they walk to where Ezra, Ophelia, and Arden are sitting and extend the invitation.

Arden stays back, leaning back on his hands, his face turned toward the sun. Ophelia and Ezra stand and dust their hands off before they push their trousers from their hips and toss them in a pile on the corner of the blanket.

Ezra strides up beside Wren and rocks on his heels as they walk toward the lake. "Hey, Wren. I dare you to cannonball from the rope."

Wren stops at the edge of the water. "What?"

"The rope," Ezra repeats, pointing to Lex as they swing out over the water and let go. The rope swings back until it hangs loosely from the tree branch. "I dare you to cannonball from it."

Wren puts her hands on her hips. "You think it's gonna take a dare to get me to jump from the rope?"

Ezra crosses his arms over his chest. "I dunno," he says. "Will you do it?"

Wren watches Lex climb out of the water and stand, the rope in their hands, getting ready to swing again. She'd watched them from the rock with Clare. They would run on the now-worn grass, holding the rope until they jumped and swung over the surface of the water. Sometimes they tucked into a ball, other times they flailed as they hung in the air before falling into the water. When they surfaced, they'd swim to the rope and grab the end before walking back to their starting point on the grass, and they'd do it all over again.

Wren shrugs. "Yeah."

Ezra cocks his eyebrow as he watches her walk up the hill to the tree.

She stands at the spot where Lex stands before they take off running and watches as Lex grabs the end of the rope and walks back up the slope.

"Hey Wren!" they exclaim. "You want a turn?"

Wren flicks her eyes toward their friends, watching from the water near the blanket. "Ezra dared me. I think he thinks I'm too scared."

Lex laughs. "No, he doesn't think you're scared. Last time we were here, he bragged about how good he was at rope swinging. He said he could do a back flip and when he tried, he starfished and landed on his stomach."

That explains Ophelia's "Hey, starfish" comment when she and Arden joined Ezra on the blanket earlier. Wren cringes. "Ow," she says, rubbing her hand over her bare stomach.

"Yeah," Lex nods. "He's probably hoping you'll mess up as bad and the starfish title will be passed to you." They hold out the rope to Wren.

Wren takes it and runs her fingers over the fibers of the braid. Then she looks at Lex. "Any tips?"

Lex smiles. "Run as fast as you can." They hold an arm parallel to the trail they'd run in the grass. "When you get to the end, jump up and out, not just out. You won't get enough altitude. Let go of the rope once you get to the highest point in your jump. Then curl and fall." Lex gives Wren another smile and steps back, then holds their arms out as if to give Wren the stage.

Wren nods and turns to the water, pointing her feet forward. She takes a deep breath and grips the rope tighter before she takes off. The runway is short, but she's able to build up enough speed that when she pushes off the edge of the bluff in a jump, she's able to get good altitude. She holds onto the rope and for a split second, she feels like she's floating. She turns her head to look at her friends. Lex is jumping up, their arms above their head. Ophelia and Clare shout and clap. Ezra is scowling, his arms crossed over his chest.

Then she's falling and there's a burning sensation in her palm. She opens her fist and lets go of the rope, pulling her legs up to her body and wrapping her arms around them. She remembers at the last second to take in a breath and hold it.

The water is cool as it envelops her, closing over her head. She unfurls herself and kicks her legs, smiling as she breaks the surface.

Ophelia and Clare run to her, splashing as they shout and cheer.

"That was amazing!" Ophelia shouts. She pushes the hair from Wren's forehead.

Wren laughs. "It was really fun," she says. Her heart thunders against her ribs and her legs itch with the desire to climb out of the water and do it again.

"Yeah, yeah, you were great," Ezra says, walking over to them, his steps barely moving the water.

"You can always try again," Wren says, reaching for the end of the rope. "Starfish."

Ezra's jaw drops open and Ophelia and Clare gasp, hiding their mouths behind their hands.

Ezra rips the rope from Wren's hand and trudges out of the water. "Better get out of the way," he calls over his shoulder. "Don't wanna land on your big head."

The girls move out of the way and watch as Ezra plods up the hill to the oak. As they wait, Wren looks at the burn over her palm. It's red and stings a bit in the water.

"You okay?" Ophelia leans over and takes Wren's hand in hers.

"Yeah," Wren says, shrugging a shoulder. "Better than a belly flop." She runs the fingers of her other hand over the raw edges of the burn and lets her fingertips heat, steadily speeding up the growth of new cells.

Once the burn has been reduced to little more than pink skin, she dunks her hand in the cool water before turning back to Ezra. He stands at the end of the runway, the rope clutched in his hand. His shoulders heave with a deep breath before he takes off running.

Ophelia stands next to Wren, her arms close to her chest, her hands clenched into fists. She's almost vibrating in the water. Despite her teasing, it's obvious she hopes Ezra does better this time than the starfish incident.

And he does. His steps are swift and steady, and his jump is up and out, just like Lex told Wren to do. Ezra lets go of the rope at just the right time and he does a half-flip before straightening out and diving into the water. There's a splash, but it doesn't even reach the girls.

Before his head even comes up again, Ophelia shrieks and dives into the water, swimming over to where he'd gone under and they break the surface together.

Lex comes near the edge where Wren and Ezra had jumped off and crosses their arms over their thin chest. "Nice work," they call, impressed. Then they smirk and say, "Starfish."

Ezra lets out a groan that echoes off the cliff face and makes a few birds take off into the blue sky. He relaxes in the water and sinks below the surface.

The rest of the afternoon is spent perfecting flips, dunking each other under the water, and playing many games of chicken. There's a break somewhere in the middle for snacks that Arden brought along and short naps in the sun.

Grace and Jez join them for a game of chicken where Grace sits on Jez's shoulders, and they face off against Wren and Ophelia. Ophelia jokes that Wren should get on her shoulders and then laughs when Wren gives her a horrified look.

Wren and Ophelia start off easy on Grace and Jez, but all that time spent with Arden in the kitchen, lugging sacks of potatoes and lifting pots of water has made Grace strong and she ends up dethroning Ophelia from Wren's shoulders. When Ophelia surfaces again and looks at her surprised, Grace has a haughty look of triumph on her face, her arms crossed tightly over her chest.

Ophelia scrambles back onto Wren's shoulders, causing her to stumble and almost lose her balance. "Rematch!" Ophelia yells.

Grace and Jez win again.

"Okay, okay," Ophelia says, her hands up in surrender when she stands up again after another dethroning, "you win." She bows. "An honor to lose to you, my queen."

Grace giggles and hops down from Jez's shoulders.

After a few more rounds of chicken, where Ezra and Lex go against Eli and Kiara—the captain and her first mate win—the crew splits off into smaller groups and nap, or snack, or read. Wren sits on the blanket with Ophelia, Ezra sleeping beside them, his arm draped across his eyes to block out the sun.

Ophelia talks about her sister, how she hopes someday soon she can bring Evey here and show her the waterfall and how to use the rope swing. She's peeling an orange as she talks and once it's bare, she hands a slice to Wren every few sentences. It goes like this until they've eaten two oranges, one slice for Ophelia, one for Wren.

When the sun sinks below the cliffs, casting the waterfall and surrounding grass in shadows, the crew of *The Altean* gathers their blankets and baskets of nearly finished food, and head back to the beach, where they pile in the dinghies and row back to their ship.

AKNOWLEDGEMENTS

There are so many people to thank for their support, patience, kindness, and generosity during the process of writing and publishing *These Dark Waters*. I'm extremely blessed to know all of them and so grateful to everyone that asked how I was doing and how "the book" was coming along.

Kaci, you inspired me so much. I am so glad to have had a fellow writing buddy that talked me through and talked me down and talked me up. Thank you for letting me pick your brain and ask a million questions. I'm not sure where I'd be in this process without you.

Lola and Kristen, thank you for your incredibly helpful comments on early drafts and for yelling at me periodically over the hurt I caused (I'm sorry but not really). Having you two as early readers was one of the best decisions I made.

Lola (again), thank you for your never-ending support. There were multiple times you convinced me to keep going and celebrated my little victories. I think you probably made me cry just as much as I made you cry (again, sorry but not really).

Mikayla, thank you for being my first internet friend that somehow, some way, led to this book being written. I don't think it could have existed without you.

Jeanine, Izzy, Hope, thank you for being amazing beta readers. You helped strengthen this story and I'm so grateful for that.

Gina, Faith, and Rachel, thank you for being my writer friends (and friends all the more). Seeing how far all of you have come in your own writing journeys has been a huge blessing and a huge inspiration. Having your books on my shelf to gaze at helped this story be finalized.

Mallory, Chasity, and Lena, thanks for letting me write during dinners, charcuterie dates, jam days, car rides, movie nights, and everywhere in between.

The girls I nanny, thanks for your support and celebrations, even if you didn't understand what they were for.

Book besties, your support and love has made all the difference. The friendships in this book are inspired by all of you.

Book lovers discord, thank you for being there when I needed it. Special thanks to Bee, Ry, Liv, Lexi, Kaci, and Kimmy.

This book would not look nearly as pretty as it does without the work of Andy, Rachael, and Faith. Your designs, advice, and hard work are not taken for granted. Thank you.

Thank you to Leigh Bardugo for writing Alina and giving me the best friend group someone could ask for. You wrote a series that changed my life and this book wouldn't have existed without our beloved Sankta Alina.

All of my teachers have been so influential throughout my life but there are a few who have stood out above the rest. Mrs. Williams. Mr. Nelsen. Mr. Rutledge. Even if you didn't know, your support of my creative outlets was imperative for this story to be heard.

To my Great (and great) Uncle Mike, and my poetic pal Uncle Charlie, I wish you were here to read this. Maybe the great beyond has a bookstore.

Mom, Dad, and Shelby, thank you for being supportive of my writing from the very beginning.

Seventeen-year-old me, I hope this story helps you as much as it's helped me. Remember that it's okay to not be okay, that it's important to remember who you are, and you are loved more than you know. Wren is for you.

And to you, dearest reader, thank you.

ABOUT THE AUTHOR

Photo by Emily Loftus

Kelsey Tremaine was born and raised in a rural Northern Nevada town where she spent most of her time creating worlds to escape the cornfields and dairy cows. When she isn't daydreaming about her next book, she can be found at the bookstore or watching the same three shows.

Follow her on social media for writing updates and news.
@thinkingbookish
kelseytremaine.com

www.ingramcontent.com/pod-product-compliance
Lightning Source LLC
Chambersburg PA
CBHW060814120726

47909CB00006B/1912